BLOOD LIST

'*Charlotte held on fast to the architrave of the doorway for support; she felt sick, she could taste the salmon as it repeated over and over again, the entire meal threatening to decorate the plush red carpet beneath her Vera Wang heels. To see it, to actually witness it, to watch him prepare the way for his later seduction was just too painful; each movement, each beat of the music was like a surgeon's knife expertly filleting its way around her already damaged heart...*'

BLOOD LIST

ALI CARTER

Matador
9 Priory Business Park,
Wistow Road, Kibworth Beauchamp,
Leicestershire. LE8 0RX
Tel: 0116 279 2299
Email: books@troubador.co.uk
Web: www.troubador.co.uk/matador
Twitter: @matadorbooks

ISBN 978 1789015 706

British Library Cataloguing in Publication Data.
A catalogue record for this book is available from the British Library.

Printed and bound by CPI Group (UK) Ltd, Croydon, CR0 4YY
Typeset in 12pt Adobe Garamond Pro by Troubador Publishing Ltd, Leicester, UK

Matador is an imprint of Troubador Publishing Ltd

To my dear mum Betty
who always did love a rattling good read
and kept encouraging me to keep going
with this one years ago.

I'm sorry I didn't get it finished
when you were still with us but
I really hope you'd be proud of how it turned out...

PROLOGUE...

KIRKBY-OVER-SANDS. A SMALL TOWN OUTSIDE
KIRKDALE, CUMBRIA 1982

Forty-seven-year-old Maggie Rowlands stared at her much younger sister in sheer disbelief. The red weals on the girl's face glared back defiantly, the eyes matched, and the suitcase hanging from her clenched fist spoke volumes; but when the younger woman opened her mouth there was no defiance in her voice, only urgency – *and pain*.

"Mags I need a place to stay – *please* – just till Davie and I can get on our feet – be together *properly*. He hasn't got a flat or even a regular job yet, *you're the only one I can turn to.*"

The older woman snorted. *Not again* she thought disparagingly.

"And what about your face, did your precious *Davie* do that too?" The girl smarted then, and not from the vicious marks across her cheek. Stiffening, she lifted her chin;

"You know *damn well* who did that – or has the distance made you forget *your* childhood so easily?" The young woman had suddenly found that defiance, just as she always did when her sister scoffed, when she'd not believed in her.

Rose remained on the doorstep, the tension between them overwhelming; air thick with resentment, with repetitions – *with decisions.*

"Maggie are you *gonna* let me in or not? *At least put a brew on and give me something t' eat.*"

"That Davie of yours is no good. He's uneducated, no money and no prospects; a useless waste of time just like the other three before him. I don't know where you *find* them Rose, really I don't. Since you were seventeen you've made bad choices in men and taken no advice from anyone. Every time there's upheaval at home and every time you come to me. *Why* Rose? *You never listen to a bloody word I say!*"

"Mummy, I'm *thirs*-ty, want a… Aunty *Ro*-sie!" A small child had wandered into the hall holding a bright red beaker, on seeing her Aunt her eyes lit up and she let the cup fall. With arms outstretched she rushed towards the door in pure joy, auburn curls bouncing with every step. Rose dropped her suitcase in anticipation and swung the three-year-old up into her arms for a long hug.

"Hello darlin' heart, you gotta kiss for Rosie then?" The child obligingly puckered her lips and planted a wet mouth on the sore cheekbone. She traced a finger along the mark and kissed it again.

"All better!" she announced importantly then sat back in her arms.

"You cummin' to stay – like last time?"

Rose Emmerson looked questioningly at her sister as the toddler twisted around and looked pleadingly at her mother. The hope in that little girl's eyes brightening the hallway like nothing else could.

"No, she is *not*. Now go into the lounge and play with your toys. I'll get you another drink in a minute."

"But *mummee* I *wan*–"

"Now Em!"

Rose kissed the top of the child's head then put her down gently, watching sadly as she ran off along the passage to disappear into the front room. The door slammed with frustration and both women jumped at the sudden bang. Maggie rolled her eyes, *the sooner that one went to school…*

"You have to go Rose," she blurted out suddenly, arms crossed, and avoiding direct eye contact. "If I don't stop this repeated bouncing back and forth now it'll never end. D'ya *hear* me now?"

"But it's *different* this time I –"

"It's *always* different though isn't it? *Every* time, and now it's got to *stop*. It's unsettling for…" she looked over her shoulder, "for everyone. I suggest you go back to mum and dad, knuckle down at the factory and behave like a daughter they can be proud of; instead of all this… this *nonsense!*"

Rosemary Emmerson stood in shocked silence.

Tears glistened then ran free and unashamedly as she bent down to pick up her case. On hearing the door click shut before she'd even straightened herself – an overwhelming fear unfurled. Stirring coldly it slid upwards – *rising like a cobra from her belly.*

ONE

KIRKDALE, CUMBRIA

PRESENT DAY

Charlotte Peterson threw two tablets to the back of her throat, took a large gulp of water and swallowed. She stared hard at the bottom of the glass, then back to the oversized container of anti-depressants before stuffing it deep into a large Prada bag.

Reaching across the table, she automatically picked up a box and poured herself a small bowl of muesli, quite oblivious to its bland appearance. As the milk fell from the bottle she heard the click of the front door and winced edgily. For the second time that month Miles had arrived home from somewhere unknown the night before, let himself in and gone straight upstairs to change for work.

She set the bottle back on the table and lifted a spoonful halfway to her mouth; it hovered there briefly before she replaced it on top of the fruited oats. Pushing the bowl away she sat motionless for a moment — *then reached purposefully back into the designer bag.*

A mile across town Missandra Gale yawned widely. Stretching her lean young body she rolled over to snuggle closer, stroking his chin, savouring the last few minutes before the radio alarm. Nuzzling into the nape of his neck she tickled it seductively with her hot tongue.

He lifted a bare shoulder in sleepy response as she worked her way up to his rough morning cheek. His eyelids flickered in the hot August sun that streamed through the gap in the curtains, and long legs stirred beneath the quilt. She loved this time of day the most, those first few minutes of morning; w*ell, as much as she adored the last few minutes before dropping off at night anyway!*

All too soon the excited tones of DJ Tony Frizzell launched the breakfast hour as Andrew Gale tried to force his groggy brain to wake up. He turned over slowly and leaning up on one elbow gazed down into her brilliant green eyes. A gentle hand followed a soft smile as he began to stroke her pale shoulders.

"*Morning* Missy," he breathed huskily, "who needs a cruddy old clock when they have a real live wake up call, *huh?*" Stretching once more, the white Persian closed her eyes and smiled in sheer delight, purring even louder as he ran his fingers lightly over her soft fur. *Life was certainly sweet when your best friend was Andrew Gale.*

2

"Guess you want some breakfast then kiddo?" He scratched the back of his head and yawned, "Let's hope our cupboard isn't bare then."

To the strains of an old Beatles song drifting from Tony Frizzel's early morning slot, Andrew threw back the duvet, stood up and stretched in a final attempt to wake up, then walked the very short walk to the tiny kitchen. He reminded himself yet again, that it really *was* time to look for a larger place.

Missy reclined princess-style on the crumpled quilt, and washed an immaculately clean paw. *Yes, life was very sweet indeed.*

"You're in luck Missy cat!" called Andrew from the depths of the fridge, the cupboard having indeed been bare. "Gina must have dropped off some fish last night while I was at the gym." This of course was not news to Missy who had enjoyed a glorious half hour of Gina's undivided attention. Had Andrew not dumped his holdall on the lounge table when he'd got in, he would've seen her fishy note which now sat under said bag.

The sound of metal fork against metal bowl soon reached her antennae ears and her appearance in the kitchen was instant. She entwined herself around his legs meowing hungrily as he placed the dish on the floor.

Cat fed, Andrew gathered together a typical (when on a semi-health kick), Gale breakfast – strong Italian coffee and a couple of slices of rye toast. Soon the aroma of both filled his one-bedroom flat as he moved into the lounge and plonked himself on the sofa. It was then that he noticed the corner of Gina's note protruding from beneath his sports bag. He pulled it out and read as he ate;

Coley in fridge for Missy, see you in Carpenters tomorrow lunchtime
Luv G x
P.S. Your sports gear won't get washed on the coffee table!!

A broad grin developed as he sipped his coffee. She knew him well – washing machines were *not* his strong point!

Andrew checked the time and realised it was getting short; he wasn't the tidiest person in the world, or the greatest at laundry, but he *was* known for his punctuality. After a top speed shave and shower he dried and dressed even faster, eating and drinking as he went.

He flew out of the flat taking the stairs to the ground floor two at a time, mindful of the weekend's games he would need to write up that morning. Senior sports reporter at the *Kirkdale Courier* wasn't the greatest job in the world, but he enjoyed it for the most part. One day he would make crime editor – *if* Stella Gray ever retired!

Andrew pointed the tired Ford down the narrow side street that fronted the office and drove to the end. The car's clock was on side, he would just make it by nine if he didn't hang around with Frizzell's morning quiz.

The Saloon swung into the little car park behind the large Georgian cottage that had housed the *Courier* for the past fifteen years, and then came to a sudden halt almost colliding with a rear bumper. Andrew was so used to his morning *'drive and arrive'*, that when he cut the corner on auto pilot he expected to turn straight into his bay. However, today he nearly slammed into the boot of a rather smart black and yellow Mini Cooper. A Mini Cooper that sat very smugly in his space. Suitably surprised, he reversed and drove straight into Rachel's bay. *It'll teach her for treating work like one long holiday* he thought mischievously. Now she would have to do the 'squeeze' between the Grays' Mercedes and an oak tree that was even more ancient than the building; nerve-racking at the best of times but when you park like Rachel Dern *nigh on impossible!*

He threw a glance at the Cooper as he walked half facing the yellow intruder, and half toward the gabled office door. *Well whoever it is, if they're going to be a permanent fixture, they'll need to get a bike.*

He depressed the black iron latch remembering to bend his head as he entered the office. At six foot five a million bruises over the years were a painful testimony to old fashioned doorways.

"*Andrew!*" Peter Gray yelled from the top of the office as soon as he saw him. "*Have you got the Kickers game written up? We need to set the back page.*" But Andrew's attention wasn't on his boss.

Ms. Mini Cooper, who had bedded her car down for the day in his bay, now appeared to be occupying his work station. Peter noticed Andrew's inquisitive gaze travel from the new face back to his own in the editor's suite. Realising the oversight he hurried down the steps into the main office where the young woman stood up, anticipating the overlooked introduction.

"I'm sorry guys, apologies, apologies," gushed Peter, "I should've introduced you first. Jenny Flood, this is Andrew Gale, Andrew – Jenny. Jenny's joined us from a position in Bradenthorpe – great potential – we're lucky to have her."

Andrew held out a hand. "Welcome to the Cuddly *Courier*, I've only one question:" he said in feigned annoyance, "when are you getting a bike?" Jenny looked puzzled and threw a glance at Peter who shrugged, his expression matched hers.

"I…don't understand," she stumbled, "I don't need a bike I've a –"

"A rather neat Mini Cooper, I know – *it's in my bay.*"

"Now, stop teasing Andy," Peter interrupted fully aware now. "We'll sort something, no hassling it's only her first day."

"So… err what exactly is she going to be doing, or

has the lovely Rachel finally started at lunchtime once too often?"

"No – Miss Dern is still with us Andy – hanging on by a thread mind but she's still with us. Stella was very friendly with her mother, same class at school and all that *soooo*...... well you know how it is. Young Jenny's going to take some of the strain off Stella, learn on the job so to speak, take over when she retires." *Yeah right,* thought Andrew, *that'll be the day, Stella Gray would still be chasing a story twelve feet under.* Neither had it escaped him that *he* wanted crime editor – if Stella ever let go.

"Anyway Mr. Gale, Kickers report please!" Peter bellowed over his shoulder as he strode back up the main office to his own.

Jenny apologised for the parking mix-up and moved to the reception area to wait for Stella. Andrew was now at his desk, a home from home with messy drawers and yellow Post-it notes dancing across his computer screen. He looked over at Jenny as he began to tap out a brief Kickers resume. It wasn't grabbing his attention.

"Fancy a coffee?"

She looked up and smiled, "Milky, no sugar... *thanks.*" He pushed back his chair and made his way down to the little kitchen. As he walked, something through the window caught his eye, a predictable scene had ensued and he beckoned Jenny over. They watched in anticipation as Rachel Dern fought hard to squeeze her car in the only available space between Peter's maroon Mercedes and the large oak tree. As Andrew predicted she would make a complete hash of it. The sound of crunching headlamps spectacularly hit the air as they both winced and then attempted to stifle their laughter.

Andrew made the coffees and passed one to Jenny, feeling their tension too had broken. As he stirred, the door of the *Courier* suddenly burst open. In swept a furious Rachel twenty minutes late and exceedingly hot under the collar, or in her case bubblegum pink bandeau. The latch handle still reverberated from it's collision with the stone wall whilst she stood with elbows out, fluorescent nails flashing on full black leathered hips.

"Well thanks a *bunch* Andrew Gale, thanks a *bloody bunch!!*"

"Calm *down* Rachel, have a decaf." He pulled a stool out and passed her a mug he'd already filled, saccharined and set on the counter. She took it sulkily and sat down, her usually full pink mouth now set in a thin concrete line.

She's steaming a damn sight more than that decaf thought Jenny. Eventually Rachel relaxed, but then her bottom lip began to tremble. Dropping her head, a free hand tried to prevent a tear from escaping. The tear won. Overly laden black mascara began to streak as it was followed by several more. She placed the mug on the work surface and struggled into her pocket for a tissue. Andrew noticed this would not be easy, her skirt was pretty tight and she wasn't really getting anywhere. He tore off a piece of kitchen roll and slid it along the work top. Rachel smiled weakly and picked it up. Jenny said nothing.

"So... who is it this time... *hmmm?*" he questioned gently, trying to look underneath her blonde fringe. "You get yourself into such a state each time Rachey; you really must find someone decent, preferably working and *definitely* single." Rachel groaned, looking skyward to imply that was *exactly* what she wanted but it was simply not achievable. A bitter divorce endured three years previously involving her husband's secretary, had led to Rachel bedding half the town's married men since. It was as if she was carrying out some kind of spurned wife's revenge but there was never a happy ending. Habitually 'falling in love' with all the wrong men meant Rachel was regularly disappointed; it appeared that was exactly what had happened the night before resulting in her pre-coffee parking fiasco and subsequent outburst. She appeared un-phased by Jenny's presence despite her being a stranger; this new girl had a sympathetic face and had begun to make all the right noises – Andrew was always nice to her. Right then, being with two people that cared was all that mattered.

She fiddled with the thick tissue replacement and between sobs and gulps relayed her latest romantic disaster. It was pretty much the usual stuff:-

Girl meets married man; girl falls in love; married man has his cake and eats it until wife gets suspicious; married man dumps loved up girl; girl ends up in tears…

As the three drank and Jenny and Andrew did their best to console Rachel, Stella Gray swept through the front door, past the kitchen and into the main office. Noticing it wasn't exactly a hive of activity she retraced her steps and found her entire full-time staff nursing mugs of coffee. One look at her late friend's daughter was all she needed to understand why no work was getting done.

"Ye Gods girl not another one?!" she questioned exasperatedly. The usually bubbly blonde who was anything but that morning, looked up at her 'Aunty' Stella and winced as a fresh tear rolled south. "Will you *never* learn Rachel?! *If your poor mother could see you now she'd turn in her grave!"* Andrew patted his soulful colleague on the shoulder, ushered her past his boss leaving her to settle in the latest member of the paper.

As Jenny sat talking with her new employer, she wondered just how this new post would work out. All things considered they weren't quite what she'd expected. But then to be fair……… *neither was she.*

TWO

Gina Rowlands felt her phone vibrate through navy summer trousers. She pulled it from her pocket to read the new message whilst holding the phone discreetly under the reception desk.

> *'Thanks for the fish, Missy loved it! See you at 1p.m. in the pub, will have a friend with me. Hugs, Andy XXX'*

She smiled at the words on the tiny illuminated screen for a few seconds until Miles Peterson broke the moment. He swung through the double-fronted arched doors flashing his usual appreciative smile in her direction. Gina felt her cheeks flush hotly and noticed her hands had begun to sweat yet again.

At forty-two he was more than twice her age, but that didn't seem to stop her from being affected every time he paid her attention. Nor did it prevent *his* enjoyment of the same beautiful view every morning.

Miles hadn't experienced any real job satisfaction for a very long time and Gina's presence at work made it worth his while coming in. She was one young lady, however, that he dared not *actually* pursue, considering his wife consulted in the same building. No, Miles was not *that* stupid, he would just enjoy every moment of her delicious presence that he could. Not being able to do anything about it somehow made it all the more intriguing, exciting even – *particularly as she was so young.*

"Morning… Miss… *Rowlands…*" the words lingered a little as his gaze washed over the rich red waves that tumbled loosely around her shoulders. At only twenty years old Gina had already inherited her mother's fiery beauty and bright personality. *If only she could have seen just how stunning her daughter had become.*

Miles' embarrassed receptionist snapped the cover shut and slipped the phone back into her trouser pocket.

"*Morning Doctor Peterson,*" she called dutifully after him as his back disappeared down the steps at the end of the corridor. She knew exactly what Miles thought of *her* of course, it was patently obvious. She just hoped nobody else had noticed – particularly his wife. Charlotte Peterson seemed to scrutinise every female member of staff every time she spoke to them. Gina felt sure she was trying to read their minds in order to discover exactly what they thought of her husband. If her boss had known the truth she would probably have fired the lot of them, any woman with a pulse couldn't fail to appreciate his appearance, *whatever age they were.*

As she turned on the computer and began to start

the day, Gina wondered why Miles had ever pursued a medical career in the first place. At least if he was going to be in medicine she'd imagined him as a specialist in some cosmetic field, something a damn sight more exciting than a village GP anyway. Miles' extraordinary good looks were noticed by everybody; his sharp blonde hairstyle, brilliant blue eyes, *enhanced greatly with coloured lenses*, and year-round tan *courtesy of a sun bed*, meant he was undeniably very handsome. Expensive designer clothes finished the look, and she knew of at least three forty-something practice colleagues whose hearts skipped a beat when he appeared. Despite this, although it irritated her, Gina somehow enjoyed his admiring glances whilst at the same time wished she didn't. It was all very confusing.

She didn't want to lose her job as it wasn't all that easy to find work in Kirkdale. As a small town with an area already overpopulated with claustrophobic Londoners after a slice of the Lake District's space and beauty, it wasn't exactly overwhelmed with career prospects.

The phone lines suddenly burst into a jangling chorus and another busy morning began against the backdrop of patients' calls, nail-tapped keyboards and the repeated swing-thud of the heavy surgery doors. *Gina was already looking forward to lunchtime.*

With a large mug of coffee in front of her, Charlotte Peterson was sucking the end of a red pen with one hand, and doodling aimlessly with a blue one on her desk pad with the other. She'd arrived at the surgery about twenty minutes ahead of Miles, having left home before he'd come back downstairs. She should have used this time to prepare for her first patient, but hadn't. Whenever Miles went AWOL there were always three questions on her mind. *Who, where and for how long?* No doubt he would have a reasonable explanation for his absence last night, he always had in the past. *Why though? Why now?*

Things had been so much better over the last few years since they'd moved from the city to Kirkdale and taken over the village practice. Miles would always be a bit of a flirt, she knew that, but until this month had no real reason to doubt him. She'd actually started to relax a bit over the last couple of years and even their love life had been back on track, not that Miles had ever failed to continue *that* side of their marriage. Even through his last three flings. Well… the ones she knew about anyway.

Charlotte took a sip of her coffee and drew some more. *Her patient could wait.* A sudden thought occurred to her as she snatched the pen from her mouth. *There was that conference on alternative thyroid meds., the one held at the Grange Hotel. It was recent – only last month. Could he have met somebody there? Another doctor? A lecturer? A sufferer?* Her head was spinning so madly with all the possibilities of yet *another* affair, she barely heard the knock on the door.

The rapping was repeated, a little louder, faster and with some impatience. Charlotte tore the page of scribbled doodlings from her notepad, screwed it up and dropped it in the bin.

"*Come in!*" she called as she laid both pens down. Miles walked in briskly and appeared to be on edge himself. She sat back expectantly, arms now crossed. For once she just waited for *him* to speak. He did so in a low voice, quickly, a little urgent, almost in a whisper, as if he feared he would be overheard by someone passing by outside despite the door being closed.

"Just in case you were running around in your head adding two and two and making seven and a half, I was at the gym last night. We, *Bill – you know Bill –* we met some guys, went for a beer, on to a curry house, more booze and decided I shouldn't drive so stayed over at Bill's place. You remember Bill, he runs the training sessions in the leisure centre?" *Miles didn't wait for an acknowledgement of her recollection.* "Anyway, he offered me a bed to be on the safe side, I couldn't risk driving now could I?" Her husband finished his quick-fire explanation with a hunch of his shoulders, arms held wide in that '*you know how it is*' manner.

Charlotte still stared at him steadily. *Her* arms still folded, saying nothing. Bill was clearly the alibi here.

"*It was late sweet pea!*" he implored, "I didn't want to wake you and you disappeared so quickly this morning before I could say anything – I guess I should have rung?" He looked sheepish now, it all sounded so plausible, *but then it always did.* She remained silent. *"Charlotte?"* She tried to think rationally for a moment, wanted to believe him but… Eventually the corners of her mouth lifted reluctantly, not quite a smile but it was enough for Miles.

"O-*kay… let's just forget it!*" she snapped, and with one eye on the door herself lowered her voice, "but *next* time you *damn well ring me, whatever the bloody time is!*"

Miles jumped at the opportunity of being let off the hook so easily, marriage to Charlotte had taught him to expect a great deal more aggravation than that.

"You got it sweetness!" He smiled broadly, now visibly relaxed. "We'll have a meal out tonight shall we?" he chatted on quickly before Charlotte could reconsider. "A drive over to the Carpenters Arms, yes? It'll make a change from the microwave and we won't have to cook after a long day." She could feel herself being cajoled into the acceptance of his latest explanation, and the idea of eating out on a weekday *was* tempting.

"Okay… I'd like that," she said grudgingly, won over for the umpteenth time as she pushed to the back of her mind that last night was the *second* time that month he'd stayed out till morning.

Miles blew her a kiss as he backed out of her office and clicked the door shut. He looked heaven-bound, closed his eyes and let out a sigh. *Boy that was a close one* he thought as he turned from his wife's office and made his way down to his own consulting room.

Behind his desk Miles sunk into a deep leather chair and twisted it thoughtfully from side to side. He retrieved a phone from his pocket and swiftly pressed a few buttons till the name search appeared on the screen. He scrolled the list and quickly brought up the one he wanted.

"Goodbye Kelly love, it was nice while it lasted". He pressed delete, flipped the cover shut and returned the spare mobile to his inside jacket pocket. Miles then tapped a few words into his computer, brought up the correct screen and rung through to reception for his first patient. An arrogant smile broke – *it would take a lot more than a neurotic woman to catch him out again.*

The weather had changed since Molly Fields had opened the Carpenters Arms that morning. Despite most of the country basking in a heatwave, Cumbria was used to a damper, wetter climate altogether. The high mountainous peaks and large expanses of water from the beautiful lakes lent themselves to producing a good deal of all season rain.

Earlier it had looked quite promising, blue skies and sunshine all around, although there had been quite a breeze coming off the river. Now though, the clouds drew closer together over Kirkby Pike, the sun was struggling to find a gap and Molly sensed a slight chill in the air. Even for the Lake District, that was strange in mid August.

At twenty she was an intuitive girl who noticed the subtlest of changes within seasons, the mood and 'feel' of the lakes and pikes and the shift in nature's wildlife – but right from childhood she'd felt a strong pull towards her psychic side although hadn't really understood what it meant.

There was also her perceptiveness to certain people, situations and events. At first it had been simple predictive episodes, who would walk through the door first, or who would be on the other end of a ringing phone – but recently stranger events had occurred.

Years ago she'd dreamt of a plane crashing into the side of a mountain followed by the media eruption of the twin towers tragedy twenty-four hours later. The dream may not have been identical, but there was a chilling similarity to the events that followed.

More recently though she'd just finished her first shift in the bar when a sense of danger connected with a small child completely engulfed her. That night's news reported the disappearance of a four-year-old who was thankfully found safe and well the following evening. Again, the exact details weren't apparent, the sex of the child or where she'd been, she hadn't even *dreamt* anything that time – just felt it, she just *knew*.

Molly stood close to the doorway of the lakeside inn and peered through the leaded light window. The breeze ruffled her long dark curls – she sensed something was amiss then as she gazed out onto the river, but had absolutely no idea what it was. It was nothing specific… just not quite *right*, in the same way a person might enter a room and know something was missing, but not knowing what. It was a sense of change without reason – without rational explanation.

"Molly? Molly!! Are you working this bar or day dreaming again?"* Her father's voice broke through loudly, it made the empty beer glasses jump in her hands. Psychic dreams, night time or otherwise had no place in his busy day.

"Coming Dad!" she called, as all thoughts of strange feelings left to be replaced by the very real throng of the lunchtime trade. She wiped down the tables, served food and drinks, worked busily alongside her parents and at the same time looked out for her friends to arrive.

Gina Rowlands was like a sister to her and had been taken into their family at fourteen when her guardian Grandmother had needed to go into a nursing home. Legally she could have returned to the house when she was eighteen, but a medical receptionist's salary didn't meet the costs of running a fairly large house. Besides, the monthly rent it fetched was needed to pay her Grandmother's nursing home bills.

From her point of view Molly was glad Gina still lived at the pub, as an only child herself it had been wonderful to have a 'sister'. As children they'd been practically inseparable, well until recently when Gina had met Andrew anyway. They didn't spend much of their spare time together these days but that was understandable, he *was* gorgeous.

Speak of the devil, she thought as a familiar face breezed in through the doorway. He held a rain-splashed leather jacket above someone's head exposing his to the rain, but when it was removed the girl that emerged wasn't Gina. It *should've* been Gina, Molly thought, but it definitely wasn't.

Andrew caught her suspicious glare;

"Molly this is Jenny Flood," he said quickly before Molly's protective thought processes got entirely out of hand, "she's recently moved to Kirkdale and just joined us at the *Courier*. I promised her lunch." Molly relaxed and smiled at the newcomer.

"Hi Jenny, nice to meet you," she said, then glanced at Andrew; "and is our answer to Fleet Street buying?"

"Sure, a pint for me and have one yourself Molls – *Jenny?*"

"Vodka orange with ice – thanks." Andrew looked above the heads at the bar and scoured the pub.

"Gina should be here soon it's nearly a quarter past," he said as he checked his watch. Molly grinned, Andrew *was* pretty cute but his obsession with punctuality definitely wasn't!

She dropped some ice into Jenny's drink, pulled his pint, then raised her eyebrows at him and nodded towards the entrance. Gina was doing battle with the heavy double doors, a used umbrella in her right hand, and a shoulder bag that threatened to leave its place and fall into her left. She was finally rescued by Andrew who'd reacted to Molly's hint.

Gina's hair was windswept but at least it was dry, *she had no qualms about carrying a brolly.* Andrew slipped an arm around her waist and guided her back to the bar where he'd saved her favourite high stool with the little bow back. She rolled up her umbrella, rammed it into her bag then downed half the iced Scotch and coke Molly had already poured. This time it was Jenny's eyebrows that were raised.

"Jeez I needed that!" exhaled Gina, eyes closed, enjoying its cold sweet kick, "it's turned ghastly out there again." Then she noticed somebody else in their group – a stranger. She was so used to it being just herself, Andy and Molly – *although Molly officially worked it never felt like that* – she'd only just realised the woman must have arrived with Andrew. A quick glance around established she didn't appear to be with anyone else. Jenny sensed her question;

"Hi – I'm Jenny Flood." She extended a hand. "I just joined the *Courier* this morning."

"Nice to meet you," Gina replied tipping her head forward in acknowledgement and holding a false smile. She raised her glass but ignored the offered handshake. The twenty-nine-year-old dropped her arm back and picked up her vodka.

Gina's eyes were watchful. The woman was noticeably a few years older than her, nearer Andrew's age, she looked mature, intelligent and sophisticated.

With herself at only twenty and Andrew at twenty-eight, some people had already commented, but he'd always laughed it off as unimportant. Gina never really noticed it before either, but she noticed it now.

Jenny was very pretty. At about five ten with long straight raven hair, legs up to her armpits and an ultra tiny waist *she was like a slender, beautiful Indian squaw* thought Gina, *but how did she stay so slim? How did she get that shape in the first place come to that?* Gina felt a jealous twinge, and unusually for her, totally inadequate. Although a generous size fourteen and five foot five max, striving to be a size zero had never interested her – nor had university. From where she was standing, she suddenly felt uneducated, plain and dumpy – *the complete unholy trinity.*

If Jenny was a journalist she must have gone to uni or at least college. Brains and beauty then, she thought sipping her drink. *Still, it was her shoulders beneath Andrew's arm, not Jenny's, and he was just as attentive as ever – but for how long?*

Molly took everything in, despite having reached both ends of the bar and served half a dozen new customers in the process. She knew *exactly* what her best friend was thinking, but she also knew Andrew adored the very bones of her. The woman was beautiful it was true, but Andrew would never cheat on Gina. Molly smiled knowingly as she dried a glass and set it back on a shelf. Gina would no doubt have a long and involved rant about it after work where Molly would put her friend's mind very firmly at rest.

"Are we eating today then?" she asked the trio on the other side of the bar.

"Too right," replied Andrew, "I'll have your mum's shepherd's pie and special spicy beans, how about you two?" He turned to the others. Gina studied Jenny more closely now and wondered just exactly where she would put even a *small* portion of Maisie Fields' pies, *whichever* one she chose.

"Me too sweetheart," Gina said looking up at him, thinking she should probably have a salad but knew she wasn't going to. He grinned at her and gently brushed her nose with the bar menu, then looked at Jenny.

"Molly's mum makes the best shepherd's pie in the village, you really should try it." Jenny hesitated, her eyes darted to the lunchtime chalkboard on the wall desperately searching for a light menu. She looked distinctly uncomfortable. *Pale even,* Gina thought as she sat quietly, almost *like a rat in a trap.* She awaited her delayed reply with interest. Sensing an atmosphere, Molly came to Jenny's rescue and offered her a range of freshly prepared sandwiches for which the new girl was extremely grateful.

Fifteen minutes later there were two huge plates of Maisie Fields' shepherd's pie and beans sitting on the bar, together with a tuna mayonnaise on brown and salad garnish. It looked very small and pathetic despite being made with chunky granary bread and enjoying a generous filling. Jenny felt the familiar hard knot in her stomach. She now wished she'd just gone along with the damned pie – it really made very little difference in the end.

The three chatted as they ate. Gina and Andrew devoured Maisie's familiar homemade food whilst Jenny quietly picked at her tuna and mayo. The granary bread grated all the way down.

The lunch hour passed very quickly during which work issues were discussed, hobbies and interests swapped, and a new friendship tentatively made. Gina began to relax which was in no small part due to Andrew ensuring she felt entirely at ease. He'd sensed her initial discomfort regarding Jenny and made sure she had nothing to feel insecure about. A protective Molly had also kept a sisterly eye whilst she managed her side of the bar. She was as observant as she was intuitive and it wasn't lost on her that Jenny had left the group to find the loo immediately after she'd eaten. In fact she never did actually finish her lunch. On her return, she couldn't help but notice the tiny pale fleck on the lapel of her dark navy suit. For a brief moment their eyes met, it was then that the attractive newcomer checked her watch and reminded Andrew she didn't want to be late back on her first day.

By the time they left the rain had stopped, the sun was out and had tried its best to dry the little puddles in the furrows of the garden's flagstones. Andrew reminded Gina of the film they were going to see that evening then kissed her goodbye before they walked in opposite directions. Now that lunch was over, Gina wasn't entirely happy at her man walking side by side with a slim, stunningly sophisticated career woman. *Next time it would be the salad* she decided firmly.

Jenny felt infuriated at her carelessness and wished her head had not started to thump so relentlessly since Molly had noticed. She also wished that her life could have been different; but it wasn't, it couldn't and now she was here.

As she walked alongside him headed back to work, the blue-eyed dark-haired woman slid a sideways glance at Andrew. His endless chatter floated completely over her head. He didn't seem to notice she wasn't contributing too much to the conversation – *or that she had just wiped a small speck of vomit from her collar.*

THREE

The enormous wrought iron gates to Kirkdale Riverside Park loomed in front of the two young journalists. Two huge posters, one on each of the gate's concrete pillars, advertised the annual country show to be held there that weekend.

Andrew nodded his head towards them and Jenny followed his glance, glad any attention given to her stained collar earlier, appeared to have gone unnoticed – *by Andrew at least.*

Although new to the area, she'd already received the spec on the event from Stella who'd broached the subject that morning after she found them comforting Rachel in the kitchen. A piece covering the four-day event with some pictures alongside was to be her first real assignment.

As they made their way back to the *Courier's* office, Jenny silently acknowledged just how much she was looking forward to that assignment, in more ways than one.

For Andrew the rest of the day passed uneventfully. He'd enjoyed the film that evening, a dark creepy thriller, and Gina's reaction to spend most of it clung to him in all its scariest places, however sexist that made him, was enjoyable too!

Jenny had meanwhile continued to unpack and got herself sorted in a rented flat on the outskirts of town. She'd managed to eat and keep down, a very small plain salad for dinner, an achievement in itself, but then she knew she was going to need it to keep her strength up.

Molly had enjoyed a break in the afternoon and was back on the bar that evening when Charlotte and Miles Peterson walked through the Carpenters' door.

The Inn was a hive of activity, the Petersons had to squeeze past a couple of darts players as they passed through the 'Snug' doorway at the side of the pub. This was not their usual watering hole as they lived on the other side of the village on the outskirts of town; in fact Miles couldn't remember the last time they'd drunk there. The Wheat Sheaf was their local, not far from their Victorian farmhouse at Willows Copse and therefore convenient at the end of a long day.

This evening, however, Miles was keen to placate his long-suffering wife in an endeavour to divert her attention away from his recent night-time absences. Things had got a little too close for comfort that morning – *he didn't want the boat rocked too violently.* Another move just wasn't feasible, nor did he think Charlotte would tolerate knowledge of a fourth full-blown affair. He'd also been advised by friends who'd been equally disparaging of their marriage vows, that divorce could be exceedingly expensive. Miles was not in any way ready to relinquish a large Victorian home and six acres of land, nor a very healthy 'pension plan' by way of future inheritance from Charlotte's filthy rich parents.

No, this restless village doctor had every intention he would have his cake and eat it for as long as possible. It was just a case of being one step ahead, or as Miles liked to think of it, *the amount of cake eaten balanced with the amount replaced – at speed – before the missed piece was noticed.*

Charlotte found a table whilst Miles waited on a couple of drinks from the crowded bar.

In the corner by a large oak fireplace, a couple of women chatted intently, heads bent over a small round table full of glasses and a couple of bottles of wine. One bottle was already empty and the other well down. It didn't take long for Miles to lock eyes with the eye-catching thirty-something blonde with large baby doll eyes and short denim skirt. She seemed a little quieter than her friend, a touch upset and almost...... needy.

He shifted his position and now had his back to Charlotte. His short-lived 'decency' obliterated from his mind, he smiled invitingly into the sad blue eyes of Rachel Dern. Just for a moment her tired expression brightened and full red mouth lifted at the corners as she caught his approval. The familiar low flutter now active, she raised her ruby filled glass to matched lips and drank deeply as she held his gaze. Against her better judgement, Rachel began to wish that her evening was not going to end at her friend Josie's house that night, a friend who'd followed Rachel's equally inviting eyeline, and sighed heavily.

Even through the busy evening trade, Miles and Rachel, who could no longer even see each other in the crowd, still sensed a strong, physical and distinctive link. It was an invisible connection, almost painful in its need; an electrically charged cord that ran in and around the crowds that mingled between their tables. This was no surprise to either of them. As seasoned veterans in affairs of the heart, they were both well aware of the situation.

People like Miles and Rachel needed very little in the way of small talk or introduction, *they just knew*. It didn't take long for the opportunity to present itself, after all when a lady needs to *'go'* she needs to go.

The minute Charlotte had entered the female cloakroom, Miles negotiated his way swiftly back to Rachel's table where once again their eyes locked. With sleight of hand he delivered a small note discreetly into her lap. Like a scene from a Bond movie, one second he was there and the next he was gone. Back at his table in seconds, he'd sashayed through a surge of chattering diners, ignorant of the moment as at breakneck speed they shovelled hot roasted meats and various buttered vegetables down their throats.

Rachel unfolded the small white square and entered the number of Miles' spare mobile into her own, her latest hurtful break up already eased as the proverbial warm glow slowly enveloped her body. That weekend might now see a new comfort. It wouldn't last she knew that, she didn't expect much in the way of real relationships anymore, but at least she could enjoy the short time they would have......*and pretend that it might.*

Molly, rushed off her feet behind the bar, seriously wished she'd also been at the cinema that night.

The new menu had certainly proved popular, its reputation must have spread wide enough to bring the Petersons across town she thought wryly. Gina had told Molly many times of Miles' flirty looks towards her at work, and Molly too had felt uncomfortable in his company when she'd met Gina from the surgery.

As she served customer after customer, cleared the bar of used glasses and wiped the tables, the continuous 'ching' of the cash register and hubbub of the throng began to sound very loud and buzzy in her tired head.

She watched the Peterson table as she worked, tried hard not to stare, but Charlotte caught her eyes and just for a second Molly was hit by that lead-eyed, dead-eyed expression Gina had warned her about. Shark-like and cold as steel, it induced a shudder from that young barmaid in a hot summer pub. For the second time that day she felt distinctly uncomfortable about her environment with no real explanation as to why.

An hour's train ride away, a troubled and moody young man watched over a dark concrete landscape. From the open window of his soulless high-rise flat, he could hear some youths laugh and swear below as they kicked out the headlights of a resident's parked car. He leant out a little and saw they'd ensured the lamps were rendered useless before they ran off to find some more illegal fun.

Jason Flood turned away from the view feeling utterly despondent. It was what he saw regularly, several times every week…and he hated it. His home was on the worst estate in Bradenthorpe, but at twenty-two he couldn't afford anything else on a supermarket wage.

Jason knew he wasn't exactly whiter than white himself, but to commit vandalism for kicks was definitely not his thing. Due to his medical condition he probably wouldn't have the energy to kick the crap out of a paper bag anyway, let alone a set of car headlights.

At the age of sixteen following his parents' death in a plane crash, he'd dabbled with cannabis to help deal with his anger and grief, and discovered how well it subdued his frustration at the world. It relaxed his mind, allowed him to smile occasionally and left him with some breathing spaces of calm and peace. Unfortunately it had also led to his heavier and more regular usage and the development of schizophrenia. By nineteen an official diagnosis had been made, and permanent anti-psychotic medication prescribed.

Jen was wonderful, his sister had practically monitored his condition single-handed for the last three years, now she deserved the very best... *and that definitely wasn't Miles Peterson.* That bastard had devastated her, practically destroyed her that spring six years ago when he'd left her high and dry and disappeared to God knows where with that sullen wife of his. If only things had been different. If only his parents hadn't died maybe he wouldn't have gotten ill, maybe he could've gone to uni, got a good job, *made* something of himself. Maybe Jen wouldn't have got involved with that user Doctor. *If, if, if... maybe, maybe, maybe!*

As things stood, his Clozapine tablets made him sleepy a lot of the time, driving or operating any machinery was impossible, concentration and therefore study wasn't easy and the weight gain and sometimes the shakes affected him adversely too. *And Jen hadn't had a relationship in six years.*

No – life hadn't been that great for either of them, and without his sister around he had a feeling it was about to be even tougher for him than he thought. Especially as he'd also promised Jenny he'd be fine if she left town and took up the chance of a more senior post in Kirkdale.

"Hey – Jase! You cummin' out tonight man?" flatmate Stevie Ross called out from the bathroom, then stuck his head round the door as he rubbed his spiky orange hair dry with a pink towel. Jason looked up from his left

hand as it trembled and managed a smile at the tenth white towel to be mixed in with Stevie's red underwear that month.

"No you're alright Steve, I'm gonna do me some packing, goin' away for a couple of days. Can you square it with the boss? He knows I'm due some leave." Stevie took the towel off his head, let it hang down beside him and smiled.

"No probs. You tell Jenny hi from me, okay?" He turned and disappeared back into the steamy bathroom as Jason walked into his bedroom, took down a holdall from the top of his wardrobe and began to pack.

That night Molly had difficulty in sleeping. She'd tried to read, tried a sheep count, a flick through her Facebook newsfeed, but her head fuzzy from the packed bar and restaurant, had developed into a right stonker of a migraine. She knew her phone had made it worse. When she'd finally felt she might drift off it was a blessed relief – *until...*

Suddenly her eyes flew open! She was wide awake and alert now – her head still pounded but she barely noticed as beads of cold sweat broke out across her forehead and ran down her face.

It was dark outside, the car park lamp was blown but the moon reflected on the river which sent a glimmer of light through her flimsy curtains. Lying prostrate across the foot of the bed with her head thrown back, face distraught and suspended in a desperate, agonised scream, was the image of a young woman. Her eyes were wild yet still – her blonde blood-spattered hair framed moonlit skin, porcelain white in stark and final shock.

And the hole in her chest was like nothing Molly had ever seen.

FOUR

That weekend, the first day of the country show dawned dry and not too hot. This, thought Charlotte as she let herself into the stable, would be a great deal easier for the livestock that would be there, including Greta. The only thing in her life that was constant, had kept her sane for the past six years were her horses.

With Miles' affairs seemingly behind them, their relocation from the city of Bradenthorpe at *her* insistence, and the arrival of Greta and Gizmo soon after had been a real life-saver for her.

As she began to use the body brush on Greta's strong muscular neck she became aware of Miles' muffled voice from the house. Charlotte sighed heavily then appeared from inside the stable to acknowledge him as he walked down towards the cars.

"Charlotte! Charlotte – can you hear m –? Oh, you're there."

"Yeah – I hear you." Her eyes narrowed as she eyed him keenly, took in his smarter than usual 'travelling to gym' clothes, his body language – *his fake smile.* Her heart missed a beat and she waited for the thoughtful caring comment. It always started that way...

"I'm going now sweetness, I'll see you later okay? Good luck – no, no need, you're gonna do *great!*" He gave her a brief wave before she could respond with anything, jumped into his Morgan and drove smartly out of the drive. Charlotte remained where she was and watched him go. One eye started to twitch.

She could hear the scrunch of the tyres on the gravel even from the paddock, like another dirty graze it scraped grittily across her heart. Her damaged ego tortured her equally shattered confidence. *Was he really meeting up with Bill?* It bounced around her head like all those times before – like the other night.

Charlotte stepped back inside the stable, walked over to the mare and ran her hand over Greta's black velvet coat. Gradually she began to feel soothed. With them she could be herself; calm, relaxed and at peace with her world. No patients, no black clouds, no anxiety… no Miles. Nonetheless – a tiny seed was planted, started to germinate, and began to take root deep in the insecurities of her mind. As she worked, Gizmo's head appeared over his stall to remind her of his existence. Charlotte turned round to rub his nose softly and brought her face close to his dark wide nostrils where his breath warmed her cheeks.

"Hello my gorgeous boy, you'd never let me down would you? No……course not." She patted Gizmo's rich chestnut neck, smoothed his mane and then returned to brushing her show girl.

With Greta basically ready, she carefully led her

into the horse box in the courtyard, then returned to the stables to turn Gizmo out into the field. She'd already double checked her tack box for a complete kit, and with the paddock gate securely locked was ready to leave.

Jenny walked through the grand entrance to the Riverside Country Park with her DSLR camera in a shoulder case, and presented her press pass to an official.

The event was massive. There were tents and stalls of all shapes and sizes with a huge variety of items for sale from home-cooked baking to new age amulets. Electric chainsaw artists carved elaborate birds and animals out of giant tree trunks, medieval-styled potters threw bowls and chalices, and stands of beautiful handmade clothes and jewellery were around every corner. There were even trained owls and hawks being flown by experts and people were able to hold them with special gloves and supervision. From everywhere there came a sensuous mixture of wonderful smells that included rich barbequed meats, home-made spiced chutneys and saccharin sweet candyfloss. With the backdrop of the Pike, the sunshine, and the river's watery music as it ran along one side of the park, it was a heavenly setting for the village's annual country show. *But cosy Kirkdale could not have foreseen what was to come.*

Jenny wondered if she could cover everything adequately, her confidence had taken a nosedive since her national press days. She interviewed some stallholders, bought a few pieces of handmade jewellery, and made sure there were enough pictures and material to choose from to make up the final piece. She couldn't afford to mess this job up – and not just for financial reasons.

Around the corner of one particularly large tent, she found the showjumping arena and decided to sit down for a while near the perimeter fencing. The horses and riders practised their jumps over the course prior to the start of the event and Jenny scanned the view with her camera to wait for the best shots. After a few frames she edged around the other side of the ménage nearer the course's starting and finishing posts. The crowd was thicker there as excited children begged their parents for horses and wary parents placated them with candyfloss. Jenny carried on walking and snapping until she came close to the competitors' preparation area.

Charlotte stood behind her horsebox with her back to the crowd. She'd completed the final grooming, applied fly repellent and checked Greta's hooves for stones before her class was called. It wasn't due to begin for another twenty minutes so she decided to ride her horse gently nearby to loosen the mare up.

As she rounded the tent's extended awning, the sun suddenly appeared from behind a cloud and shone straight into her eyes. Charlotte instinctively lifted her arm to block the glare, when she removed it her hands involuntarily snatched at the reins, her leg muscles tightened and her world began to implode. *Jenny Flood.* The horse sensed the tension above and shifted uneasily. *It couldn't be* thought Charlotte stunned. *Surely she didn't know wh… it must be a trick of the light – dear God not again!*

Greta snorted, her massive frame precariously stepped forward and back in heated agitation, sweat glistened on her flanks as Charlotte's head spun and her stomach clenched tight – locked down like a Rottweiler's jaws on a cushion. The nausea rose from her guts, an eruption of bitter acid saturated her mouth as almost simultaneously Greta's front legs reared skyward, her nostrils flared and eyes rolled into her head. It took all of Charlotte's riding skills to bring the horse to a safe stand, and when she did, it was directly in front of Jenny Flood. The younger woman stood before her and barely flinched as she almost tasted horse hoof – snapped a photo of the rider astride the black mare, then immediately backed off.

Charlotte wasn't even sure if Jenny had realised who she was. A black peaked riding hat and a shorter hairstyle in the last six years could've seen to that.

An anxious crowd had now gathered. People began to stare up at Charlotte and repeatedly asked Jenny if she was hurt. High above the ground astride Greta, the older woman felt acutely aware the crowd considered her responsible for the incident. Her cheeks flushed hotly. Embarrassed, she pulled the peak of her hat down a little further and mumbled an apology, then with a click of her heels turned Greta around and rode off towards the other side of the arena.

The throng gradually dispersed, and Jenny thanked the concerned onlookers that remained with one eye on the mare and its rider as Charlotte disappeared behind the large marquee. She hadn't felt quite as calm as her behaviour may have implied. Jenny knew *exactly* who the rider was, and the whole encounter had left her stunned. Her stomach gnawed with hunger; no breakfast had passed her lips that morning nor dinner the night before, but she welcomed the discomfort and pain – *it took the edge off the rest of it.*

Jason Flood stepped down from the carriage onto the platform. His purple holdall matched the latest luminous stripe in his otherwise black floppy hair, and his left eyebrow sported a small gold ring. Despite the warmth of the day, a long black coat swirled Gothicly around his ankles and skimmed purple laced boots whilst baggy slouched jeans hung relaxed and low beneath his hips.

He sauntered lazily to the exit barrier, handed in his ticket and pulled a bar of chocolate from his pocket. As he ate, music from a fairground carousel met his steps and a boyish grin spread across his face. He'd intended to go straight to his sister's new flat but decided she'd probably be at work, it *was* Friday. A bit of fun at the fair was just what he needed right now and it didn't take long to find it. He followed the melodic strains and within minutes was standing in front of the huge gates to Riverside Park.

Once inside he meandered through the stalls and felt his spirits lift a little. His hands had been better today – hadn't shaken so much. But then he *had* reduced his medication from his regular much higher dose – that always helped, with the twitching anyway. Sometimes though, sometimes... *they* came back. He would hear them in his head, they told him to do things, things he knew he shouldn't; bad things; wicked things; and he would argue with them – but not today. Today he felt good. Today he would have some fun at this country show and then he would go to see his sister. Jason did not notice the girl turn across his path until it was too late.

Molly Fields had pleaded for the afternoon off. It had been a long queue but the extra large Mr Whippy with the double chocolate flake, strawberry sauce and toasted nuts had definitely been worth the wait! She'd reached up to take it, turned from the van and with her head tilted had begun to lick her way to an extra inch on her hips. Human anatomy being what it is, however, meant her eyes were unnaturally close to the '99', and her view of Jason impaired as he walked across her field of vision. In seconds he was wearing half of the cone's topping whilst Molly had the rest of it spread unflatteringly up her nose and across her chin.

"*Oh God!* I'm *so* sorry!" she exclaimed, face cold, wet and a complete mess. She frantically rummaged in her handbag for tissues whilst she tried to keep her head down and apologise at the same time.

"No – definitely *my –*" came half a reply from Jason – "please, let me –" he fished unsuccessfully into each overly deep pocket.

"I've a tissue somewhere... *damn it!*" Molly faltered – "here..." Having finally found some, she handed a few to him whilst she tried to clean herself up.

"Oh God your tee-shirt and coat, they're covered!" She winced, quite mortified now.

"I should've looked where I was going," he said, "*my fault – really.*" He accentuated the point. "I'm always being told I'm a daydreamer." They finally looked at each other properly after a wipe down then burst into laughter. Molly looked away briefly, then back at him and smiled slowly. His last comment sounded familiar. She'd spent most of *her* life being told to concentrate on what she was doing – 'get her head on straight'; but then people didn't understand her, not really. Not about her dreams, her senses... *and now the visions.*

"I know what you mean," she said. "I'm always being told I'm away with the fairies."

"Well in that case," he added with a grin as he slung the used tissues in a nearby bin, "we should get on great! Hi – I'm Jason."

"Molly, Molly Fields," she replied as she absorbed his colourful appearance. The streak of purple on the left side of his zigzag parting, the eyebrow adornment, the long coat... she found him quite attractive in a creative sort of way. Not naturally gorgeous like Gina's Andy but... well, kind of *different*. Nice different.

Molly dumped the remainder of her squashed cone into the bin and mentally praised herself for the saved calories. She wasn't obsessional about dieting, not like that Jenny, but she did worry about her relationship with ice cream...

They walked away from the van together and into the main show area. Molly had arranged to meet Andrew and Gina next to the forestry demo at two o'clock – it was the one place everyone could find because of the noise from the chainsaws.

As they approached the noise got louder. Broad-shouldered men in lumberjack shirts and worn jeans carved an amazing array of animals and birds from gigantic logs as sweat glistened on their foreheads... *and elsewhere in some cases Molly noticed,* as shirts were cast off in the heat.

She couldn't see either of them. Molly checked her watch; it was only twelve thirty so there was still an hour and a half to kill. She slipped a tentative arm through Jason's leathered one and they smiled comfortably at each other. Molly nodded her head towards a coffee bar that stood opposite the forestry event and pulled him towards it. A snack and a long chat would be just perfect.

It was four o'clock. Miles Peterson sank back on to the mauve silk sheets and lit an extra long menthol

43

cigarette. The pretty blonde sighed in contentment as her hair fell over the squashed pillows, one arm draped across his overly tanned well toned chest. Miles *did* actually spend a fair amount of time in the gym – it was just that he managed to fit in a few extra activities whenever he could get away with it.

"Miss Dern, that was *more* than extremely satisfying." Rachel giggled and snuggled up even closer.

"Miles…" she trailed a finger in deep thought across his stomach… "when can I see you again?" The need to hear that commitment to a further meeting, to know he wanted it as much as she did, overpowered her common sense not to push it. "I get my car back from the garage in a couple of days," she continued quickly, desperate for a positive response, "we could meet somewhere out of town, maybe have a nice –" She broke off suddenly as he moved her arm and sat up.

"Don't get clingy now, *there's* a good girl." His tone had changed. It was clipped, patronizing – *and absolutely stone cold*. Rachel flinched. He was already out of the bed and had his jeans on before she could protest.

The half-burnt cigarette dangled from the corner of his mouth and ash fell to the floor with every jerky movement. He double bent the long stub in a bedside ashtray. Experienced fingers fastened trouser buttons at speed and his eyes avoided hers and swept the face of the radio alarm before he dragged his shirt over his head. When he was fully dressed, Miles reached for his designer blazer on the back of the dressing table chair.

"I'll call you sweetness, *okay?* Just don't *bug* me about the whole relationship thing. You know as well as I do – this… it's just fun – *for the both of us.*"

"Please don't –" it sounded lame as she leant up onto her elbow, but he'd already disappeared through the bedroom door. The rapid thud of his steps as he ran down the stairs left her lost as it always did when they went – lost and worthless.

In seconds she heard the roar of his Morgan Roadster start up as tears splashed onto the sheet. She watched the blurred spot darken and spread to purple against the lilac silk before she crossed over to the window, jaded and empty. Her lips tasted salty but she barely noticed as his car tore down the road until it was out of sight, the engine gradually tailed off in the distance to leave…*nothing.*

Her head remained against the alcove. Rachel stared long and hard at the space the burgundy and silver car had left behind, it was as if she could bring it back if she concentrated hard enough… as if she could bring *him* back.

Eventually she turned from the window and slumped down heavily onto the bed. Her worn heart was lost and alone that much was certain, but there was no way she could have predicted it would never shed lilac tears again.

FIVE

She clung to the white melamine cabinet. The room spun in white, huge whirlpools of it streaked liberally with red as she shook uncontrollably – hands, face, arms – all smeared with blood. Patchwork scarlet handprints decorated the door's architrave, the walls, the vanity unit, the toilet seat. She'd aimed herself at the toilet to throw up, although considering everywhere else...

The bathroom mirror forced her to lift up her head, look into its glass – *dragged* her eyes open to make her view the reflection. *It wasn't one she recognised.*

After the encounter with Jenny, Charlotte hadn't just ridden to the other side of the arena to calm down, she'd trotted Greta over to the river that ran around the edge of the park and dismounted.

On a peeling iron bench beside the water, with Greta tethered to its arm, her hand had instinctively pulled a couple of pills from her pocket. She never went anywhere without them these days. Some anti-depressants in high doses had been known to cause nightmares, but what the hell – she was already *in* one! It hadn't been easy swallowing on spit alone but she'd managed. As they'd tracked awkwardly down her dry throat her mind had flashed up long past images, haunted memories and stinging rows from six years before. Her rocked world had left her numb back then, and it did so again.

Greta had grazed quietly, looked every bit the champion, her champion for sure, but she'd known she wouldn't be jumping *that* day. It had been Charlotte's decision to go home early from the show that had transformed the rest of her afternoon... *and the rest of her life.*

By the time she'd returned to her horsebox, loaded Greta and arrived home, it was one o'clock. The house had been empty and Miles' car was not in the courtyard, but then she hadn't expected it to be given she'd just spotted its rear plate through a thin hedge in a side street on the way home. The dual shock of Jenny Flood's arrival in Kirkdale, *and* spotting the Morgan so badly hidden, had finally destroyed something in Charlotte that nobody can safely live without – *rationale*. It would have taken no longer than ten minutes to lead Greta into the field, change her clothes, jump into her own V6 and roar out of the courtyard back to that sparse hedge. Back to what could have merely been his scuppered afternoon and simply another major showdown. But that wasn't what had happened...

As she'd waited from a concealed vantage point for him to exit the property, Charlotte had trailed a finger across a blue nylon bag that sat on the passenger seat. The house had been unknown to her, but it was irrelevant *whose* house it was, what *was* relevant was that her husband was inside it. Inside it, almost certainly, with another woman – and there were no prizes for guessing what they'd been doing. Her nails had made that zippy sound over the top of the bag as she'd worked them backwards and forwards whilst she'd waited, whilst she'd concentrated her thoughts.

When he'd finally emerged, her stomach had lurched, her throat sandpapered and her eyes had remained glued to his Gucci jacket. The same jacket she'd bought him the previous Christmas. The jacket she'd queued over two hours for in the Harrods sale on a London weekend break.

As he'd leapt over the Morgan's low silver door into the burgundy leather seat, her gaze had been drawn upwards to the movement of curtains. Lilac curtains. Lilac curtains that hung in a room above the ground floor bay window – *bedroom curtains*. Charlotte had seen the blonde lean against an alcove wall and gaze after Miles, *her* Miles, as he'd disappeared down the road back to their world, their life and their shitty, fake marriage.

What had happened after that, Charlotte could barely remember. She'd tried but she simply couldn't. There was the clunk of her car door, the squeak of the garden gate, the front door that'd bounced off the snib – *Ms. Blonde had obviously left it open for Miles* – and that hideous stair carpet. She recalled all of that, but then......*nothing*.

The mirror held her gaze for a moment longer before Charlotte switched to auto pilot. Her movements were slow and deliberate at first as she began to wash herself, then the basin, the toilet, the floor, the architrave. After that she stepped up the momentum, moved more quickly as the need to be clean and get out of that house filtered through.

Panic began to surge then; it rose from the very depths of her stomach at an alarming rate, until it sat square and obtrusive in the back of her rasped throat.

As she stepped out of the en-suite back into the bedroom, a hand flew to her mouth in response to a scene that met her amnesic gaze. She heaved again and again but somehow managed to keep the threatened wave of bile in check. Her head swam for the umpteenth time as she eased herself slowly past the body, back pressed hard against the only clean wall until she reached the door to the landing.

Once out of the bedroom she staggered down the stairs, stumbled halfway and grabbed at the handrail to prevent a fall. At the bottom she suddenly stopped – eyes wild they darted uncontrollably, Charlotte gasped as her breath coursed in and out of her lungs, *hyperventilated lungs fit to bust! Think* – she ordered herself – *think first!* The front door had a little oblong viewing glass in its centre, through it she quickly checked the road at the front and from the hall's aspect window the neighbour's gardens to the right. Her heart thumped as blood pumped loudly in her ears; *it was too fast, too fast!* She leant heavily against a hall table, tried to stabilise her breathing then jumped away sharply as a lamp crashed to the floor. Her head swam, wave upon wave until she thought she would surely faint! She reached for the bronze Yale knob, paused for a moment to control the shakes, then cautiously opened the door. Charlotte reset the snib as she'd found it and checked the street both ways before she walked straight down the path to the waiting gate. She saw nobody, *and prayed that nobody had seen her.*

The change of clothes hadn't been easy. With the car parked in the quietest part of Clovelly Woods, Charlotte had flicked the switch to slide the electric hood shut and struggled to strip off in the cramped two-seater. At any other time it might have seemed erotic, fun even to be stark naked in the open air, *no doubt Miles had experienced it many times over the years,* she thought acidly. On this occasion, however, she couldn't get re-dressed fast enough – however, Houdini she definitely wasn't. Once changed, her blood-soaked clothes were stuffed into the black bin liner that had held the fresh set, and then hidden under a blanket in the boot. They could be burnt when she got home. The next ten minutes was spent breathing very slowly, very calmly – *in… and out… in… . and out* – until she was quite – quite relaxed… *almost serene.*

The tyres scrunched on the courtyard gravel at Willows Copse. Charlotte pulled up alongside Miles' Roadster and turned off the engine. She sat motionless for a moment, heart still racing a little – then a flash bulb moment made her glance down to examine her hands. *Had she cleaned them well enough, got all that……muck out from under her nails?* She didn't even want to *think* the word *'blood' and her a doctor! Even with the gloves the red…stain had soaked through. Damn – should have used surgical ones. Well…next time then.*

'*Step out of the car in an ordinary fashion*' she instructed herself with silent lips. '*Be ready for any questions about the show, and above all……act normally*'. Charlotte surprised herself. Maybe she should've been an actress instead of a GP. She giggled as she let herself into the house, one hand over her mouth to try and stifle the rising hysteria…

The rest of the weekend had passed without any unusual events. Miles had even played landowner and took the sit and ride mower over the paddocks; he usually employed someone to do that. As the seconds slipped into minutes and the minutes into hours, her prolonged calm manner continued to amaze her. It was so *realistic*, it was almost *scary*. Not even pills could have achieved *that* sort of result. Still, she *had* come to see Miles in a different light now and it had made everything so much clearer, cleaner – simpler. No longer was he the erring husband she'd decided; no, from the day of the show he'd become something very different as far as Charlotte was concerned. As of four fifteen that Friday afternoon, Miles had become... *dispensable*. Yes... that was the word. If she cut her feelings dead it would make life a lot easier, more practical – *tidier*. No point in getting all jealous and upset over these silly girls, just make everything – *everyone*, inessential, superfluous, like life's hardware – *completely disposable*.

Monday morning dawned bright and sunny.

Like everyone else, Andrew had paid little attention when Rachel didn't turn up for work. It was such a normal occurrence for her to walk in at five to ten, that when everyone else had arrived, made coffee, sorted mail and got on with their respective day, there was nothing out of the ordinary for anyone to be aware of.

As the morning turned into lunchtime however, Andrew had found himself looking out of the window to the high street, Rachel's car still being in dock, he'd kept watch on the bus stop. His screen had precious little more in the way of work displayed on it than it had at eleven thirty, but he just couldn't concentrate – particularly after he'd got no reply from either of Rachel's phones.

Something Gina had said about Molly's latest daft dream, or *vision*, or whatever it was, *did* actually pop into his head, just for a split second, but he'd immediately chucked it out again.

The clock on the *Courier* wall said ten past two. Andrew dropped a pen down on to the desk and bounced it back through his fingers. He repeated it again and again, glanced up at the clock for the umpteenth time, but it was only ever a couple of minutes later than his previous check.

Jenny had gone across town with Stella at noon to interview the owner of a new restaurant that'd just opened up, and Peter was busy with whatever he found to do in his office. Rachel, however, had still not turned up and hadn't rung in either. Although she was notoriously late *every* day, she always rang in if she wasn't coming, and she was *never* later than eleven.

Andrew tried her again, but there was still no answer from the landline and her mobile was turned off. He considered how upset she'd been the previous week over her latest romantic disaster. Surely she wouldn't have done anything stupid? *Would she?* Andrew threw the pen across the desk, really anxious now. He bit his bottom lip as his eyes got pulled back up to the clock. There had never been anything between them and it wasn't as if he was responsible for her, she was a grown woman for God's sake. But they *had* worked together for over five years, and there was just something about Rachel, something that'd always made him feel, well......*he just wanted to look out for her.*

Two thirty. He released an audibly impatient sigh and ran agitated fingers through his hair. At the other end of the office Peter's head was still bent over his work. He hadn't seemed particularly worried about his employee's absence, but then he knew very little about any of his staff's personal life, and he'd *always* left Rachel to Stella. Andrew on the other hand had been at the receiving end of Rachel's despair since her ex-husband Roger's adultery three years before. In fact, he'd been the one that supplied the kitchen roll, coffee and a sympathetic ear at the end of *every* relationship she'd indulged in, *and lost*, ever since.

Andrew leant forward, and with both hands on his desk pushed the chair sharply away and got up. He swept his jacket off the back, strode down the office and marched straight out of the door to the car park. Peter Gray barely managed to look up from his desk.

It was sheer luck Andrew didn't attract the police with the speed he ramped up on the way to Rachel's. Once out of the *Courier's* side road his foot floored the accelerator. He hung a left at Turners Garage along the high street, straight through a red – over to the middle of the road then threw a right into Grangers Crescent. Even his old Ford could turn up trumps when his back was against the wall! Down to the end of Grangers – where he narrowly missed a car backing out of its drive – and round into Darcy Avenue. Every corner was cut, every red light was run and his gearbox didn't sound too healthy either. The usual fifteen-minute journey took no longer than nine as he screeched to a halt outside Rachel's house. There was a long path up to the front door, a door which looked kind of distorted from the gate. *Surely his eyesight wasn't going* he thought as he ran past rose bushes, pansies and a whole row of geraniums – all of which persisted in growing despite Rachel's aversion to gardening. Her dislike of anything that involved getting close to the green and earthy was something he'd always teased her about.

Once Andrew reached the door he realised why it had appeared 'off set'. He pushed at the snib with his thumb but it wouldn't retract until he released it. The door had been unlocked and was resting on the latch then – *but for how long?* And more to the point – *why?*

"Rachel?" He called out tentatively from the threshold then listened for a reply as he stepped into the hall. There was a scrunch beneath his feet. He looked down to see a smashed lamp and swallowed the lump in his throat as he stepped gingerly over the glass. He felt awkward walking uninvited into a woman's house however well intentioned, particularly as she hadn't answered him, and there was broken glass all over the hall floor…

"Rachel love, are you in? It's Andy." Nothing. He took a few steps towards the kitchen and wondered if he should try and find something to protect himself with. Gently his foot nudged at the half-open door. It

creaked slightly. The room was empty. He picked up a carving knife from the counter and gripped it tightly as he stepped back into the hall.

"Rachy are you there hun?" Nothing. He pushed at a door nearest the kitchen. *"We were worried at work but nobody's mad at you, not even Stella."* Still no answer. It was the dining room and a quick glance through its patio doors to the back garden told him she wasn't outside either.

When Andrew had checked the lounge he returned to the hall and negotiated the area around the bottom of the stairs to avoid the broken lamp. He held the knife out in front of him and began to climb. *Maybe she'd just had a severe migraine, knocked the lamp over and went to bed to sleep it off,* he thought. *Or maybe a chronic stomach bug? Still, it didn't explain the front door – and what in God's name is that bloody smell?* A heavy sweet odour hung in the air. He'd noticed it immediately he entered the house, but as he mounted the stairs it grew stronger. When Andrew had reached the top he felt quite nauseated; the smell was overwhelming, it clung to the carpet, the curtains, his clothes, everything. *Shit! Could it be some kind of gas leak?* He stood quietly and listened, but couldn't hear anything. It was then that he realised he'd stopped calling Rachel's name.

There were four white doors set around a single galleried landing and all were closed except the one to his right, the one opposite a streaked lead paned window. It had begun raining again. Andrew turned at the top of the stairs and walked along the landing towards the door that was ajar. He lifted his arm to push it open, afraid now of what he might find. His hand hovered in mid-air for a second; then he allowed the knifepoint to connect with the door until it moved inwards – and walked hesitantly into the room.

"Rachy…are you…?" No more words were needed. After he dropped the knife and introduced his breakfast to the bedroom floor, he staggered backwards onto the landing, grabbed the stair rail and collapsed. In two short steps, Andrew Gale's world had gone from caring colleague and smalltown reporter, to reluctant psychic believer and amateur sleuth.

Dazed and trembling, he fumbled blindly in his pocket for his mobile and rang the police. Afterwards he punched in the private family number of the Carpenters Arms… *and asked for Molly Fields.*

SIX

At forty-nine, Harry Longbridge had been a DCI for ten years and an experienced cop for over twenty. He hadn't always lived in a country town, the move to Kirkdale was his wife's idea, but even including his Met days, he'd never seen a murder scene quite as grotesque as the one in front of him. When a couple of the more seasoned Scenes of Crime Officers had embarrassingly made use of the victim's en suite, he wasn't exactly surprised. The young guy who'd found the woman had missed it, judging by his 'eau de vomit' cologne and damp shirt sleeves during his interview. Harry's stomach was made of sterner stuff, however, years of his wife's culinary non-delights and readily available fast food outlets had seen to that.

He wandered slowly around Rachel's bedroom, fast sharp eyes flashed into every corner, every surface and every drawer. He was known as *The Magpie* in the squad for rarely missing a trick. Nobody could have missed the knife, but it had already been ruled out as an attack or murder weapon. There was ash on the floor and a cigarette stub bent over in an ashtray on a bedside table next to it. The victim still had the remains of bright pink lipstick on her mouth, the butt did not. The thing that most puzzled him about this murder scene though wasn't the fact there was no lipstick on the stub, or even that the weapon was missing, that was often the case, no, the thing that puzzled him most was that Longbridge had absolutely *no* idea what could have been used to kill Rachel Dern. The gaping hole in her chest was huge, he knew of no gun that could have caused that without making a lot more mess. Anyway, that would have been like using a sledgehammer to crack a nut. The direction of the blood spray didn't correlate with any type of bullet entering and leaving the body, and SOCO had been all over the room – there *was* no bullet. Neither was there any wood or glass splinters in the wound, just a gaping hole to the left-hand side – *straight through the heart*. Whatever had been used to make that hole had been held by someone who wanted to make a statement. They'd already used chloroform as their first weapon of choice, presumably to make the job easier. That sickly sweet smell was everywhere; *God knows how much they'd used*. The chest wound had almost certainly been unnecessary to affect death; the amount of anaesthetic alone would've been enough to affect death. *That*, thought Longbridge, as he turned to leave the room, *was exactly why a statement was being made by the killer*. One he intended to get down officially.

"*Walker!! Get yourself up here!!*" yelled Harry over the banister to the young PC on sentry duty at the front door. "My belly thinks my throat's been cut, and my mouth's like a gorilla's pit. Get down the baker's and sort a pile of sausage sarnies and coffee, all round."

"But – *sir*," he called as he ran halfway up the stairs from the hall. "What about the front –?"

"Don't you worry about playing garden statues for the day son, I need a grub runner. Just get down that shop; *and don't hang about!*" One thing that definitely wasn't going to get overlooked was Harry's lunch, even if it was twenty to four. Rookie Joe Walker realised that yet again, he was going to get stung for the take-out…

On the drive to the Carpenters Arms, Andrew went over the shock of the last few hours in his head. He wasn't just remembering it, he was analysing it. *Why was the door on the latch? Did Rachel leave it like that deliberately? Did that mean she knew her killer then? Who was he and why murder her? What possible reason could there have been? He could have barely known her! Unless it was the guy she'd split up with. Was that a possibility? Had she thought they were getting back together again? Was that why the door was unlocked, so he could let himself in?*

The questions just kept coming and demanded answers that Andrew simply didn't have. Not yet anyway. The sight of his friend lying on the floor at the side of the obviously well-used bed, her body prostrate, the copious quantities of blood, that… that *grotesque hole* in her chest – all of it played repeatedly, movie

sized in his head. Somehow he had to find out why –
how – and most importantly – *who?*

The chloroform, so heavy in the air, had attached itself
to the fibres of his clothes, mixed with the vomit and
walked out of the house to climb into the car with him,
as this time he drove at a normal speed across town to
meet the girls.

*That DCI was something else. Boy had he been
watching too many American cop dramas,* thought
Andrew as he wrinkled his nose at a sniff of his sleeve.
His full statement was due to be taken at the local
station the following morning, but as he drove to the
pub he recalled the initial brief interview with Harry
Longbridge following his 999 call in Rachel's lounge…

"Ah… Mister… er…" – Longbridge had consulted
his notebook – "Gale. Mister Gale, I understand you
were the gentleman who reported finding Miss Dern in
this most… *unfortunate way."*

"If you mean did I find her *dead*, then yes I am!"
Andrew had shot back; angry at the description of how
he'd just found his long-time colleague and friend. He
hadn't liked the officer's phrasing one *bit.* It wasn't *bloody
unfortunate,* it was *tragic! Terrible! Horrific! Devastating!*
Any number of alternative adjectives, but it definitely
was *not bloody unfortunate!*

Longbridge had just waited patiently, staring at
him. Andrew had continued on. "She didn't turn up
for work so I came over to check she was okay."

"Bit of an over-reaction wasn't it Mister Gale, just because she hadn't arrived for work at the usual time you decided to check up on her? Do that often do you if she's late? What time *was* this exactly?"

This was going to be one sarcastic bastard, Andrew could feel it. "About two forty p.m. Rachel was always late, it was a thing with her everyone kind of accepts… accepted it. Her mother had been a longstanding friend of the *Courier's* owners," *but that wasn't the point.* He had already explained why. "She was *never* later than eleven a.m. and she always rang in if she wasn't well or couldn't make it for some reason. *She didn't call.*"

Andrew remembered how Longbridge had scrutinised every word that had come out of his mouth. It had felt like he was suspicious of anybody who had vaguely known Rachel, mainly if *they* were still breathing.

"Even so it seems a little… shall we say *full on* for want of a better expression," Longbridge had replied, and eyed *him* full on then. "Were you having a relationship with this young woman Mister Gale? Or if not recently, have you at any other time?" Andrew had felt distinctly uncomfortable about this line of questioning. He'd never actually been out on a date with Rachel, but he'd always been very fond of her, and for some ridiculous reason felt he should keep an eye on her. Look out for her. He'd even done a couple of odd jobs around the house, but then so had his boss, Peter Gray. *How would all that sound to Columbo here though?*

"No, Rachel… Miss Dern… and I had never had anything other than a friendly working relationship – *at any time,*" he added pointedly. The policeman had carried on looking at him steadily for what seemed an age. Eyes level with his own he'd remained very quiet in the opposite chair and waited for Andrew to add something extra. He didn't. It had felt as if he hadn't *quite* believed him. He could imagine exactly what Longbridge had been thinking at that moment. *They were of a similar age these two, worked together for quite a while. This young woman had been very attractive until some sadistic bastard had put a crater in her chest.* Finally he'd dropped his eyes back down to his notebook before suddenly flicking them back up as if something had occurred to him. He'd begun again…

"Do you know if the deceased had been seeing anyone else recently? I understand that she was single, a divorcee I believe?" Andrew held his gaze. *What did he mean by 'else'* he'd thought; *'else' implied he was suggesting she'd been seeing him at some point – didn't it? And he hadn't for God's sake – he'd just told Longbridge that.*

"Yes, that's right, Roger Dern." Andrew had continued calmly. More calmly than he'd felt. "Three years ago. He had an affair and Rachel threw him out." Anticipating the next question he added; "I don't know his whereabouts now." Andrew watched as Longbridge continued to fill in his little black book. He carried on. "After that she… she had a lot of – boyfriends."

"*Really* – and do you know any of these men, these... *boyfriends?* Did you meet any of them socially?"

"Actually – no, no I didn't." It was only then that for the first time Andrew had realised that nobody really knew any of the men Rachel had gone out with since being married to Roger. Well nobody at work anyway, nobody *he* knew. "The relationships never seemed to last very long," he added. "I think a lot of them were doomed to fail... if you know what I mean?"

"No I don't know what you mean Mister Gale – explain." *That bloody look again, why couldn't he talk normally* he remembered thinking. *I know he has a job to do but I didn't kill her and this guy would make Mother Theresa feel guilty.*

"Well they were mostly already married or in long-term live-in relationships. Rach was always getting hurt, let down. Nobody ever thought it would end like this..."

"Nobody? And who is... *are...* nobody? Friends? Relatives? Neighbours?" Andrew had sighed then, something else the Inspector had noted down. Obviously he'd thought him 'twitchy' and impatient – *he was.*

"I was referring to people at work," Andrew had explained. "Rachel often arrived in tears when a relationship had finished, we used to mop her up, make her coffee, *listen –* you know, *be a friendly face?*" It had been *his* turn to sound sarky then. It was ignored. At that moment he'd thought DCI Longbridge probably had very *few* friends. He'd imagined him sitting at home every night trying to solve the Jack the Ripper case or something similar. Anything that needed unravelling or sorting out effectively, something somebody else had failed to do, failed to wrap up and conclude to *the Magpie's* standards. The young PC on the doorstep had spilt *that* little morsel; he certainly couldn't imagine the *Magpie* having fun with friends. Hell he'd never even seen the guy smile yet, not even to shake his hand, but he'd noticed a wedding ring and Andrew had felt sorry for whoever *she* was. The Chief Inspector had spoken again then.

"So… in that case you think a jealous woman could be involved do you?" *Making assumptions again* Andrew had thought.

"I guess that's possible. *Anything's* possible, but as I said, I never knew who she was seeing. Anyway, she broke up with the latest one last week; as far as I know she hadn't met anyone else." Andrew hadn't mentioned that Rachel had seemed a little happier over the previous few days, as if she *had* actually met somebody new. At the time he didn't know why he'd kept that information back – he just had.

"Okay Mr Gale, that'll do for now, thank you for your time." The little black book had snapped shut indicating an abrupt end to their 'chat'. "Perhaps you could make arrangements to call in at Kirkdale Police Station tomorrow morning sometime, make a full statement?" It's on River Street – just in case you aren't familiar with it." Harry had stood up then, at which point Andrew had felt dismissed, like a naughty schoolboy – but there was something else too. It was as though Longbridge had decided he'd had enough of interviewing him, like there was some urgent event waiting. Andrew had left and assured he'd call in to River Street the following day, but he was also curious as to what it was he'd appeared so suddenly agitated about.

By the time Andrew had arrived at the pub and persuaded Molly to swap shifts, and Gina had returned from visiting her Gran in the nursing home, it was six o'clock before the three got a chance to talk together. Now they sat in the private lounge at the Carpenters Arms, doubles poured all round – all three in shock.

"It was just… *awful,*" said Andrew quietly – he looked over at Molly with renewed respect for her 'abilities'. Sat next to him, Gina watched in surprise as he knocked back his brandy in one go and set the glass back on the coffee table. He picked up the bottle Ron Fields had left and poured himself another. Just as he was about to replace the bottle he changed his mind, topped it up a bit more and drank it down. He winced as it kicked the back of his throat. Gina noticed Molly's surprise too.

"I've worked with Rachel for more than five years," he continued, "I know she always got herself into disastrous relationships, often with married guys, but she didn't deserve to *die* for it. I want to find out who *did* this. I know the police are doing their job but I can't just sit around and do nothing." Gina and Molly glanced at each other again, they both knew once Andrew had made his mind up the deal was done – neither of them would be able to change it.

"Don't think you can go into this alone," Molly reasoned, "the last thing Rachel would want is for something to happen to you too – and what about *Gina?*" Her friend drank deeply of her second double Scotch and coke – it didn't help her pallor. Molly persisted; "Just exactly how do you propose to start and where?" You're a reporter of events not a policeman who investigates them, and *they* aren't going to thank you for nosing around." Reminded of Harry Longbridge's interviewing techniques, Andrew snorted and drank some more, he knew *that* officer would definitely not want him anywhere near. Andrew decided not to go into his opinions of the local constabulary, or a detailed description of his 'interview'. The girls eyed each other again and waited for him to speak.

"Rachel had seemed… I dunno… *lifted* somehow, *brighter* at work over the last couple of days. I think she'd met somebody else since her recent break-up. I know he smokes for a start because *she* didn't, not anymore anyway. I know she occasionally used a bit of weed when she was *really* down, but she gave up regular cigarettes a couple of years back." He paused. *"There was a stub in an ashtray beside the bed."*

"Oh *great!*" exclaimed Gina, exasperated by her boyfriend's apparent simplistic summary of the evidence. *"That would narrow it down then!"* She folded her arms and threw herself back against the cushions in frustration. Andrew turned to her…

"Gee I *have* to do this." Their eyes held each other's in a desperate mix of love, concern, determination – and the unknown. Molly stumbled a little over her next comment and broke the uncomfortable silence in a quiet and resigned voice.

"I… I had another dream."

"Yes we know," said Gina, "I told Andy that's why he rang you pretty much straightaway after… after he found –"

"No Gee – no, not that one… not the vision, I had another *dream,* on Friday after the country show. You know I told you I met that guy Jason, and never got around to meeting you two by the forestry demo?" Andrew and Gina nodded in unison. "Well that night I dreamt I was suffocating, had some kind of… *cloth* or something held over my face. There was this smell – heavy, sweet – and then I passed out. I woke up about two a.m. feeling cold, *very* cold. I even felt kind of… *'heady'.*"

Andrew turned grey, looked like Molly really *did* have some kind of psychic thing going on – *not just a one off then.*

"She was chloroformed first." He started uneasily, "before… before she was stabbed with – " Andrew hesitated as Gina's bottom lip began to quiver, "with – something," he finished cautiously. Their horrified expressions left him uncertain whether he should be too exact or even go on at all. He decided to tailor it. "Even the police don't know what it could be yet." His eyes glazed slightly as he lowered them toward his hands and ran a finger up the side of his brandy glass. Gina enclosed her fingers around them as Andrew went on. "The wound to her chest was… not small, and completely the wrong shape for a knife or a bullet. I've been racking my brains all afternoon trying to work out what it could be. Just keep on seeing her *lying* there, covered in blood and that… *sweet, thick* scent of anaesthetic filling the room, in my nose – my mouth." He screwed up his face and grimaced… *"I can still taste it…"*

Unbeknown to Andrew, Harry Longbridge *did* have something else waiting on his attention just before Andrew had left. When Harry's stomach growled and his caffeine withdrawal kicked in, his brain ground to a complete halt. It had been the same way for years, his glucose levels were shit. A round of sausage on white and a much-needed cup of caffeine had been waiting fifteen minutes in the kitchen whilst he'd questioned Andrew – he'd hung on as long as he could. It was semi-warm polystyrene coffee, but it was coffee. As the well sugared liquid had slid down his throat and the comfort food hit the right spot, he could feel the sharpness return and spread through his system.

'*You know something else Mister Gale,*' he'd thought, eyes narrowed as he drained the cup – '*I don't know what or who yet – but I will.*'

SEVEN

The plate sailed past the oak cupboard doors, drifted to the ground in slow motion and crashed spectacularly onto the ceramic tiled floor to shatter beyond repair. As his white knuckles gripped the edge of the work surface the blood drained from Miles' face, in those first few moments his sunbed tan was unable to deliver its usual golden hue. *Rachel... dead? How? Why?* He continued to hold the worktop for support as he stared through the window across the courtyard to the horses in the paddock and beyond – but he didn't see any of it. He didn't see the stables or the ménage, the Willows or the Oaks. He didn't see the hedgerows or the numerous rabbits that had taken over their land. He didn't see *anything* except the imprint of those deathly dark images the news item had concocted, delivered – then so selfishly left behind.

He was thankful at least that Charlotte was still upstairs when he'd heard the gut-wrenching instalment of his latest short-lived fling, but she soon came running down when the sound of smashed china echoed through the hallway. She rounded the door into the kitchen and gasped as she recognised the tiny delicate blue flower on a piece of their best dinner service.

"Oh *Miles* how *could* you!!" That's the *fourth* plate you've broken! *For Christ's sake my parents bought us that collection for a wedding present and it's not cheap!* She began to pick up the larger of the jagged sections and pushed him aside from the sink cupboard door to find the dustpan and brush. He didn't hear her as she ranted on about not looking after their things, how he *always* managed to break something important, something that was important to *her*. He didn't hear as she carried on sweeping and accusing, brushing and shouting, until all the shattered pieces were in the pan and then finally dumped unceremoniously into the bin. The radio news slot had already finished as she'd first surveyed the damage, now an old Stones number rocked the airwaves as it stomped noisily around their 'quiet' country kitchen.

"Why do you always have to use that set anyway?" she yelled above Jagger's scraping vocals. "*I'll* tell you why Miles because you *always* want the best of *everything*, *all* of the time, *that's* why!" He was still staring out of the window.

"Miles are you *listening* to me?" She walked over to the window stood right behind him, pulled him around by the shoulder and pointed accusingly towards the open bin.

"W – what?" He looked at Charlotte's irritated expression, at the bin and back to her face again, then realised why he'd been able to hear her voice in the distance somewhere, but hadn't registered it.

"Oh... *God – I'm so sorry!*" He held his head in his hands, ashen-faced when he saw what he'd done. "It just... slipped, must've been wet, *I'll replace it, buy another!*" He tried to placate her; he knew she was right, *she was always right...* Miles reached for an everyday plate from the rack and fervently hoped she hadn't noticed the real reason for his absent-mindedness, then shoved some bread in the slots and pushed the toaster lever down. Charlotte snorted – an irritated moan escaped as she threw both hands in the air, pulled cereal boxes from the cupboard and milk from the fridge. She began to set the farmhouse table for breakfast completely oblivious to the fact her husband had just unwittingly learned he was living with a murderess...

The doors to the surgery swung open with an unusually heavy force when Dr. Peterson barged through and marched into reception. His face was stern as he swept past the admissions desk, walked quickly down the corridor and turned left to his consulting room. Gina's mouth dropped open in surprise as did several of her colleagues, but not for the same reason as the young redhead. She couldn't remember the last time she hadn't reluctantly flushed hot with embarrassment because of Miles winking at her or flashing one of his appreciative morning smiles. As he flew past the wall of the nurses clinic his elbow caught the edge of a painting and sent it askew, he ignored it and carried on. Without exception and regardless of age, every woman within view of that reception area watched in a mixture of lustful amazement as the tails of his navy pinstripe jacket disappeared around the corner.

Inside his office the seriousness of his predicament began to sink in. The news report had mentioned that the pathologist had placed Rachel's time of death as sometime on Friday afternoon. Whoever killed her *must* have arrived soon after he'd left which meant he had to have been the last person to see her alive prior to the murderer. He fished a half empty packet of Consulate and Zippo out of his pocket and a glass ashtray from the back of a drawer in his desk. Smoking was expressly forbidden anywhere inside the building, but at that moment his nerves weren't interested in rules. He leant worriedly against the desk and lit the cigarette. As he drew heavily on its pure white menthol he began to think straight for the first time since he turned on the radio that morning. There were no details of him with any police station in the UK, he'd never been in trouble with the law, and no DNA had been collected anywhere to his knowledge. *And he was innocent for Christ's sake!* No. There was no need to panic. He was the local GP and a respected pillar of the community. Well – maybe the pillar part was a bit of a stretch but he hadn't done anything wrong, therefore there was no reason to be concerned. He wasn't even her doctor. If he kept his head down, carried on with his work and let the police get on with theirs, everything would be fine. One thing he certainly *wouldn't* be doing was walking into the local station with even a scrap of information about his relationship with Rachel. If Charlotte found out what he'd been doing whilst she'd been at the country show there would be hell to pay. *More than that...* He flicked the ash off the end of his cigarette, took a last couple of drags and after spraying the room with a mini air freshener, double bent the butt into the glass tray. He felt a lot better – *things never looked so bleak when you analysed them properly.*

Charlotte had the day off. She pointed the remote at the lounge TV and sat back. It was no surprise to her to see the local news carried a slot on Rachel's murder or that the police hadn't a clue about the weapon used. She snapped a ginger biscuit in two with her teeth and chewed one half slowly; the other she drowned in her coffee a couple of times and put that in her mouth too. She calmly brushed some crumbs off her lap, popped a couple of pills and relaxed into her black leather recliner with a smile. As she listened, her eyes were drawn to an area above her oak mantelpiece. An area that displayed an ancient Chinese replica bought on a long-ago trip to Hong Kong, a trip, place and time when she'd been happy. She was lost for a few moments in that memory, the voice of the news reporter faded into the distance, her eyes briefly glistened at blurred mental images...

Suddenly cymbals and trombones crashed loudly in her living room as a brass band appeared on screen. She blinked away the past, extended her arm and changed channels.

Across town the *Courier* was a hive of activity, everyone was in deep shock over Rachel's murder. The police had been in to take statements from all of the *Courier's* employees regarding their own relationships with her, and any knowledge they'd had of her home and social life. Only Andrew had needed to report to the station to give a written statement as he was the one who'd found her.

Stella sat utterly mortified with Peter in his office. Although she'd always appeared exasperated by Rachel's lifestyle and behaviour patterns, deep down she'd really been very fond of her. She'd known Rachel since she was born, in fact Stella had *seen* Rachel being born, helped her friend Pam through the labour and the first few years that followed till she got on her feet. Rachel's father had disappeared pretty much after the conception and hadn't been seen since, so the nearest she'd ever got to a father was Peter. Despite not getting involved with Rachel's personal life, Peter Gray was nevertheless in an equal state of shock to Stella. The young woman had been the daughter of a close friend who'd died ten years ago, and his wife had promised she would always keep a caring eye on her. Now Stella felt she'd let Pam Delaney down – *and Peter knew this was a story his wife would not leave to anyone else – including the police.*

Andrew arrived back at the *Courier* from Riverside just as their officers from the murder squad were leaving. He still didn't know how or what he was going to do to discover the truth behind Rachel's death, including who'd killed her, but he thought maybe a really well written report in the *Courier* might help. *Some*body must know something *somewhere*. He just needed to find them. He also knew he had to convince Stella to let him work on this story with her, let one of the 'bods' upstairs cover his sport reports for a couple of weeks. It was the first time a murder had occurred in the village for a very long time, certainly the first since he'd been working at the paper. Stella would be all over it, dominate and devour it, particularly considering her personal involvement. *But Andrew wanted in too.* Two days later they ran the story between them, Stella Gray had just broken the habit of a lifetime and Andrew was not going to disappoint her.

On the Thursday, three days after discovering Rachel's murder, and publishing day for the *Courier*, the front cover hit Kirkdale like a gigantic tidal wave. A newly discovered volcano in the middle of town would have been less of a shock. Their village just did not *have* murders, a few burglaries, the odd pub brawl, even a suicide once, but not murders. Andrew sat at his desk and read Stella's final draft once more, this time in their paper published that morning. Before he realised it, a quiet mousey haired young woman in a green wax jacket and matching Hunter boots stood in front of him. He noticed the brown footprints that led from the front door all the way down the office to his desk, getting lighter and lighter as the carpet sucked up the wet rainwater from the owner's rubber souls.

"Hello, Miss… err… ?"

"Kinkade, Josie Kinkade. I'm a… *was* a close friend of Rachel Dern's. I've been away for a few days, came back this morning – to *this.*" She threw a copy of the *Courier* on his desk. *"I can't believe it."* She bit back a tear, "I only saw her last week." Andrew took in her broad Scottish burr, clear complexion and minimum make-up. "Rach and I spent the evening in the Carpenters Arms over by the river. That's why I've come here today, soon as I heard, to tell you what I know. What I *think* I know anyway." Andrew sat up, attentive now.

"How do you mean…what you *know*?"

"You know how she was… about… *men?* Well that evening she was so upset about the latest one that'd dumped her, we went out to drown her sorrows. Then this man walks across the bar and drops a note in her lap. It was his mobile number. Rachy was back on track the moment they locked eyes, then he sauntered off back to his table in the restaurant."

"What point are you making Josie?" asked Andrew. "Did Rachel see this man alone after that evening?"

"I don't know. I can't be sure, but it's my guess she did. She said she was going to ring him, said he was too gorgeous not to. I told her to forget it that he was *bound* to be married or involved, but you know how she was, always craving love; craving attention. I had to go home to Glasgow the next day, on the Saturday. I've only just got back. I *can't* go to the police with this." Andrew's eyebrows rose slightly. She continued on quickly. "I've got my reasons and I'm not prepared to go into them, so don't ask." He didn't. "I was hoping you could do something. Rach often spoke of you lot here, her friends at work, she thought of everyone here as family you know. She didn't have any of her own after her mum died."

Andrew looked Josie Kinkade straight in the eyes – "Finding Rachel's killer is uppermost in my mind. I found her – feel I owe it to her."

"Oh *God*... I'd no *idea!*" Josie felt for the chair to her left, legs now buckled she made use of it. *"It didn't say anything in the report!"* she exclaimed as she sat down grabbed the paper back off the desk and hastily scanned the two pages.

"You won't find it, it's not there. I didn't want to publicise it, didn't want to... alert anyone to the fact that it was me who'd found her." He automatically glanced around even though he knew was in a safe place. It was almost as if he felt the killer was already aware he was looking for them, and on their trail. "What did this guy look like; the one in the pub?"

"Tall, fair, tanned, rich and with a cocky attitude even though he never actually said anything, just stood at the bar eyeing Rachel. He stared straight at her, like he held her in a trance or something, she was glued to it. Then he walked over, dropped the mobile number in her lap, walked back to the bar and picked his drinks up and disappeared to wherever his table was. It was pretty crowded, I didn't see him again – that's all I know. It just seems too much of a coincidence that by the Monday she was dead."

"I agree, but it's not much to go on. I do have a friend in the Carpenters though. I'll ask her if she noticed anything that night." Josie nodded quickly, looked at her watch, stood up and thanked him for anything he could do. She gave him her mobile number, picked up the paper and left the building just as Jenny Flood came off her phone.

"That was Molly. She said to tell you she's had another dream."

EIGHT

The discovery of the second body wasn't just a shock to Harry Longbridge it was more like an intrusion. Like many people he'd relocated to the quiet Cumbrian village for exactly that reason. It was quiet. Two bodies in under a week with no leads was just bloody inconsiderate.

The young woman had been found by a dog walker under the Bridge at Devil's Drop, an historical beauty spot along the river that was popular with gundog owners who liked to give their dogs a swim. It was a Labrador that had sniffed this one out from a badly disguised hideout which was basically a few fallen branches roughly dragged across the body. It was almost as if the killer had wanted it to be found so little effort had been made to conceal it. It was obvious that the murder weapon was the same as before... an unknown one, and the gaping chest wound dared every one of the CID team to hold on to their lunch.

He recognised the newspaper reporter at the scene immediately as the guy who'd found the first victim. He also realised that if this killer hadn't ended his or her work with this poor woman, it was likely Andrew Gale was going to become a fixture in his life, certainly for a while. Harry Longbridge disliked newspaper reporters. They got in his way, complicated investigations and invariably hung around like a bad smell. All to gain a few team points with their bosses by trying to solve the crimes themselves. He had a sneaking suspicion that this was *exactly* the situation that faced him with Andrew Gale and he didn't like it. He didn't like it one bit. Not only that, this young man had an extra axe to grind that would keep him beavering and digging away at this case until he'd found the murderer. No doubt he would put his own life at risk and cause Harry more trouble in the process. The first death had been one that was very close to this particular journalist, quite how close Harry had yet to discover, but he knew that somewhere along the line there was a connection with Mr. Gale. He may have been plagued with hypoglycaemia most of his life, but it hadn't skewed his senses, and thirty years in the force had sharpened his nose for a mystery for sure.

"Mr. Gale. We meet again. Strange that wherever I find dead bodies you are never very far behind." Andrew ignored the implication and took out his notebook.

"Just doing my job Detective Inspector," said Andrew with an overly broad smile, "it's the news that makes the world go round, without it the public would be ignorant of the facts." Harry snorted. The amount of rubbish that found its way into most rags informed nobody of anything but hearsay, red herrings and sometimes downright lies. It also often completely fouled up some cases, murder cases in particular. Where the Crown Prosecution Service believed certain evidence could no longer be admitted in court, it caused the loss of many prosecutions, thus dangerous psychos walked free. No, Harry did not like the press.

"But it appears that you are somewhat like a dog with a bone on this particular news story. You appear to find murder of particular interest – am I right Mr. Gale?"

"When it affects my friends and colleagues – yes *undoubtedly*. You can't blame me for wanting to find out the truth behind Rachel's death."

"And what makes you think that this poor woman is linked to Ms. Dern's unfortunate demise?" That bloody word again. *Unfortunate!* Andrew took a sharp intake of breath and held back an angry retort.

"How many murders do you know of that have occurred in this town? I only know of one before Rachel and that was ten years ago. Even I can work out that this latest one must be connected. There could be a serial murderer out there. Did this girl die in the same way, and do you know who she is?"

"Unfortunately for us......yes... she did, and no, we don't know her identity as yet." Andrew began scribbling.

"So you are no nearer to discovering the murder weapon then?" He knew he'd touched a nerve.

"No – look Mr. Gale, we're too early on in our investigations to make *any* comment whatsoever about these murders. *Understand?* They are less than a week apart which in itself is difficult enough without you running around playing Sherlock, unless you have any further information to give *me* of course." Andrew *had* actually spoken to Molly on the phone about her latest dream, he was now convinced this psychic… 'thing' she had going on was going to lead him to the killer eventually, but could hardly mention that to Longbridge. He'd think he was a complete nutter. Molly had described the woman in her dream as having long ginger hair of medium height and slim build, that she was lying on leafy soil near some kind of water… *with a massive hole in her chest.* As soon as Andrew had heard the unfamiliar police sirens screaming through town he'd jumped in his car and taken an educated guess as to where they were coming from. It hadn't been difficult to follow the noise and find them all over Devil's Drop.

"No, I haven't any more information for you, I wish I had."

As the paramedics stretchered the body away from the crime scene and up the bank towards a waiting ambulance, a muddy blood-spattered arm fell lifelessly from underneath the heavy grey blanket, thin strands of rich ginger waves flew freely in the breeze. Andrew's eyes strayed to the dirty marmalade coloured hair where they remained a little too long. It was a gaze not missed by Harry Longbridge.

The young reporter turned to walk back up the grassy incline towards the road and his car. He'd discovered what he needed to know, Molly was spot on – he just wished she could *'see'* a bit more that would help him. The detective eyed his back as he climbed the slope.

"Mr. Gale!" he called out, "you're not thinking of going on holiday anywhere at the moment are you? Only I'd rather you didn't if you wouldn't mind." Andrew stopped at the top by the roadside and hesitated for a moment before he turned round. He sighed heavily…

"No-o-o- Mr. Longbridge," came the tired reply, "I'm not going on holiday, or anywhere else for that matter." He couldn't resist a sarcastic smile before adding; *"Are you?"* Harry shoved a hand in his pocket, pulled out a paper bag full of barley cubes and popped one in his mouth. He sucked down hard, felt the sugar rush into his bloodstream and pushed it over to one side with his tongue.

"It's DCI Longbridge to you *Mister* Gale – I've earned *my* title!" He turned away sharply, strode back to his team and began barking orders.

As Andrew drove down the narrow road past St. Peter's, he barely registered the newish but still mud-splattered Range Rover coming up the hill towards him. He was well on down the road back into town when Charlotte

Peterson took her foot off the accelerator and slowed slightly beside the seventeenth century church. A poker-hard expression hid privileged information of the previous evening's events as she turned sideways to look down on to the scene beneath Ratcatchers Bridge. Her eyes quickly scanned the white uniforms, noticed they far outnumbered the blue ones, the suits too as SOCO gathered what evidence they could. As they carefully packed little plastic bags with the tiniest of clues, hands gloved, she was barely able to repress the laugh that tickled the back of her throat. She satisfied herself with a smug smile that crept to the corners of her mouth. *There will be little to find down there boys, or anywhere else for that matter.*

The ambulance had pulled away from the kerb just as she'd arrived, and less than twenty seconds had passed since the Range Rover was in neutral. Now Charlotte engaged first, and the four by four roared its way further up the hill. As he heard the engine's efforts, DCI Harry Longbridge turned aside from a colleague and briefly caught the Rover's tailgate out of the corner of his eye before it disappeared around the back of the graveyard. Just for a nanosecond a flash of something hit a dim memory in the recess of his mind – then it was gone. Slowly he turned back to the SOCO officer and finished his conversation.

As Charlotte drove round the back of the church and on down the lane, her left hand delved into her handbag to root for cigarettes. She had given up a few years ago since the move to Kirkdale where she'd decided that from then on everything in her life would be fresh. Clean, fresh and healthy. However, the shock of seeing Jenny at the country show had sent her straight back to a forty a day habit and she hated her for that too. It was so bad for the skin, and apart from anything else had made her look a complete idiot where Miles was concerned. She'd nagged him for years to give up and now she'd reverted to the disgusting habit herself. How he'd laughed when he found out. The memory of it made her grimace. *She hated it when he poked fun at her.*

The knack of a packet retrieved one handed from an overly large, overly crowded handbag as she drove, still hadn't left her. The hot car lighter popped just as she managed to extricate the cigarette from its box. Soon she felt the warm nicotine kick leap into her lungs. Her body relaxed but her head spun and she let up on the accelerator. The long dark hair and slim body of Jenny Flood swam in front of her eyes. It was of course *all* her fault that everything had turned out the way it had. It was always Jenny's fault. It had been then and it was now. If only she hadn't turned up again all this… *messy* business wouldn't be necessary. She, Charlotte, would not have missed her class with Greta at the show the previous week, and she wouldn't have caught Miles out with that… that bitch *Rachel*. Not that in some ways she wasn't *grateful* to Jenny for that of course, but generally speaking it hadn't been helpful. It caused the need for

87

Charlotte to kill her – which naturally of course she had to do. The second woman hadn't *actually* bedded her husband (well not that she knew of), but she'd caught her *looking* at him in the surgery once, in that… sexy flirty way. No patient should look at their doctor like that – look at her *husband* like that. It wasn't healthy, it wasn't right. Under the circumstances what else was there to be done? It had become distinctly obvious that if these women weren't… *removed*, Miles would just succumb every time. It was utterly impossible for him to be faithful. Like most men, she thought as she inhaled and exhaled, Miles was simply *incapable* of keeping it in his trousers, so she, Charlotte, would remove *all* of the temptations that might stand in his way. The distinct flavour of her old favourite brand began to soothe her now. It probably wasn't really his fault anyway; completely irrational now as ash got tapped into the tray, she was… helping him, helping *them*, their *marriage* – their *future*. Yes, she thought as she checked the rear-view mirror, pulled up outside her two o'clock home visit and yanked on the handbrake. She was preventing a marital breakdown. It was the most practical answer. She flipped down the visor mirror, checked her hair and lipstick and smiled a long slow smile – it didn't quite reach her eyes. It never did. Contented, Charlotte stubbed the cigarette out in the ashtray and flipped her favourite car accessory back up into place. She reached over to the back to retrieve her doctor's bag, heaved it through to the front, opened the door and jumped down from the high seat. There was a spring in her step as she swung the black case up the path of the elderly, very safe female patient's cottage.

***

NEW YORK

Emily Stone leant back into soft beige calf leather. Her legs were crossed, her long fingernails exquisitely polished and manicured, her Ben de Lisi suit and Jimmy Choo shoes fitted her perfectly, *but her patience was wearing thin.*

In her plush editor suite of McCarthy Stone's New York office the phone on the desk in front of her hadn't stopped ringing all day, but as far as she was concerned it might as well have remained silent. She checked her watch again and added five hours. Still time then. She stared across the chicly designed room, out of its huge panoramic windows and over the water to Brooklyn and beyond, as she twisted her white gold wedding band round and round her finger. Manhattan Island had been her home for nearly half her life, yet every time she saw the Hudson River it pulled her further out, towards the ocean, towards home. The knock at the door and entrance of Megan Calder dragged her mind back into the present.

"Ms. Stone, I don't want to interrupt, but you *do* have a board meeting in five." Emily looked at the earnest face of the young PA and nodded curtly. She had been in her shoes once, taken orders from the upper echelons, but not for very long. It had been a prudent and quite cynical decision on her part to marry publishing giant Gareth Stone, but nonetheless it had been the right one. The marriage had been more successful than most in spite of everything.

"Thank you, I'll be there. Please ensure there is plenty of fresh ground Brazilian coffee, a variety of fruit juices, and that the handmade Swiss chocolates and cakes are available."

"Yes Ms. Stone, everything is ready."

Emily's gaze reclaimed her memory through the giant window as Megan left the room, instinctively knowing she'd been dismissed. It was then that the single long ring of the red metallic phone caught New York's most famous crime editor off guard. Emily's whole body twitched in anticipation as she leant forward to pick up the receiver…

NINE

Gino's was buzzing. It was a warm, muggy evening and although everyone wore thin light clothing, they were grateful for the three large ceiling fans. Even with the door open it was still an overly hot night. Unfortunately the pavement in that part of town was not wide enough to take exterior tables like some of the other bars and restaurants, but it was still packed which proved the extent of its popularity. There was the usual happy friendly atmosphere it was known for, the reason it was their favourite watering hole after the Carpenters. Situated on the corner of Main Street, Gino's had originally been a two-bedroom cottage, but like many other old buildings in town had been transformed into a thriving little bistro a few years ago. The original whitewashed walls and modern crimson window canopies worked well together.

Andrew stepped inside and welcomed the breeze across his face. It would probably be cooler inside anyway he thought as he stood in the doorway. His eyes scanned the room until he spotted the girls in a far corner by a large cheese plant; its green stalk climbed the white brickwork and worked its way along the edge of the ceiling to create a leafy vineyard feel. He smiled when he saw that Gina had got her favourite spot as usual and there were already two bottles of wine and three glasses on the table. Two of the glasses were half full and Molly and Gina were well into the first bottle of Bordeaux. It took little more than four long strides to reach them. Much as he liked the place it *did* remind him of his ultra small flat. *Still, it stocked the best selection of wines in the village and had a great reputation, so two out of three wasn't bad.*

"Got your favourite little corner then?" Andrew teased Gina as he gave her a peck on the cheek and lovingly stroked her back before he squeezed in next to her.

"Molly managed to grab it actually, I was a bit slow!" Gina replied as she rested her hand lightly on his knee. These two were made for each other thought Molly who'd begun to feel like an extra on a film set. She was truly happy for them but it had been a while since her last real boyfriend, and although surrounded by people every day, she'd started to get lonely. Pity that guy she met at the country show wasn't around but she hadn't seen or heard from Jason since that day, even though he'd taken her number. Molly had felt a bit peeved about that considering they'd got on rather well. *She'd* felt a spark. Obviously *he* hadn't.

"Molly are you with us? *Hello –o-o-oh, earth to Molly.*"

"Very funny Gale," she retorted, "just thinking about... *something*."

"Some *one* more like," Gina cut in. "Still not heard anything then?"

"No. I guess he was just passing through – doubt if I'll get to see him again so let's just forget about it."

"Who's this then, a lapsed boyfriend?" Andrew added.

"No, just that Jason I met at the show – remember? I didn't get to meet up with you and Gee by the forestry thing. I mentioned it the other day." Andrew nodded his recollection of the conversation. Molly continued. "Well I just... kinda *liked* him. He was different, hasn't rung though."

"You say he was just passing through Molls, so nobody had seen him before that day?"

"Nope, not that I know of..." Andrew narrowed his eyes in thought. "Now don't you run away with any ideas, you said that vet lady Josie insisted it was a tall *blonde* guy that gave his number to Rachel that night. Jason is medium height and *dark*. Unless he dyed his hair between Tuesday and Friday *and* bought stilts he's not our man. The only guy I clearly remember that fitted Josie's description was Dr. Peterson, but I never saw him talk to anyone other than his wife or the bar staff. They came in for a meal and were sitting restaurant end. If it *was* him Rachel got the mobile number from I didn't see it. To be honest I didn't really know her that well Andy, I can't even remember seeing her that night. I've certainly never met Josie, so the two of them together wouldn't have registered with me anyway."

"Well it's not impossible to buy hair tint," Andrew pointed out, "you can pick up a bottle from practically any chemist but – "

"What – *and stilts?!*" said Molly exasperated.

"Andy it's *not* Molly's Jason," Gina interrupted, "she's gone on about him for days, he's a nice *guy!*"

"Well he *seemed* really nice, bit secretive about his past admittedly," said Molly, "I didn't really learn much about any personal stuff but would never put him down as a killer – no *way!*"

"Did he tell you where he was staying or why he'd come to Kirkdale?" Andrew pressed.

"He said he was visiting his sister for a few days but didn't really say much about her, just that they were very close and she'd moved here recently. We mainly talked about what we were into. You know bands, books, films, food, usual stuff you chat about when you first meet someone."

"You usually talk about family, work and where you come from too," Andrew added pointedly, *"unless there's a good reason not to."*

"Well if there *is* a reason," replied Molly, "it's not the one we're here to discuss. We need to make a plan, and damned fast, before trails and clues start to dry up and go missing." Molly threw a large mouthful of red down her throat and re-filled her glass – suddenly she was the one setting the pace for the evening *and not just with the wine.*

"These dreams are getting to her a bit, aren't they Moll?" Gina put a supportive arm around her friend's shoulders.

"You haven't had another since Wednesday have you?" Andrew asked worriedly. *Surely the murderer wouldn't strike again so soon? That would be three in just over a week if her visions were a definite connection.*

"No, not yet but it's stressful… *really* stressful I *hate* them. I just want this to be over I feel so… *responsible* somehow. When I first noticed I had a gift, thing, whatever it is, I didn't expect it to develop into this… this series of predictive *nightmares.*" Andrew and Gina swapped concerned glances. Both emptied their glasses together and Andrew opened the third bottle just delivered by the waiter. He began to fill all three glasses to the rim, *much more of this and they wouldn't be able to work out anything at all* he thought. With the wine back on the table he looked up at the girls and made the first real suggestion as to how they might attempt to discover Rachel's killer, and of course of the poor woman that had been found that morning.

"I've an idea," he said, eyes squinted slightly in apprehension of their response.

"Go on," they both whispered, as if the murderer was actually eavesdropping, their voices barely audible above the hum of the bar. Gina was especially worried at what he would come up with – it was bound to involve something dangerous and she wasn't entirely sure she wanted to or even *could* cope with it. She certainly didn't want *him* in any danger.

"It may sound ridiculous, off the wall even, but we've got to start somewhere."

"*Not* Jason!" Molly heard herself immediately pre-jump to the defence of someone she barely knew. She was mystified why when he hadn't even bothered to contact her, but nevertheless felt he had nothing to do with this.

"No, not him, I don't think he's a suspect. With your intuition Molls I think you would have sensed something. No. I think we start with our Dr. Peterson. You've often mentioned he's a bit of a womaniser Gina and we know he was in the pub on the same night, maybe, just maybe it was him who dropped the number in Rachel's lap. Maybe he arranged to see her and... I dunno, just lost his temper for some reason."

"*What?!* And caused that that awful... *wound...* that *ghastly* hole in her chest, in *both women's chests?*" Gina was aghast. She knew Miles was a bit *slimy*, for want of a better word, but she couldn't believe he would actually *kill* anybody. "He's a *doctor* for chrissake! He *heals* people he doesn't *hurt* people." Andrew turned to her with eyes widened pointedly given she was no longer anywhere remotely on the whispering scale.

"Keep your voice *down*," he hissed, furtively looking around at the other tables as if they were guilty of plotting a bank raid. No one was interested in them, they were all too happy with their own friends and conversations to notice Gina's unexpected outburst. Andrew picked up her hand and went on more softly. "It's just a place to *start* Gee, we have to start *somewhere*, and Peterson was in the Carpenters on the same night as Rach. His ID fits and I told you on the day I found her that she'd seemed happier recently, as if she'd met someone new. Well maybe she had."

"But... *Miles?*" whispered Gina horrified as she checked groups on either side of them now and then leant forward.

"Look, this is what I suggest," said Andrew firmly. "Molly, the next time you have a vision or a dream, ring me immediately *whatever the time is, day or night.* So far the murders have occurred at least two days after your predictions. I'll follow Peterson home from work on the first day and hang around all night if necessary, just to make sure. Then repeat it again on the second day if nothing has happened. Gina – you text me half an hour before he's due to leave and I'll make sure I'm near the surgery but out of sight. At least his car is easy to recognise. Has he still got the Morgan?"

"Yes, it's his pride and joy," said Gina, recalling how she'd once seen him run his hand lovingly along the car's long silver-grey bonnet.

"Right – I'll follow him home then and just wait somewhere secluded until he leaves the house again that night – *if* he does. Of course if he goes out later it could be perfectly legit, probably will be, but at least

I'll *be* there to tail him and make sure it is – *and if it isn't…"*

"I guess that's reasonably safe," admitted Gina. "You'll have your mobile with you and you'll only be following in the car won't you? You won't *do* anything Andy will you? I mean, I know it's a helluva long shot, but if it *is* Miles he's pretty damned fit. Promise me you'll ring that DCI and not get involved." If he was honest Andrew was a bit miffed his girlfriend thought Peterson was in better shape than he was, especially considering her boss was fourteen years older than him! He didn't know if Miles did train at all, but *he* was in pretty regular attendance at the gym.

"Gina. Do you *really* expect me to stand aside and let an innocent woman get brutally murdered when I might have been able to do something?" Heavy red waves masked a fearful expression as they fell across her cheek. She reached forward for her glass. This time it was his girlfriend who knocked back the Bordeaux in one gulp. It was only as it slipped down that she suddenly remembered Miles Peterson's unusual behaviour following Rachel's death. Her eyes glazed in stark realisation. It was the first time he'd ever left the car park without the ritualistic proud glance over his shoulder at the Roadster, the first time he'd ever walked straight past reception without looking in her direction, and the first time he'd worn that sickly grey expression as he'd hurried down the corridor to his consulting room. Equally though, it had been the first time he'd arrived at work on the same day news of a horrible murder had been released, the murder of Andrew's female work colleague and long-time friend.

The room swam as Gina slid sideways off her chair.

TEN

Jason Flood crouched behind the low flint wall that separated the surgery car park from the large open recreation ground, his back pressed uncomfortably flat against its sharp jutting points. The night was warm and muggy and his tee-shirt thin, it offered very little protection against the cutting edges. His heart thumped wildly now as he looked back across the rec through a sparse hedge that gave pretty inadequate cover. It was completely empty. A quick look over the top of the wall into the car park at the front of the surgery also revealed nothing – all was surprisingly quiet and desolate. If this had been a rec near his estate in Bradenthorpe, the kids' swings, roundabouts and slides would be getting a right hammering from local gangs at that time on a Saturday night. On *any* night come to that.

He hadn't seen much of his sister since he'd arrived that first weekend. To be fair Jenny had been working every weekday, but he'd still felt a little ignored considering he'd made the trip to see her. Most evenings had been spent in her tiny flat above the dress shop in front of the TV – she certainly hadn't invited him to meet any of her new friends. He'd thought that really odd, she would surely have made *some?* It had hurt a bit if he was honest. Still, it was Bank Holiday soon, they'd be able to spend some time together, go out, meet some new people. He held on to that thought as he prepared himself for what was to come.

With a final check of the car park and surgery building for any signs of life, Jason heaved himself up, over the wall and down to the gravel the other side. The gritty surface scrunched noisily beneath his trainers as he landed – grass would've been better but beggars can't be choosers. If only *they* would stop telling him to do these freaking things he could be in that pub now where that pretty Molly worked – he *really* liked her. They'd had a good time at the country fair thing the other day, she was one of the few girls he'd felt comfortable with – chatting had come easily, effortlessly. Her number was on his mobile but every time he went to call his finger stopped short of actually pushing connect. In some ways he was worried about meeting up again… in case *they* found out. Well they would wouldn't they, they always found everything out. They always whispered to him, instructed him, told him to do things he shouldn't, they were *bound* to know if he met up with Molly again. His hands were better now since he'd halved his medication, but the voices had come back, and Jason knew he had to obey or the shouting would start. Then the yelling, the hollering, and then the full-on obscenity screaming, all multiplied, all mixed up and deep inside his mind. He couldn't stand that, not again. The headaches were agony and the confusion unbearable. It was 'they' that started the need for the meds in the first place, why he'd been put on the Clozapine in his mid teens after his parents' death. The side effects had been awful though, the weight gain the tremors… so sometimes he'd reduce the dose to half for a while, just for a few weeks to find some relief – *and a less embarrassing social life.* Anyway – '*they*' told him to.

He scouted round to the rear of the building and ensured he constantly scanned the area for people and security cameras. His brain was on overtime and stomach giving him gip – always did when he was nervous. He cursed as the 'tool' belt banged heavily against his jeaned thighs and wished he'd brought a rucksack instead. In truth he wished he wasn't there at all. Suddenly his hands flew to his ears, he pressed hard with his palms, his eyes screwed tight and lips twisted to match as he shook his head and spat a resentful hushed reply through clenched teeth.

"Yes, yes I *know*, I *am*, I *will*, I can *hear* you, *stop… shouting!*"

The voices came thick and fast now, echoed repeatedly, demanded, ordered and egged him on. The closer he got to his target the louder and more hysterical they became. Jason shook his head fiercely now – they just frustrated him, hindered him, delayed him.

He found a single back door, took a small suction cup and glass cutting tool from his belt and set to work on an individual oblong pane. The neat circular hole was soon scored and Jason gently pulled the suction cup towards him which brought the pane with it. He slipped his hand through the gap and felt for the key. It was there. Within seconds he was standing nervously inside the small surgery kitchen expecting some kind of an alarm to go off. Would there be one? He remained absolutely still, held his breath as the voices reduced to a whisper now, waited nervously with him. Nothing. His controlled breathing sounded too loud as it moved slowly in and out of his lungs. Still nothing. A trickle of sweat slid irritatingly down his left shoulder, made him want to twist his arm up his back and scratch. He didn't. There was very little space, he could barely see and didn't want to start swiping mugs and coffee jars off the work surface. Inch by inch, Jason felt for a clear area, laid the glass disc on the end of the work top, removed the suction cup and replaced it into his tool belt along with the cutter. As he stood still again almost too afraid to move, he heard the hum of the town traffic in the distance and the electronic tick of the clock in the room he'd just broken into. Now though he had to listen closer – *to receive his orders*.

Without the street lighting, the corridor that led from the kitchen was even darker than the room Jason had just left. He didn't want to leave the door open behind him because of the window directly opposite, so decided to forgo the small amount of light it would have shared. He began to work his way carefully down the hall. Almost immediately his shoulder offset a heavy object, and as it see-sawed dangerously against the wall, a wave of adrenalin coursed through his body. Both hands flew to the picture's corners as he sensed its shape and somehow managed to set it right again in the pitch black.

Every now and then he acknowledged the voices as their excited and annoying chatter buzzed inside his head, but his hands were now surgeon steady as he felt for the first door handle. He depressed it slowly downwards. Once in and the door closed, Jason stroked the wall either side of the entrance until his fingers ran over the light switch and pushed it down. The brightness made him blink, it had not taken long to get used to the dark. He mentally kicked himself then as he remembered the mini torch he'd packed in his tool belt. A quick glance revealed it was just a regular office – desk, phone, laptop, flash black leather chair and a wall of medical books and stationery items. Not what the voices were interested in. He couldn't resist a quick swing in the large soft swivel chair though, just for a moment, but almost immediately his hands shot to his head. He jumped out of the seat as if it had burnt his rear and held his ears.

"Okay, *okay*… I'm going, I will… *yes* I'll *find* it. Yes I'm *doing* it, *right now*. Don't… *yell!*" He walked swiftly back to the door, snapped off the light and stepped out into the corridor again. His legs began to tremble now, not from his medication, but from the sheer terror of what he was doing. He couldn't believe the extent to which the voices could control his actions, but he also knew he had very little choice.

It wasn't long before he came across another door, used the torch this time and noticed a further one opposite. It had been left ajar and Jason could see right into the room. Just more office space similar to before though, he thought, not the one he was being instructed to find.

He made a brief search of each room as they appeared, until finally around a left-hand corner he found a glass window sat above a wide counter. Jason flashed the beam onto the handle of the adjoining door and tried to open it – *locked*. He pushed against the door with his shoulder, it stood firm. A quick rummage in the tool belt produced a simple piece of long bendy wire which he fed it into the key hole. Expertly he tickled the inside of the lock until a couple of minutes later he heard the familiar click. Jason winced at the sound, he could almost become a professional burglar at this rate – *it had become far too easy.* The door swung open and once the wall light was on, the room revealed its prize.

The surgery's pharmaceutical department spread out in front of him. Jason dropped the mini torch inside the tool belt as the voices laughed and squealed with delight, and with his heart in his mouth, a very, very dry mouth, he quickly searched for the opiates. Pethedine, Dihydrocodeine, Diconal, Palfium, Temgesic, and Methadone. His eyes ran swiftly over the labels on the neatly stacked canisters careful to memorise where each drug was stored. He was also 'told', *very specifically*, not to forget the Prozac and Seroxat or any similar 'A' grade drugs. Jason knew with every fibre of his being this was wrong. Equally, his hands flew in and out of each cabinet as they cleared the shelves of the drugs. Repeatedly he bent up and down from the bottles and jars to fill the collapsible bag he'd pulled from his belt and shaken into shape.

It was only by chance he thought he'd heard the click of another door somewhere else in the building. Jason stopped for a second not daring to move. He held his breath and strained hard to listen, but all he could hear was blood rush in his ears and his heart pound whilst he stood with one hand outstretched to a shelf as the other held the bag. *Nothing. Did he imagine it? Must have.* Even so it was time to make a move now he'd got what he'd come for, or rather what the voices had come for. It was imperative he got out and got out quick just in case there *was* somebody knocking about. Jason placed the overly full stretchy container onto the floor and carefully and quietly closed each glass cupboard door. Then he picked up the bag and flicked off the light which left him blind once more.

With the heavy awkward shape in his left hand, he fiddled deep into the belt for the torch with his right and thumbed the switch forwards one notch – it was just enough to give a slight glow. He opened the door and flashed the low beam up and down the dark corridor but was met with nothing other than quiet emptiness. He slipped out of the room and walked quickly back up the hall towards the kitchen – *and escape.*

As he turned the last corner, his blood froze. His legs were rendered useless as his feet stuck firmly to the corded carpet. Suddenly the corridor was fully illuminated which made his little light pathetically redundant. Jason let his torch arm fall to his side – his bowel juddered violently as he held on tight. Eyes wide with shock, he still looked briefly behind him even though he knew it was a dead end then returned his terrified gaze to his calm captor. Directly in front of him, arms crossed and barring his way, was somebody he actually *knew.* The woman stood with hands on her hips and a sneer on her face, clearly enjoying her surprise find which she intended to put to good use – *very good use.*

As Jason tried desperately not to lose control of either end of his digestive system, she casually pulled a half empty pack of cigarettes from her trouser pocket, shook the lighter from the box along with a cigarette and lit up. She drew heavily, eyed her prey and exhaled slowly as she replaced them. Jason felt a steel chill creep down his spine as he watched the warped satisfaction spread across Charlotte's face. Through an icy smile, she spoke with sheer malice and manipulation.

"Well… well… well, if it isn't young Jason Flood. *Looks like I've been delivered two for the price of one."*

ELEVEN

Jason's voices were uncannily quiet. Nobody offered any wise counsel now. No orders, no directions, no explicit instructions, not even any yelling... which meant it was down to one person and one person only to get him out of a very tight spot.

"I... can't believe you're here." He started carefully, not wanting to antagonise her. "How come, I mean... *why?... Why here?*"

"*Why not?*" Charlotte replied crisply. "It's as good a place as any to get away from that *trashy husband stealing sister of yours.*" She spat out the words like they actually tasted of the poison they represented to her. It was clear she'd still not gotten over Jenny's and Miles' affair – even six years down the line. What was *also* clear though, what stood out a mile and he'd thought rather odd, was that Charlotte was wearing a coat. A shortish lightweight summer coat admittedly, but the nights had got so unbearably hot in the last few days, a jacket was hardly necessary. Everyone in the streets and pubs had been in thin, cool clothing, as little as could be respectably got away with even at closing time, and here was Charlotte Peterson, in this surgery, at nearly midnight – very odd anyway – and wearing *a coat?* A coat with two large bulging pockets as well come to that, what the hell had she *got* in there and why come for it at this hour? Never mind him, *she'd* started to sweat! Charlotte caught him staring at her unusually swollen jacket, with the heavily drooping shape to each pocket. She instantly covered them with her hands, the left holding her cigarette awkwardly away from the material. Almost immediately she realised her guilty mistake and quickly removed them again. She switched her attention to *Jason's* stretched bag that was now lying at his feet and held her free hand out.

"*Mine* I think." She spoke pointedly, a distinct granite edge in her voice. "Hand it over but stay exactly where you are – *thief! Just like your sister!*" Jason passed the drugs over to Jenny's most hated rival and couldn't help but think how surreal it all was. He hadn't even thought to run, not really, it was almost as if everything was in slow motion or on a film set, and he *knew* her for Chrissake! He'd been caught robbing in a strange town by someone he actually *knew!* Jason watched almost trance-like as Charlotte quickly rummaged through the contents and noted the types of medication he'd stolen as she lifted each one to the top of the bag. What would she do with him? His insides were really churned up now – he wished he could get the hell out of there and find a toilet. Charlotte looked back up at him, took one last drag of her cigarette and let the butt fall to the floor.

Jason watched transfixed as she extinguished it with her heel.

"*Where's* your sister?" The question came as a shock. He'd expected; '*Why are you stealing these drugs?*' Or '*Why are you in Kirkdale?*' Or more to the point, '*I'm phoning the police*'. He certainly wasn't expecting questions about Jenny's whereabouts. He had a gut feeling it would be prudent to stay quiet about Jenny's location although how would he then be able to explain *his* appearance in the village? He hadn't a clue. Jason ransacked his brain, not an easy task when it was home to so many. Somehow he dragged what he thought would be a reasonable answer from its crowded depths...

"I dunno. I guess she's home this time of night."

"Don't play funny with me Flood. Where is she *living?* She must be local because I've already *seen* her. *So where is it?* My guess is you're staying there too, although not impossible, it's unlikely you know anyone else here. So where *is* she?" Jason started to feel more uneasy at this than he would've been if she'd just called the cops and he'd been collared for the job he'd pulled. Or *tried* to pull, but *this?* This was just plain creepy. They were still in exactly the same spot in the corridor, he'd been caught fair and square attempting to steal drugs from a locked-up surgery late at night, and the only thing this doctor wanted from him was Jenny's address – *and she wanted it pretty badly*. Well she wasn't getting it. He began to feel a distinct and urgent need to protect his sister.

"I don't know *exactly*, as you said I'm just visiting."

"You're *living* there you must *know* where it *is*." Charlotte swung the drugs bag angrily at the wall, her eyes flashed dangerously as its contents clattered together. She took a step towards him. Nervously, Jason took a step back and blurted out a quick response.

"It's over the other side of town – somewhere – don't ask me where, I haven't a *clue!*"

"You're *lying!*" Charlotte hissed – "*Where* on the other side of town?" The bag was swung again, this time there was the sound of glass breaking. She didn't seem to notice. Jason hesitated, tried desperately to think of something – anything that would satisfy her without giving away Jenny's actual property details.

"It's on the outskirts of the main shopping area, I can't remember the precise address I just… recognise it as I walk along, as I get nearer to the fl– " He bit his lip as Charlotte smiled. If Jenny was in a flat she at least had a rough idea of where she might be. There were certain areas that definitely had no flats at all, and others that had large designer-built loft conversions with amazing panoramic views over the lakes. They were hideously expensive – it was unlikely to be one of those. *The rented quarter then…*

"Why do you want to know where my sister is? She has a whole new life now she's not going to interfere with you and yours again."

"Maybe – maybe not." Charlotte hesitated herself now, she didn't want to appear *too* hostile… no point in raising any kind of suspicions, however slight. She calmed down a little and breathed deeply. "I… just like to know where trouble lies sleeping, Jenny caused me plenty of that six years ago, if she's in the area I want to know about it." Jason held her eyes and waited for the next development. What the *hell* was she going to do with him? They couldn't go on like this all night.

"Go now." Charlotte suddenly jerked her head sharply towards the kitchen, guessing that's how he'd got in. "Go – and if you tell *any*one you've seen me, I *will* report this incident to the police. That includes Jenny. *Do* you understand?" Jason paused for a second before he replied – why did she seem even more worried than *he* was about being found at the surgery? "*Do you understand Jason?* Because if you *do*, I'll see to it your feet don't touch the ground. It'll be a police cell followed by court and at least the next three years in a very small room without a key." Charlotte stood menacingly close to him now, and everything about her was hostile, challenging – and very, very threatening. The young man could feel her warm breath on his face, smell her perfume and sense her power. Even through her agitated behaviour her eyes held his steadily – waiting… Jason eventually nodded, resigned to the fact he had very little choice if he didn't want to spend the night in a cell, or several hundred come to that. He was also a little apprehensive of, but also intrigued by

Charlotte's odd behaviour. He knew all about odd behaviour after all.

"Yeah… got it," he murmured.

A few minutes later Jason had slipped out of the kitchen door and counted himself lucky he was all in one piece and still a free man. He hadn't wanted to be there in the first place, it wasn't *his* idea and it wasn't his fault. Whilst he congratulated himself on getting away with what was essentially a forced entry, criminal damage and an attempted drugs theft, at the same time he tried to push aside an uncomfortable and unsettled feeling Charlotte had implanted. It was a feeling that was fast taking root. He walked back across the park and kicked out at a loose tuft of earth. He wished now he hadn't wandered around that part of town on his own and noticed the damned surgery in the first place. Jenny had got an appointment that evening, *more likely a date he'd thought when she'd mentioned it*, and Jason had been left to his own devices. Well this was what happened when he was left alone *and on reduced meds*. The latter of course *was* his fault, but he quickly kicked that out of his mind too.

As he made his way towards the high street, a pair of blurry, but watchful eyes, studied him carefully from the damp rim of a large paper bag. They followed him back across the recreation ground, past the swings and the roundabouts, through to the road on the opposite side and eventually out of sight. They had also observed him earlier, from their hiding place behind the surgery's enormous willow tree as he'd snuck round to the back of the building. Presuming he was breaking into it, they'd let the paper bag be still for a while for fear of missing his reappearance. *The youngun di'n't look like he were carryin' nout though, not when he did come back inta voo,* the owner had thought as they strained hard with hazy vision. It was a struggle to focus properly these days, a real struggle in *order to be absolutely sure.*

Those eyes had also seen Charlotte Peterson let herself in through the front entrance, bold as brass and at eleven thirty at night, for the second time that week too. The eyes didn't like Doctor Peterson, didn't like her one bit. *Too stuck up bee arf if ee ask me* they thought as the next arm raise brought another vodka shot comfortingly home. *Allus shoutin' 'n' movin' us on 'en she seen us, e'en though we's not mitherin no one.* She exhaled in appreciation of her liquid friend then scratched a permanent itch from another. She cuffed the snot from her nose, wiped the residue across the already stained skirt and smiled knowingly as she recalled her interactions with Charlotte. She may have been old and dirty with no posh house or flash car, but she knew a 'wrongun' when she looked 'em in the eyes. She had looked deep into that woman's eyes, *and Charlotte Peterson was mad as a box of frogs.* No, there wasn't much that got past old Mary, even if she *was* three sheets to the wind most of the time, not that she'd ever admit to that. As far as she was concerned hers were just quiet empty evenings spent minding her own business, and occasionally she'd be joined by a bottled pal. Well, often joined by a bottled pal, *"but that di'n't make me no drunk. No Siree! Not Mary Tattershall!"* She'd lived rough for many years and the nights were far more pleasant to endure in still warm summers than in cruel icy winters, but come rain or shine Kirkdale's most famous vagrant slept that way every night in a whole variety of places. She took another swig in defiance of an angry memory before she let her arm drop loosely to her side for the last time that evening. As she sat propped up against the trunk her eyelids began to drop... *"Yip – mad as a box of frogs..."*

TWELVE

It was four a.m. when she startled awake to the noise of her best friend's favourite music toy. With the heat of the summer nights, the duvet had long since been kicked off the bed and lay in a heap on the carpet, fortunately for Missy she'd been snuggled up in Andrew's floored dressing gown rather than in her usual quilt position. As usual he lay sprawled at an angle across the bed in a deep sleep, and she watched the mobile light up and jitterbug its way off the side unit to bounce against his cheek. He half woke up, swiped the phone off his face which promptly fell on the floor just out of reach. Andrew groaned as he hung out of bed and scrabbled around in the dark with his hand till he found it.

"Molly – Molly is that you?"

"Yep – I've had another dream vision Andy. I couldn't see her face this time thank God, just the body in undergrowth and trees, but there were boats in it too for some reason."

"Could be Dorrington Sailing Club?" suggested Andrew, as he switched the table lamp on then got out of bed and looked for his jeans, "there are woods behind there."

"That's it – yes of course, I didn't think... I just wish it would stop Andy, I've had enough now... same hideous wound as well." He felt for her, it must be pretty horrific lying in bed wondering if you were going to be able to get eight hours without a nightmare.

"Try and get back to sleep Molls, I'll get out to the Petersons' place and see if there's any movement in the next few hours."

He knew he'd either not be able to help the latest victim, or may just have a very slim chance to prevent their death, particularly if his first suspicion of who the assailant actually was, was correct. The police weren't likely to give any serious interest to Molly's visions so she hadn't told them, and as far as the three 'sleuths' were concerned, the chances of a further death being prevented by the professionals was significantly reduced because of it.

It took less than five minutes to throw on some clothes, slip out of the flat and drive over to Miles Peterson's property on the other side of town. Gina had given him the address the other night in the wine bar and it was already in his Sat Nav.

Andrew had parked his old Ford up the lane a little distance from the Petersons' Victorian farmhouse. He was now slouched low in the driver's seat to wait. His heart beat uncomfortably fast and he could feel his hands start to sweat. There were no street lights and he stared at the long-fingered branches that looked quite eerie as they almost concealed the entrance to Willows Copse. He'd seen no one, and nothing had happened – *yet*, but still his heart raced with what *might* happen. At the end of the day if it *was* Miles who was responsible for the murders, Gina could be in serious danger. He shivered then as an icy chill spiked the otherwise humid air.

By eight fifteen a.m. Andrew had followed Miles in to work. Having hidden in the lane for almost four hours and waited for him to either leave or return from something illicit, he realised nothing was going to happen that night and – certainly unlikely for the next few hours anyway. Miles swung the Morgan into the surgery car park and Andrew threw the Roadster's rear window a last glance as he drove past, then turned his car in the direction of the flat for a quick wash and change before work. His stomach rumbled loudly and he made a mental note to pick up bacon rolls and coffee from Gino's sister's place opposite the wine bar on his way back. After the Café Calisé he would phone Molly and fill her in on the night's events.

It was nine ten a.m. when Andrew pulled into his bay at the *Courier*, which bugged him because he was always on time. It appeared his latest chosen 'career' would mean he'd need to ditch some of his long-held principals. *Oh what the hell,* he thought, *what did a few minutes matter, there were more important things in life than being obsessed with punctuality.*

With his Calisé bagged meal between his teeth Andrew grabbed his phone, locked the car and walked into the office as he fought a yawn and a rumbling belly. He dumped the stuff on his desk and immediately slumped into his chair to dive into breakfast where he devoured every unhealthy morsel including the custard doughnut that really shouldn't have been there. He swallowed the final mouthful and aimed the screwed-up bag at the bin. As it clipped the edge and bounced off into the aisle his mobile rang.

"Hi Gee, how's you this morning?" he said as he reached down to pick up the paper and eyed a now crowded front door.

"I'm fine, but Molly told me she texted you at four a.m. You didn't go out *then* did you?"

"Yeah but nothing happened. He's still there at work I take it?"

"Mmm yeah... oh... *can't talk now*," she said suddenly in a hushed voice. "*He leaves at six tonight,*" she whispered. "*Best try then – make sure you call me later.*"

"Okay, and don't worry I'll be fine, love you – bye." Andrew sighed, envisaging another long and very boring evening – *thank God it's summer.*

The busy front entrance had brought a bouncy Beano and a harassed Peter in for the day, together with the news that Stella had broken her ankle over the weekend walking the dog and was holed up at home for the next few weeks. That really *would* make her mad, thought Andrew, if there was one thing Stella Gray couldn't stand it was missing out on a major story, which to be fair, was as rare as hen's teeth in Kirkdale.

Jenny on the other hand appeared to be almost completely indifferent. The newest member of the *Courier* had been nigh on *disinterested, complacent* even when it came to talk of the latest murders. The possibility that Miles Peterson had been the last one to see Rachel before she died hadn't seemed to provoke many questions either. Considering she was new to the area and would need to register with a GP, that seemed a little odd too. He eventually came to the conclusion that as she came from a large city outside the area, murders had probably been, if not a regular occurrence, still more frequent than somewhere like Kirkdale. Maybe recent village events didn't seem so unusual to her. *Didn't answer the question about needing a GP though…*

By ten to six that evening Andrew was waiting for the distinctive silver Morgan to pull out of the surgery car park. He wasn't disappointed. Shortly after five to, Miles exited the front door immaculately dressed and carrying a black case. He threw the bag into the passenger seat before opening the driver's door and lowering himself into the sumptuous luxury that a local journalist could only ever dream about. The V6's engine roared into life and slunk out of the car park onto the road and headed immediately in the direction of home. The old red Ford was soon on its tail but not too close, Andrew didn't want to blow his cover and alert 'Crippin' he was on to him. That was of course assuming Miles was responsible for the recent spate of events.

Twenty minutes later Andrew was back in the same place he'd occupied at four that morning and very annoyed he'd stupidly forgotten to stock up on some provisions for the night. He turned the radio on low and reached into the glove compartment for one of his many crime thrillers. They were mostly stored at the flat in pride of place, *a fake oak bookcase which he intended one day be the real McCoy*, with maybe one or two on his sofa for choice – but there was always one in the car for 'emergencies'. Crime fiction was a long-held passion, no surprise then that he now found himself sat alone in his car in the bay of a quiet country lane waiting for a murder to be committed…

An hour later a second silver and burgundy Morgan V6 came around the corner of Riverswood Lane and rolled into the concealed driveway of Willows Copse. *Matching cars – how quaint,* he thought. It was only after Morgan number two had killed its engine he realised he hadn't taken a note of the number plate and now it was out of view. *Damn!* Miles could use either of them. Not a mistake Poirot or Marple would have made. Oh well – too late, he wasn't about to risk creeping around their property until he was sure of his facts. He leant back against the stark reality of his ten-year-old torn Escort seat, and unfolded a marked page of an Inspector Wexford mystery. Well settled for the evening he soon became engrossed in Ruth Rendell's *'Some Lie & Some Die'*, and seriously wished the Café Calisé wasn't sited at the other end of town.

It was 9.30pm before one of the Morgans slipped quietly beneath the Weeping Willow that graced the entrance of the Petersons' home, and gently purred its way out into the lane. Andrew had been so engrossed with his book he'd almost missed it as it turned the corner only to pick up momentum when out of sight and on its way back into town.

He flung the paperback onto the passenger seat, fired up the engine and rammed the gear box into second, then braked sharply as he passed their entrance to make a mental note of the 'sibling' Morgan's reg. number. Driving one-handed, he kept a discreet distance behind Miles whilst he rummaged inside his door panel for a pad and pen, and at the same time watched the road. It took a couple of sweeps before he found a biro that worked. With the pad balanced on his leg he tentatively wrote down the memorized registration, surprised it wasn't actually personalised – he'd imagined Miles would have something really sleazy like *I.90.4.MLS* with the bolts in the relevant places, or at the very least *Doc 1!* As it was he had a regular plate – *Andrew felt a tad disappointed.*

The last of the late evening summer light had gone by the time the two cars hit the town square. Miles indicated left into Kirk Street and had rounded the next corner as Andrew left the square behind him. He was careful to hang back on each turn in case the Morgan came to a sudden stop in the following road. After a few minutes and a few more side turnings the pace began to slow and Andrew had to be extra vigilant. It soon became obvious Miles was looking for a particular address, but these were mainly very small shops off the high street, not residential homes. He stopped ahead of him and Andrew slowed to match, but unlike Miles, Andrew was not parked under a street lamp. He watched intently, heart pounding, not quite sure what his next move should be.

Miles got out of his car and locked it. He could see him clearly now, tall and chicly dressed, and then watched closely as he carefully checked up and down the street before he disappeared down an alley. *What was the check for then – witnesses?* Andrew slid down his seat into the protective darkness of the Ford's black interior. *What should he do? Follow him? Check out his car? Stay put? What?* For the first time that evening, or since the great *'plan'* had been devised in Gino's, Andrew realised he hadn't got a clue what he was actually going to *do* when faced with step one in private detection. Annoyed with his indecisiveness, he reached forward, punched at a radio button and then fell back and began to drum his fingers on the edge of the seat.

The local evening news drifted quietly over his head unheard. By the time he'd decided he should probably have followed Miles down the alley, his gaze was diverted upwards to a window light that had suddenly appeared on the alley side of the road. In a room over a rather old-fashioned dress shop, he could clearly see a man and woman entwined in each other's arms. Clothing was being discarded urgently and passionately, and it was obvious they were snogging the face off each other completely unaware of the show they were putting on. Whoever she *was* he reasoned, they must've known each other for a while, somehow he couldn't see Miles Peterson visiting a 'working girl'. He wouldn't need to for one thing, and it didn't look like that kind of a clinch anyway. Not that he had any personal experience of working girls he reminded himself quickly...

Andrew could see the signature blonde hair and floppy fringe very clearly as Miles faced the window that overlooked the street. All he could make out of the girl was a swathe of long dark hair that dropped clean down her naked back. When the young woman reluctantly broke away from her eager partner, she moved towards the window with her dress held up in front of her and began to pull awkwardly at the long cream curtains with one hand until he helped her yank them shut. In those few moments her face was lit, her river of straight black hair now fell loosely across her chest and what he could see of her ultra-slim figure looked thinner than ever. Andrew's jaw dropped – with one arm stretched up to close the curtains in full illuminated view... *stood Jenny Flood.*

He was still sat in shock with eyes on the window when the radio station kicked into his trance.

"Tonight's victim, the third, was found three miles outside Kirkdale in Dorrington Woods behind the town's exclusive sailing club on Dorrington Lake. She has yet to be identified. Locals are said to......" Andrew's head shot towards the radio, his hand flew to the volume control and spun the dial.

"......the police are still no closer to finding the killer of these young women, the first of which was found twelve days ago."

"Oh my God it's not him!" He spoke the words out loud as he shot an incredulous glance back up at the window, genuinely surprised, but also somewhat relieved given Gina was at work with Miles every day.

Thoughts began to swim around his head now. *It's not him – and another poor woman is dead. Why was he that surprised though – really? After all it was only their first suspect, somewhere to start, in reality it could be anyone.* Andrew felt numb yet frustrated at the same time. Although Molly had no time-line on her visions he didn't expect to hear of another death quite so soon. *Oh Rachy... if only you could tell me who the killer is, who did this to you too...*

With a last glimpse at Jenny's now darkened flat, he turned the ignition on, slipped the gear into first, and drove thoughtfully past the dress shop to head for home. *"So… what now then Rachy?"* he said to himself as he turned back into the high street. *"What now?* And more to the point – *what and who* is *Jenny Flood… ?"*

THIRTEEN

The following day the weather had lost some of its cloying heat almost overnight, although still uncomfortable it had become more bearable with the aid of a cool breeze.

It was 6.00 p.m. when Jason heard the street door of the flat slam shut and Jenny's footsteps run quickly up the stairs to the landing hall. Her key turned irritably in the lock as she swept into the small vestibule, marched through to the lounge and flung the jangling fob on the coffee table. Her brother looked up in surprise and switched off his attention from the late afternoon TV he'd only been half watching. His upward glance met with her jacket being ripped from her shoulders and thrown outside in onto the couch where she slumped heavily down beside it. Her arms were crossed, her eyes flashed and anger seethed from every pore – it was a look Jason had rarely, if ever, seen on his sister. The situation was quite unreal even for him as he waited for her to calm down.

A whole two minutes passed as John Thaw and Kevin Whately gave chase along the roads of Oxford on another Inspector Morse re-run. Jason picked up the remote and clicked the off button.

"So-o-o…"

"I'm fine Jase… *fine.*" She sat pensively chewing the inside of her cheek and began to fiddle with the hem of her skirt, an old habit he recognised from childhood. *She doesn't look fine* he thought, *she looks upset, distinctly very upset… and extremely agitated.*

"Just had a bad day at work that's all – I'll get us some dinner." She jumped up then as she sensed an impending tear. It welled, escaped, and slid silently into her long loose hair. Head down she walked quickly from the room. *The chances of her eating anything was pretty much nil then,* thought Jason, as he watched her go, *it was obvious her anorexia was taking hold again – certainly judging by the last few days he'd spent there. Time to restore top dose meds – Jen needs me clear-headed if she's got problems.*

Suddenly a familiar icy hand slithered swiftly through his guts and gripped hard. Its cold fingers stretched right around his stomach and alternately squeezed and churned. He sat open-mouthed at the space his sister had left when she'd walked through the doorway to the kitchen and the realization dawned. The reason she'd got her visiting brother to amuse himself in the evenings, either in or out depending on her want, was for one reason and one reason only. Jenny had met up with *him* again. She'd rekindled their relationship and walked *right back* into his emotional trap. *That's* why Charlotte Peterson hadn't been interested in his thieving when she'd caught him ransacking the surgery, and *that's* why she'd grilled him so heavily as to Jenny's whereabouts. *It had started all over again.*

That day at the *Courier* had felt very strange. Andrew could neither concentrate on anything much, nor behave normally with the paper's newest arrival since the previous evening's revelations. Jenny had suddenly become a mystery within a mystery and Andrew didn't like it all, there was enough to worry about without newcomers adding to the mix. It certainly wasn't going to make things any easier, he knew that, and now he couldn't share his and the girls' plan with her either, which he may well have done in time as they'd got to know her better. Not now though. Instinctively he felt a barrier between them, but he obviously couldn't disclose to her *why* he felt like that, *how* he knew about her relationship with Miles, because he'd have to explain his nocturnal activities. He hadn't a clue what was going on. Not about her involvement, how deep it went, how long, or if anyone else knew. Come to that *how the hell did she meet him so fast?* She hadn't been here five minutes!

According to the vet Josie Kinkade, Miles had only just met and been with Rachel in the last fortnight. No – better not to disclose anything. Anyhow, with the latest murder being announced on the radio with Miles stood in Jenny's lounge, it seemed highly unlikely he was the target. Well, not if Molly's visions were accurate. The latest media reports were that the third body had been found unusually soon after death, even Miles couldn't be that callous, *or* calm. The victim had been heard screaming in Dorrington Woods above the boating arena. An on-deck yachtsman had followed the direction of the yells, sailed back in, moored up and eventually found a horrendously mutilated woman barely hidden in the undergrowth. He'd called police on his mobile after rather messily honking up his lunch nearby… It was just unfortunate the killer had managed to slip away unnoticed yet again.

So how *did* Miles meet Jenny – and *when?* Frowning, Andrew pushed the glass door of the leisure centre open with his left hand, hauled the kit bag over his right shoulder and walked thoughtfully down the corridor. A run around after work was just what he needed to dispel the tension, and an hour of squash was the best thing to thrash it out. There was a connection there somewhere he just *knew* it, and somehow he would find out what.

As he turned the corner with his head scrambling, struggling to work out the seemingly unworkable, he careered straight into the back of a familiarly tall, blonde athletically-built man. As he turned around to face him, Andrew found himself looking directly into the eyes of Miles Peterson.

"Hey steady on, the circuit track's at the running club!" Miles laughed and bent down to pick up his dropped squash bag. There was no hint of recognition despite the fact that Andrew had met Gina from work a couple of times – or irritation at the collision. In fact the off-duty doctor was really quite friendly despite Andrew's lack of attention. He hoped the initial look of shock that crossed his face was now gone and replaced by an apologetic smile.

"Er – sorry – my fault, too much on my mind as usual."

"No probs," said Miles, "look do you fancy a game? My partner won't turn up for a half hour yet and I was just about to get in some practice shots – warm up a bit. He's a little dynamo when he gets going and I'm getting thoroughly fed up with being beaten! I'm Miles by the way – Miles Peterson." He held out his hand and just for a split-second Andrew hesitated before taking it to return a firm handshake. His hesitation went un-noticed because Miles wasn't even looking at him now. He'd spotted a couple of young girls laughing and chatting as they walked up from the courts, freshly exerted sweat glistening on their spray-tanned bodies only *very* briefly kitted out. His eyes washed over them, and in particular studied their long – oh *so* long, legs and their eyes flashed back with appreciation as they returned his interest. They looked over their shoulders with wide smiles as they carried on excitedly up the corridor like two fiery gazelles.

Andrew grabbed that time to make a swift decision.

"Yeah, sure I could do with the extra practice too, I was just going to thrash a ball around for an hour myself. I'm Andrew Gale by the way." He smiled openly at his unwitting new-found informant whose attention had now returned. If he could get close to Miles he might be able to find out something. Even though he was now pretty sure he didn't have anything to do with the murders, a glimmer of information would be preferable to blundering around in the dark. Apart from that, he wanted to find out what he was doing with Jenny, and more importantly, if he had any designs on Gina. It was pretty obvious he had the morals of an alley cat – *and that was insulting the cat.*

The two men carried on down the corridor towards the squash courts and Andrew noticed Miles catch a quick glimpse of himself in the opposite wall mirror that flanked Court 1. Andrew's eyes rolled – *was this guy for real?*

Harry Longbridge stared at the plastic bag on his desk, as his left hand fished haplessly around in his pocket and his right stirred four teaspoons of sugar into tepid polystyrene hugged coffee. He gulped down the stale black liquid in one go as his thoughts hovered around Dorrington Woods, the associated boating arena and what had been found there. Evidence that pertained to the third murder now sat on his desk having been signed out of the security store.

He growled when he realised he definitely *was* out of barley sugars and reached forward to whack at the intercom button with his free hand.

"Denise, go get me some barley cubes will you?

My head's banging like a drum – I can't think straight. Donaldson's should still be open." His long-suffering secretary glanced up at the glass partition and gave a tired half smile. *When the hell was that man going to get himself a diabetes check? Never that's when.* Still, no point in trying to labour the obvious anymore, she'd spent the last five years since his transfer from London trying to do that. It hadn't got her anywhere when he'd arrived, it still hadn't and she guessed it never would. Denise headed for the door; a fifteen-minute leg stretch would be welcome anyway considering it looked like she'd be working late again.

Harry picked up the little SOCO bag and re-read the name on the brown plastic medicine bottle that sat inside it. Jason Flood. Flood… Why did he know that name? Flood… *J a s o n…* Flood. He felt he *should* know it and yet… He jumped up from his desk then and yanked his door open to the main office.

"*Walker!*" He yelled over the heads of several un-surprised secretaries and a team of murder squad officers bogged down with paperwork. The hunt for what had now become a serial killer dominated the small town station. Several large white boards that bore photos of the three dead women, all of which shared the same grotesque chest wounds, had been erected across the back wall. Information added to them as it came in. "Get in here!" bellowed Longbridge. "I need your clear head and instant recall for a moment!" The young PC hurried across the room and presented himself.

"Sir?"

"The name *Flood*... d'you remember it? Heard it recently? Haven't we spoken to a Flood locally about something?"

"Yes sir it was at the *Courier* newspaper." Joe Walker pulled out his pocket book, flipped over the front cover and pushed the first few pages over. "There's a *Jenny* Flood, a young single woman who works for the paper, only started a week or so back – we interviewed the whole place with regard to the first murder of Ms. Rachel Dern on account of how Miss Dern used to work there."

"Did Miss Flood supply any family information? It's a longshot but SOCO picked up some medication dropped at Dorrington Woods, made out to a *Jason* Flood. Not that uncommon a surname but you never know." Longbridge picked up the bag that contained the bottle and read its label out loud. "Clozapine – from a pharmacy in Bradenthorpe. I've checked it out on the net, apparently it's a drug that controls schizophrenia. Where did this Jenny Flood come from?"

"I don't have any family information sir, but she did move here from Bradenthorpe. Got her most recent address though, we could pay her a visit outside of work – see her on her own turf this time?"

"Good idea. Do that." Take a WPC with you." Harry glanced at his watch, it was 6.30p.m. "Go now, before she gets a chance to disappear off out somewhere. To wherever or whatever it is young female reporters do of an evening."

"Right sir. I'll take WPC Moorcroft with me shall I?"

"Suit yourself. It's just for a second pair of ears and eyes… and well y'know… just in case she gets emotional." He threw Joe a 'you know what I mean' look. "Report back to me before you go off duty though – got that?"

"Yes sir, will do." Joe turned on his heel and marched quickly out of Longbridge's office as Denise McBride walked back in holding a large bag of barley sugars. A bright red *50% 'Extra Free'* star was splashed right across the front. *That* should put him in a good mood she thought as she dropped it purposefully in front of him. Harry immediately ripped into the plastic and sent half the contents scattering across his desk and the other half irritatingly out of reach as they bounced straight onto the floor. Denise made her escape before the yelling started…

"Jason – get that would you?" Jenny called out from the small kitchen that sat snugly off the flat's lounge. "The *door* Jason – there's someone at the…" Suddenly she wondered just why there would be anyone at her door at 6.45p.m. in the evening. It would hardly be Miles, not so soon, and she wasn't even sure there *should* be a repetition – despite everything. Her feelings – her plans – her life… She'd hardly had time to make any real friends, so not work. *Who* then…?

"Got it Jen," called out her brother, *"was just in the bathroom."* He was halfway down the steep narrow

staircase when Jenny's head appeared behind him at the top. His hand was on the doorknob – her mouth opened to form the words *'Jason - No!'* but it was too late, he'd already opened the door. The two police officers that filled its frame surprised both of them – but Jenny felt sick, a *lot* sicker than usual.

Jason sat opposite his sister in the lounge and couldn't understand why she looked so pale. He was beginning to think Charlotte had reported his break-in into the surgery after all, *but surely Jenny couldn't know anything about that?* Joe Walker and Suzanne Moorcroft looked at each other and both registered the same thing. With the striking resemblance between these two in front of them, this lad *had* to be *some* sort of relative to Jenny Flood if not her actual brother. Joe looked directly at Jason and came straight to the point.

"Can I have your name sir?" Jason shot a glance at his sister who still looked distinctly uncomfortable – *but why?*

He faltered slightly, eyes on Jenny but spoke to Joe.

"It's… Jason… Jason Flood". The two officers exchanged glances again but now Suzanne left the room and closed the door behind her. The occupants left in the lounge could hear her low muffled voice from the small box hall. Joe continued.

"Are you a relative of Miss Flood?" He gestured towards Jenny who sat silently.

"I'm her brother – I'm just visiting for a few days."

"And where are you visiting from sir?"

"Bradenthorpe... I live in Bradenthorpe, we both..." He broke off as the WPC came back into the room. Suzanne nodded at her colleague.

"You were saying sir?" Joe continued.

"Jen and I... we both come from Bradenthorpe... originally. Look, why are you asking us all these –?" Jenny opened her mouth then to interrupt, speaking for the first time since they'd arrived.

"The whole of the *Courier* has already been questioned regarding Rachel, is that what this is about? I don't know any more now than I did then, and Jase certainly doesn't. He never met her." Neither Joe nor Suzanne answered. They were now both facing Jason.

"If you wouldn't mind sir, we'd appreciate it if you could come along with us to the station. We believe you may be able to help us with our enquiries over a recent incident." Jason didn't need to ask what. *Damn Charlotte* – she *must* have gone back on her word. The last thing he wanted to do was worry Jen about his recent night's activities. His sister looked on helplessly as he followed the two officers down the staircase and out into the street. An area car sat waiting. His mop of floppy black hair with its vivid purple flash framed an anxious look on his face as he glanced up at Jenny through the vehicle's window and she watched him from the lounge.

The car moved off down the road and finally turned the corner into the high street and out of sight. Slowly

Jenny lowered herself onto the dark red sofa, reached over the side to the wine rack and pulled out a bottle of red. A few minutes later she'd worked her way through half the contents as she tried to decipher her thoughts. *Why did the police want to question Jason? It just didn't make any sense.* Jenny came to the only conclusion she could under the circumstances, she hadn't noticed anything, but Jason must have started having periodic episodes again. Bad enough news – *but this time it was going to seriously jeopardise things.*

FOURTEEN

Charlotte sat sideways to her office desk and rocked her chair thoughtfully backwards and forwards, the annoying squeak it had developed barely heard by her today.

Her mood was pensive, the images in her mind were not those that most *normal* people would conjure up on an early summer's evening – not *any* evening come to that. Her gaze flickered with recent visions of scarlet splashes, incredulous eyes that stared wide open in horror at their owner's last view, and the knowledge that she, Charlotte, had single-handedly cleared these vile threats from her troubled world.

Each time it had become easier, which was helpful really as there was so much clearance work to be done. The office chair fell silent. She twisted herself round to face the desk and returned to writing on the pad that lay there. Several women's names looked up at her in bright red ink, each beautifully scripted with her silver dragon fountain pen, each set out evenly one above the other – in the form of a list. Its newest name sat glistening freshly up at her, all bright and wet and shiny. She reached for the blotting paper *and stamped it with a smile.*

Gina bit her lip in anxious annoyance, her heart raced. Hurried whispers over her mobile to Molly whilst in the loo had been a big mistake. When she'd entered the cubicle she'd been quite certain the other three were empty, but with the loud bang followed by the swing and thud of the external door it was obvious she'd had company. *Someone* had overheard her conversation. Now, with her hands beneath the dryer, Gina racked her brains to try and recall exactly what was said that could be construed as information, however small, regarding the latest events.

It had already been decided by the three of them it couldn't have been Miles who was responsible despite his recent connection with Rachel. Gina thought hard. Molly had actually talked mostly about Jason again, wondered why he hadn't been in touch, and she, Gina, had sympathised with her. She remembered mentioning Jason's name but that wouldn't be a problem, and she'd said "Hi Molls!" in a low hushed voice when her friend had first answered the call. No particular worry there. No, it was the bit at the end that concerned her. She'd mentioned Rachel by name, *and* Andrew's when she'd referred to him discovering Miles' affair with that new Jenny Flood! *That* was the bit that worried her.

The hand drier clicked off. Gina smoothed down her skirt, breathed slowly and deeply then checked her reflection in the mirror. *She looked as guilty as hell.*

Back in reception, Gina glanced at the other girls

around her, there was nobody missing, nobody who seemed unduly surprised or agitated at having just gained an exorbitantly large slice of gossip. Maybe she'd just imagined it. The bangs she'd heard in the ladies could well have been the old pipework knocking or something. Yes that was it – of *course* that often happened! It *was* an old building after all. She began to relax a little then and started to tidy up some paper work and stationery items before she finished for the day.

By the time she was ready to leave Gina had a smile back on her face and was lost in thought of meeting Andrew later that evening. Just as she began to rummage in her handbag for car keys, Charlotte swept up the hallway then slowed down purposefully in front of the reception desk. The doctor stared directly at her young employee and paused just long enough to unnerve her;

"Goodnight Gina, I hope you have… an *enjoyable* evening." She turned on her heel, continued on to the exit and forcefully pushed open the heavy oak doors to the car park.

"I'm telling you she *heard* me", wailed Gina. "It *must* have been her! You didn't see the way she *looked* at me. God I feel sick, give me a double – *no* – *make it a treble!!*" Molly reached for the optic and poured a *single* measure of whisky then topped it up with a generous helping of Diet Coke. Her friend was drinking far too much lately. She ladled in the ice and grabbed a couple of lemon slices from the bar tubs. Gina was too distracted to notice the short measure.

"Here, get this down you, then we'll *both* head over to Andrew's, I'm off tonight. It's a good job you had next week booked out too, you look wrecked."

"Yeah, you're right." She sighed with relief. "Thank God for that! I'd forgotten it in my panic. Molly, what on *earth* will she do? We were talking about her *husband*. You *know* what she's like, she's bloody neurotic when it comes to Miles and we discussed Andrew's discovery of him with that *Jenny*! Jeez I'm really in the shit." All sighs of relief were forgotten.

"Calm *down* Gina. All we can do is wait and see what develops. If she doesn't ring you over this next week my guess is you'll be fine. She must know what he's like, and I doubt she'll want anyone else to hear about her husband being over the side." Gina wasn't listening – she was staring down into her glass. Suddenly her free hand flew to her mouth in shock *the other still nursed the whisky like it was a precious gem.*

"You don't think she knew about… *Rachel* do you?" Molly fell silent then. What if Charlotte *had* known about Rachel? What would that mean? The young barmaid picked up another glass, stuck it under the brandy optic, pushed twice, hesitated – then pushed again. She omitted the mixer. It flamed all the way down to her stomach as her shoulders shuddered. Molly usually stuck to red wine but this little germ of an idea required something with a bit more bite.

"That's one hell of a suggestion Gee – I mean, what are you actually saying? That our village doctor bumped off the local bike?" She winced then. "Don't tell Andrew I said that, he was so protective of Rach."

"It wasn't long ago we wondered about Miles, and *he's* a local doctor," Gina pointed out. "And there *was* Shipman…?"

"That's true. Still, I can't believe… I mean *Charlotte Peterson?* She's your Gran's GP too remember, found that great nursing home for her, even vetted it *personally*. No Gina, Charlotte's a jealous cat but she's no murderer. She wouldn't have the stomach for it. This is just our imaginations getting out of control – *big time*."

"I *s'pose*…" conceded Gina.

"The police haven't been round to the surgery have they?" asked Molly.

"No, nothing like that, Rachel wasn't registered with us. I *did* get back late from lunch a couple of days running this week. Maybe it was just a warning shot without actually *saying* anything."

"There you go!" said Molly and raised her glass hand in triumph. "That's more like it, and if the 'Old Bill' haven't even had a chat, she's hardly likely to be a suspect."

"They haven't come up with *anything* though have they, not according to the media, there's been nothing in the paper or on the TV."

"Doesn't mean our local surgery's at the heart of the conspiracy though does it? No, she was just being offish with you for taking a couple of extended lunches. Forget about it. Let's get over to Andrew's and see what he's got – if anything."

The message was clear. Andrew walked around the other side of his car to discover it bore something similar. Basically he was being warned off. The leisure centre car park was not yet that full, but the early evenings were still light. Whoever did this had taken a big risk. The words *'DEATH ISN'T NICE!'* and *'BACK OFF GALE!'* glared angrily back at him in large white letters – *not exactly original* thought Andrew.

He'd left Miles to continue playing squash with his friend Bill who'd turned up about twenty minutes late. Had Bill seen this on his way in? For some reason he didn't want to go back inside to ask. Miles maybe innocent but he was still unsure of him. Puzzled, Andrew unlocked the door and threw his kit bag on the passenger seat. For a moment he just sat there thinking whilst he scoured the car park to see if anyone was hanging about or acting suspiciously. *'Who could possibly know I was doing a bit of detective work? Only that Inspector Longbridge, he suspects me of just about anything at the moment, but a copper wouldn't do this. So who then?'* He actually shivered and ran a finger round the steering wheel. He didn't want to face the obvious fact that it could only have been one person, and he or she now knew he was on to them. *Time for a meeting with the girls.*

The three sat in Andrew's living room huddled around fish and chips and large mugs of tea; they looked for all the world like Macbeth's three witches. Missy cat circled round and round, head in the air and stalked the wafting scent of cod and rock salmon that emanated from the coffee table. Molly was the first to give in, as of course Missy knew she would!

"Your car's just the first warning Andy," said Gina, and anxious as always laid an arm around his shoulder and made him look at her. "*Next time they could cut the brakes!*"

"There won't *be* a next time, not now I know they're watching me, I'll just have to be a bit more aware that's all." He gave her a hug and kissed her forehead.

"Aren't you even going to tell the police? You *must* report it Andy, you can't drive round in it like that," she replied, eyes brimming. Molly leaned forwards and pushed a tissue box along the table. Gina motioned a thank you and took one. Andrew kissed her again and squeezed her elbow.

"It's an old banger I've held on to it for sentiments sake, I've already decided to take the plunge and buy a new one from Ropers. Time I left 'old Rosie' well and truly in my teens where she belongs." Molly sat thoughtfully as she ate her supper and fed Missy far more than the odd titbit. It wasn't long before the cat had eaten almost as much her.

"So what have we got?" she called over her shoulder after she wrapped up the last few bits of her takeaway in the paper and walked through to the kitchen to put them in the bin. Missy, who'd run straight after her, was nosing around the swing top lid until Molly scooped her up and returned with her to the lounge. "*You've* had quite enough young lady," she scolded affectionately as she ruffled the top of her head and dropped her back down on the sofa. She immediately jumped off and landed neatly on her cat rug where she proceeded to lick rock salmon juice from her paws.

"Well I admit Gina's experience at the surgery today was a bit odd," answered Andrew, "but I agree with you Molly – I can't think that Charlotte has anything to do with it. Funny though, I still can't help feeling there's a link with Miles, yet…" He tailed off in thought as he waved a chip in the air.

"So basically we have nothing then," added Gina – head in her hands. "That is, until something else happens that could give us a clue to go on."

"Yeah… unfortunately, and that's likely to be another murder," said Andrew. Both the girls looked resignedly at each other and then at him. "Looks like we may have to sit tight and wait for Molly to have another premonition. I just hope to God she gets it well in time so we can pre-empt the killer, or at least warn the police." All eyes then turned to Molly who flopped back against the cushions in exasperated reluctance of the inevitable.

It was then that the landline rang. Andrew reached over the arm of his chair to the side table and casually picked it up. The look on his face moments later, however, was far from casual. It was serious enough to alert the others he was listening to something, or some*one* important.

"Err… yeah… yeah I see, right. Look I understand what you're saying but… no… no I don't see her outside of work at all. I didn't even know she *had* a brother. A Jason you say?" At the mention of his name Molly spun round and caught Andrew's eyes. "Hmm… well I can't really see that I can help you with that one Inspector, as I said I've never met her brother… no never. Right, yeah… okay… I *will… yes goodbye.*" By the time he'd put the phone down and not having had the loudspeaker on, Molly and Gina had practically combusted whilst they waited.

"*Well?!!*" exclaimed Molly. "What did the police say – why did they ask questions about Jason? Where *is* he?"

"Looks like your *Jason*… is Jenny Flood's brother," replied Andrew, eyes narrowed at this surprising new development. "Very odd that she never mentioned him at work, particularly as he came to stay with her recently. They've got him in custody."

"But why is he involved with the police, why have they rung *you* about him Andy?" Gina was more confused than ever.

"Because *I* work with Jenny, obviously they think she's kept some sort of information from them. Probably wondered if I could fill them in on any history he, or *she*, may have left out. They didn't give too much away though. My guess is he's the new boy in town and it's only since his arrival these murders have taken place. Unless they've got something concrete on him, they've probably added two and two…"

"… *And made five*!" said Molly defiantly. "It's not Jason, *never in a million years!*"

"You don't really *know* him Molls," reasoned Gina. "He may have *seemed* okay but how the hell do you know whether he is or not? What does a murderer look like *anyway*? Maybe you were lucky?"

"I just *know* that's all – it's *not* him. I can… sense it." Andrew remained quiet during the girls' exchange and sat in contemplation as he stroked Missy who'd jumped up from the floor and now lay on the table beside him.

"Miles, Charlotte, Jenny, Jason, Rachel…" Andrew looked up as both girls stopped their debate and waited for him to continue. "These five people are all connected with each other somehow."

"What about the other two dead women?" asked Gina. "Where do *they* fit in?"

"I don't know, for some reason I feel they're just kind of, *'extra'* to the whole thing. It's the other five that are central to this." Then he had a lightbulb moment. "What if Miles and Jenny *knew* each other before she came here? What if they'd met years ago and had rekindled an old affair rather than just a quick fling? Now that *would* make sense wouldn't it?" The two girls looked at each other, then back at Andrew and nodded.

"Yes it would," said both girls in unison.

"I think you're right Andy," continued Molly, "this story could go way back, but why murder innocent women with no connection, and we still don't know *who*'s doing it?"

"We can't be certain there's definitely no connection with the other two girls," said Andrew. "All I know is that Miles & Charlotte Peterson, and Jenny and Jason Flood have some sort of a shared history. *We'll start from there.*"

FIFTEEN

MANHATTAN ISLAND - NEW YORK

Gareth turned over in the opulent oversized bed and looked down at his sleeping wife. It was 5 a.m. but *he* couldn't sleep. He didn't know what was troubling her lately, but there was something eating away at her deep inside. *That* much he was sure of. Gareth was well aware he'd never really *understood* Emily, just knew he'd always loved her and wanted to take care of her. Right from their first meeting in the pouring rain outside Bloomingdales all those years ago, when as she fought to open it, she'd nearly speared him with her umbrella......

"*Whoa!!* I'd like to *keep* my kidneys if it's all the same to you!"

"Oh I'm... I'm... *so* sorry this... this damn stupid, *stupid thing*." She continued shaking it wildly whilst huge droplets of water plopped all over her fast dampening hair and slid down to her shoulders.

"It's *always* doing this to me," she added fractiously. He remembered how she'd stood there looking like a bedraggled spaniel puppy, waiting for someone to scoop her up and bring her in from the rain.

"I know what you mean," Gareth had replied, "they're all a waste of time, even if you do get them up along comes the wind and blows them inside out."

"That's what happened to me *last* week, I think it must have busted then." She gave the umbrella one last angry shake and looking up at the sky sighed resignedly. "Well I guess I'm just going to have to go looking a complete and utter wreck now." Gareth raised his eyebrows questioningly. "My job interview," she explained, "it's just gone up in smoke – or in this case drowned in water!"

"Where is it, this company you need to get to?" he asked, already wanting to get to know her better, his jacket now removed and above her head in the hope of preventing further damage to her hair and interview outfit.

"McCarthy Stone, the publishing house on the corner of Water and South Street. I need to be there by 2.45p.m.," she replied, grateful for the gesture but at the same time thinking she must be mad to accept what amounted to being 'picked up' in her first week in New York.

"I'm Gareth by the way."

"Emily… Emily Blythe." She lied. They shook hands awkwardly as they both juggled coats bags and wet umbrellas. The two of them half-walked, half-ran through the rain till a loud shrill resonated through the air and a large yellow taxi slid alongside. Taking advantage of another guy's whistling technique they jumped in and mouthed *"Urgent – sorry!"* through the window.

The offices of McCarthy Stone came into view with five minutes to spare. Gareth smiled as she ran into the building and over to the lifts he knew would take her up to the Interview Suite on the 5th floor. She would ride past each level, nervous of her meeting, conscious of how important it was to get this job.... . *completely unaware his father owned half the company*. Outside, Gareth Stone opened his mobile and made a direct call to a friend in personnel to ensure the 2.45p.m. interviewee was hired. He reassured the voice on the other end that he'd take total responsibility for the decision......

Emily did eventually find out that on that crucial day her future husband had given her a helping hand, one that in time had led her to the editor's chair, although *that* was entirely down to her own capabilities. Still, through all those years there'd been something missing, a kind of emptiness that Gareth had found impossible to fill, no matter how hard he'd tried. Early on he'd originally thought it might be a baby that was needed in their marriage, but she'd never wanted children. Lucky in a way considering his own sterility, although they could have gone for donor IVF, adoption or surrogacy – but she hadn't wanted to. Lately, however, that emptiness had become an almost constant irritability, sometimes even a tense sharpness. There was a secretive... *something* about her that he just couldn't understand. It was only due to her history of her father leaving her mother for another woman, that he felt fairly confident she wasn't having an affair, but even *that* thought had crept into his mind recently.

The flat mechanical buzzing of the alarm clock rudely interrupted his thoughts as Emily stirred, eventually turning over to find him looking down at her. A nervous smile played on her lips as she lay quite still. Then she half reached up, as if to brush his cheek with her hand, till something changed her mind and she let it drop back onto the quilt. Sadly, the semi-smile disappeared, as if somehow it would show a sign of weakness. She pushed back the cover, got out of bed and walked straight to the bathroom.

***

KIRKDALE - CUMBRIA

The first few days of September remained fairly uneventful considering the way bodies had been turning up in the last weeks of August. Although macabre, it was as if the murderer had gone on holiday… *or was in custody.* Both Harry Longbridge and Andrew Gale were highly suspicious, bordering on surety, that Jason must be the culprit. He was new in town and pretty damning evidence had been found at the third murder scene. As far as Kirkdale's DCI was concerned, with the lack of anything else turning up he was hanging on tight to that theory.

This of course had been exactly Charlotte's intention. The best way to destroy Jenny Flood was to destroy her brother. Her ingenious idea of leaving the Clozapine meds at the last murder scene was not only enough to cause high suspicion, but also enough to hold him in custody it seemed. She sniggered quietly at the thought of Jason Flood behind bars, then suddenly straightened her face. Of course it would be extremely inconvenient if he wasn't let out on some form of bail *fairly* soon, because Charlotte still had work to do – quite a lot of work. It hadn't been easy fitting in her new 'campaign' whilst working as a GP, engaging in daily life, shopping, household chores etc. but it *was* nonetheless a necessity. One which, strangely enough, had become exceedingly satisfying, despite somewhere deep in the recesses of her warped, rapidly developing psychotic mind, there was a niggling feeling it wasn't really quite right. It was actually *very, very* wrong. However, if a guilty thought surfaced too close – she merely pushed it firmly away, after all, *that* sought of negativity would hardly help her cause. She checked her watch. It was nearly 2p.m. – time to grab a bite to eat – *'Campaigning' was hungry work.*

Gina carefully arranged the flowers she'd brought for her Grandmother as the sun shone through the nursing home window and lit up the violet and gold shades of the bouquet. Her Gran loved all flowers, but especially the variety in the mauve and gold pansies.

Margaret Rowlands watched her granddaughter as she worked, a girl who in truth meant so much more to her than that, considering she'd brought her up single-handedly – well up until Gina was fourteen anyway, and her damned heart and arthritis had become so troublesome. The important thing was that Margaret had always felt she was her own.

The old woman now thought of her birth daughter at Gina's age. The girl was the image of her mother, at least as beautiful and twice as impetuous. She hadn't had a baby to consider but Gina seemed to be settling down now since she'd met her young man. Margaret had instinctively liked Andrew the first day he'd been introduced to her – not like that God-awful Davey her sister had got tied up with all those years ago.

"There! How's that Gran? Will it do?" Gina finished the arrangement and turned around, a satisfied smile on her face.

"They're beautiful, thank you dear, you always bring me such *lovely* flowers." Smiling broadly she patted the bed. "Now come and sit here by me."

The young girl walked over and sat nervously on the quilt, shooting a quick glance at the bedroom door. "Don't you trouble yourself about the nursing staff, I pay enough for this place and if I want you to sit on my bed than on my bed you'll sit!" Gina laughed at her fiery Gran, it was obvious where she got her own feisty temper from.

"Look," she said as she bent down to a large carrier bag, "I brought you something else too – your favourite banana and walnut cake." She placed the package on the bed. "Molly's mum made some for the pub and asked me if you'd like one, I've sliced it so it's all ready for you." Her Grandmother's blue eyes sparkled at the thought of the treat. Home-made banana and walnut! How delicious – she would certainly make short work of that! She leant forward and kissed her granddaughter in thanks.

"You know, I used to make this for your mum before – before... *she* loved it too. We would eat it straight from the oven you know, piping hot, thick slices all smothered in local farmers butter. There were times, most times..." *she winked wickedly and whispered as if someone would hear her confession...* "when we'd polish off the whole cake before your Granddad got home!" Her frail shoulders bounced under her bed jacket as she giggled and picked up the end slice Gina had cut. She broke it in half and brought a piece slowly and slightly painfully up to her mouth. Eyes closed she munched happily, a big smile spreading across her face as she remembered the past.

"Gran…" started Gina, "tell me again… about mum. About how she was and what she liked, what she did… and about my dad." Grandma Rowlands stopped munching and swallowed awkwardly. Not for the first time did she find banana and walnut loaf sticking in her gullet.

Her eyes opened to find her granddaughter looking at the quilt, tracing the poppy pattern with her finger. Suddenly the girl appeared about four years old again. She swallowed harder.

"Gina… *dear*… It was all *so* long ago." She reached up an arthritic hand, smoothed down the girl's thick red hair and lifted it away from her face. Gina looked up as a tear escaped and plopped down into the centre of the red petals and disappeared into its black heart. She leant forward and held onto her grandmother like a baby as the old woman stroked the back of her head and rocked her just as she'd done when she was a little girl. "Your mother and father were *very* young you know – your mum didn't know what she was doing," she soothed. "Before you were even born your father had long disappeared with the fair." Gina sobbed against her shoulder now, she'd heard it all so many times before, but somehow it never seemed real, it was never… *enough*. "When you were two she… disappeared. Nobody knew why and nobody knew where she'd gone. We never saw her again. With so many years gone by, when it goes on like that, a person is registered as missing presumed dead, but you would've liked her Gina. You two would've gotten along famously. She loved all the same things you youngsters do, and she had that headstrong way with her, just like you have at times." She smiled when she heard a small reluctant laugh as her granddaughter sat up to blot her eyes with a tissue from the bedside cabinet. Margaret watched as she lovingly, gently, cupped her hands in hers, *and wished desperately she could tell her the truth.*

At that moment there was a quiet knock and a nurse popped her head round the door. Gina jumped up and guiltily smoothed the quilt where she'd been sitting, but the nurse was young, not much older than herself, so just winked and smiled at her.

"No need to worry about me, but Sister McNally's on the warpath, just thought I'd let you know." Gina sat back down. "Everything okay for you Mrs. Rowlands? Do you think you'll you be needing anything for an hour or so?"

"No Sherry dear, thank you, I have my granddaughter here, she can fetch me anything I need."

"Okay then have a nice visit and I'll see you at 6.00p.m. with dinner." She backed out of the door and closed it quietly leaving Grandmother and Granddaughter alone again.

"I wish I'd known her," Gina sighed heavily. "I always feel there's something missing. You know? It's like a piece of my jigsaw is lost and I can't settle until I find it and the picture's complete." Margaret Rowlands dropped her gaze to their hands and pulled her own gently away. Gina realised how her comments might have sounded to the old lady and immediately started to qualify her statement. "Oh Gran, look… I mean you have been the *best* mum anyone could have had, I'm not saying that –"

"It's alright dear – I understand, I *do*, I just wish… I wish that you could just *try* and accept things. The way they *are*, the way they will always *be*. Your mum was my daughter too and I miss her dreadfully. I never really understood her, not really, not as I should have." Her lips quivered. "But that night she left and didn't come back, didn't phone or write *I knew I'd never see her again*."

"But don't you *see* Gran, that's just what I *mean*? Just because she disappeared doesn't mean she won't come back *one day*?! Maybe she lost her memory or something and… and nobody knows who she *is!*" Margaret saw the look of hope, desperate imploring hope on her granddaughter's face. She knew then, *this* time she had to finish it, squash any romantic thoughts of a reunion – *once and for all.*

"There was… a body found – several months after she went missing." Gina's exuberant and hopeful expression dropped instantly, like a guillotine blade had just rammed home and cut off life's breath itself.

"But… but…" she choked.

"I know," continued her grandmother, "I've never told you this before because… well you were always so… *so hopeful*, so *positive* you might see her again. You were *very* young Gina, too young to be told. Most children would be resentful their mother had disappeared, but not you, you just kept silently marking the days off until she returned. It's not going to happen my love, and you must learn to accept that." When she saw her granddaughter's crumpled face, Margaret wondered if she'd gone too far.

"I can't believe that. I *won't* believe it!" Gina exclaimed horrified at what she'd just heard. The old lady held fast; sniffing back a tear she gripped the girl's hands tightly;

"You *must* my love – you *must!*" Gina stood up quickly, visibly shaken and strode purposefully to the door.

"I have to go now Gran, I'll… I'll be back again at the weekend."

"Will you mind what I *say* though dear?" Margaret called out as the door closed behind her granddaughter; "*It's for the best – really it is…*" She left the old woman fiddling painfully with her gnarled and stiff fingers. *They* may be of little use, but her brain was as active and able as ever, and she *knew* there was only heartbreak to be found by pursuing this particular jigsaw puzzle. She shook her head slowly, and as her eyes filled with salty memories, pushed the other piece of banana cake away.

As Gina walked back through the grounds of 'Tall Firs', she turned over and over in her mind what her grandmother had said, but simply wouldn't accept it. Her mother was *not* dead. She didn't know *why* she felt like that, she just knew she was still alive. As Gina opened the door on reaching the car and slid into the driver's seat, she was totally unaware of the eyes that had followed her every step. She reversed carefully out of her space, swung the Fiesta around to face the road and drove straight towards the exit. The eyes watched it all... *and then stepped back into the cover of the tall trees.*

At the *Courier* Andrew ran his hand angrily through his hair as he paced up and down the office.

"I'm not saying you know *everything*," he argued, "just that it seems very strange you have a brother you've never mentioned, who happens to be staying with you and is now in custody under suspicion of several murders! *One* of which happened to be a very close friend of mine!" Jenny sat nervously checking the door, waiting for Peter Gray to arrive and stop this. He was unusually late and Jenny was suffering the brunt of Andrew's frustration. "Jenny I need to find out just what happened to Rachel – *who* killed her and why. It strikes me that the police have found the right person. So tell me – *why* am I wrong?!" She looked agitatedly at the window now, anxiously searching the tiny car park for the familiar maroon Mercedes... *"Jenny?!"* He pressed, pushing her hard now for some answers. This was not how he'd intended to have this conversation, but after the fish supper with the girls at the flat the night before, and the fact that so far he'd found out pretty much zilch, he'd decided that some sort of direct action had to be taken. As far as Jenny was concerned it had become pretty obvious Peter had chosen to have a rare lie in on the very day she could have done with him arriving on time. She peered through the window and craned her head around the secretarys' cars. Still no sign – looked like she was going to have to face the continued barrage.

"Look Andy, I'm as much in the dark about this as you are. All I know is that my brother had *nothing*, repeat, *nothing* to do with any of these murders – *including* Rachel's."

"So how come he's been arrested then? Why are they still holding him for questioning? What is it about *him* that makes enough of a difference from you or I that made the police decide to keep him in?"

"I… errr –"

At that point the maroon Mercedes slid alongside the large oak tree and Peter stepped out. The door clicked shut with that predictable muffled thud of pure luxurious quality. With his love of premium cars even Andrew's attention was averted – *but only for a second.*

"I'm waiting Jenny."

"He's a schizophrenic," she blurted out, one eye on the door. "He has to have medication. They found… they found a bottle with some tablets in at the last crime scene – *okay?!*

"*And?*" questioned Andrew wanting the rest – Jenny dropped her eyes to the floor, her voice barely a whisper.

"It had his name on it...on a Bradenthorpe pharmacy label."

"Morning troops how are we *todayyy?!*" boomed Peter Gray as he strode through the door behind Beano. For once, Andrew was not in the mood to play with the little dog, and one look at his two reporters told the *Courier's* editor things weren't good. If he'd learnt one rule, it was not to interfere with young people and their problems because it usually led to issues, days off type issues usually. As long as the paper got out all in one piece and the columns and articles were read by the majority – that's all he wanted to think about. With Stella at home, ankle broken, barking murder questions at him like a fish wife – these days he came to work for a rest. All he got was how *she* should be speaking to the police and running the story, and *who* and *what* was going on – there seemed little else on her mind lately. He was only late that morning because of fetching her some painkillers from the chemist.

"On second thoughts, don't answer that," he called over his shoulder as he made his way up the office to his own whilst Beano trotted along obediently at his heels.

"You were saying?" Andrew reminded his colleague.

"It *wasn't* his prescription!" hissed Jenny, one eye on the pod, so much for hoping Peter would intervene – right now she'd even swap having to eat a three-course meal for this bloody interrogation.

"How do you know? How many schizophrenics is a town like Kirkdale likely to have? It had his name on it for Chrissake! *Wake up Jenny!* Who *else* could it be?!"

"*You* just want to pin it on someone, *any* one because of Rachel. I'm *telling* you Andrew, it's *not* Jason! It must have been... *planted* or something, *I* don't know."

"And who would want to set Jason up? Nobody *knows him!*" Andrew flopped back down into his chair exasperated, shoved a heap of half-finished sports reports away from the edge of his desk and began doodling with a pen. He was frustrated, annoyed with himself more than Jenny, and in the heat of the argument had completely forgotten his car had been vandalised *whilst* Jason was still in custody. Now it was Jenny that asked a question.

"By the way... where's your car Andrew? It's not outside."

"Oh someone scrawled graff..." he looked up. Jenny was now waiting for the rest of *his* answer. He looked deservedly sheepish then. "It's alright Jen... it couldn't have been Jason. Not unless this is a two-man team." She looked at him puzzled at his sudden climb down. "Jason's in custody and my car was vandalised last night in the leisure centre car park, whilst I was playing squash with Miles Peterson of all people. Of course it couldn't have been your brother – I apologise for suggesting it was." Jenny couldn't stop her eyes betraying her, just that slight widening of the lids at the mention of Miles' name.

"Who's... Miles Peterson?" she asked, calmly as she turned her back on him to sit down at her own desk. Andrew may have been wrong about Jason but he wasn't going to let that go…

"Oh I think you know the answer to that Jenny," he replied now back in the driving seat. "I think you know the answer to that *very well*."

SIXTEEN

Jenny flinched as she sat down. How could Andrew know about her and Miles? How could *anyone* know? She didn't have to wait long for an answer.

"I saw you together the other night, when he was at your flat."

"Are you saying you've been *following* me?" she asked incredulously. "I'll damn well have you for stalking if that's the case!"

"No of course not – I've been following *him*. But that's not for public consumption. I mean that Jen, *you keep quiet*. As it goes, I now know he can't be responsible for the murders because the third body was found pretty much at the same time he was with you. Reports state the woman was dead less than an hour. Even Miles couldn't be *that* cool."

"You really *are* a lousy detective aren't you?" she mocked, chin raised, eyes narrowed in scorn almost laughing out loud at him. "First Jason now *Miles*? You simply haven't a *clue*." Andrew was shocked at this sudden personality change, he hadn't known her long but this character assassination seemed way off course.

"And you *have* I suppose?" he replied defensively.

"Come on I'd like to hear *your* theories. I'm all ears!" he said folding his arms, waiting. Jenny held his stare, equally adamant that she was not going to be the one to lose this particular spat.

"I have no idea who is behind it Andrew, I leave that kind of thing to the police. *You know?* Those guys in blue uniforms trained to carry out *murder* investigations!" Andrew's arms remained folded – waiting…

"I've known Miles a long time. Our… *relationship* is nothing to do with you, or anyone else. Like me, *Mister Gale*, I suggest *you* keep quiet about *that* too. Her eyes flashed a warning and there was a new firm set to her raised jaw. Her whole body language said *'don't push me too far'*. He carried on looking at her for a few more seconds before averting his gaze and letting the subject drop. There was more to Miss Flood than she was giving out, but he wasn't going to get anywhere like this.

Although Miles wasn't really a suspect any longer, he now wondered if Jenny was tangled up in this mess somehow. Or was she just sensitive about Miles? On reflection, Jason was probably in the clear so why should *she* be in the frame? He looked over again – Jenny now had her back to him and appeared to be getting stuck into the morning's work. God what a nightmare! He ran a hand around the back of his neck in frustration. She was irritatingly right about one thing though – he *was* a lousy detective! Andrew got up and headed for the kitchen. Strong black coffee was what he needed right now – *not to mention a few leads.*

The rest of the day passed peacefully enough if rather strained. The two reporters pretty much ignored each other as they produced their columns and articles for the coming week. There was an atmosphere in the air though that wouldn't, and probably now *couldn't* be shifted. This just left Andrew more confused and suspicious than ever. Who *could* he trust anyway? At that moment his mobile vibrated – somebody he knew he *could* trust. Molly.

'I JUST VISITED JASON – HE'S BEING RELEASED ON BAIL IN THE MORNING AND I'M GOING TO MEET HIM AT GINO'S TOMORROW NIGHT. I NEED TO BE SURE...'

So even Molls was having doubts now... Andrew shut the phone and tapped it with his fingers. He shot a glance at Jenny before reopening the mobile and flipping through the address book to Gina's name. He pressed *send SMS*, and worked quickly tapping out a message to meet him at the Carpenters for lunch. They would need to arrange a 'watch' for Molly the following evening. He couldn't let her meet a suspected murderer alone, *and a schizophrenic one at that.*

Andrew wished he could have taken as much pleasure in his new-ish car as he would normally have done, particularly as Ropers had got it in so quickly for him. However, given his current position, was wondering if it would also soon fall prey to whoever 'decorated' old Rosie.

He parked the metallic blue Mondeo carefully between a tired Jag and a not so tired Mercedes, in the vague hope if he *was* being watched they might think twice about graffitiing his car whilst it was flanked by two fairly decent vehicles. He noticed a maroon and silver Morgan Roadster was nestling alone in a corner bay, and this time took down the number plate. If it *was* one of the Petersons he'd soon know. Very few people in Kirkdale drove a car like that. One day he thought, glancing back at the Morgan as he sauntered through the rear patio entrance of the pub. Once inside he gave Molly a nod and she got to work pulling him a pint whilst he scanned the room. He couldn't see Miles at first, lunchtimes were always busy, but then noticed him head down in a corner booth with one of the *'gazelles'* from the squash club corridor. *Moron* thought Andrew, as he grabbed a stool and ordered a Scotch and coke in readiness for Gina. With a week off work she was already on site, and now entering the bar from the private quarters she shared with Molly's family.

"So are you here to warn me off meeting him then?" Molly whispered under her breath. "Because it *won't* work, *I have* to know." She looked furtively over her shoulder at her father who was fortunately now serving on the other side of the bar, so safely out of earshot.

"No Molls, I know when you've got a bee in your bonnet about something you're as bad as I am for wanting to see it through. But I found out something very interesting from Jenny today, and what I *do* want to do is for Gina and me to be in the wine bar as well – at a discreet distance."

"What? What did you find out Andy?" she asked excitedly, her back half towards him, half towards the optic as she pushed up on the nozzle for Gina's drink.

"Jason Flood is a schizophrenic. Jenny says the police found a bottle of his tablets at the last murder scene, but she insists they're not his *actual* bottle. As you know he's being released on bail in the morning and is still a suspect."

"He never told me he had that condition" she said, disappointed Jason hadn't confided in her. "Maybe I can get him to open up a bit tomorrow night. It doesn't *mean…*"

"No I know, but I'd rather Gee and I were both there. He doesn't know us so he won't suspect anything, and I'd feel happier knowing you aren't totally alone with him. Allow me that much *eh?*"

"Okay," she conceded, smiling. "You've got your 'Surveillance Op.' Secret Squirrel!" Molly grinned as Gina arrived then and sat down on the stool opposite her boyfriend. She leant forward to receive his *'Hi – missed you babe'* kiss. Their eyes held for a second before including Molly into their little bubble. It'd been a long time since they'd spent any real quality time alone together lately. Andrew squeezed her hand. He knew she was thinking the same and made a mental note that when this was all over he'd make it up to her. Smiling, she knew what he was thinking too, and knew that he would. Lovely thoughts of a romantic break somewhere popped into her head as she reached for her drink.

It was just then Miles spotted Andrew and looked decidedly alarmed, particularly when he noticed who was with him. The two men stared hard at each other before Andrew reluctantly gave him the 'boys' nod', inferring he wouldn't say anything about his indiscretion. Miles returned the gesture with a weak smile, quickly drank the last of his brandy then leant forward to speak to the young girl before slipping out of the pub as swiftly and covertly as possible. He certainly didn't want his receptionist seeing him cosying up to anyone other than his wife.

"So what are you hoping to gain from tomorrow Molly?" asked Gina, with one eye on the bar menu.

"I'll know if he's telling me the truth, I just want to be a hundred and ten percent certain he's not involved. I liked him that day at the fair – a lot, and I felt he liked me. I just want to give him a chance."

"Okay, but *be* careful, at least we'll be there to keep watch," replied Gina reassuringly.

"Fair do's," Andrew added. "It will be interesting to find out a bit more about him anyway, what he knows about Jenny and Miles, their history and so on. I *still* think there's a connection with that man but for the life of me I haven't a clue why."

"Well while you're trying to work that out I'll have a brie and salad baguette and a bowl of cheesy chips – I'm *starving!*" Her two friends looked at Gina and then burst out laughing. *"What?!"* she exclaimed. Andrew wrapped his arms around his girlfriend, pulled her into him and gave her a bear hug.

"My little hungry horse – I *do so* love you!" he laughed then kissed her firmly on the lips.

The following evening found them in their favourite wine bar. Gino's was quieter than a Saturday when they would normally have been there, consequently some conversations could be more easily overheard.

It was eight o'clock. Andrew and Gina sat two tables away from Molly who, as arranged, had arrived earlier. They watched the door impatiently, intrigued to know which guy would make for their friend's table in the corner, and what he'd be like. Molly had brought a magazine to read to prevent her looking over at the others.

Ten minutes later they were all sipping house white when Jason Flood walked through the door. Several of the older clientele looked up in disapproval as he swept through the entrance. His long Gothic coat skimmed his pointed boots and the purple flash in his hair had been joined by a strip of luminous green. Emblazoned against the rich black, they flopped lazily across his forehead as he searched the room. Molly looked up from her magazine on hearing the door, and seeing Jason, smiled and beckoned him over to her table. When he saw her face, *his* lit up, Andrew and Gina noticed that his smile was no different from any other young guy pleased to be meeting his girlfriend. Jason strode eagerly over to Molly's table, bent close and gave her a friendly peck on the cheek before sitting down.

"It's great to see you again, I never thought I was going to get a chance to explain – why I never contacted you I mean. I couldn't believe it when they said you'd turned up at the station."

"I knew there had to be a good explanation," replied Molly as she went to pour him a large glass of wine. Immediately he placed a flat hand over the rim to stop her.

"No! Err… I can't… thanks." She put the bottle down. "I have to take some… some medication," he continued. "It clashes, makes me drowsy and stuff, so I just stick to Coke generally." This was true, but he was speaking from habit. Jason had not taken his Clozapine correctly in months…

"No problem, I'll join you," said Molly as she gestured to a waiter, ordered two Cokes and tried hard not to look past him at her two 'minders' while she did so. She managed – *just*.

"Looks like he doesn't drink then," observed Andrew glancing at Gina.

"No. Very odd for a young guy isn't it, sooo…" his girlfriend slowly stroked the stem of her Chardonnay. "Either that's because he doesn't *like* it or…"

"…Because of his *medication*," finished Andrew."Well maybe we'll be able to hear something if Molly can get him to talk." Just as he finished that sentence, the air filled with instrumental music which basically put the kybosh on them hearing *themselves* clearly, let alone anyone a few tables away. They both let out a sigh and simultaneously reached for their wine glasses.

The next few hours passed by very slowly. Molly appeared to be having a good time with Jason, and they both stuck religiously to Coke. By eleven o'clock, and without being able to hear much at all above the music, Andrew and Gina had become rather relaxed and not quite as sharp as they'd been at the start of the evening. Even Andrew had wound down considerably. Before they realised it, Molly and Jason had slipped past them and were walking hand in hand through the open door and out onto the street. It was only because Gina felt Molly's sharp dig in her back, she realised her 'ally' had been far more astute than either she *or* Andrew. Next time they'd better stick to Coke too she decided.

"Andy!" Gina kicked him under the table.

"Ow! Wha'… what babe? D'you wanna another…?"

"No! Sharpen up!" his girlfriend whispered urgently. "They've just *left!*" Those few words seemed to clear his head faster than any good night's sleep. They pushed back their chairs, and carefully followed them out into the night.

Jenny looked up at the lounge clock and lit one of her emergency cigarettes. Jason's release had been good news, and relieved, she had gone to pick him up. However, his meeting a friend of Andrew's that evening definitely wasn't. She'd tried to cajole him into staying at home with her, said she'd cook a nice meal, even promised to eat properly too. *But he'd insisted on going out to meet that Molly from the pub Andrew had taken her to that day.* She was far too cute for her own good that one thought Jenny, squinting as the smoke rose, making her eyes sting and water a little. A vivid memory played out of Molly noticing her vomit-splashed jacket after returning from posting her lunch down the toilet. *If anyone was going to dig for information it was that one.*

And so she had eaten very little again *that* day too, but surprisingly was now feeling a bit hungry. She ignored the pangs. Better to be totally in control of a least *one* thing than nothing at all she reasoned irrationally. The minutes ticked by. Eleven o'clock – eleven fifteen – eleven thirty… Eleven forty-five and *still* he wasn't back. By midnight she was really beginning to get worried. Had he been taking his tablets properly she wondered? Did he remember to take them regularly and without breaks? She drew heavily once more on the nicotine and flicked the end off into the ashtray.

The police had suggested the tablets found at the last murder scene were *his*, but they both knew the dosage on the bottle was incorrect. They *couldn't* have been one of his prescriptions. That meant *somebody* was trying to frame him for murder – but why? Why *Jason?* It didn't make any sense. It was then the obvious occurred to her for the first time, and the reason slapped her right in the face. *Had his prescription changed?* A sharp pain shot straight into her already aching stomach.

Jenny stubbed out the cigarette and jumped up from the sofa. She walked quickly through to the spare room where he'd been sleeping and began rummaging franticly through his holdall, throwing tee-shirts and jeans this way and that. They weren't there. Her heart began to thump wildly as she spun round. Where could they be? They *had* to be here, they just *had* to be! In one crazy moment she had turned the room upside down. Wardrobe open and rifled, dressing table cleared, chests of drawers pulled out! Nothing! In a frightened daze she lowered herself gingerly onto the edge of the bed and began to feel the threat of tears welling up. She was shaking visibly now. It was only when she reached for a tissue that she noticed the Clozapine had fallen behind the large Kleenex box on the bedside table. A nervous laugh escaped as she heaved a huge sigh of relief and picked up the bottle to check the dosage. Thankfully it was the usual strength – she felt guilty then for doubting her own brother. Her relief was short lived however – the bottle was almost full and the date stamped on it was more than a couple of months old. Silently and carefully Jenny replaced it back on the table with slow deliberation, as if the tablets were some form of miniature explosive device.

Nausea washed over her then, she knew from past experience that seeing the quantity left unused...... *could represent exactly that.*

SEVENTEEN

The warm summer nights had suddenly disappeared as the first September evenings opened with a distinct chill. Gina shivered, wishing she'd brought a jacket out with her, or at least a cardigan. Andy sensed it immediately and pulled her in closer to him as they followed Molly and Jason down the high street, holding well back to avoid being seen. Their distance further behind meant they still couldn't hear anything – they just had to be satisfied knowing Molly was safely under surveillance. Both of them watched carefully for any change in Jason's behaviour, but none was apparent, and Molly appeared to be relaxed and happy in his company. That was, until they reached the market square.

It was quite subtle at first, the strange movements the young man made as he walked beside her. Initially Molly thought he'd just tripped on a raised paving slab, but after a few more yards realised he'd begun to walk a step behind her. She saw he was shaking then, having some form of spasm, bending down, holding his head and rocking as if in pain. When he began talking to someone *'else'*, then progressed to have an *argument* with 'them', she *really* began to get worried.

"No! No I *won't* do that, I *won't,* you can't *make* me!" He spat the words out under his breath, struggling to control his composure, horribly but only partially aware that Molly had now noticed his seizure.

"Jason! For God's sake – *what's wrong?!"* Molly tried to put an arm around him, but as himself, he cowed away, trying to protect her.

"*Not* her, I *won't, no, don't* say that! I won't *listen* to you I *won't!"*

He tried to walk away in the opposite direction but it was as if his legs were wading through treacle, then his whole body was being held back. Molly pulled him round to face her and tried again.

"Jason *look* at me, it's Molly, *look* at me!" He tried his best, fought as hard as he could, telling them to leave him alone, to leave *her* alone, but as the voices grew stronger he knew he had no choice. They were shouting now and the pain inside his head was just too much, he *had* to stop that yelling. He *had* to.

Suddenly he looked up, his eyes seemed to be staring straight through her, not seeing Molly, not seeing anything at all. It happened in seconds. He grabbed her by the shoulders marched her into the next side street where Jenny's yellow Mini was parked, and before she realised what was happening, Molly found herself in the car with the doors locked and Jason behind the wheel. He had the car started in seconds and dived out from the kerb just as Andrew and Gina came flying round the corner.

"*Stop! Jason – stop the damn car!*" Andrew yelled helplessly.

"*Molly! Molly!*" Gina cried out as the car screamed up the road and around the next bend.

"Damn! Damn! Damn!" Andrew flung his arms in the air, whizzed round full circle and punched the wall. Pacing up and down – he clasped his hands behind his head, angry and disorientated, clueless as to what to do next. "This is *my* bloody fault. I should *never* have agreed to her meeting him."

"It was… down to her Andy," gulped Gina through frightened tears. "She would never have backed down once she'd decided… you *know* what she's like." As she spoke she dug into her trouser pocket, retrieved a tissue and dabbed the blood from his knuckles. He let her tend his hand without even noticing.

"What do we do now Gee? Is it the police or do we try and track her down ourselves? The police are gonna want to know what we were doing setting up a surveillance, but… oh God why does every frigging thing go *wrong?!*"

Gina fished in her handbag and pulled out her mobile. She pressed a preset button. The line connected and she willed her friend to answer as she cradled it against her ear, groaning loudly as Molly's phone went straight to voicemail. Andrew had *his* phone out then – decision made – he punched in 999 just as the yellow

Cooper appeared at the top of the street. Hearing the engine, they both looked up as it sped down the road towards them. He slapped the phone cover shut. The brakes shrieked as the car came to a sudden halt and the passenger door flew open. Jason was screaming at their friend, begging her to get out of the car.

"Molly GO now! GO! For God's sake before they come back – I can't fight them anymore, I'm sorry, PLEASE hurry!!" There were tears on his cheeks as Molly faltered, not knowing what to do for the best, *knowing* this wasn't *his* fault, this wasn't the *real* Jason, but also knowing she couldn't help him. She hesitated for just a second longer before leaping from the car and landing in Gina's arms. The moment she was safely on the pavement he drove off at speed steering the Mini erratically through the market square, past the Soldiers monument, clipping the kerb and heading out towards Riverside Park before disappearing from view. All three watched helplessly, stunned at how everything had happened so quickly but grateful Molly was unhurt, if a bit shaken up.

"It's not his fault!" she sobbed. "He wouldn't have hurt me – it's the condition, he's hearing voices. All the way up the road and back he was… fighting… fighting him*self! Arguing* with… *nobody… it was horrible!"* Gina pulled Molly's head down onto her chest and stroked her hair, talking comfortingly, trying to calm her down as Andrew wrapped protective arms around them both. These two girls were the most precious people in the

world to him, but he'd let them down this evening – *badly*. They stood there numb, huddled together on the street, staring at the space the car had left behind.

Once they were all safely back at the pub, and several strong coffees consumed all round, Andrew called a cab so he and Gina could head back to his flat. It had been a tough night and they were feeling the need to be together more and more as events unravelled. Andrew had been toying with the idea of asking her to move in with him recently anyway, but the flat was so small, he'd ideally wanted something bigger and better for them. As it was, she was there most nights anyway so it probably didn't make that much difference, but her gear would take up major amounts of space and that was something he didn't have.

All these thoughts were milling around his head along with what had happened to Molly, as the cab swung into the twelve-block car park and came to a stop. Andrew paid the fare then hand in hand they walked to the entrance hall door and made for the stairs. They first became aware something was wrong when Missy met them halfway to the first floor mewing plaintively. She danced up and down the steps in front of her friends, entwining herself gratefully around his and Gina's legs in a figure of eight and then began jumping up at them. Andrew's heart lurched at the thought she could have got outside, at least she'd had the good sense to stay within the building and not go roaming when the exit doors had been opened. To him, this was more important than the state he expected to find his flat in…

He swept her up into his arms and made comforting noises as he and Gina climbed the rest of the staircase. They could see the crowbarred door through the window of the hall landing when they got to the top. On reaching it, Andrew put a finger to his lips indicating quiet and passed Missy to Gina, then held both hands' palms upwards to signal she should wait there. Gina nodded swallowing a large lump in her throat as Andrew gently pushed at the already open door. It creaked as it moved a little further ajar. After checking behind it he walked inside and disappeared from view…

When Missy suddenly mewed in protest, Gina realised she was stroking her harder and faster than normal just through sheer tension. At that moment Andrew reappeared.

"All clear, there's no one about and not much mess either considering what they could've done. It's not a typical break-in though, obviously looking for something specific but heaven knows what. Unless it's just another warning – letting me know they can get to me." Gina walked into the hallway and through to the lounge before letting Missy jump from her arms onto the sofa.

"You've really attracted someone's interest haven't you Andy?" she stated pointedly, looking around her as Andrew began to pick up books from the floor and place them carefully back on the shelf.

"Yeah – certainly looks that way. This isn't an opportunist thief; whoever did this probably *is* linked to my old car being trashed, and maybe even tied in with everything else. If we involve the police though it'll just magnify Longbridge's attention on me – and *that* I can well do without. I'm pretty sure nothing's gone missing and I can sort the door out temporarily for tonight. I'll call a locksmith first thing in the morning."

"Just promise me one thing Andy," said Gina firmly, "if things get *really* dangerous, you *will* stop this damn competitive male pride thing from getting in the way, *give* up this amateur murder hunt and *call* them!"

Andrew stopped fitting various crime thrillers back in their respective order and placed the ones he was holding down on the coffee table. He turned to face her and for the first time saw raw fear in her eyes. He reached over, took her by the shoulders and brought her in close to him brushing his lips across her hair.

"Don't worry, it'll be fine, I'll be fine… we'll *all be* fine. This is just a setback."

"*Promise* me Andy," she repeated looking up at him with eyes brimming.

"I promise," he replied as he stroked her hair and then gently tipped her chin up to kiss her lovingly on the mouth. "Now, let's get that door secured, some food inside us all, and bolt the hatches down for the night." They smiled weakly at each other, both understanding what was needed, what was important – both knowing where the line would finally have to be drawn. *Gina just hoped her boyfriend wouldn't be too late with his pen…*

In the early hours of the following morning, sleep was determined to evade Andrew. Gina slept restlessly beside him and he instinctively placed an arm across her. She stirred and turned over to face him, snuggling deeper into his body as if trying to prevent anything, or anyone from capturing her in her dreams.

Andrew knew he couldn't risk anything happening to either her or Molly, and given the choice of this serial killer's method of operation, it was only women he was interested in. Or she… She…? *She?* Where did *that* come from? What made him suddenly think it could be a woman? He rolled over abruptly onto his back and stared at the ceiling, wide awake now. Gina moaned at the sudden movement, turned over and pulled the quilt higher up around her shoulders. This little revelation was not something he'd expected to come up with, but it must have popped into his subconscious none the less and catapulted straight from there into stark clarity. *Not Jenny though,* he thought, brain ticking over at full throttle now, *no not Jenny, although she was also new to the area, but she was with Miles shortly after murder three took place. Made both their alibis a touch awkward should they need one* though. Andrew smiled grimly in the darkness. *So who then?* He couldn't imagine any of his secretarial colleagues being a suspect. Rachel didn't exactly socialise with any of the staff, but had got on well enough with all of them when she was at work. He didn't know either of the other two women who'd met their death at the hands of this freak, so maybe *they'd* had a contact with him... or her...

Dawn broke – Andrew was still thinking. Still analysing the small amount of information, adding it to possibilities, impossibilities, probabilities and improbabilities – in fact scrutinizing it so succinctly, it was bordering on OCD.

Gina screwed her eyes up at the light that shone through the gap in the curtain and stretched. Yawning, she slowly awoke to see Andy looking down at her with that decisive look on his face and blinked hard.

"It's a *woman*," he said. Then threw back the quilt swung out of bed and headed for the kitchen. "Coffee? I've got the Calino, you said you..." Gina was quickly behind him as he reached up to the cupboard for the strong Italian blend.

"A *woman* Andy? Where did *that* come from? What makes you so *sure?*" He picked up the coffee, shut the cupboard door and turned round to face her.

"I'm not a hundred per cent certain, but we've always assumed it was a man and I'm pretty damn sure the police are thinking the same thing. A strong woman of average height could overpower one of her own sex just as easily as a man, and none of the victims were particularly tall or heavy."

"You may have something," said Gina thoughtfully… "It's a horrible thought though, bad enough it's happening – but a *woman?!* That's creepy… although… after Dr. Peterson, *Charlotte* that is, looked at me weirdly the other day even Molly and I were throwing around a woman's name – *hers!* We dismissed it though – as Molls pointed out she's been nothing but lovely with my Gran." Andrew agreed;

"I know you've mentioned before Charlotte can be odd sometimes, but then we all have our foibles…"

They sat in the lounge drinking the rich dark Calino, his black as always, hers as ever topped with evaporated milk, Missy getting a good half a can in a saucer and whiskers duly creamed.

Gina, now in one of Andrew's shirts, was nursing her mug and sat crossed legged in her favourite squashy old leather chair. She still had the rest of the week off work and was in no hurry to get dressed, but Andrew still needed to get into the *Courier* by 9.00 a.m.

Once the last of the cafetiere was finished he began to get ready, and as he dressed, decided to pay a certain person a visit later that morning. Someone who because of a leg injury had been left out of the murder hunt up until now – someone who *because* of that, wasn't at all happy.

Stella Gray had lived in Kirkdale all her life, run the local paper with her husband Peter for two decades, and was the best damn 'digger and sifter' he knew. She'd known Rachel since she was a child and had gone to school with her mother. If anyone could shine a light on this – Stella could. Maybe she'd have some information from the past that could help. Something, *anything,* however small, that might just lead him in the right direction. *It was time to bring her in from the cold.*

He told Gina of his intentions, and left her to have a lazy day with Missy cat and a pile of magazines whilst she waited for the locksmith to turn up.

The river flowed past the garden of the Carpenters in just the same way it always did. In the height of summer it was so beautiful with the sun sparkling on the water and Kirkby Pike rising up majestically behind it, vast and breathtaking. It was a sight she'd always loved – always pointed out to visitors enjoying a drink on the garden terrace. Now Molly stood alone in the bay window of her room and watched the trees begin to lose their foliage to the rushing water. Reds and golds dancing on the moving surface tossed helplessly downstream, disappearing forever into the autumn.

The sky had turned grey. It seemed summer had all but gone. She pulled the dressing gown around her more tightly and shivered as she looked out beyond the river – beyond the Pike. But it wasn't cold that made her hug herself, made her wrap her dressing gown more tightly across her chest…

Surprisingly, after her ordeal with Jason, she'd slept soundly, fallen into quite a deep sleep, might even have needed an alarm to wake her any other day. No, it wasn't cold at all. In true visionary style, Molly Anne Fields had woken from that blissfully happy slumber a few minutes earlier as if hit by a thunderbolt. Lying flat on her back and facing the ceiling, her eyes had shot open… *whereupon she immediately and indisputably witnessed her own death.*

EIGHTEEN

Stella Gray placed her teacup back on its saucer and leant heavily into the cushions of her armchair. Her foot was throbbing and itching again under the cast which caused a foul mood.

Just then the doorbell went. *Ye Gods! That's all I need!* she thought irritably. It had taken fifteen minutes just to get up and out to the loo and back again. Now there'd be another bloody circus, necessitating complex and intricate balancing, just to get on those damned crutches to hobble back out to the hall and now open the front *door!* She'd never get used to the wretched things, they may as well have been chopsticks – *she couldn't use them either!* Stella sighed heavily as she pushed herself forward to the edge of the chair for the second time in the last twenty minutes.

"Hang on!" she called out – both hands found a wooden support as gingerly she eased herself up, engaged one carefully under each arm, and after a fashion began to head slowly for the hall again. The bell rang a second time, faster and more urgently. *"I'm coming darn it, be patient!"* she yelled at the top of her voice, wobbling un-rhythmically through the hall, and

more by luck than judgement, managed to reach the front door.

"Sorry Stella," Andrew called through the glass. "Forgot you'd have a problem what with…" *His boss now stood before him, the door opened,* "… the foot and… everything," he finished lamely.

"Not to worry Andy, lucky it's you. I'd probably have been very uncharitable to anyone else." She winked. "To be honest I'm glad you've called. Come in lad." He helped her through to the kitchen where she sat down gratefully at the table whilst he made them both a coffee. As the kettle boiled he rifled through the biscuit barrel for the Bourbons he knew would be there. Andrew Gale and Stella Gray went back a long way. Many's the time they'd sat at her kitchen table with mugs of tea or coffee, digging into the biscuit or cake tin, *or both!,* and pondered over local burglaries and street muggings. Often they'd agonised over Rachel, *but there had never been anything like this to fuel their conversation.*

"What the *hell* is going on with that murder business?" she questioned straight out, exasperated. "Have you turned anything up yet? With poor Rachel being… *ohhh…*" She shook her head slowly – clearly upset. "I know it's not strictly your area but with this damn foot I'm stuck here in these four walls, it's driving me *crazy!*" Andrew could well imagine what it was doing to her. Stella Gray was known for scratching away at the surface of a story and uncovering a whole new world of information beneath – he secretly called her the 'Iceberg Detective'. For her not being able to zoom around town unearthing anything and everything, must be like finding a fountain in the desert locked behind a triple glass wall.

"I know this may sound odd to you because you hardly know her," he began – "Well, *I* hardly know her, but I think that somewhere in the middle of all this is… *Jenny Flood.*"

"What our new *reporter?* Are you *sure?*" He nodded.

"*Our* Jenny?" his boss continued incredulously. "Why on earth should *she* be involved?" Andrew brought Stella up to speed with what had happened since she'd broken her ankle over the next fifteen minutes or so and left nothing out. Molly's visions, their suspicion of Miles via vet Josie Kinkade and the note to Rachel in the pub, Andrew's following him and discovering Miles at *Jenny's* flat, and his and the girls' plans so far. Right up to the surveillance op that had gone so badly wrong the previous evening, and Jason's psychiatric condition. When he'd finished she was surprisingly quiet.

"So… what do you think?" Andrew asked hesitantly. He wasn't used to silence. This half of the *Courier's* editorial executive team was never stuck for words.

"I think we don't alert Jenny or question her anymore," she said decisively. "*If* you really think she's connected?" Andrew hunched his shoulders, the expression on his face screwed into *'well I think so but can't be absolutely sure'.*

"Thing is there's definitely history between *her*, Miles and Charlotte Peterson," he replied, "probably Jason knew about the affair in the past and I've witnessed it recently. Jason has been under suspicion from the police but is now out on bail. According to Josie Kinkade, Miles *definitely* gave Rachel his mobile number that night in the pub. Connections are there. Molly hasn't had another dream or vision, so we don't know what, or more to the point, *who* is next." Stella stroked a finger up and down her coffee mug her eyes darting around in thought.

"I remember the Petersons coming to this town from Bradenthorpe about six years ago. That's where Jenny moved from, at least that's what she *said* in interview, and her landline STD confirmed the area when I rang her. I think you're right. She's followed them here, presumably to locate Miles, albeit six years later, but how does all this fit in with actual *murder* – other than the fact she and her brother are new here and arrived just prior to Rachel's death?"

"Exactly – we haven't a clue – *as yet.* The girls and I came to the conclusion because Miles was with Jenny for at least *part* of the night of the third killing he couldn't *really* be considered a suspect. He was far too cool and relaxed when I played squash with him the following evening anyway. I think it's a woman doing this Stella, obviously not Jenny but… don't ask me why, I just had a feeling about it out of the blue this morning."

"*What are you suggesting exactly?* Charlotte Peterson's

had a hand in this? *Is that what you're getting at?"* Stella asked. Andrew remained quiet. "She isn't a big woman you know, and from what you've described, the victims' injuries are quite grotesque. She *is* a GP after all. I know I don't always hold the greatest respect for the NHS, ankle aside, but I draw the line at *murder!"* Stella sat back in her chair in exasperation – arms open and palms upwards.

"Well I didn't actually mention *anything* about our Dr. Peterson *female,* but interesting you should have jumped to that conclusion Stella…"

"No, no Andrew you're barking up the wrong tree if you're even *thinking* that lad. All my instincts tell me this is the profile of a male, probably with inadequate sexual abilities, *and opportunities."* Andrew raised a tired eyebrow. This was typical of Stella, blaming the male sex for everything from moaning to murder. She was a good clue sifter, but when it came to pointing the finger, dear old Stell tended to lean a little too automatically towards men as a uniform aggressor. Andrew put it down to a miserable childhood. Her father had been a nasty piece of work, something she'd let out in a weak moment during one of their kitchen table *tête-à-têtes.*

"There was no evidence of sexual interference," he replied. "Not even clothing removed. Usually in cases like that the man would want to humiliate the female victim, expose and control physically as well as emotionally and psychologically." Stella eyed him quizzically.

"So what about Rachel – I'm damn sure that wasn't the case with her was it?" This was true. She was the only one of the three women where evidence of sexual intercourse *had* taken place. It didn't necessarily mean it was down to the murderer though.

"Yes you're right," he said. "But she could have met someone *else* for a liaison, *prior* to the killer arriving at her house, whether that killer was male *or* female. Neither of the others was personally interfered with, which unless there are *two* attackers, could imply a woman aggressor. In Rachel's case I believe she'd simply agreed to meet someone earlier in the afternoon. *That* person I'm convinced was Miles Peterson. That's his connection with this, but he *didn't* kill her, which is why I've not said anything to the police. You know what they're like, they'll hold on to anything with a remote possibility whether it's relevant or not." Stella looked approvingly at her young reporter.

"Time you came off sports columns lad – you're way beyond cricket and football league now." Andrew smiled appreciatively. He drained his mug, popped one last Bourbon in his mouth and one in his pocket before replacing the lid on the barrel. Stella grinned. "Just like my grandson, you lads never grow out of your favourites!" He laughed as he made his way to the front door.

"I'll see myself out, take care, and *rest* your foot – *that's* an order!"

"And *you* young man, *you keep me in the picture a damned sight sooner from now on!*" Andrew acknowledged her with a backward wave as he strolled down the path. He walked round to the driver's side of his car, opened the door and slid into the seat of the new Mondeo. *This*, he thought, holding the steering wheel, *is infinitely better than the tired old saloon I held onto. Not a Morgan Roadster granted – but definitely an improvement. That graffiti artist did me a favour.* He stuck the key in the ignition, slipped the gear into first and gently pulled away from Stella Gray's front gate. *Time to seriously consider some new possibilities* he thought as the car made its way back to work. *Not least of which could lead to a promotion.*

Miles was out that evening… *again*. Charlotte paced the lounge floor, occasionally glancing up at the oriental mementoes above the fireplace. *Hong Kong…* Things had been really good on that trip, so long ago now – *so forgotten by him… .*

She reached up to trace a finger along the black and gold striped mask that sat next to a rare silver sculpted horse head. The mask's diamond was centred just above the nose bridge, and the huge gold swirls, like spider leg eyelashes, surrounded the slanted sensuous eye slits. She took it down and stroked the velvet surface. Her heart began to beat faster, thudding densely, heavily, drumming Black Sabbath style in her ears as she realised what she was going to do next. What she *must* do next. Charlotte looked back up at the horse head handle and *placed the mask over her face.*

Molly refused to be scared, going out and about carrying on with day-to-day activities as usual. She wouldn't take any undue *chances,* but *nobody* was going to stop her from living her life, not even under present circumstances.

She hadn't told Gina about her latest death vision yet because she'd stayed over at Andy's the previous night. Had she been in her bedroom that morning, Molly would have told her immediately, but as it was she hadn't so actually nobody knew at all. She could always have texted or rung her or Andrew, but it had been really busy in the pub and now it was nine in the evening. Gina had stayed at Andrew's all day too, and wouldn't be coming back *that* night either. Molly felt sure it wouldn't be long before her friend moved out altogether, which was understandable, but sad nonetheless. It would feel like the end of an era somehow, the end of the 'sibling' closeness that had always been there, always been strong.

She watched the customers carefully from behind the bar – scanned the room over the heads of those she knew well and had been chatting to. Everything was normal, there were no disturbances and nothing seemed out of place. She began to think that rather than an actual *visionary* prediction, it had just been a bad dream in the early hours due to last night's abduction by Jason. She was obviously hoping that was the case.

A glance at the clock reminded her it was still only ten past nine. Maybe she should just take a quick break and phone Andrew and Gee – let them know? As her mind tossed the idea around, her father came over to suggest she took an early finish as she'd worked the bar all day. For once Molly would have preferred to have kept busy, but it *had* been an exhausting shift. Smiling at her dad, she finished drying a glass and walked through to the private quarters where she slumped down onto the lounge sofa and put her feet up on the coffee table. Just as she picked up the TV remote, her mobile buzzed noisily from the floor. Molly reached into her handbag, retrieved the phone and turned it over in her hand. It wasn't anyone she recognised.

Meet me in park by swings 9.30p.m. tonight
I need to explain to you about Jason.
Jenny.

Well, that's a turn up for the books thought Molly dropping the phone back into her bag. *Maybe Jason told her what had happened and asked her to speak to me? He must be really concerned – feeling guilty I guess. Maybe that means he does like me and thinks he's blown his luck? To be honest he probably has but...* well, everyone deserves a second chance, an opportunity to explain themselves, she thought rationally. *At least I know he has a problem, can understand to a certain extent. Maybe his tablets aren't agreeing with him for some reason?*

It wasn't long before Molly had slipped a jacket on, grabbed her car keys and left by the rear entrance. She longed to know the full story behind Jason Flood, and now it looked like she was about to find out.

The lights from the pub together with the street lamps were deceiving as they mixed with the last of the low dusky hue of a September evening. It made one think it was brighter than it actually was, that there was still some daylight left.

Soon she was driving along the river road, with the pub lights far behind her and the night suddenly became darker and her mood less upbeat. It wasn't long before the chug chug lurch of her little Fiesta brought her up sharp. *Shit! Dad said he thought the engine sounded dodgy last week.* She now cursed her procrastination in booking the car in. The noise became louder as she drove over the bridge at Devil's Drop and around the corner past St. Peter's Church. It became worryingly obvious the car wasn't going to make it all the way to the park. Once she hit the hill she was able to coast down to the bottom, but a few metres of lunging on the level road brought her to a grinding halt. Molly looked at her watch. It was twenty past nine. *It shouldn't take me more than ten minutes to walk from here if I don't hang about,* she thought.

Standing outside the car it felt distinctly chilly. A cool wind had gained some ground since she left the pub and was now quite nippy. She pulled her jacket collar up around her neck and locked the door. The steering wheel clamp her dad had insisted on buying when he bought the car for her eighteenth lay idly in the passenger well and stared up at her through the window. Molly sighed. *Well it's not like it can go anywhere is it?*

Impatient to meet Jenny and discover more about this brother of hers, she began the rest of her journey on foot, quickly walking through town and out the other side towards the children's park. There were plenty of people and cars around – it was after all not even half past nine yet. As she neared the recreational area the tree density increased and the brisk autumn breeze whipped up, howling through their branches. She hurried along a little faster. *Jeez it feels like winter's arrived already, how this country's climate can change overnight beats me.*

Her footsteps picked up even more quickly as she consoled herself with the knowledge it wasn't too much further. At least there would be the comfort of finding out some more about Jason, after all that *was* what she'd been trying to do the previous night.

Just as the roundabout, swings and slide came into view beside the huge oak trees her mobile bleeped. She dug it out of her pocket and read the text.

Sorry I'll be a little late
Please wait by the bench
Jenny

Molly sighed heavily, snapped the lid shut and dropped it back in her pocket. As she sat down on the bench beneath the massive old trees, she felt something cold and wet on her cheek. Looking up into the dark sky the rain plopped selfishly onto her hair, slipping in and out of her carefully created waves that hung past her shoulders. *Great! That's all I need – and no umbrella or hood on this jacket either – typical!* She hunched crossly into the collar even more. At that precise moment, Molly couldn't possibly have known that the classic Cumbrian weather was the least of her worries…

Jenny Flood tensed in his arms and waited for the final thrust. When it came, the experience was not new to her, but as always it was exceptional, as satisfying for her as much as it was for him. Her whole body shuddered violently, clinging on to him, not just with the ecstasy of it, but with the relief he was there with her, and not with another woman. For a selfish bastard like Miles, one might have thought his consideration relatively lacking in the bedroom, but in truth his vanity would never have allowed that, and anyway, not with Jenny, *never ever with her.*

He fell back onto the once crisp hotel sheets, panting with the exertion of their lovemaking, but still he covered her hand with his, stroking it affectionately. Something she recalled he'd always done, so they remained connected – to let her know he loved her, let her know *she was different from the others.*

"I've missed you Jen, you know that don't you?" He squeezed her hand now, reassuringly, reaffirming that memory. She was quiet at first, thinking how best to answer this, knowing full well he'd almost certainly been bed-hopping ever since their break up. Realistically, he could have left Charlotte for her six years ago, at any time during their three-year affair – *but he didn't*. Miles would never commit to anything that would risk his slice of a massive inheritance. Money always came first. She turned over on her side and watched him lying there, tiny beads of sweat glistening across his forehead.

"I've missed you too darling," she breathed huskily – then added, "*More than anyone.*" She kissed his cheek gently, then immediately slipped naked from between the sheets and disappeared into the luxury bathroom. Jenny didn't want to be questioned over who *'anyone'* might be, particularly as it was a reference to anyone *else* who might have missed Miles, rather than any guy *she* might have missed from her past. *Let him think he's the main man,* she thought – which of course sadly for her, *he was*.

As the massaging spray of hot water washed away the previous hour, she heard the muffled strains of the BBC ten o'clock news through the bathroom door.

At the point of attack Molly instantly realised she couldn't breathe! The thick sweet scent was suffocating her. She had tried twisting around to see whoever, or *whatever it was!* Someone had come from behind the bench, but they were too *strong! Oh God the killer… the killer was too strong!* In gut-piercing realisation, her arms and legs flailed desperately in vain as she tried to pull the hand and cloth away from her nose and mouth! *That smell! It was so pungent!*

There was pressure on the back of her skull as they held it tight with their other hand against their body. *Why couldn't she hear herself scream? Her brain was screaming!* Her hands tore blindly, haphazardly in frenzied panic! *Incessantly, repeatedly she scrabbled at the assailant's grasp, but nothing worked!* She could feel the stickiness of the perpetrator's blood beneath her nails, smell it as she scratched and clawed – *a trapped animal fights for its life!* For a few brief unyielding seconds every fibre in her body was strung taut against the strike, but resistance was futile! *Where was Jenny?! Why didn't somebody help her?! Anyone for God's sake!* Molly rapidly felt herself losing consciousness; muscles became heavy, no longer under her control, *abandoning her at life's vital moment.* A brief upward glimpse of blurred black and gold brought nothing. *Why is your face so… Dazed – she slipped swiftly into black.*

"Don't 'ee be wurryin' moi lover, th' ambulance is a comin'." Mary Tattershall cradled Molly's head in her arms, stroked her damp hair as the aroma of whisky meth attempted to rival the chloroform. "Ol Mary'll stay with 'ee as long as it takes, as long as 'ee needs me, oil be 'ere – you'll see…"

But the young girl could hear nothing of the old vagrant's words. *To all intents and purposes – Molly Fields was dead.*

NINETEEN

Nobody could have been more surprised than Charlotte when the interruption had occurred. *That damned vagrant woman was always hanging around the surgery,* which unfortunately for her, just happened to be opposite the park. As soon as she'd heard the slurred protest, Charlotte had spun round to see a swaying bundle of alcoholic fumed rags – the stench of which had her retching in disgust. She was of course oblivious to her *own* abhorrent behaviour… *but not to the fact that this was nonetheless, a bundle of rags that could see, talk and hear, despite the inebriation.*

She'd instantly released Molly, who'd immediately slumped sideways unconscious onto the bench. Charlotte had then grabbed her blue nylon box, shoved Mary to the ground and run like a deer to the woods opposite. It had been a shock and a warning. *Next time she would be more careful, she wouldn't choose anywhere near work just because it was convenient for supplies.*

Charlotte remained hidden until the ambulance had come and gone, before pocketing the mask and taking the long route back to where she'd left the car. Sitting comfortably inside now, composure regained, she pushed away the enormity of the risk she'd taken, and of what had actually just happened. The familiar hysteria seed began to sprout – and rise, the corners of her mouth began to twitch, and her mind began to re-plan as she rhythmically drummed her fingers on the blue box beside her. *That one would have to be a double appointment…*

Somewhere far away in the deepest recesses of her mind, Molly was aware of a screeching siren. It was faint, very faint, and she wasn't sure if this floating tinny noised fuzziness was some halfway spiritual platform between death and heaven.

Everything felt heavy, lead ran through her veins and there was a kind of 'tugging' and a repetitive pressurised sensation somewhere. She didn't know where, it was just there. Muffled voices struggled to get through the 'mist'. Were they coming to greet her: grandparents, great aunties and uncles and other long ago relatives? Were they coming to welcome her to the other side, to guide her through the darkness? Or was she developing medium tendencies as well as psychological abilities? No, well… *not if she was dead…*

"Get her on to that damned stretcher – now! We've got less than fifteen minutes!" The two paramedics from Kirkdale General lifted her lifeless body swiftly and skilfully onto the stretcher and into the waiting ambulance. The flashing light circled slowly, throwing

an intermittent shadowy blue hue across the playground apparatus.

"*The oxygen mask Geoff, one band's bust, it keeps sliding off her face!*"

"*Then hold the bloody thing on and keep that blasted saline drip in!*" He thumped the back of the driver's wall to alert him to get moving. As it pulled away the siren built up to full volume, the blue light revolving at speed.

"*BP's dropping – down to eighty over forty and falling – pulse 30, it's gonna go Geoff, she's gonna flatline, Geoff we're gonna lose her!*"

"*No we are NOT! Charge her! I'm NOT losing this one!*"

The ambulance defibrillator shot up to two hundred as Geoff Ransom hit the charge button, and his newly qualified trainee slapped the defib paddles on Molly's exposed chest. Her body jumped like a bucking ram then fell back motionless onto the board. The oscilloscope beeped and ran a single line across the monitor.

"*Again – dammit!*" yelled Geoff! Sally Gordon attempted a repeat charge just as the speeding ambulance hit a large pothole in the road. The violent lurch sent her sprawling to the floor, her head smashed viciously against the metal. Blood poured from her temple and the pain made her release the paddles sending them flying out of reach under the stretcher.

Geoff threw himself across his colleague and

scrabbled under the makeshift bed. His long rugby arms managed to grab hold of the wires as he yanked them back, ordering Sally to hit the button. She crawled back to the de-fib., her vision impaired by the blood running in her eyes, and brought both hands down on the control. Geoff slammed the paddles back down onto his dying patient and released the power. *"Come on! Come on! You've got to make it!"* A weak signal blipped faintly on the black background, their hearts and faces jumped together as they watched, prayed the peak would remain and repeat, but it was not to be. Their heads dropped as hope was dashed again and again, at every attempt the weak ripple fell to the floor into one long continuous screeching line. The siren of the ambulance screamed through the town as the driver expertly handled corners, traffic and red lights.

"She's gone Geoff, we can't get her back now."

"Yes we *can! We will! Charge her again – four hundred joules this time!"* Sally responded to the increase without question, just as her training had taught her, and for one last time the paddles were brought down on Molly's bruised body. The shock jolted her so violently she nearly fell off the stretcher, so grotesque were the current's effects, Geoff thought he had surely killed her himself. They waited, tense, anxious seconds. There it was. They both heard it. The beep beep of the oscilloscope, they saw the peaks of the heart's rhythm in luminescent green, like alien mountain terrain scrawling its way across the night. It wasn't strong but it was a reasonable rhythm – it was *there.* Then...

"I've got a pulse!" exclaimed Sally, jubilant at its reappearance.

Both paramedics exhaled in exhausted relief and strangely, almost laughed with the stress of it all. Sally, however, at a similar age to her patient, couldn't prevent the tears escaping as they mixed with her blood and coursed down her cheeks.

"Thank God..." sighed Geoff, his tense muscles relaxed for the first time since arriving on scene. He sank heavily against the side of the vehicle as Sally cuffed salty blood across her face and temple, and for the first time he realised her injured condition. Geoff pulled some gauze from the first aid box, blotted her tears and pressed it against her head wound with a smile, as the ambulance swung into the A & E forecourt of Kirkdale General.

Three nurses shot through the glass doors to meet the docked ambulance. Geoff and Sally had now checked her bag for personal details, and already rolled Molly out with the help of the driver as everyone ran with the gurney into A & E.

They rushed through the hospital corridors past wards and turning heads, Geoff competently reported her name, age and medical condition whilst sprinting alongside. Once the information was conveyed, the paramedics slowed to a walk and left the doctors to continue on at high speed. Shoving the gurney through the first set of double doors, monitoring vital signs and radioing ahead to intensive care, they disappeared into the nucleus of the hospital.

Geoff stood gazing up the corridor after Molly, standing back to let doctors shoot past him as they headed in the same direction as the crash team.

"Well done," said Sally quietly, "you've probably saved her you know." She looked up at him and ran a hand affectionately over his back.

"Yeah… well, let's hope so."

"It wasn't your fault Geoff… the last time. Even *you* can't save them if they've run the perfect pill gauntlet." Geoff delivered a half-smile appreciating her logic, took her elbow and steered Sally towards A&E.

"Come along, paramedic Gordon, *let's get you patched up!*"

Her head was banging like a drum. It felt as though the Royal Philharmonic had been rehearsing in there all night! Molly opened her eyes to find a room full of people in white clothing.

"Jeez, looks like I made it to the *good girls'* place then!" she quipped as she struggled to lift herself into a sitting position.

"You're in Kirkdale General Miss Fields, *and lay back down!* Not heaven fortunately, or not, as you may decide after experiencing the dinner tray!" The girl in white approached her bed with a smile, pushed up Molly's gown sleeve and strapped a blood pressure monitor on her arm.

"I'm Staff Nurse Bradshaw by the way, *Clare to the well-behaved patients!*" She winked wickedly. "The others are students," she gestured to half a dozen people behind her. "But if you don't feel like a party…"

"No, no that's fine." Molly smiled weakly.

"Let's see how we're doing today then, you've had quite a nasty experience you know. Do you remember anything abou–?"

"Anything at all?" interrupted a man in a slightly crumpled grey suit who'd slipped in unnoticed behind the group of students.

"*Inspector?!*" Clare Bradshaw turned abruptly from the bed. *"I asked you to wait outside until I'd determined the state of my patient!"*

"That's okay, I'm fine, well… obviously I'm not completely…" Molly massaged her forehead with her spare hand – eyes wincing.

"Inspector Longbridge, will you *please* wait outside until I've finished my observations? You can see Miss Fields is in no fit state to answer questions!" Harry obliged and left. He decided a large caffeine shot was needed anyway.

Clare finished her obs., wrote them up on the chart at the bottom of the bed, and ushered the students out of the room.

"How do you feel about the police Molly? Do you

think you could manage a few questions? They *really* need to speak to you if you can. I'll make sure he's not here too long."

"Yeah I guess… I've got to get it over with. Send him in." *Longbridge though*, she thought sighing to herself. *Now I'm going to encounter an ultra-grilling if Andrew's experience is anything to go by.*

Harry Longbridge didn't need a second invitation. Luckily the drinks dispenser was close by, and listening from the corridor was inside the door the moment the words were out of Clare's mouth.

"Miss Fields, I'm Detective Chief Inspector Long…"

"Yeah I know who you are," Molly interrupted. He glanced up at Nurse Bradshaw and Clare in turn raised her eyebrows at Molly to check if she was happy for her to leave. Her patient nodded affirmatively and Longbridge waited for her departure before he continued. Harry settled himself in the visitors' chair and took a mouthful of the machine's unappetising brown liquid, grimaced then placed the beige plastic cup on top of Molly's bedside cabinet. He gathered his thoughts before opening his line of questioning, breathing in deeply then exhaling loudly as if he had bad news to deliver.

"I believe what happened to you Miss Fields, is very relevant to a current case we're working on. You can't fail to have heard about the murders in Kirkdale over the last few weeks."

"I'm aware... *very aware,*" she replied, her eyes holding his.

"So what can you tell me about what brought you here two nights ago?"

"Two – *two nights ago?!*" exclaimed Molly. "I didn't realise I'd been here *forty-eight hours!* Have my parents been inform– *my friends...* do *they know?*

"They would have been told, probably saw you when you were out of it. Look, don't concern yourself with that now, I'm sure you'll see them later. I don't want to appear harsh but I need to know all you can remember about that night in the park. First off, why were you there?" Molly instinctively didn't want to tell him *why* she was there. Safer to play the memory loss card, the last thing she wanted was for the trio's private detective work to be discovered. *Imagine* what Longbridge would make of *that*, particularly where Andrew was concerned.

"Not much – not really, I... don't remember much at all to be honest. Just recall sitting on the bench, don't know *why* I was there. Suddenly someone held a cloth over my face. I smelt this awful perfume, heady, you know, like chloroform or something, and that was it. Bosh! I was a goner. Didn't *see* a thing, well... not..."

"Not *what?* Not *what* Miss Fields? *What* was it you thought you *didn't* see?" A pause...

"Well it sounds... *stupid* really."

"*Try me.*"

"Well when I looked up, I saw a... a sort of swirly black and gold... *mess.* That's all I can describe it as. Just those two colours all wound together. Then I passed out." Harry eyed her suspiciously. *Was she making this up? And if so why?*

"I *told* you it sounded stupid." She looked at the wall, arms crossed. He decided not to pursue the scepticism tack.

"That's okay. If that's what you saw… you *were* very heavily sedated, probably couldn't make a thing out once the pad was over your face. The brain does funny things." *Didn't answer why she was there in the first place though,* he thought.

Just then Harry's stomach began to rumble, it *always* began to rumble at crucial moments. He fished around in his jacket pocket and brought out a small bag of barley sugars. *His* brains would soon feel like they'd been chloroformed without one. Molly watched as he popped the sweet in his mouth, and just before he returned them to storage, extended his arm out to offer one. She declined. Longbridge shrugged, and replaced them into the sugary grey depths of his suit jacket. He continued – with difficulty as he swapped the cube from one side of his mouth to the other.

"You've yet to inform me why you were there alone at ten o'clock at night. Particularly with the dangerous situation we have at the moment. It's hardly a safe and sensible thing to be doing, on your own, is it?" She flushed then dropped her head to concentrate on fiddling with the bedding. When she looked back up Molly answered him with a newfound coolness.

"I simply can't remember Inspector. I'm sorry." She began to massage the sides of her head trying to relieve the 'pain', then pushed the call button at the side of her bed. "I'm really feeling very tired now, I think I'd like to rest." She spoke confidently, her tone practically dismissive. At that moment Nurse Bradshaw re-entered the room and held the door open with an arm extended pointedly towards the gap. There was no mistaking her body language.

"Thank you Inspector. *Have a good day."* Harry Longbridge vacated the visitors' chair and walked to the door where he paused and then turned around.

"If you *should* remember anything, *anything* at all…" Molly inclined her head. "You were nearly killed – three other women *have been."* His face softened for a second, displayed just a trace of vulnerability, his voice low, almost despondent. *"Quite frankly Miss Fields – I need all the help I can get."* With that he thanked the nurse and disappeared into the hallway. Bradshaw closed the door on her way out.

Molly was now alone, staring at the space that just a few minutes ago had been inhabited by half a dozen people. The room felt isolated, and with the door closed, unconnected with the busy wards outside. She lay there determined not to feel either scared or pressurised, but hospital was the one place in the world she hated to be, and illness had nothing to do with it. It was the lack of familiarity, freedom of movement, her clothes and routines, *and the feeling of having absolutely no control over what happened to her.*

Molly now felt completely uptight and thought to herself – *I wish I'd accepted that bloody barley sugar now!*

"Surprise!!" The door burst open and what appeared to be a huge bouquet of talking flowers floated in its entrance. The blooms shifted to one side and behind them stood Andrew and Gina, beaming like two Cheshire cats. Molly giggled. Her parents had visited earlier after her sleep, but only these two could *really* lift her spirits.

"Hi guys, thanks for those they're *gorgeous!*" Gina laid them on the side table, assuring her friends she'd get the nurse to find a vase before they left. Both of them gave Molly a big hug and sat either side of the bed, just needing to be close, to reassure themselves she really *was* okay. It was a good thing it was a room in the 3rd floor private wing otherwise they would most certainly have been turfed off it, and probably not allowed to bring flowers in either.

Once they'd both convinced themselves she really was mentally and physically okay, it was down to the serious stuff. Andrew picked up her hand and asked the most obvious question first. *The one that Longbridge had wanted answered.*

"So what were you doing there Molls?" Molly automatically glanced up at the door as if the police were about to burst in to take her confession. In the absence of such an inquisition she related the whole story. Her latest vision, how she'd received a text from Jenny to meet her in the park, the car breaking down and the actual attack, *what she could remember of it.* Andrew and Gina looked at each other, horrified at what their friend had been through, then Andrew suddenly realised something. In their relief that Molly was okay, nobody had thought of it.

"Strange that Jenny should want to see you anyway though Molly isn't it?" said Andrew puzzled; "Do you think it was to do with your relationship with Jason? I mean we haven't actually *touched* on the fact that Jenny texted you one minute and the next thing you know is you're fighting for your life!" There was quiet in the room then as all three absorbed what Andrew had just implied.

"Jenny Flood *is* new around here," exclaimed Gina, eyes wide now as she looked at Andrew, "and you *work* with her every day!"

"But she was with *Miles* when the third murder took place, remember?" Molly pointed this out very calmly, but was secretly relieved she'd remembered it. Apart from obviously not wanting Andrew to be in any danger, she didn't relish the idea that Jason's sister could be a murderess. *He* may be schizophrenic, but she felt certain of his innocence and hoped that when back on his meds properly something might come of their relationship. She didn't need his sister being a whole other personality too.

"Maybe we'd just better forget the whole thing." Gina was looking at Andrew now, her eyes pleading with him.

"*No way!*" Molly interjected, "don't even consider that for one minute! Look – just because we hit a bit of a glitch that's no reason…"

"A glitch – *a glitch?! Are you crazy girl?!*" Gina had leapt off the bed now and was pacing up and down the hospital room, her red hair flying this way and that as tears filled her eyes. "*You nearly died Molly Fields, do you realise that?!*"

"*Exactly* – it was *me* who nearly met 'Granny gone over', not *you!* Therefore *I* get to make the decision on whether we keep going or not. If we *do* stop searching for the killer I don't want it to be because of this!" She waved her hands wildly backwards and forwards over the bed. Gina was now looking at Andrew expectantly, exasperated at having to wait for his support. She had never been in full agreement with their amateur sleuthing, *obviously now,* she thought, *he will put an end to this.*

"Molly, maybe we…" he started lamely;

"*No Andy! Not because of me!* I won't be the reason for quitting, *and I won't be sidelined either.*" Andrew looked up at his girlfriend who was now standing opposite the bed hands on hips, eyes flashing and tears brimming. His *'you know what Molly's like'* expression, resulted in her throwing her hands skyward, and emanating what could only be described as an incensed guttural screech. Molly and Andy both glanced at the window next to the door as Nurse Bradshaw paused on her way past with eyebrows lifted at the raised voices. Molly smiled, waved an 'okay' and Clare carried on down the corridor.

Gina had turned her back on them and faced the wall in frustrated anger. In reality though, she was merely trying to prevent the tears from falling, *and a feeling of utter foreboding.*

"Gee, I'll be *fine.*" Molly tried to placate her but she remained with her back to the bed. "I won't go anywhere at night on my own again, *okay?* I promise." Gina began delving into her jeans pocket for a tissue, and giving up on finding one, blinked back a tear and turned to face her closest friend, *the girl who was like a sister to her.*

"Don't you *see? I can't lose you too!*" Andrew, who had already raised himself off the bed in anticipation, now dashed around to the other side and pulled Gina into his arms.

'Her mother,' he mouthed silently to Molly as he cradled his girlfriend's head against his chest and held her tight.

"Come on Gee – sweetheart? Eh? We're here to cheer her up, not for all of us to get upset." He pulled some tissues from the box that Molly had held up to him and dabbed Gina's eyes, trying carefully to avoid her make-up, which to be honest was pretty much now wrecked anyway. He kissed her gently on the lips and stroking her hair, waited until she'd calmed down before letting her go.

"I'm sorry… I just can't bear to think…" She sat down close to Molly and took her by the shoulders. *"Promise me* if you do anything it'll be with Andy or all of us, *never* on your own, *not at all Molls."* Molly nodded and hugged her friend close whilst looking over her shoulder at Andrew who was heaving a huge sigh of relief. Whilst he obviously didn't want any harm coming to her, he knew that out of the two, Molly was the one he could rely on for staying the course. He loved Gina dearly and always would, she was his soulmate, *but he needed Molly for her sheer tenacity.*

Staff Nurse Bradshaw came back to check all was well and popped her head round the corner of the door, noticed the flowers and returned with a vase of water.

"Visiting time is over now thank you," she said briskly, arranging the bouquet in the glass holder. Gina and Andrew kissed Molly goodbye and promised to return the following evening. Once they'd gone and the dinner round was over, the room and ward outside was quiet and she was alone again.

The evening passed slowly. Molly glossed over a few magazines, dozed and watched a little TV. By eleven, as she was dropping off at the end of a film, a new doctor was about to start the night shift. *Having just stubbed out her second cigarette in the hospital car park she now walked purposefully through the ground floor corridors towards the lifts.*

TWENTY

Jason had spent the last three days laying low in Jenny's flat. He'd managed to persuade the police to contact his doctors in Bradenthorpe and proved the dosage on the bottle they'd found was *not* his prescription, but in the absence of any other suspect they'd ordered him to stay in the vicinity.

Since Molly's abduction incident, he'd been in and out of self-control, and although he was taking his tablets regularly again, he knew they weren't working fast enough because of his lapse. Even though he'd increased the dose, the voices now almost always governed his actions. From past experience several months could pass before full effectiveness would be restored, *but he didn't have several months,* and the thought, *and guilt,* of not being there for his sister really weighed him down.

The depression was building again *and the voices were everywhere.* Jenny had said she needed time to sort some 'things' out, would be away for a couple of nights. Well he guessed what *that* meant and it wasn't good news. Jenny continually ignored his fears, refused to admit she'd resumed her relationship with Miles, what more could he do except be there when it all fell apart again? He'd promised her faithfully to stay indoors, not get into any trouble, but how could he do that when *they* wouldn't let him? When they were holding court inside his head? *Where they were gathering right now...*

The clumping and shuffling re-focused his thoughts – *his orders for the night.* Access to Jenny's car these last few days had proved extremely useful, not that she needed to know that of course. Following Charlotte home from work on one of them had proved very lucrative. If she intended to harm his sister in any way, then he would harm *her* and he'd discovered precisely the way to do it, the most wounding way the *most effective.*

After she found him in the surgery that night and demanded to know where Jenny lived, Jason believed it was only a matter of time before that mad witch struck. This was one occasion when he agreed with the voices, and they had no need to shout – *he wasn't fighting back anymore.*

The padlock that should've been linked through the bolts had been left hanging carelessly. After slipping it off and placing it quietly onto the stone floor of the block, he drew back the first bolt on the top door, then the joining bolt to the bottom door, and the last one that connected to the upright framework. They gave a soft snort on hearing him enter. It was black inside, the only light coming from the moon shining through the top opener. It cast a pale strip-shadow across the walled partitions, the hanging riding hats and crops, the floored Hunter boots – *and Charlotte's precious horses*. The smell of dung had hit him the minute he'd opened the top stable door, along with the warm hum of urinated hay and nine hundred pounds of horseflesh. When Greta and Gizmo actually became aware of him, their agitation was instant. Shuffling their feet, eyes wary, heads swinging this way and that, *they were not accustomed to strangers in their stable – especially at night.*

Jason set down the bin liners he'd been carrying and quickly opened them both, the horses were getting twitchy and he didn't want to hang around any longer than he had to. From inside the bags he pulled out armfuls of what had originally been pretty yellow flowering plants. Pretty – but deadly. Hundreds of limp daisy heads like mini baby suns fell to the floor, *each head, each petal, each stem, a killer*. He smiled nervously each time he delved into the black plastic bag, nodding manically in agreement with *them* as they began laughing wildly in his head…

He moved cautiously towards the two horses, held the Ragwort just out of reach of their muzzles and shook it encouragingly. The animals leaned forward eagerly now and took the out of hours offering. *Food could always override a little nervous tension where greedy horses were concerned.*

Jason had always bemoaned at his flatmate's interest in watching *Countryfile* every week, it had always seemed a really odd choice for a twentysomething latent punk, but now it had proved extremely useful. *Amazing what you could actually learn,* he thought as he watched the horses gratefully munching – *and all from Sunday TV!*

As the bin liners slowly deflated, his head rang with insane whispery chants for him to finish the job quickly and go – experiencing only a flash second of regret from somewhere far away as he scrunched up the bags and squashed them into a ball...

It hadn't been that difficult to discover Molly's whereabouts. Charlotte had simply donned her old white coat from her hospital days, stepped into the revolving glass door and walked straight into the foyer of the building.

Kirkdale General was a large teaching hospital, to all intents and purposes it just looked like she'd come on duty. It would be highly unlikely for somebody to suspect her, particularly with all the agency staff that were constantly coming and going. All she had to do was sling a stethoscope round her neck, stick some files under her arm, walk positively up to the reception desk *and give a false name.*

Charlotte got lucky. The team on was the same as night duty two days ago, they remembered the pandemonium, the yells of 'chloroform poisoning' and 'resus'. They were also extremely busy *that* evening, it was a Friday, and as a weekend night always a challenge. *No one bothered to check any credentials.* A confident woman in white bearing medical equipment and an apparent stack of paperwork would easily pass for staff amongst the chaos of a busy night in A & E. After all, she *was* a doctor – *just not one of theirs*. Charlotte simply asked which floor the girl had been taken to. *They even gave her the room number* – 121.

Her comfortable flat brogues walked her silently along each corridor, rode stealthily with her in the lift and carried her smoothly and sedately out of the elevator when it reached the third floor. It was here that the private wing of the hospital was set out, where patients were nursed in individual rooms able to enjoy real peace in their own space, sleep better, and could use personal TVs and laptops if well enough. Usually this was a jackpot bonus for the recuperating individual who could afford it – *but not tonight.*

It had taken Charlotte a full fifteen minutes to locate the correct part of the hospital where it would be easiest and quickest to reach the upper floor area she needed. The sheer size of the building meant that there were plenty of corners, cupboards, toilets etc. to duck behind or into if she noticed anyone particularly worrying.

Unfortunately she would be unable to complete the job in her usual trademark style, carrying the relevant equipment would have aroused too much suspicion. *Truly a shame*, she thought, *it depicts so much. Still, the end result is what really matters, and this girl is extremely unhelpful to my work – needs must.*

As Charlotte rounded a corner she nearly walked straight into a couple of young interns enveloped in each other's arms. She was getting close now, a less busy section, questions could very well be asked by a keen student wanting to score points. However, these two were clearly not thinking about their patients, or their duties. Even so, Charlotte still ducked behind the wall, heart pounding, neatly pressed into the convenient telephone alcove she'd just passed. *The Gods are surely smiling down on me tonight* she thought looking up – which ones she didn't care to dwell on. *As for the first-year post grads, what bloody appalling behaviour – in my day there would've been hell to pay! Still, seems they're only interested in themselves so guess I should count my blessings.*

She looked to her right again, checked the length of the corridor behind her as she'd done repeatedly, it was still unusually empty. *Probably why the youngsters had chosen that area to meet,* she decided disapprovingly, not for one moment appreciating the hypocrisy of *her* intentions...

The young voices fell silent and what could only be described as kissing and moaning sounds followed. Her eyes rolled. *Dear God! How our hospitals need their army of matrons back!* After a couple of minutes the lovers' noises fell silent and she could hear both pairs of footsteps as they moved away from the area. Still in the alcove, she waited for a few more seconds, held her breath tensely and strained to hear – *it had to be now.*

Despite the last five minutes, there surely wouldn't be *too* many moments when there was absolutely no one due to appear in this section. Charlotte ventured out of the recess and craned her head around the corner; nothing. She re-checked behind her for the umpteenth time *then began walking quickly towards room 121.*

Jason checked his watch. 10.20p.m. He'd already spent far too long in that smelly stable – time he wasn't there. The voices were reasonably happy although there was still some Ragwort left on the floor. Enough ingested to see the right result, however, *long-term and short.*

He peered out of the top door opening but could see and hear nothing untoward, just the horses munching contentedly behind him, *for the moment anyway.* It took less than two minutes to close and bolt the doors, replace the padlock, run along the tree-lined stable block using the bushes as extra cover and out of the gravel drive into the lane. It wasn't pitch black but with no overhead street lighting there was very little illumination, he could slip unnoticed along the quiet country road to pick up the car from the clearing at the other end – *job done.*

As her hand rested on the door knob she felt the nausea rise from her stomach, when it reached her throat the familiar burning made her shudder automatically. Although it was a necessary act, there was still that nugget of sanity that continued to lurk in the farthest recesses of her mind where it tried to break through – each time manifesting itself in a spurt of reflux. Charlotte reached irritably into her trouser pocket for a tissue bent her head down and spat. She folded over the unpleasant contents and returned it to her pocket but the sour odour still hung tartly in the air; remained on her breath…

She removed the Chinese ball mask from the deep white surgical pocket, depressed the handle gently, entered the room and closed the door slowly and carefully behind her. It made the quietest click…

Molly lay in a deep sleep. *Not deep enough though eh?* she thought. The oriental face now covered her own as she began to approach the bed. Her heart hammered violently, her head throbbed with concentration, with the sheer terror of being discovered. *She was not used to such a public place – it was a massive risk.*

Suddenly Rachmaninoff was striking loud melodious tones from her inside pocket! She froze. *Her mobile!* The files tucked under her arm fell to the floor in that splattering whoosh only stationery could effect as she cursed her stupidity in leaving it on. Charlotte groped at her clothes, desperate to stop the ringing, located it and saw Miles' number. She swiped the answer icon with one eye on Molly. *He would never bother to ring, particularly when she was out, not unless there was an emerg…*

"Charlotte! Where the *hell* are you? The horses are sick, *really* sick, they're snorting, stamping, there's

Ragwort all over the stable floor!" She staggered then, clutched at the bed rail as an iron jaw clenched viciously down on her stomach and ripped at her guts. Her feet didn't work, her mouth didn't work. Her ears heard all the words but her brain was totally redundant. "Charlotte do you *hear* me?! *For God's sake!*"

"I… I…" she started then glanced at her 'patient'. Molly was stirring. The noise of the folders falling and the mobile ringing had partially roused her. Charlotte suddenly regained her composure. The phone was snapped shut and thrust into her inside pocket. She left the plastic wallets where they fell, ripped the mask from her head and pushed that deep into an outside pocket. With all the self-control she could muster, she opened the door very, very slowly, extraordinarily quietly, just a crack so she could see. Once she'd checked the corridors both ways, she closed it silently behind her… *and ran!*

Molly moaned, turned over, and oblivious to everything began to snore…

Charlotte got out of that hospital a damned site faster than she'd got in. She flew down those corridors and gave no thought to her predicament, how she should be more careful in letting people see her running through the hospital without explanation, without her beeper going off, without any Tannoy announcements – without anyone *else* running. *All she could think about were the horses.*

Luckily it was late at night, there weren't any visitors wandering about which cut the body count down somewhat. Even so she was now not only taking a huge risk by even *being* there, she was drawing attention to herself by those that *did* see her. A couple of doctors looked up in surprise as she ran past the end of their wards, but she didn't care. Greta and Gizmo meant *everything* to her, they were her *life*. *Who could have done this? Who?*

Her head was spinning now, her legs composed of jelly, her lungs fit to burst through her chest, *and still she ran*. She didn't bother with the lifts, couldn't wait, couldn't be contained and hampered by fluorescent floor-stopping lights. Instead she found the stairs, took them two at a time as her white coat tails streamed out behind her, heart pounding, blood rushing through her ears like a red tsunami! Only when she reached the ground floor and approached the corner to the reception area, did she force herself to slow down and resume a normal walking pace. Front of house was always full of people, *even she wasn't that suicidal.*

Once outside and away from the hospital's entrance, Charlotte picked up speed, tore off the coat, rolled it into a ball and shoved it into a plastic bag she'd pre-placed in a spare pocket. She glanced furtively around her like a street urchin then started to run again, grateful for her flat shoes. Her car was parked in a side street nearby. On reaching it she threw the carrier into the back, jumped in and pulled the silver Morgan from the kerb in seconds. Her chestnut hair buffeted in the wind and the soft crimson leather hugged her body as she flew the Roadster home on autopilot.

And in the private wing of Kirkdale General's 3rd floor beneath Molly Field's hospital bed, laid a wet mauve plastic folder *emitting a sweet and heavy scent.*

TWENTY-ONE

The Morgan's wheels skidded spectacularly halfway along the gravel drive of Willows Copse. Wide arched lines cut deep into the gravel and sprayed tiny stones across the paintwork of Miles' own Roadster.

Charlotte hauled aggressively on the handbrake, wheel spinning the car to a sudden crunching halt and narrowly missing its twin. Scrambling out of the low door as it fell open she ran for the paddock screaming her husband's name. Suddenly she needed him, she needed him desperately no matter what he'd done. *This was one nightmare she couldn't face alone.*

Miles appeared from within the stables, sleeves rolled up, his usual polished, confident appearance distinctly lacking. There was horse shit on his beige slacks, hay in his hair, and even in the poor light she could see his ashen face, his expression full of genuine concern. He may not have much respect for his marriage vows, but he would never want anything bad to happen to the horses, *he wasn't completely heartless.*

"I've called the emergency vet. Callum wasn't on, there's a locum working this weekend, a Josie Kinkade." He paused. "But... but even on the phone she doesn't hold out much hope. You'd better prepare yourself."

"But I need him, I need *Callum! Miles ring him! Ring him at home! Make him come! He can do something!"* Her voice rose higher and more hysterical with every word.

"He's away Charlie, late summer holiday – Cyprus. Don't you remember him mentioning it when he did their shots last month?" As she knelt beside her babies she could barely hear him, let alone recall the conversation with Callum Westcott. He was the best vet in Kirkdale. She needed him. She needed him right *now* and he wasn't *there!* Charlotte stroked her darling Greta then Gizmo and the tears fell quickly as the affectionate nickname Miles had used in their early days fell on deaf ears.

Josie Kinkade pulled up alongside the two Morgans and jumped down from the mud-splattered jeep. She yanked out her medical box flipped up the two end catches and lifted the lid. On this occasion it contained a bolt gun. There was going to be little to nothing she could do for these two horses and depending on what the owners wanted to spend she might need it.

As she checked the firearm, her eyes swept briefly over the large Victorian house and the Scots vet made a derisive generalisation of its occupants. Even in the dark it was obvious her own upbringing in the working-class areas of Glasgow was a stark contrast to this idyll. *Barbiturate shots then* she concluded. She shrugged the chip off her shoulder, put the gun away and screwed her eyes up against the dark to look for the paddock gate. It was barely visible beneath a large untrimmed willow tree. Reaching back into the jeep for a Maglight, she tossed it the right way round with one hand, flicked the button and walked behind its beam towards the stables.

The dark wooden building was set at a right angle to a row of tall, equally dark conifers that bordered the two-acre field. As she rounded the end to access the front of the shelter, Josie froze. Every nerve in her body vibrated, her throat sandpapered and her hands became slick as the vet box slid from her grasp to thud heavily on the soft earth.

"Quickly in here!" Miles was waiting at the door, his voice urgent, desperate. *"They're down already, my wife is with them!"* Noticing the dropped box he automatically reached down and picked it up before disappearing into the stable.

"Th… Thank you," she replied to the back of his not so white designer shirt, hoping her voice didn't betray an internal swathe of fear and recognition. She followed him into the equine 'mortuary…'

Charlotte was kneeling by Greta, eyes glistening, not feeling the sharp hay poke through her expensive linen trousers, not caring about the mess they were in, not knowing which of her two horses to comfort first.

Josie glimpsed her surroundings under the illumination of what she hoped they'd intended was a *temporary* light. Her gaze landed on the single bulb and followed a very long cable that led along the stable block wall and out over to another farm building. *Really safe and professional* she thought – *it's always the ones with money.*

She placed the torch on top of a large tack box and left it burning. Looking down she saw the evidence of the horses' condition. The scattered Ragwort told her all she needed to know. The poison had been brought in and she didn't know the size, but even an average bag densely packed would have been enough to finish them both off – *eventually*. This was just a case of client hand-holding, a sympathetic ear and euthanasia – *there was absolutely nothing else she could do.* Josie just needed to do it without Miles Peterson recognising her, and get out of there as quickly as possible. If he remembered seeing her in the pub with Rachel and he *did* have anything to do with… well at least her hair was pulled back into a ponytail for work. *She winced at the unintentional irony.*

Her quiet disposition and slow movements had not gone unnoticed.

"Don't just stand there for God's sake, *do* something!" Josie walked over to the now utterly tortured Charlotte and knelt down beside her.

"Mrs. Peterson there's –"

"It's *Doctor Peterson* and don't start yacking at me, just *get working, and save my damned horses!*" Charlotte bent back over Greta, her shoulders were shaking, she was visibly sobbing now and both animals were uttering painful throaty noises. Their bloated stomachs were plain to see. *It was absolutely heartbreaking.*

Josie stood up again, chanced eye-to-eye contact with Miles and shook her head slowly from side to side. Uncomfortable though it was, she held his gaze until certain he knew what she meant. Miles sighed – felt utterly beaten. He ran a hand stressfully through his hair and fully acknowledging the situation now his gut instincts had been confirmed. He showed no signs of recognising the young Scottish vet, turned to his wife and swallowed hard before he spoke very softly…

"Charlotte." She didn't hear him. She moved erratically between the two horses, not knowing who to hold, who to caress, her clothes reeking of horse sweat, fodder and urine, she was in another world that was simply delaying the inevitable. Miles tried again, this time he raised his voice slightly.

"Charlotte." He bent down and stretched out his arms, both hands cupped her shoulders. For the first time in years he actually felt compassion. "She can't do anything for them Charlie, you *know* that. Ragwort's a killer, look how much they must've *eaten*." She spun round suddenly then, her face contorted in resentment.

"Callum could!" she screeched, *"Callum could save them!"* She shook herself free of his touch, her voice soared higher and higher, her eyes grew wider, the whites shone madly in the half-light. *"Why aren't you doing something?! Call yourself a vet – you've not even tried!!"* She wiped a clammy hand irritably across

her forehead, forced an escaped clump of hair back behind her ear. Her eyes narrowed sinisterly now as she looked directly at Josie. "*If you don't do something I'll hold you personally responsible! When Callum gets back I'll... I'll...*" Josie paled and shot a glance at Miles for direction.

"*Do it.*" He instructed crisply; then took hold of Charlotte's shoulders more firmly this time and pulled her on to her feet. He wasn't about to let the woman he'd spent the last twenty odd years with witness the destruction of her only friends.

"*Nooo!!*" Charlotte desperately tried to shake herself free from his grasp. She clawed at the air with her expression distorted on a face that spoke volumes beneath the streaked mascara as she fought to stay with her only 'children'.

"Which meth–"

"Injection."

With that, Miles dragged his grief-stricken wife out of their stables and half-coaxed, half-marched her firmly back towards the house. Every faltered step, every stumble was accompanied by haunting wails and sobs of protest railed against it – this blackest of nights. *But even she couldn't silence the sound of death.*

Josie Kinkade sat at her kitchen table nursing a half-drunk mug of tea. A glance at the clock above the sink immediately made her yawn long and hard. *One a.m., time for some shut-eye* she decided. The chair scraped noisily backwards across the flagstones as the young woman got up to head for the little winding staircase of her rented cottage.

She trudged her way slowly up to the landing where two bedrooms sat snugly next to each other and pushed open the door of the one she was using. Mentally exhausted, *and not only from a long day*, Josie flopped fully dressed onto the bed and began to doze. Behind heavy lids she reflected on the past hour in a mixed haze of sympathy, and anxiety that Miles may have recognised her. She had absolutely no possible realisation it wasn't Miles Peterson who was her problem.

There were no more call-outs that evening and she slept deeply until six a.m. when her uninvited alarm clock – *the infuriating yap of next door's Terrier* – woke her as usual.

Charlotte lay very still. It had been a tortuous and sleepless night where she'd refused to take anything to help her rest, had refused any form of comfort from Miles, *and to his credit, he'd really tried* – and refused to take any time off work.

It was just after seven and although she lay on her side, legs pulled up to her chest in a protective ball, motionless and seemingly numb, *her brain was operating at full capacity.* Molly Fields was no longer a top priority. '*Ms. Vet*' Josie Kinkade, however, *was another matter entirely.*

Miles placed a mug of coffee on her bedside table and sat gingerly at the edge of the quilt. She pretended to be asleep.

"Charlotte? Are you awake?" Nothing… He guessed at her pretence, her need for seclusion. "I'm going to work now, why don't you take the day off eh? A few days even. I know you said you didn't want to but I *can* manage you know, I honestly feel you're not in a fit state to consult at the moment. *Understandably* so, you've had a *terrible* shock, a *dreadful* emotional loss." He waited for a response. There *was* none. "If you really won't, then I'll see you later, but at *least* have a long lie-in, maybe just do a few home visits this afternoon." Her answer was to turn away and face the opposite wall. Miles sighed heavily, then stood up and walked slowly towards the door where he hesitated for a few seconds before he retraced his steps. He bent over his wife, hovered momentarily then placed a light kiss on her ruffled hair. With still no response he straightened up and walked swiftly from the room.

Charlotte waited for his footfall on the stairs before she opened her eyes. They were dry. There would be no more tears. She had only three sensitive points: her inability to have children, unconditional love for her horses and an excessively irrational sense of self-preservation. The first she could do nothing about, for she was not prepared to house anyone else's cast-offs. The last two she would avenge to the death – *anybody's*.

Charlotte threw off the covers. *It was time to get back to work.*

TWENTY-TWO

Cordon tape vibrated noisily in the crisp breeze, the red and white blurring with the very speed of it. Behind him, the river beneath Tiddly Bridge ran fast over its stony bed as it blew bush twigs and silver birch leaves along its ripples. It was only mid-September, but the wind was already singing and the promise of a cold winter lurked around the corner.

Harry Longbridge turned up the collar of his grey padded jacket and rammed his hands deep into his pockets. He nudged gently at a piece of dirty glass with the toe of a black loafer and expertly flipped it over. Bending down the object became clearer than on his first sharp-eyed flash – most would have missed it, but not the *Magpie*. With a clean handkerchief he turned the broken segment over to reveal a gold stud earring.

"Walker! Over here!" PC Joe Walker left his other colleagues to search the small rear garden that belonged to Josie Kinkade's rented cottage, and joined his boss at the side kitchen door.

"Sir?"

"I need a SOCO bag." Longbridge held the find up between forefinger and thumb, the hanky carefully between his fingers and the earring. Joe produced a bunch from his pocket, pulled at one and opened it along the seal as Harry carefully dropped the small gold stud into it. "Don't forget to write the details on that and ensure it gets included with the button we found earlier."

"Sir." The young officer nodded and turned to go.

"And Walker –" Harry added, "make sure you log *everything* when you get back to the station. I don't want to find half of it left in the squad car."

"To be honest sir, there doesn't seem to be a lot of evidence here."

"*That* Walker is why you're still getting sent for take-out." There is *always* more evidence than you think Walker – *always*. You've just got to look hard enough." The rookie reddened, dropped his head and shuffled his feet awkwardly.

"Yes sir. I'll remember that sir."

Harry turned back to the broken window, depressed the kitchen door handle and crunched his way across the stone slabs.

He wondered why the house felt so hot it necessitated the removal of his jacket, but a familiar smell soon gave it away. Even with the killer's chloroform trademark vying for dominance, the Longbridge nose could sniff weed out a mile off. He reckoned *this* house had been privy to regular use. The smell had attached itself to the fabrics: curtains, cushions and carpets, just like nicotine would.

He made his way up the steep staircase to the landing where it didn't take too long to find the source. He popped his head round the door of the larger of the two bedrooms where one of his officers was already recording details and taking photographs. It was basically an indoor greenhouse. Trays of cannabis plants – some mature, some seedlings, were stacked floor to ceiling on neat rows of light aluminium shelving. Oil-filled radiators that trailed end to end along the floor and in-between each shelving stack, were belting out full blast. Super bright extra large bulbs hung along a crude spaghetti junction-style cabling system. Heavily taped and tacked, across the ceiling and down the walls, all the hooded reflectors carefully aimed at the plants. *Ms. Kinkade obviously liked gardening as well as animals then. She'd certainly been a very busy girl.* He moved next door to the smaller of the two bedrooms.

Andrew sat in the car outside the Kirkdale Veterinary Practice and looked down at the card Rachel's Scottish friend had given him. Ms. Josie L. Kinkade BVSc MRCVS. *She never mentioned she was a vet* he thought, flicking at it with his thumb, *but then why should she I guess? It wasn't like we were chatting socially when we met. She wasn't the sort of person Rach would've hung about with though, that's what I can't understand.* A stab of guilt pierced then. He knew Rachel may not have studied for any kind of degree, been professionally trained or particularly well versed in anything much, but she would've helped anyone who needed it and had possessed a heart of gold – one that had been cruelly and brutally ripped open...

Not having been able to reach Josie at the mobile number on the card, he'd decided it must have been the practice mobile, and called in to the surgery to see if she was on duty. The receptionist had informed him she was a vet down from Glasgow working six monthly posts around the UK to gain a range of animal experience. She currently floated between the Kirkdale and Leighthsham village surgeries as a locum, and wasn't working at the Kirkdale practice that week. Andrew had used all his charm to persuade the young receptionist to give him Josie's home address after showing her the contact number she'd given him. The mobile apparently *was* Josie's own, not the practice one, so the girl had thought it'd be okay to give him her private address.

Andrew stuck the card in his pocket and started the engine. *A home visit then*, after all, he *had* promised to keep her in the loop.

His car approached Leighthsham's Tiddly Bridge and as he scanned the cottages on the far side for the house number, the police cordon fluttered into view. Suddenly his stomach lurched. He slowed right down to squeeze the car through the ultra-narrow bridge road as sweat broke out on his forehead. *Not again – surely?* He caught sight of the cottage's number behind the tape and realised it must be Josie, or someone living with her. Once on the other side Andrew slid the window down, breathed deeply and gestured to the youngest officer he could see on the cordon. Joe Walker strode importantly over to the car, head up, shoulders back, doing his best to look commanding at nineteen. He bent down to the Mondeo's open window.

"What's the deal here then?" Andrew asked coolly as he flashed his press card, "not *another* murder surely?" *He* tried very hard to look nonchalant, as if he regularly reported on murders.

"There's been a suspicious death sir, but I'm afraid I can't say any more than that at the moment." Walker wasn't going to make any *more* mistakes that day. Andrew nodded politely and murmured his appreciation of the officer's position.

"Is Harry Longbridge on scene by any chance?" He stared straight ahead though the windscreen towards Josie's cottage.

"Yes sir, Mr. Longbridge is leading the investigation."

"Ah good, that's good. He'll be pleased I'm here then," he said matter-of-factly looking at his watch in feigned hurriedness. "We've talked at length regarding the first victim, I'd better get inside. I take it he's already in the house?" Andrew now looked assertively at Joe, straight in the eyes, and saw unease hover there. "He'll not want to wait for this," he said patting a folder of sports column notes that sat on the passenger seat. "I've managed to collate it all now." Joe weighed up the pros and cons of his boss not getting the information he wanted quickly enough, versus him letting non-constabulary through the cordon. What was that the Guvnor had said though? There is *always* more evidence he just had to look for it? Joe relaxed, straightened up and gesticulated to his colleagues ahead as he waved Andrew on through. Once he'd driven past the youngest officer on the squad a wry smile crept to his lips as he shook his head in sheer disbelief – *amazing how that one always worked – every single time!*

A dried, dark red 'BITCH', was scrawled in two feet high letters on the wall opposite the bed. It was enough to disturb anyone's steel resolve, *even Harry's.* He'd met some sickos in his time, but to use a freshly bloodied corpse as an ink pot was a bit ripe. It was also indicative of the murderer becoming less concerned about the length of time they spent at the scene, the strength of their anger, and their twisted mental and emotional state.

The flies were everywhere as were the forensic guys. White overalls collected fingerprints and carefully lifted papers, clothes and other items with gloved hands and long tweezers. The body had already been photographed, and a meat wagon been requested and despatched out to the house to transfer it to Kirkdale General's morgue. Harry stood beside the bed that held Josie Kinkade for the last time as the police surgeon examined her.

"Nasty business this Harry, I've never had to deal with anything like it in the Lakes, not ever."

"Tell me about it, I thought I'd come up here for an easy last few years. London was a playground of naughty kids compared to this. We still need to talk to the landlord – *he* seems to have gone AWOL."

She ran a hand round the back of her neck, beads of perspiration broke out on her face. "*Phew*, it's warm in here for an old place isn't it?" She swiped irritably at a fly that buzzed past her ear. Harry nodded and 'hmmed' in agreement, he'd already discovered why.

"O-*kayyy* time of death somewhere between thirty-six and forty-eight hours ago, 'fraid I can't be more precise than that. Rigor's been and gone, she's cold right through, we've got flies…" *she swatted the air again…* "and new eggs in the wound," *then pointed to a crop of white dots.* "The coroner will fill you in on anything else." She pulled off her latex gloves, sealed them in a plastic bag, dropped them into her case and snapped it shut.

As she picked it up to go, she sensed he was about to ask a question. Harry's eyes had narrowed, his right hand pulled on his chin as he glanced from Josie to the wall and back again, studying the length of arterial spray from her chest. Shorter bursts than he would have expected from such a large entry wound, but almost identical to that of the other two bodies. *What the hell had been used to create that puncture?* That's what it looked like, a form of deep, very wide puncture. They *all* looked like that. Not a knife, it was definitely not a stab wound. Well, not unless the murderer had spent a good deal of time gouging huge circles and removing lumps of… *he shuddered.* Maybe he was getting too old for this job.

The doc began to sigh impatiently. Harry looked back at her. She raised her eyebrows, her face twitched in hurried expectation as she waited for his comment.

"The coroner's reports on the first three victims confirmed the use of chloroform. They also discovered traces of material embedded in the tissues, which would be understandable considering they were dressed at the time." *He pointed at Josie who was clearly naked.* "Yet the distance of blood spray here was still short, even with no material, no jacket or even a thickish top to partially stem the spurts. The sheets are obviously saturated with the victim's blood, but that's mainly beneath her from continuous loss, not distant, not just from the initial point of attack." Harry waited as the doctor considered his observations. She looked back at the bed.

"Well, I would say either the chloroform *almost* killed her, which would've reduced the blood pressure enough to create shorter bursts of arterial spray, *or* it *had* killed her, in which case the heart would have stopped pumping altogether prior to the external trauma, which would give the same result." Harry nodded and thought for a moment.

"What if only a *small* quantity *of* anaesthetic was used and she was still half-conscious before the trauma occurred? Wouldn't some sort of material be needed to cover the chest before weapon impact to help reduce initial blood spray?"

A pause… "Yes, probably, I – I would think so," she agreed turning to look at Harry. "Have you found any type of cloth with a hole in it that would match the opening in her chest?"

"No. No I haven't," he replied. She looked at her watch now as if late for another appointment.

"You'll need to get any finer details from the coroner I'm afraid, I really *do* have to go."

Harry looked back at the girl on the bed. He was approaching the end of thirty years in the service, known down South precisely *for* his detail, for nailing the really tricky ones – but this? *This was another kettle of fish altogether.* This was straight out of a blockbuster, a nasty one at that, one he began to think he might not solve before his golden handshake. Christmas was only three months away and Harry could see himself retiring on a bum note. He heard an impatient sigh and looked up. This police surgeon really *did* look like she needed to be elsewhere.

"Thanks doc, I appreciate you coming out straightaway, I know it's not usually your call." He offered his hand and she shook it briefly before turning to leave the room.

"No problem, no problem at all," replied Charlotte.

TWENTY-THREE

Harry wondered if the drugs had any link to her death, or whether that was simply a coincidence. It was certainly unlikely they'd have found this little 'hot house' anytime soon, the semi-detached cottage was an unlikely venue for a trafficker even if it *was* only 'C' class drugs. With the amount of shrubbery in that bedroom, this vet had been cutting off more than the local dogs' bollocks.

According to neighbours, the owners of the adjacent house lived in South London and had bought the property as a holiday retreat. It was just one blow after another with this case, even basic local contact was unavailable.

A movement outside caught his eye and he looked up from the contents of a dressing table drawer. Members of the SOCO team continued to work around him. He walked over to the window and scowled deeply at the sight of Andrew Gale, notebook open and pen in hand. He seemed to be in deep conversation with one of his men. *Now how would our Mr. Gale have known anything about Ms. Kinkade? It hasn't even hit the media yet.* The only reason the police were called in was because the milkman noticed broken glass in the kitchen door and two days' bottles on the step.

Harry began to feel the familiar rise of angry frustration mingled with the development of a light head and grumbling stomach. He instinctively moved to throw open the sash frame and give Andrew a piece of his mind, only to stop seconds before a surprised SOCO officer had intercepted him. The window area still needed to be dusted for prints, and Harry's personal irritation had momentarily made him forget official procedure – *something he never did.* This hypoglycaemia thing really *had* started to get to him.

He mumbled a barely audible apology to the surprised officer, *apologies being a rarity*, as he realised what he'd nearly jeopardised. Turning sharply, he began to head for the door when he was brought up short as he noticed something else – *an unadorned right ear.* The red message on the wall opposite the door had taken his immediate attention on entering the room. The bed was positioned behind the door. Now on the opposite side of the body he could see there was an earring missing, and the stud in her left ear matched the one he'd found outside the kitchen door. *Damn! Not the killer's then,* he thought – frustrated yet again. It seemed what he'd initially believed was the first *real* piece of evidence in this case, was in fact the victim's own property. Most likely it had worked its way loose and just fallen out.

Harry disappeared down the staircase and out into the street already wired…

"… but can you at least tell me if…?"

"Mis-ter Gale!" Harry Longbridge stood in the front doorway hands on hips, his voice at yelling pitch. *"How the hell did you get through my cordon?!"* Andrew's covert glance led to the youngest member of the Longbridge team. PC Joe Walker swallowed hard, eyes first looked upwards then down to his boots, then sideways, *both directions,* before he finally had to look at his boss. Feeling guilty, Andrew interjected.

"Come on Longbridge it wasn't his fault, he's only a kid, I told him I'd got some information you were expecting. I was just about to come into the house. *He* wasn't to know."

"*Were you?* And just why are you here at *this* murder scene as well Mr. Gale? *Hmm?!* Considering nobody is *aware* of this latest victim – apart from the *perpetrator* of course?" Then in delayed realisation added loudly, *"And it's DCI Longbridge to you and **don't** tell me how to deal with my damned officers!"*

"Actually I…" began Andrew.

"Damn bloody funny if you ask me! Feeling extra protective of this unfortunate woman as well are you?" Harry flung his arms towards the open front door. Andrew smarted then. *Why did this ex-London cop always refer to murder as unfortunate, was it a Southern thing?* He decided he may as well tell him now – how he came to know her.

"Look – Josie came to me at the paper after Rachel's death. She read the article I ran in the *Courier* and told me…" he hesitated. *If there was any mention of Miles meeting Rachel in the pub Longbridge would jump at it, yet he knew Peterson wasn't the killer,* "… . She told me she'd seen Rach three days before the murder, in the Carpenters Arms. She was very upset but said she couldn't go to the police with anything. She refused to tell me why." Harry ran a tongue around the inside of his top lip in thought as he eyed him closely. *Well that made sense at least,* he thought, *considering what's just been discovered inside that cottage. However, maybe Gale here was a customer. Maybe he'd just turned up to cut a deal.*

"Let's go inside Mr. Gale – *I'd like to have a chat.*" He extended an arm. Andrew was more than a little surprised at Longbridge's invitation, but walked ahead of the policeman who followed him into the cottage. In the little hall Andrew stopped, not knowing which way to go. Harry gestured for him to turn right, into the lounge and they both sat down.

Andrew had not seemed familiar with the property so… thought Longbridge…*maybe he hasn't been here.* Harry watched as Andrew wrinkled his nose, turned his head from side to side then lifted his chin to sniff the air. Andrew narrowed his eyes like he was trying to work out something…

"Anything wrong?" asked the detective. "Apart from…" he glanced up at the ceiling – "The obvious."

"It's that… *smell*. I think it's… it smells like… *cannabis*. Did she – Josie – did she smoke *weed?*"

"And how would you know what that smells like?" replied Longbridge sarcastically. Andrew hesitated, then realised it hardly mattered now.

"I think Rachel sometimes indulged, I noticed it occasionally but never said anything. It was all tied up with her unhappiness, the failed marriage through her cheating husband three years ago, the endless unsuitable – '*boyfriends*.'" He made air quotation marks in disparaging inference of the men who'd littered her 'post-divorce' life. Harry thought for a moment.

"Nothing I indicate here is to reach that newspaper of yours until I say so. *Deal?*"

"Deal," agreed Andrew, surprised at what felt like Harry's slight change of heart regarding reporters, especially him. He hoped it meant he was going to get some inside information.

"Miss Kinkade was a drug dealer. Nothing major, not heroin or cocaine, but she had a fair little cannabis emporium up there." He looked back up at the ceiling again. "I take it you knew nothing of this?" Andrew's eyes widened in surprise – *this* was why Rachel had been friends with Josie.

"No. I definitely did *not*. I didn't actually *know* her, not really, I just promised to let her know if… if I found out any…thing…" Andrew paused as he realised where this was heading… "Found out anything about Rachel's killer," he finished awkwardly. There, he'd admitted it now; he was trying to do this police officer's job for him. Andrew waited for the fall out.

"*Mis*-ter Gale…" Harry sat forward elbows on his knees. "I realise that from *some* form of *misguided loyalty* you want to play detec–" Andrew stiffened.

"There's nothing misguided about my loyalty." His tone was firm, unwavering. "Rachel just needed a friend at the end of the day. I feel I owe it to her to show that at least *someone genuinely cared*, that they would fight her corner, even if it was only platonic. *I intend to fight her corner.*" Harry studied this young man opposite him and realised he probably wasn't going to go away anytime soon. He reminded him of himself thirty years ago, bull dogmatic, tenacious and downright bloody-minded. *He probably had the makings of a damned fine officer.* A smile began to tickle the sides of his mouth. He stopped it immediately.

"Maybe you're just in the wrong profession Mr. Gale, but for now you are a newspaper reporter *not* a police officer. I would appreciate it if you'd remember that." Andrew remained silent and tight-lipped. Harry could feel his head beginning to swim, hunger now beginning to eat through his stomach. He began to fidget, rubbed his tired eyes and looked about him agitatedly for a 'grub runner'. Andrew noticed and immediately cottoned on. His father was diabetic and the signs were pretty much identical. He reached into his pocket and produced a KitKat. Chocolate being Andrew's other great 'foody' love apart from fresh Italian coffee, he always had some form of confectionary on him. Harry's eyes lit up in appreciation and he leant forward to receive it. As he peeled off that wrapper and broke the biscuit along its length, there was a definite feel of a temporary truce in the air. Harry snapped the chocolate stick in half, popped a piece in his mouth and developed a resigned lopsided smile as he chewed. This lad had good intuition as well, right now he'd be worth ten of his current crew – *Pity that* he thought, swallowing.

Charlotte Peterson had driven away from Josie's cottage, back across the bridge and down the road before detailed thought hit. She'd just held a thorough ETD *(estimated time of death)* conversation with a senior police officer, and coolly conducted the official medical examination of *her* latest victim, *in the girl's own bedroom*. The familiar hysterical twitch tugged at the corners of her mouth. *Well*, she'd reasoned to herself, *considering that was where I'd despatched her, she could hardly be anywhere else really could she?*

Charlotte had emitted a tight high-pitched laugh as she'd scrabbled in the parcel shelf for her lighter and cigarettes. One-handed, she'd lit up and inhaled as Andrew Gale had approached and passed her from the opposite direction. Her more distinctive maroon and silver Morgan had been left at work and the surgery Range Rover used instead, but despite *his* different car, there was no mistaking *that* young man's clean boyish good looks. The appealing Hugh Grant fringe and his more than a passing resemblance to actor Richard Armitage was *quite* unmistakable. *She'd rather liked him as Guy of Gisborne a few years back* she thought smiling – *then quickly brought herself back from her little lust fix…*

There'd been nowhere else for him to go other than across the bridge, it was a dead end and harboured only four cottages, three of which were usually holiday rentals. It meant he *must* have been going to the dead vet's place – but why? Surely the news couldn't have reached the *Courier* yet?

Charlotte tapped the cigarette into the ashtray, quickly inhaled again and narrowed her eyes. The receptionist Gina Rowlands was back from a week's holiday and knew she'd been called out to do an ETD… *and* where the location was. Those two were an item – one that had taken no notice of warnings so far. She and Gale were also friends with that pretty little barmaid, who'd up till now, inconveniently avoided 'removal'. Yes – *that* much she'd gathered when she'd overheard Gina's recent mobile conversation in the surgery ladies, *plus a whole lot more* – and *both* of them could turn a man's head. She winced at that last realisation…

Andrew hadn't noticed *her*, she was sure of that, but as she continued on towards town, she mentally marked *his* card too – a shame really as he was so cute. It appeared graffiti warnings and a ransacked flat were not enough to put Mr. Gale & Co. off the scent. Despite their complete and utter amateur detection work, it seemed those three needed upgrading. This time there must be no avoiding their promotion – *up the List.*

TWENTY-FOUR

NEW YORK

Emily Stone's outstretched hand held the last crime thriller manuscript of the day. Thirty odd titles already screened by half the editorial team and pruned down from almost two hundred had swum about her large oak desk for most of the afternoon. Now tired, her hand hovered over the slush pile for a few more seconds before she let it drop on top of the other twenty-eight rejects. She congratulated herself on managing to find two really good thrillers for McCarthy Stone that season, one by a fledgling British author. When she considered what else she was working on at the moment, it amazed her she still had the concentration for editing, but then she *did* always love a good piece of crime fiction.

She picked up her suit jacket and purse, walked out of her office and headed down the corridor towards her husband's. The door was ajar and the back of his soft leather chair faced her as she stood in the entrance.

"Gareth?" Silence. She remained on the threshold, preferred to wait there instead of going up to him. He knew she would and waited, the chair stayed in its reverse position. Emily sighed impatiently and walked smartly across the soft wool carpet to the front of the desk. He sensed her closeness, detected her light citrus perfume… Gareth Stone swung the chair round slowly to face her and sat resignedly, patiently, *knowingly*.

"Emily?" He questioned back, his eyes pleaded and waited for an explanation of her current reticent behaviour. Gareth knew the chances he would actual get one of course were nigh on zero. He'd still not questioned her fully, kept putting it off in the hope it was no more than a hormonal blip, that despite everything she was still committed to their marriage… and hadn't started seeing someone. Emily held his gaze and took a deep breath;

"Gareth, I'm meeting Faithe for a quick bite to eat at the little Mexican place on 4th, couple of hours of girly catch up, you know? God knows I could do with a break, it's been full on this month." Her words spilled out quickly, easily, *too* easily, tumbled one upon the other without much care. *Why didn't he believe her?* "I won't be late home, nine-thirty, ten maybe, okay?" *And why was his heart jumping, pounding as if it would shoot upwards, burst right into his throat and stop him from speaking – breathing even?* His eyes dropped to the desk looked at nothing at all in particular as his hands shuffled a few papers about before he brought his gaze back up to meet hers.

"That's fine Em it's… fine…" *it didn't feel fine…* he waved a hand in the air to demonstrate just how *'fine'* it wasn't. "No problem I'll… grab a pizza or something." She dipped her head in quiet acknowledgement and half-turned to leave before turning back to face him. She managed a weak hesitant smile, an expression worn so often with him lately that it had become almost permanent. She spoke softly, coaxingly…

"Tomorrow – we'll have dinner together tomorrow. I'll cook something special, okay? Her husband returned her tentative smile with a gentle one of his own, the one that said; *but you still won't really talk to me about what's troubling you, will you – and it still won't make anything any better, will it?*

His voice said:- "Sure sweetheart, that'll be great – I'll look forward to it." They both knew what their smiles *actually* meant, and as Emily walked from his office, Gareth made a decision. The following day *must* be the day he discovered what was eating into the heart of his very beautiful, but very distant wife.

Emily took the elevator to the ground floor alone, and trance watched the orange light flick past each level. The manicured nails of her free right hand the only sound as they tapped anxiously against the metal of the wall behind her.

She felt guilty, she *always* felt guilty when Gareth was unhappy, looked lost, concerned, obviously worried about them as a couple. Emily did *love* her husband, he was a good kind man, a wonderful caring partner, gave her more financially than she could have ever thought possible – but she wasn't *in love* with him. She couldn't have wanted for more, she knew that, but still there was that… that *something* missing. Something she had felt once a very long time ago, something she couldn't let go of, something she would never forget and never feel again. Like a Terrier with a bone, her past had always been there to haunt her – taunt her, *and tomorrow at dinner he would press for some answers, answers she could not, dared not give him. Somehow she'd have to stall him long enough to…* her ride reached the ground floor with that slight 'bounce back', and she was jolted out of the one-way conversation in her head.

She stepped briskly from the elevator and quickly snapped out of her reflective mood. With a lift of her chin, Emily Stone crime editor adopted a more positive expression, the one worn for her public. She smoothed imaginary creases from her jacket, marched across the marbled reception and disappeared through the revolving doors into the throng of an early Manhattan evening.

In a quiet corner of Pepe's, Emily sat in front of a 'Chicken Fajita Salad' for one. She sipped at the second glass of chilled white Prosecco and studied the room over its rim. It was a Thursday and the Mexican restaurant was still pretty empty, too early to have filled up just yet, which is *exactly* why she'd come straight from work.

She replaced the glass on the table and flicked the screen on her mobile to locate the number. As it connected, Emily checked her watch. It would be 11pm there and she would either be in bed, hopefully not alone – or out somewhere. Either way she needed to be with *him* – and *regularly*. It hadn't been easy to accept *that* part of the plan, but it was necessary nevertheless and although dangerous, there was no other way. Anyhow, although she felt uncomfortable, it'd never been about the sex for her.

A voice answered, it sounded tense:-

"Hi, I'm glad you've called."

"How are you? Do you have any more news for me?"

"Things are hotting up over here Emily, and I don't just mean with her. I'm not sure how much more of this I can take – it's doing my head in."

"Why? What's happened since we last spoke? You have to hang in there, it has to be completed!"

"Another murder, everyone has been questioned since the first one, and *not* just by the police."

"What do you mean, not just by the police?" She whispered now as one or two people had started coming through the door for an early meal.

"There's this guy he –" there was a hurried rustle of bed clothes – "Hold on –" Emily heard a door close.

"Sorry about that just being careful, I don't want to be overheard."

"You're not on your own then, is he –?"

"No, no, not tonight, he's got a dinner and dance thing on with *her.*"

"Who's questioning you? You said that –"

"Yeah, some guy at work – thinks he's *Columbo* or something, it's got very uncomfortable Em."

"How clever *is* he? At digging and discovering I mean?"

"Actually, not that great, which is the only saving grace, but he could hit home at any time by pure accident, you know? Throw enough balls in the air and he's bound to catch one or two isn't he?"

"Hmmm... just be careful then. *Your* job is to make *damned* sure she's put under enough pressure she falls apart completely – *makes an irreversible mistake.* At the moment she's crazy, but still in that shrewd, controlled auto-pilot mood thing she does so well." Emily's eyes narrowed in pure hatred then, and as she scanned the room quickly hissed into the phone; "*I want her destroyed!*"

"I'll be seeing him tomorrow night and again on the weekend. I just hope she doesn't follow *him* to *me* Emily, I'm taking a massive risk here and if –"

"I know I know... look – just keep something with you at all times, for protection I mean just in case. You can't get a gun easily over there, not without arousing suspicion, but – a knife? *You can get a knife.*"

"Already do!" The woman caught her breath in a nervous laugh. "Look, I need to get some sleep if I'm to be on form tomorrow. I'll catch up with you at the weekend, and ermm… Emily –" she paused long enough to give the impression what was to follow would not be well received, – "I know it wasn't part of the plan but I…" Emily could sense what was coming next, her stomach tensed; she did *not* want to hear it…

"I have to go," she threw back quickly; "I'm meeting someone and I'm already late – we'll speak again on Saturday." Emily stabbed at the red icon abruptly, cut off the words she didn't want spoken and leant back heavily into her chair. She stared hard at the cell phone in her hand. Love *could* not, *must* not come back into this. It was why she, Emily, had waited… allowed enough time to move on, move from hurt to anger, from love to revenge – waited this long in order to be ready.

The chicken fajita suddenly looked very unappetizing. She took another large gulp of wine, chucked some dollars on to the table, got up and walked out of the restaurant.

Earlier Gareth Stone had looked at his pizza with much the same interest which was why it now lay at the bottom of the bin.

Alone in the lounge of their Bay Ridge home, he'd poured himself a generous measure of Jack Daniels. It had been cradled in his hands for ten minutes as he sat deep in thought on the edge of the sofa. He looked down at the whiskey and wondered what would happen next – because it could, *would*, affect everything. If he drank it, it would be the first he'd had in fifteen years – his battle with booze had been a long hard one… *an ongoing one*. Alcoholism was *not* pretty *or* healthy.

It swirled around in the crystal glass as he glanced up at their wedding photo above the fireplace. His eyes glistened, blurred out her white *Angelo* creation as the rich aroma filled his nostrils. He hesitated for a second more – then in one swift move the whiskey was warmly caressing his throat…

TWENTY-FIVE

CUMBRIA, UK

The annual dinner dance in aid of the Kirkdale Children's Foundation was an obligatory must. Miles and Charlotte always attended but it was one event he could have really done without this year. However, he was there as usual and now stood at the bar in the hallway just outside the Wordsworth room in the Grange Hotel. *He was also in a reflective mood.*

Miles was more than happy to donate money to needy kids; he would've liked some of his own if Charlotte had been able to have them, but she couldn't and had refused all other routes to achieve motherhood. That fact had always saddened him, even though he'd tried to suppress it and hide his feelings from her. Maybe a son or daughter, *or both*, would have kept him from falling into other women's beds, although even *he* knew he couldn't make that an excuse for his bad behaviour... *or* frankly, guarantee it would've made much difference. It just seemed to be in his blood.

He wasn't overly keen on these events, particularly that night when he could have been elsewhere with someone special, someone *very* special. However, it wasn't all bad news, this year was a nineties theme so apart from requests mostly music from his era, the food was classy for once, and thankfully every person allotted to their table was under sixty. In addition, the evening so *far*, had proved highly rewarding.

Whilst he leant on the bar to wait for drinks, his eyes scanned the tables once again as he searched for the leggy blonde tightly hugged in deep turquoise. He'd noticed her return from the hallway during dinner and zoned straight in on her perfect poise and fabulous figure. If Charlotte had been aware of his evening's 'discovery' then she'd not made any comment so far...

Frustratingly, Miles couldn't see Ms. Turquoise anywhere; what he *could* now see during his detailed sweep of the room, however, was his wife's poker-hot blistering glare. Seething from her seat at their dinner table, she looked decidedly explosive. He raised both eyebrows and smiled confidently back as if it was *her* he'd been looking for since he'd left to get the wine – *of course they both knew this wasn't true*. He gave a brief wave and mouthed the unnecessary; *'Red?'* She responded by turning to look massively interested in a group of large cheese plants... Lucky for Miles his drinks were put in front of him at that point and the tension was temporarily shelved.

He paid the barman and picked up the two huge glasses of Merlot. As he turned to head back to the table, the size zero turquoise walked purposefully across his line of vision, *she too* had noticed *him* earlier. He couldn't help but give out a smile that said he hadn't been 'fed' in ages, but a glance at Charlotte realised anything further was quite futile, *not to mention financial suicide*. She sat stony-faced now as her eyes watched him like a hawk, and her chin rested on bridged hands as she dared him to step out of line.

Their six dinner companions, who were really no more than annual acquaintances, hadn't been able to engage her in much conversation since Miles left for the bar. Due to the awkward silence that had arisen, some had already got up to socialise elsewhere.

Ms. Turquoise caught his flash of appreciation and smiled right back at him. She briefly dipped her eyes beneath her blonde fringe, before shiny even blonder waves were tossed over her shoulder and down a bare spray-tanned back. She also made full use of freshly glossed apricot lips as she continued on past – this one knew *exactly* the effect she delivered, thought Miles. He was surely hooked, but his attention was inevitably brought back to his 'watcher', and he quickly headed across the hall into the function room towards his table, *and his wife*.

The nineties tribute band had started to play and he wondered if it would encourage her onto the dance floor, he thought a mix of hits from their early years might loosen her up a bit.

"Okay sweetheart?" He placed Charlotte's wine in front of her and offered a nervous smile at their few remaining diners. They smiled uncomfortably back at him.

"Fine darling – *thank* you," she replied crisply. Her steel shot eyes couldn't have sent him a clearer message. Miles at least had the good grace to flush at his planned indiscretion and at the same time pretended to fuss over her. She accepted his arm around her shoulders and a light peck on the cheek as their last few dinner companions mumbled something about dancing and left them to it.

They sat in awkward silence and listened to the music for a few minutes. It felt odd just the two of them sat alone at such a large empty table, although in some ways thought Miles, it aptly reflected their marriage. The music had slowed to a sultry romantic tune and he decided he really ought to take Charlotte onto the dance floor to try and 'reassure' her. Somewhere deep down he did *care* for his wife, although had to admit that some of that *was* due to her predicted substantial inheritance... *particularly as she was the sole beneficiary.* It was just that women seemed naturally attracted to him, a lot of very beautiful *young* women, and he found it so very difficult to say no. This 'affliction' was not easy to live with, keeping one step ahead of Charlotte was even harder. She was incredibly intelligent, very shrewd and he'd been caught out more than once. Suddenly his thoughts were interrupted…

"I'm just going to the ladies Miles I won't be long," said Charlotte curtly. He could just make out her words above the music and squeezed her shoulder as he removed his arm. The song's lyrics increased to a crescendo and he mouthed back;

"Okay, see you in a moment."

As if she were kept in a completely different mental compartment that he could conveniently change gear and shift over to, his mind immediately switched to Jenny. They had planned two nights together that weekend and he had yet to work on a realistic excuse. It was getting harder and harder to find workable reasons to be away from home overnight, but Jenny was extra special and somehow he would come up with something.

In reality, to revive their affair was utter madness. It had been six years since they'd last seen each other and he'd made his choice back *then*. He should have left the past where it belonged but since her unexpected arrival in Kirkdale he was drawn right back to the beginning again, and it had been his intention to see her as often as possible. He'd genuinely missed her, and had only ended it to safeguard his share of Charlotte's massive inheritance. Much as he had adored Jenny, he could not live his life without the prospect of a very great deal of money.

The move from sprawling Bradenthorpe back to his small hometown of Kirkdale had been at Charlotte's insistence, a last chance for him and their marriage. Miles had to admit he'd been more than a little surprised the day Jenny had turned up out of the blue and walked into the leisure centre cafeteria. Since then they'd met up regularly, he'd enjoyed every minute of their renewed relationship and tried to condense those lost six years into the last few weeks in the hope of making it up to her. *Yet despite all that... even Jenny wasn't enough for him.*

As he racked his brains to think of something believable to tell Charlotte as to why he would be away that weekend, Ms. Turquoise walked directly up to the table and stood closely in front of him. His eyes began to drink up every inch of her soft young skin, from her painted toes in silver jewelled sandals, to the lobes of her ears where neat little diamonds nestled erotically. He was completely captivated. Jenny was well and truly back in her compartment...

"Would you like to dance? I'm a *very very* good dancer," she purred with a quick flick of her shiny blue hips in time to the music to demonstrate just how good she was. Miles felt that familiar feeling stir deep and low; and with all thoughts of Jenny now boxed, shot a quick glance towards the large open doors that led to the hallway. Charlotte would be a few minutes yet he reasoned; hair and make-up would need to be checked – he might *just* get away with it.

Under normal circumstances most women might not have minded if their husbands danced with someone else, but Charlotte was not like most women. As a couple they were different; they had *always* been different – and they always *would* be different. Jenny was now in the far recesses of his mind; he smiled wickedly, took the girl's hand and pulled her onto the dance floor.

She watched their bodies blend and move together in time to the love song. His fingers stroked the small of her perfectly tanned back, then slowly returned to her shoulders to caress them, to pull her close to him; their eyes glued to each other, their lips barely a breath apart…

Charlotte held on fast to the architrave of the doorway for support; she felt sick, she could taste the salmon as it repeated over and over again, the entire meal threatening to decorate the plush red carpet beneath her Vera Wang heels. To see it, to actually *witness* it, to watch him prepare the way for his later seduction was just *too* painful; each movement, each beat of the music was like a surgeon's knife expertly filleting its way around her already damaged heart.

Her eyes stung as she turned away sharply and leant her head against the wall, her mind a fast reeling picture house of cinema photography, each clip a shiny turquoise image splashed heavily with red.

She blinked through salty tears, looked away embarrassed from a concerned woman that had hurriedly approached, and made her escape back to the ladies' room. It was empty, and as Charlotte leant on the washroom unit and looked slowly up into the huge elongated mirror, she noticed that its very size seemed to magnify how dreadful her face looked at that moment; *and just how important her campaign had now become.* She remained staring at her reflection for a few moments, tried to concentrate, to focus on what must be done; there was just so *much to* be done now, *so much* to complete. *There was no time for tears.* Charlotte was well aware she'd given herself the bathroom mirror chat many times before, but this time would be the last. There would not, *must not* be anymore weakness.

She worked quickly with tissues, mascara and eyeliner, her makeup soon repaired – *the only thing that could be.* Finally with lipstick renewed and hair revived, she looked at the reflection of a very different Charlotte. A harder, stronger, more determined Charlotte; one who would not be made a fool of and would remain in control – *one who would reap another revenge, another despatch before the weekend was out.*

Back in the hotel hallway at the entrance to the Wordsworth room, Charlotte saw Miles as he left the dancefloor with the simpering twentysomething bareback. The child smiled and giggled stupidly, whispered something in his ear and slipped something in his pocket. She watched as they behaved like a couple who had the whole damn universe in front of them, certainly not like polite acquaintances, or like they'd been married for almost twenty years. She winced at the last comparison, and at Miles' clear enjoyment of Miss Perfect's girlish charm. How could he not enjoy it? She was young, carefree and beautiful just like the others – *and how she hated her right now just as she had hated them back then.*

Over a perfect spray-tanned shoulder, Miles caught sight of his wife as the music cranked up to a faster key and *Fleetwood Mac's* 'Little Lies' hit the air. He paled significantly. He was in trouble, *big* trouble. Once home there would be hell to pay. The thing was Miles *knew* what was to come… but the girl? *She hadn't the slightest clue of just how much trouble she was in…*

Across the other side of town Molly Fields was in the Carpenters Arms pulling a pint for one of their regulars. A week out of hospital, she had begged her reluctant parents to let her get back to work, said she'd convalesced enough for a whole *ward* of patients. She was bored stiff and needed to get her life back to normal, *well as normal as it could be for her at the moment*, although Molly obviously didn't share that little nugget.

It was when the ghostly impression of a dead woman in a turquoise dress floated above her customer's head that she let go of the pump. The pint was next, and amidst the distant sound of breaking glass and someone yelling her name, she slumped heavily to the beer-soaked shard-sprayed floor.

TWENTY-SIX

Molly had only been back at work for a couple of days since she'd returned home from hospital and now been made to follow her parents' advice to rest properly. They were still unaware of her visions and investigative involvement with Andrew and Gina; so had attributed her collapse in the bar the previous evening to severe stress and side-effects from the horrific chloroform attack.

Snuggled in a blanket on the sofa and scrolling through Facebook with a pile of magazines may have been relaxing, but wasn't exactly her idea of dealing with the situation – hence she was on the phone to Andrew to check he'd received her text the night before.

"I couldn't believe it Andrew! There she was clear as day floating above his head! That's all I can remember, I crashed after that and woke up in bed this morning. Mum and dad had carried me upstairs after I passed out. I was lucky I didn't cut myself too badly on the broken glass – got away with just a couple of scratches. I've toyed with the idea of telling them what happened, but they've been so worried about me I daren't mention the visions as well."

"No best not," replied Andrew, as he stirred coffee with his spare hand, "the fewer people who know about that the better anyway. Did you mention them to Harry Longbridge by any chance?"

"No why? He did ask me if there was absolutely *anything* I could remember that might help, but decided against telling him."

"Well it's just that he'd probably think you were *bat crazy*, he already thinks I'm a bit odd – *although…*"

"Although . . ?" she pressed.

"Well… we kind of reached an unspoken understanding, a sort of truce if you like, back at Josie's cottage – the vet that was found murdered last week – Rachel's friend?" Molly 'hmmed' an acknowledgement…

"Well I'd gone over to see her as she'd paid me a visit at the paper that day. I was going to tell her how we'd realised it couldn't have been Miles who'd murdered Rachel."

"Yeah I remember," she added. "It was particularly ghastly from what you told me. Strange I didn't see *that* one coming."

"Perhaps it was the stress of what's been happening, or maybe you'd had a few drinks? You've said before that with visions and all that spiritual stuff, a person needs to be clear-headed, calm and relaxed." Molly agreed that could be a possibility. Andrew took a sip of his Calino and glanced at his watch before he continued…

"Anyway, we had a good chat after his initial lecture at me for turning up so fast at yet *another* of his murder scenes. I don't think he really believes I'm a suspect anymore – he'd have pulled me in by now if he did. Longbridge understands I'm looking into this because of my loyalty to Rach even if he doesn't like it."

"Yes I guess so, although Jason's meds *were* proved to be a different strength from the bottle found near the third victim, yet I don't think the police are going to let go of *him* anytime soon. They haven't anything or anyone else to go on, and have already said they'd *prefer* it if he didn't go back to Bradenthorpe."

"Which presumably means he's still staying with Jenny?"

"Yes, that's what he told me outside the station the day they released him. I think he'll lie low for a while now though – so would I if I was him."

"To get back to your vision last night Molls, can you remember what she looked like apart from the long turquoise dress?"

"*Well...* she had long wavy blonde hair and was youngish, I guess about twenty-five, twenty-six? Then there was that... that *awful* hole in her chest exactly the same as the others, and the blood – obviously... all that... *blood...*" She tailed off and fell quiet for a moment.

"Do you think I *should* tell Longbridge about this Andy? I mean, if I'm right and we can't find *her* in time either, she'll be number five, I could've been *six*… maybe I *should* say something?" Andrew thought about it for a moment as Gina put a plate of rye toast in front of him.

"Okay *tell* him – but don't be surprised if he rubbishes the idea. We may have an understanding between us, but he still doesn't strike me as a guy who'd consider ghostly visions as a link in a murder case, or *any* case for that matter."

"Okay, well maybe I will, maybe I won't, I don't know, but he'll have to come here if he wants to interview me officially, I won't be driving anywhere with my car still in dock. Dad got it towed to the garage after that night it broke down on the way to meeting Jenny, or who I *thought* was Jenny."

"Which reminds me –" interjected Andrew a little unclearly, mouth half full of toast now as he tried to get dressed one-handed;

"I've been wondering, just how, whoever it *was,* got your mobile number in the *first* place?" Molly just *about* worked out his question…

"It was the pub mobile, we have one in addition to the landline in case that's engaged, because of all the deliveries and bookings for the new restaurant, you know? It's freely available in all our advertising so anyone could find it – I often have it on me."

"Mmmm… Molly, did you see *anything* else, or *feel* anything else when you had the vision last night? Anything at all we could go on?"

"No, not really, except…"

"What, except *what?*" pushed Andrew – he began to sound as desperate as Harry Longbridge…

"Well… there was this sort of big 'S'… in her hair, I don't know, it could have just been a wave I suppose, but it looked a kind of thicker, *darker* blonde strand than the rest. It sounds stupid out loud that's why I never mentioned it."

Andrew swallowed his last piece of toast, picked up his coffee and walked into the hall.

"Okay, well it could be something I s'pose, maybe a personal name initial? You've not had that before so at least it's a start, but from previous experience, there's not much gap between your premonition and the actual murders." Molly gave a long impatient sigh, she felt exasperated and quite useless at not being able to help any more than just getting creepy warnings. Andrew sensed her frustration even through the phone. He checked his watch again and quickly drained his mug, he was rushed now;

"Look – I've got to get to work. Gina just yelled out *'Hi'* and said to tell you to *rest!*"

"Yeah right!" Molly only half laughed – reminded that her long-time 'step-sister' spent more and more nights over at Andrew's flat these days. She missed Gina – missed her a lot, although she *had* come back to stay the first week Molly was out of hospital.

They said their goodbyes and Molly remained on the sofa, knees peaked under the throw, her chin tapped in thought with her mobile. The letter 'S' had certainly been very strange, as if the visions weren't strange enough, but she'd never seen letters before. She wondered what the police *would* make of her apparitions; it certainly wouldn't be easy to speak about them, *or* to receive any scathing scepticism.

She only hesitated a few moments more before a quick root around her handbag produced what she was looking for. Having found the card Harry left with her at the hospital, she decided there was only one way to find out. She brought up the keypad again, punched in the direct line number for Kirkdale's Detective Chief Inspector – and waited…

The mauve plastic folder had been the first piece of *real* evidence Harry Longbridge had been given in this case, and it had been rendered pretty much useless. He'd not been a happy bunny when it had arrived smothered with the fingerprints of half of Kirkdale General's medical staff. One of the nurses had found it beneath the bed of the girl who'd been subjected to the chloroform attack, complete with the wet chloroform pad inside. By the time it had reached his station half the town could have been considered suspects, which at that point in the investigation was probably about right. He'd sent it for DNA testing, but with no suspect to match anything up to, and no prints that corresponded with anyone on their files, it may as well have been binned. He just prayed something could come of the chloroform pad as he'd 'been *assured*' that the folder hadn't been opened.

When the call had come through from Molly Fields, she was the last person he'd expected to contact him. For a moment his heart had jumped at the thought of something, *anything at all frankly*, that might kick-start this damned case and give him a lead. When he'd heard what she had to say, however, that initial ray of hope dissipated rapidly. He leant his elbows on the desk, rolled his eyes and massaged his forehead with his thumb and forefinger to ease the tension, *and the disappointment.*

"Visions of *dead* women you say – that float in the air; and you see one shortly before each murder takes place, except for the one time when you *didn't?*" He listened to Molly's detailed encounters with tired disinterest.

"Tell me, does Mr. Gale have any views on this?" On learning that Andrew appeared to be going along with her mediumistic 'experiences', Harry felt a twinge of disappointment. He'd come to quite like the lad, even respect him, grudgingly of course, but still felt he was wasted as a reporter, even if the boy hadn't realised it himself yet.

Harry politely declined Molly's suggestion of a formal interview with regard to what *she* felt was of relevant help. Unless she remembered anything tangible with regard to the attempt on her life, he wouldn't need to speak to her for the foreseeable, and hoped she would soon make a full recovery.

He leant back in his chair and sighed heavily; *four grotesquely murdered women, no real leads, a misguided reporter and now a budding clairvoyant. Terrific! Topped his day right off – roll on retirement...*

As he massaged his head again he half-heartedly lifted up the piece of paper he'd been doodling on whilst talking to Ms. Fields. A rough outline of a woman in a long dress with the words 'blonde hair' and 'turquoise' sat beside it. He was about to screw it up and aim it at the bin when a large overly inked letter 'S' stopped him. Instead he folded it in half and in half again, opened his top drawer and dropped it inside. *No harm in keeping an open mind.*

Two days later Charlotte was parked in the surgery Range Rover in one of Kirkdale's most respectable leafy side roads. A quick glance up and down '*Farringdon Avenue*' had the area evaluated in a nutshell and to be honest she was quite surprised. The houses were all rather nice, in fact very nice indeed; maybe not opulent, but certainly up market – *in a modest way naturally.*

She flipped the contact card over and under, running it through her fingers repeatedly back and forth as she watched the house she was interested in through the window. It had not been difficult to lift the card from Miles' pocket the night of the dinner dance. He'd barely noticed what his wife was doing in the sheer relief she hadn't created a scene over Susie – '*Ms. Turquoise Spray Tan*'.

Charlotte didn't know if he was aware the girl's contact details had been dropped in his pocket as she enveloped her body around him, and she didn't care. That night she'd continued to watch them from the hallway outside the Wordsworth room, and saw the girl's hand disappear into his jacket. It was quite obvious what she'd done, and all Charlotte needed to do was get that card, something that had been achieved more easily than she'd imagined. Charlotte also didn't know if Miles was now frantic the card was missing, racking his brains at how he'd lost it, or worse still worried sick that somehow she had found it. And Charlotte didn't care about that either. The important thing *was* that *she* was the one who now knew where to find Miss Susie Sarrandaire – *and find her she would.*

The blue nylon zipped box sat in its place beside her on the passenger seat. On top of it, neatly folded, a new pair of opaque surgical gloves. The black and gold oriental mask lay snugly in one deep Barbour coat pocket, and the chloroform-soaked pad, tightly bagged, waited in the other. She glanced at the box... there was not much time.

Susie Sarrandaire was an aspiring young actress. She'd worked hard at drama school and kept working since leaving five years ago. A few walk-on parts in the odd soap opera and drama, a bit of extras work, commercials and so on were all okay, but now she was waiting to hear from her agent about a lead role in a new family saga set in the Highlands. If she got *that* part, and there was a good chance as the audition had gone *brilliantly*, the name Susie Sarrandaire would soon be on everyone's lips. Of course Susie Sarrandaire wasn't her *real* name, but Danielle Mogg didn't have quite the same ring to it. It hadn't taken much to persuade her to change – like a lot of people she'd never really liked what was printed on her birth certificate anyway.

Susie was also waiting to hear from a rather gorgeous looking mature blonde guy she'd met at a charity function a couple of nights before, and was rather disappointed that so far she hadn't. Today though was all about a lounge lazy afternoon flipping through magazines, large frothy cappuccinos and waiting for her agent to give her some exciting news.

Her comfortable four-bed detached nestled in the sexier part of Kirkdale if it could be described as that. She certainly wouldn't have purchased anything in the drab-looking apartment block area. London was where she would have preferred to be based, but until work really took off her hometown would have to suffice.

Licking chocolatey froth off her lips, Susie idly turned glossy pages not really interested in what lay between them. It was the silent phone that held her attention – *that was of course until the doorbell rang.*

TWENTY-SEVEN

Jenny watched from a covert position having parked round the corner from where Charlotte had left the surgery Range Rover. Owning a bright yellow Mini Cooper maybe helpful when searching for it in a supermarket car bay, but it definitely had its drawbacks when undertaking a surveillance operation.

She watched intently now as the local doctor stood waiting for the householder to answer the door of a large attractive new-build property. Jenny noticed Charlotte had a large blue box with a wide strap handle that was carried over her shoulder. It certainly didn't look like any doctor's bag she'd seen before.

When the door opened and Jenny saw Danielle stood there, she nearly collapsed in shock. Danielle Mogg had been one third of an all-girl band at Bradenthorpe High School. Jenny had been another; a third girl, Fiona Blake, had made up the trio. It was hardly a band in reality, but they'd had loads of fun with their karaokes and cheap microphones in each other's bedrooms, and one performance at a school pop concert. Jenny hadn't seen her in donkey's years, but even at 80 metres and through a hedge, could never mistake those up to the armpit legs and trademark blonde hair – *they were both legendary.*

When Charlotte walked into the house Jenny quickly scanned the area for cars and neighbours. Once it was clear she shot across the road and up Danielle's drive. The angle of it swung out and around a large grass frontage which was offset to the house. This helped to keep her from being seen from the ground floor windows. A wooden gate with a simple open and shut latch flanked the right-hand wall. She made for that, squeezed the black iron handle and desperately hoped it wasn't bolted from the other side. It wasn't and opened easily. Cautiously she let herself into the back garden. It was at that point she wished keeping such close tabs on Charlotte hadn't been such an essential part of this plan. Renewing an affair with Miles to send her loopy and get her committed was one thing, to follow her about whenever she got the chance to see how all that was coming along was quite another. *Emily Stone certainly owes me* she decided.

Along a pink and yellow squared pathway, Jenny eased herself past an overgrown holly bush at the corner of the house, and briefly scanned the lawn and fenced perimeters at the rear of the property. *Anyway this must be a medical call if she's in the surgery Range Rover,* she thought quickly. Then logic kicked in. *Danielle seemed healthy enough, why the home visit? And that definitely wasn't a doctor's bag she was carrying… To get a doctor to come out these days you had to be practically dead anyway*

– unless she had kids of course – even then… Kids though?
No not Danni.

She recalled Danielle attending Drama College after High School and remembered her being utterly driven where achieving fame was concerned – children would've hampered her game plan.

All these thoughts whizzed around her head as Jenny kept close to the back wall of the house. She instinctively ducked when she reached a bay window and crouched low beneath the sill, flattened herself against the brickwork as much as possible in order to avoid being seen from inside.

A fanlight was open and Jenny could hear Status Quo playing from somewhere inside the house; *Danielle always did like a bit of 'Quo'* she thought. Then, without warning and to her abject *horror* – *'Sweet Caroline'* was suddenly drowned out by muffled cries, falling furniture, *and what sounded like piles of glass and china smashing to the ground!* Without warning, the level of Rick & Co. shot up just as she gingerly lifted her head and peered through the window, eyes at sill level…

Charlotte had followed Susie Sarrandaire down the hallway. It had not been difficult to pose as a very exclusive, very chic cosmetics agent. Luckily for Charlotte, Susie was very bored and agitated that day – but unluckily for Susie, she was also very conceited and very vain *every* day.

"Wowww!! How absolutely 'abfab'!" she trilled, using the double adverb incorrectly; "An up-market Avon lady! I had no idea there *was* such a thing!" Susie had eagerly beckoned Charlotte in and walked ahead of her down the hall towards the lounge, her incessant chatter babbled all the way. She then threw her arms wide and exclaimed in delight;

"*Do* set up in here while I make some coffee, I'm just *dying* to try out an exceptionally select designer range – it'll be such *fun!*"

"Oh yes," replied Charlotte, close behind her with a derisive smile as she tapped the blue zipped bag, heart pounding with every step;

"I can assure you, you'll definitely not have experienced anything like *this* before…"

Susie's neck felt as if it was going to snap right off, such was the force with which it was wrenched back as she stepped across the threshold to the lounge.

The thick pad that now covered her mouth and nose was pressed heavily down on her face. A strong and heady chemical smell invaded her lungs – made worse with every attempted gasp for air. At first, sheer adrenalin worked her arms and legs as she tried to struggle through a mix of outright terror, panic and confusion. She managed to kick out at the coffee table and saw her empty mug spin through the air and crash to the floor. She heard the volume of the internal audio system suddenly increase as both hands tore at the thick noxious fabric across her face in frenzy but it was hopeless.

Her left arm swept in a wild arc to the side as her hand air scrabbled – she was frantic, hysterical now for something, *anything* she could use as a weapon. It merely caught the lip of a crystal vase which similarly smashed to the oak floor. Water, roses and splintered glass bounced back up, sprayed across her legs with the impact. She realised her limbs were failing fast, the already blurred cream and caramel lounge decor had swirled incessantly into one – *then in an instant cut to black.*

Susie Sarrandaire dropped like a giant puppet whose strings had been snipped. *It had taken less than twenty seconds.*

Outside Jenny Flood, both hands clamped over her mouth in utter horror at what she'd just witnessed, could nevertheless not stop herself from looking through that window. It was as if she were held rigid on all sides, hypnotised and trapped in her worst ever nightmare, compelled to continue with that unfolding scene in front of her. Then she felt a nauseous rush and removed her hands to let her precious breakfast spill onto the Battenberg stone patio. *For once, it was not a premeditated act.*

Her vomiting was not heard over the music, but what came next was so abhorrent, so horrifically violent, the shock sent her in a backwards sprawl to fall against a stack of earthenware flower pots and the noise as they fell created a loud clatter outside the window. Jenny was mesmerised for a split second before she tried to get to her feet, legs now jellified, octopus-like in her scrambled attempts to stand upright.

Charlotte's attention, suddenly removed from her now heavily bleeding victim, was sharply diverted to the lounge window. When their eyes met both women were in total shock and disbelief. Not only that the other was there, and what had been witnessed, but that there was only a few feet between them separated by a pane of glass. For Charlotte there was an extra stab, a jolt as she realised the oriental mask lay unused in her pocket. Bent over the body, mallet in hand, she was soon up and began to head for the front door.

When she realised where she was going, Jenny suddenly found her feet and launched herself at the path! She ran straight past the bush ignoring its barbs; grabbed at the iron latch and was through the gate in a flash. Her head screamed but she was too horrified, too nauseous and too scared to cry. She didn't dare look back, just ran straight down the drive and across the road, didn't check for traffic – didn't check for her pursuer, just kept right on running to the corner until she literally fell across the bonnet of her yellow Mini – lungs spent.

She shook uncontrollably now, terrified Charlotte would be seconds behind her. Normally nimble-fingered Jenny suddenly began fumbling hopelessly as the large bunch of keys caught on her jacket lining and wouldn't pull from her pocket. She yanked hard, heard a rip as they came out awkwardly, in her panic she tried to separate flat and work keys from the car one but they slipped from her hands down onto the kerb's drain grating and skid precariously across the gaps!

"*No!*" she cried as she fell to her knees, lunged out for them as she heard fast-running footsteps closing in behind. Her fingers clasped around the large oblong photo fob that had thankfully prevented them from slipping through the grid out of reach into the murky depths.

With the bleep of the lock, she grabbed at the door and was inside with the locks hit and the engine started not even aware it wasn't Charlotte she'd heard behind her – *just a sports-type making use of his fit tracker!*

The gear was rammed home as Jenny accelerated out from the kerb and never saw Mr. 'Fitbit's' shocked face, any other pedestrians, cars, or which direction she was headed. As long as it took her away from that road, that house – *and that insane murdering bitch!*

Charlotte had decided not to follow Jenny. Her first instinct was to get her and shut her up quickly, but then realised that would be her second mistake. A public chase and subsequent assault in broad daylight would not be clever.

She was back in the lounge now angry with herself. How could she have *been so stupid?* Charlotte trembled as her fingers reached into her pocket and pulled out the oriental mask – and with it came her surgical gloves. She winced and studied both for a moment before she replaced them. *I've got sloppy, too many stupid mistakes, far too many, and all in one place.* Charlotte was scared now, didn't feel in control and she didn't like it.

For the first time she heard how loud the music was and pushed the wall panel sound system off then cleaned her prints with a hanky. The house fell instantly quiet.

Susie Sarrandaire's beautiful long blonde hair was splashed heavily with her blood, her perfect body and porcelain skin violated in the most foul and grotesque way. *It's not enough though* thought Charlotte irrationally as she gazed down at her work. *Not for what she did, what she planned to do, but there's no time for anything else. No time for wall messages, no time to set anyone up, no time to leave anything for the police to muse over. No time...*

Charlotte picked up the small mallet and returned it to the damp blue nylon bag, pulled out her gloves again and put them on. She must leave and leave quickly – it wasn't entirely impossible neighbours hadn't heard anything although statistics usually bore out people turned a deaf ear to 'domestics', checks were rarely made to see if anything was seriously wrong.

She tried her best to slow down her breathing, to be as calm as possible as she stepped over the body and eased herself past the broken glass and scattered roses into the hall. It was quite hard to avoid stepping in the blood – *it was everywhere.*

Now she just she needed to be gone – needed to clear her head, be able to think. There was an important message to deliver, and it needed to be delivered quickly. *Charlotte just hoped Jenny really did love her schizophrenic brother as much as she remembered…*

TWENTY-EIGHT

Jason Flood had turned his sister's flat upside down and still couldn't find it. Now he was seriously worried. He had re-checked his wrist, *both* wrists a million times, but the skull and crossbones was definitely not amongst his many other Gothic bracelets. Had it been the only one he would have noticed its absence pretty much straightaway, but with half a dozen jangling heavily at the end of both arms, he had no idea it had gone until that afternoon. Somehow the clasp must have worked loose.

The bedside table had been emptied and searched twice, the lounge sofas and chairs pulled apart, and the small galley kitchen had its pots, pans and cutlery drawers completely rearranged – *still nothing.* If it had been any one of the others it might not have been quite so desperate, but that particular one was special. It had his initials carved on it. There was one at either end so when they were brought together and fastened it formed J. F. very clearly... *and it had been a gift from his sister.*

His heart sank as he collapsed on the bed, head in hands. There was no getting away from it; it must have slipped off in Charlotte's stables. That was an episode he was acutely and deeply ashamed of. He would never have done such a wicked destructive thing had he been in his right mind. He'd not taken his medication properly for weeks prior to visiting Jenny, now all hell had let loose and he was breaking into pharmaceutical surgeries and murdering horses. Even worse, *both* incidents involved that evil bitch Charlotte Peterson.

Jason quickly tidied up the flat. He didn't want Jenny asking questions on her return. With only minutes to spare and the last sofa cushion back in place, he heard the roar of an engine scream up the road and tyres screech to a halt outside. He looked through the window down on to the street where the roof of Jenny's yellow mini looked back up at him from a very strange angle. He watched the door fly open, his sister jump out, arm extended behind her to lock it as she dashed for the flat's street entrance.

What the... Jason was flummoxed for a second – then Miles Peterson came to mind. *If he's hurt her again I'll...* at that moment his sister burst through the flat's tiny hallway and into the lounge where she barely acknowledged him, instead Jenny ran over to the window parted the nets, quickly checked the street up and down then drew the curtains sharply.

It was only three p.m. and she should have been at work. Her complexion looked very pale, which wasn't unusual given she barely ate enough to feed a sparrow

– but this time it was different. *This time there was terror in her eyes.*

She lowered herself gingerly onto the settee and began to rock backwards and forwards, hands clasped together, she bit her nails, her eyes were jittery, and she whimpered like a frightened child. Jason sat down next to her and momentarily forgot his own problems. Gently he cupped his hands around hers, this seemed a little overkill for a Miles rebuff but he went with it anyway…

"When will you ever learn Jen, you're my big sister but you still behave like a kid running after that…'

"*It's not him Jase!*" she said through gritted teeth; "It's not Miles – it's… it's *her!*" Jenny turned her face to his and he could see she was utterly and completely petrified. Her eyes were wild – white with fear; he'd initially hoped she hadn't noticed *his* guilty expression but needn't have worried, Jenny was totally self-absorbed about *something, and it had left her traumatised in a way he'd never seen on her before – on any face before.* What on *earth* was it? What could have got her into this state?

She continued to rock back and forth clearly in a state of shock. His arm was round her now and he could feel the fear radiating off her body.

"What about Charlotte?" he tried gently; "Have you seen her then?" Jenny nodded. Slowly at first, then her head seemed unable to stop nodding, faster and faster as the tears began to brim, spill down her cheeks and onto both hands. Hands that gripped each other tighter and tighter until the colour drained from their knuckles and matched her white cheekbones.

"She… k -*killed* her Jason! Sh… She *murdered* my, my… oh *God* it was just so *vile*… it was so *bloody vile* Jase, like nothing I've ever…" she broke off and sobbed hysterically then.

"Whoaaahhh… *now just wait a minute!* What do you mean… she *killed* someone? Who? Where? Do you mean she ran them over, an accident or something in her car?" Jenny looked up at him then, her eyes wide and staring as she held his gaze.

"No Jason, *I don't. I don't* mean a… a *car accident or something!* I mean she *killed her*, my old school friend Danielle, she killed *Danielle Mogg!*" Now it was Jason's turn to pale visibly as her voice rose and became even shriller.

"Charlotte murdered Danni – in *Danni's – own – house!*"

Jenny grabbed some tissues from the coffee table and dabbed at her eyes before she crushed them all against her face. *Jason's* eyes were glued to his sister, he tried to understand what she'd just said but wasn't able to process it properly… or his brain wouldn't let him. He moved closer to comfort her, both arms now protectively around her shoulders he hugged her to him, too stunned for a moment as he fought for words.

"What… what were you doing there Jen, you haven't mentioned Danni since fifth grade?" Jenny pulled away from him then and fumbled with the Kleenex, looked down at them so as not to have to look her brother in the eye. She took a deep breath;

"Danielle came into the *Courier*," *she lied*, "asked if there was a spare copy of last week's paper. We couldn't believe how we'd now met up after all these years and she invited me over to her house this afternoon to catch up." Jenny was uncomfortable at how the lies tripped off her tongue so easily; *that's what plotting with Emily has done for me,* she thought.

"When I got there, her car was in the drive but there was no answer from the front door so… so I went round to the back. When I got there I heard some… some crashing noises and… and then…" She broke off suddenly and began to shake again, her hand came up to her mouth as she ran for the bathroom and slammed the door. His ears could not shut out the noise of her throwing up, he'd heard it many times before but knew this time she had good reason.

Jason waited for her in the lounge and intermittently rolled his lips in uneasy tension, then flicked his teeth nervously with his thumb nail. Beads of sweat broke out on his forehead. He heard the flush of the toilet then the door opened. Jenny walked slowly back into the room, agitated, drawing heavily on an emergency cigarette. He decided this was not the time to badger her over her obvious lapse in trying to give up.

"You do mean *Miles'* Charlotte don't you?" he asked incredulously as she sat back down. "I mean, I know she's an evil sarcastic cow but… *murder?*"

"Yes… it was Miles' Charlotte, and *yes*… she murdered her alright. She murdered her in the sickest – foulest way you could possibly imagine." Her voice shook with every word and her mouth snatched at the cigarette as she inhaled deeply.

"*How* Jenny – *how* did she kill her?" It sounded weird as soon as it was out of his mouth. He couldn't actually believe he was sat there in her flat asking that question. The tension in the air was like a thick fog, yet edgy, charged with the anticipation of just exactly what his sister had just seen. She turned to him, removed the cigarette slowly from between her lips and opened her mouth to speak;

"I saw h –" At that moment the phone rang which made them both jump apart. Jenny shot an apprehensive glance at her brother before she picked it up off the coffee table. Warily she brought the phone up to her ear. It seemed to Jason to take an age. The expression on her face was enough to alert him as to exactly who the caller was.

Charlotte was brief. "I know you're aware of who this is so I shall come directly to the point. You mention *one word* of what you witnessed to the police, to *anyone*… and your brother goes down for a drugs theft. Ask him. He knows what I'm talking about, *and he knows what I can do.*" Jenny stared suspiciously at her brother then spoke as steadily as she could manage into the phone;

"How did you get my number?"

Charlotte sniggered. "I made it my *business* to find out where you worked." She sneered. "A very co-operative little junior gave it to me when I explained our computer system was down. Told her I needed to contact you urgently regarding some test results. She was most obliging. I now also have your home address Jenny – so I'm warning you, *don't – cross – me.*" The line went dead.

Jason had paced the lounge throughout. Jenny now sat with the phone in her lap; she stared blankly down at it then looked slowly back up at him.

"That was –"

"I guessed…" scowled Jason; "What did she say?"

"She *said* she could get you sent to prison for stealing *drugs Jason* – what the *hell* is *that* all about?" Jason winced. *Time to come clean… but only about the surgery break-in…*

Charlotte flipped the cover of her mobile shut. Sat with her left leg outstretched in the hay, and the other peaked, she wondered just how much she'd frightened her, how much she could count on Jenny Flood not to squeal her adulterous little head off to the police – *or anyone else for that matter.*

Apart from the horses, the stables had remained exactly as they were that terrible night, Charlotte couldn't bear to change *anything*. Not the halters, the grooming equipment, saddles, boots, rugs or nosebags. None of it… She could still smell them; Greta and Gizmo, her babies, *her only real friends.*

As she sat there facing their stalls, their blankets thrown over the partitions, she fiddled with bits of hay and felt a tear well up, sting and escape down her cheek. It was as if it could dissolve all her callous thoughts, as if the salt could cleanse her destructive madness. *For that one fragile moment she was almost human…*

With her head hung low and her right leg now slid down and along the stable floor to relax with the other one, *she realised just how very, very tired* she was as she reflected on the whole hideous nightmare. The sliding action caused her shoe to scrape through the dried-out grass and create a metal clinking sound, then she felt something beneath the sole of her flats. Puzzled, she wiped the tear away, sat up straight and felt through the matted floor covering. When her fingers found it, they lifted it out slowly. She sat back against the stable wall holding it in her lap.

Charlotte turned the silver bracelet over and over looking incredulously at what she'd just found. When the 'J' fell right side up across her left palm she pushed at the skull and cross bone with her right index finger and straightened all the links into a neat line. The 'F' was clear to see at the other end. She brought the broken clasp and eye together – to create the Gothic silver circlet.

Realisation of who was to blame for the murder of her beloved horses hit like a taser. Her fingers closed over the garish carved letters and squeezed until she felt them cut into her flesh. Her eyes narrowed and she spat his name out between tightly clenched teeth. *Out loud – and with venom.*

TWENTY-NINE

Harry Longbridge rubbed the strong menthol stick on his upper lip in preparation. Josie Kinkade's cadaver lay on the mortuary slab in front of him, and although he'd served nearly thirty years in the service and attended many autopsies, he'd never got used to the unpalatable aromas of *'dice and slice'*.

He tried his hardest not to grin as young Joe Walker looked as if he was about to pass out despite the mortuary's 'best pocket buddy', and had to respect Suzanne Moorcroft's steel resolve not to follow suit. For both recruits it was their first autopsy and they were doing their level best to remain in situ for the duration.

"O – *kayy…* are we ready folks?" asked the forensic pathologist, eyes bright, smile wide and tools held mid-air. The pose made her look as if she were about to serve Sunday lunch.

One of Kirkdale General's finest, buxom American expat Kay Winford was known for her dry sense of humour and no-nonsense execution. She never meant to be disrespectful to the deceased, just simply felt it helped to lift the atmosphere a little if she viewed death as acutely interesting, rather than deeply depressing –

from a forensics point of view of course. To avoid morbid thoughts most of the time made for an easier ride all round.

Harry and his two charges swapped raised brows as Kay made the first incision. The previous three victims had all turned up very little in the way of real evidence, no more than the content of their stomachs, and the fact that Rachel Dern's lungs were none too clever after fifteen years of nicotine. He sincerely hoped Josie Kinkade's body might offer up something a good deal more informative than the early stages of lung cancer, or the fact that her last meal was a pepperoni pizza.

The two rookies watched with advanced apprehension as the pathologist's scalpel slid silently between small neat breasts down the torso to the top of the pubic bone; *it's like she's unzipping a banana*, thought Joe Walker irreverently. An immediate guilty flush followed, his conscience pricked at what his devoutly religious father would have made of *that* idea.

The nasal rub did little to help reduce the shock of the odour emitted, it was barely tolerable. As she noticed her colleague's plight, Suzanne offered Joe a handkerchief. He took it and threw her a grateful wince in thanks, held it to his face and prayed he wouldn't introduce it to his breakfast.

Kay Winford first parted and then peeled back the pale chilled flesh and thin layers of subcutaneous fat to expose the rib cage. Josie Kinkade had been a slim woman, not much work was involved there. Heart side, it revealed several already broken ribs from whatever had been used to create the hole in her chest after the initial chloroform attack. It was this that Harry was most interested in, to see if there were any buried splinters from some form of stake, or if the end of the weapon had made any chip marks to the bone which would imply some sort of metal chisel. *It would have to have been bloody big though,* he reminded himself.

The heart, Kay could see, was a splattered mess. She reached for the bolt cutters to prize back each of the intact ribs after a tweezers job on the bits of broken bone. Suzanne visibly flinched at each loud crack but managed to stand firm. Kay then lifted the mangled organ into a Petri dish just as Joe's drained face sailed past the head end of the slab. Harry stifled a grin, left him to a male assistant who'd just entered the room, and imparted a rare wink of respect to Suzanne who remained on her feet. She smiled – *weakly.*

The cavity organs were next: stomach, large and small bowel, liver and intestines; all plopped redundantly one after the other into a deeper larger bowl; all glistened slickly, eel-like under the brightness of the lab's overhead lamps.

"Anything?" asked Harry hopefully.

"*Well* – at first inspection there's no trace of wood splintering in the heart or surrounding tissue, just like the other three," replied Kay.

"I'll run a more detailed surgical check after you've gone, and let you know if there's any change on that, but I don't think there will be. If a wooden stake or similar weapon had been hammered into the chest and then pulled back out, at least *some* visual splintering would have been left behind."

"What about a metal stake – or a chisel or something?" Suzanne suggested.

"Hmmm… it's *possible,* the edges would be smoother, there would be no material to be caught up in the tissue, but there's no chip from a chisel end on any of the ribs. Breakage yes, but no chisel-type marks, either of those would have left indented lines on the bones and there aren't any. Here, do you see?" Suzanne leant forward and examined each of the snapped-out ribs more closely now that Kay had laid them individually on a separate tray. Harry also looked more closely whilst he tried not to breathe in – it didn't really help much. He acknowledged he understood, covered his mouth and stepped back smartly again. Joe remained seated by the far wall, head between his legs. *Of the two, it was Suzanne who was destined for bigger things* thought Harry.

"What about if the stake or… whatever it was, had been made of something else?" pursued Suzanne.

"How do you mean?" asked Kay, "like plastic or rubber or something?"

"No… more like… I dunno, stone or –"

"*Or ice?!*" shouted Joe excitedly, he'd jumped away from the wall now and quickly re-joined the group – albeit behind Suzanne. Harry's mouth dropped about a foot in surprise as he turned around to his young constable.

"Well where the hell did that come from?" he asked, eyes wide. Joe gave a modest smile.

"Just a mixture of what was being said I guess," he replied. "Is it possible though Dr. Winford?" The stout pathologist leant back on her heels and re-studied the open cadaver, then the wasted heart in the Petri dish. Josie Kinkade had been naked when she was murdered; there were no clothing particles in her body tissue; no wood splinters and no evidence to suggest a knife; *the hole was the wrong shape for a blade anyway*, nor a poker or any chisel-type of metal implement. More importantly, nothing had been found at the scene or in the vicinity… of *any* of the murders. Kay was quiet for quite some time before she looked up…

"Young man… *I think you may just have something."*

Back at the station later, Harry filed a report on the Kinkade autopsy. Joe's ice stake theory was not one he wanted to go with, but with nothing else on the table, and Kay Winford having admitted the idea had legs, he couldn't exactly rule it out. Hadn't he seen some drama on TV where a large ice stalagmite or something had been used? *Hardly realistic though surely,* he thought; he ran his hand through his hair in frustration.

An hour later, Harry had found a reminder note scrunched up underneath half a corned beef sandwich and a cup of cold coffee. It was from his secretary,

Denise. He groaned; checked his desk diary, then his watch, then rolled his eyes in irritated impatience. Mrs. Longbridge had made a doctor's appointment for him, *against his wishes*, to sort out the hypoglycaemic/diabetic symptoms that had plagued him for so long. Just to make her happy, he'd promised to keep it – and now he was late. As if to make a point, a foggy head descended at that very moment. He snatched a barley sugar from the supply dish on top of the desk, grabbed his jacket and headed off for a consultation – with Dr. Miles Peterson.

It was two a.m., Jenny stood outside Jason's bedroom door and strained to listen – his radio had finally gone off and she could hear faint muffled snores.

Things had gone too far, way too far she thought as she punched in Emily's mobile number to tell her so. She stepped away from his room, heart pounding, and walked into the lounge. He *mustn't* find out about her six-year transatlantic link with publishing giants McCarthy Stone. *Nobody must find out.*

Jenny repeated the number impatiently as the line kept connecting to voicemail. She needed to speak to her, and she needed to speak to her *now.* It was nine p.m. U.S. time. Her finger hesitated over the buttons; *she's got to be home* she thought desperately – *surely fancy New York publishers can't be entertaining clients all the time!*

The sound of the soft intermittent burr of the American landline continued on for much longer than she'd anticipated. She kept her eyes on the lounge door in case he woke. Jenny had never rung Emily at home before – it was expressly forbidden, but this was an emergency and she intended to tell her exactly what she wanted. *The instigator of this crazy plot on the next plane out of JFK!* The line kept on ringing.

"*Come on, come on, come on,*" she muttered under her breath, her eyes still on the door. Finally someone picked up.

"Yup?" it was a man's voice. Jenny didn't quite know why she was surprised but she had to think quickly;

"Oh hi – it's – uh, Faithe, a friend of Emily's. I was just ringing to check wheth –"

"Hold on I'll call her. *Emily! It's Faithe !*" A pause – then – "She'll be with you in a sec." Jenny heard the phone put down onto a hard surface, *obviously the husband didn't feel chatty,* she thought relieved.

Her anxiety increased as she waited… Jenny hoped she'd remembered the friend's name correctly from the other night. Emily had mentioned she was supposed to have been with Faithe whilst in fact she was on the phone to *her* when she'd called from the Tapas bar or Mexican bistro *or whatever it was*. More than that though, right now she hoped the older woman would be able to bluff her way through this conversation when she realised who it actually was.

Jenny heard footsteps in the background and the rustle of the phone as it was picked up…

"Faithe? You okay sweetie?"

"Emily — it's me, Jenny," she hissed. "I know I shouldn't have rung you at home but I *have* to speak to you! Pretend I'm a friend who's just been dumped — *it shouldn't be difficult."* Emily winced and turned away from the mouthpiece;

"Gareth… could you pop down to Larson's and pick up another bottle of that nice sparkling wine sweetheart?" Jenny heard a male's distant acknowledgement at the other end followed by a mumbled; *"Every time a bloody interruption!"* Then a door slammed. Once he'd gone Emily couldn't hide her anger;

"What in God's name are you doing?! Do you want everything to go tits up?"

"Too late for that," Jenny replied. Emily felt an unwanted rush of adrenalin. The younger woman then spent the next ten minutes on speed talk as she brought her up to date with what she'd witnessed that afternoon, including Charlotte's subsequent blackmail attempt. Emily listened in stunned silence, absolutely staggered at what she'd heard; then delivered a bombshell of her own. A very much *wanted* bombshell, however, as far as Jenny Flood was concerned.

"Look — I'm sorry I jumped down your throat Jen, I can hear how upset you are; it must've been truly… *truly horrible*, especially as you knew this girl. Listen, the reason my mobile was busy for so long was because I had another call from England earlier this evening. I've had some bad news, it's my mother. The owner of the nursing home rang me herself and advised if I wanted to see her... *before it's too late...* it's got to be soon – *very soon.*" Jenny gave a sharp intake of breath;

"You're coming over?" she whispered excitedly, then immediately re-analysed Emily's news. "Oh... I'm sorry I didn't mean to sound –"

"No – it's okay. I know what you meant. Look – I've just booked on the 10.00 p.m. flight Tuesday evening, JFK to Newcastle. I'll hire a car and drive down. Can you make me a reservation at the Kirkdale Grange? I assume it's still there?"

"Yeah – yes of course – I'll see to that, sure, no problem... Emily –I'm *so* glad we're meeting up again after all this time, *and* that I won't be alone with this any longer. I've lost an old friend, my brother's in danger, my work colleagues are digging for answers – *I'm scared Emily.*"

"Don't worry, I won't let anything happen to you, I –"

Jenny heard the sound of an exterior door again and Emily's voice suddenly altered to a hurried whisper. "– *I have to go, Gareth's back. I'll see you Wednesday night – keep your head down now, no more till I get there.*" The phone suddenly fell silent and Jenny was left alone in the dark again. Alone – but a little stronger. *Emily Rowlands was finally coming home.*

***

The package sat next to the pilot in the Cessna light aircraft as it tracked an arch and coasted towards the crude runway. He was unaware what he was carrying but a pretty good guess told him it was some form of illegal merchandise – he just hoped it wasn't drugs.

The plane picked up speed as it thundered along the course ground, then lifted like an eagle to begin the five thousand foot climb into the blue. If the weather held it would hopefully be a routine and safe trip, *apart from the extra delivery.* If not, old Davey Jones had better have the pot on…

THIRTY

Monday morning at the *Courier*, Andrew noticed Jenny looked both paler and more frail than usual. In fact she looked pretty wrecked. Her eyes were sunken, her hair lank, she appeared utterly exhausted – and very *very* much on edge. She hadn't even acknowledged him when he'd arrived for work, and had been pretty cagey ever since the day he'd discovered her affair with Miles.

"What is it Jenny?" he asked tightly. "Have you realised that a relationship with our Dr. Peterson isn't the *smartest* move you could have made?" Andrew saw her wince and immediately felt bad. As soon as the words were out he'd wished he could've taken them back, it wasn't his style and he knew it. He also knew that this constant riling wouldn't get him anywhere. The theory proved right as she ignored him completely and continued typing up an article about a new restaurant launch to go with some pictures she'd taken.

He got up and went to the kitchen to make some coffee, brought back two mugs and set one down in front of her. The typing stopped.

"Here," he gestured to the extra milky one, having

learnt that was how she liked it – then leant against her desk. She traced her finger up and down the handle before she looked up at him – *a ghost would've had more colour* he thought.

"Thanks," she said softly, all fire gone from her voice. *Where was that bristling passionate woman who'd argued so strongly with him a few weeks back?* He decided it was now or never, but spoke more gently this time.

"*Is* it Miles that's upset you Jen? Or have the police hauled Jason in again? They haven't actually *found* something to connect him to the murders have they?" The girl in front of him looked like she was having a really tough job not crying into her coffee. *Or was it simply that she was trying desperately not to say something? Something she longed to get off her chest but couldn't?* "Jenny?" he prompted.

"I'm fine Andrew – *really*." She smiled a broken smile and blinked back a tear, then closed both hands around her mug and blew lightly across the top before taking a sip. "My brother *is* innocent you know," she continued shakily, "there's no way he'll be called back in for questioning. Not for any murders any –" She stopped short of finishing the sentence, stingingly aware of her implication that Jason could be guilty of something else. Andrew was about to press her about it when his mobile buzzed. He took it out of his pocket and read a brief text from Gina at the surgery;

'5th woman, 25 Farringdon Ave, Charlotte's attending – 30 mins.'

His eyes widened; he shot a glance at Jenny and then at his watch.

"I have to go out Jenny, there's been another murder. Charlotte Peterson's attending – I… I take it you don't want to come with me?"

The look on Jenny's face in response to that question had troubled him all the way to Farringdon Avenue. It wasn't the expression of a woman who was nervous of being in the same room as her lover's wife; it was the expression of a woman who was *totally petrified* of her lover's wife.

He tapped the steering wheel impatient for the lights to change in the centre of town as his eyes darted about insanely with a myriad of crazy thoughts. When they turned green he drove straight across and took the first left into Broad Street. *Why was Jenny so uptight – no – wrong word; why was she absolutely totally and utterly terrified at the thought of even being in the same room as Charlotte Peterson?* Just for a second he let himself consider his theory of a few weeks ago, that the serial killer was a woman. *Might she actually be a woman he knew? The three of them had thrown that idea around before – and thrown it right out again…*

Andrew realised his speed had gradually increased to fifty in a thirty zone with each crazy thought. When he pulled into Farringdon Avenue he slowed right down and looked for number twenty-five. As he searched, he recalled Molly's last vision – *long blonde hair, turquoise dress and the darker letter 'S' formed in the waves of her hair.* He wondered how detailed the vision would turn out to be – *if it was the same woman.*

Harry Longbridge crouched beside the body of Susie Sarrandaire – *or Danielle Mogg* as he'd since discovered from some old bank statements in her office. The double name thing appeared to be innocent enough, borne out by some commercial photo shoots she'd been working on. There was also a message from her agent on the landline's answering facility to say she'd won a part in some new drama which backed up the acting background. *This girl had obviously been going places* he thought as he glanced over at a glamorous photo on the mantelpiece. In it she was wearing a long black evening dress, her hair cascaded casually over her shoulders in waves.

A lightbulb moment flashed as he remembered the conversation with Molly Fields. He got up and walked out to the hall.

Joe Walker was searching the first floor to see if there'd been any disruption up there.

"Walker!" yelled Harry; *"have you gone through those rooms yet?"* Joe's head appeared over the banisters;

"Yes sir, nothing unusual to report, in fact the whole of the upstairs looks fine – very clean and tidy actually. On the face of it there's no evidence to suggest disruption at all – to any of the rooms."

"Did you find any turquoise evening dresses amongst her clothing by any chance, in *any* of the bedrooms?" asked Longbridge.

"Well, I wasn't really taking too much notice of the col–"

Harry was already halfway up the stairs and Joe straightened up as his boss rounded the corner post to the landing. This wasn't important for evidence reasons, the Field girl had nearly been a victim herself and had the perfect alibi even if she'd *had* any prior knowledge of Miss Sarrandaire's evening wear. No, this was a personal mission. Harry just wanted to prove to himself that all that vision nonsense was precisely that – *nonsense.*

He checked every garment in the main bedroom and quickly scanned the wardrobes in the others. Only one room had an overspill wardrobe with a woman's items in it, the others were empty. Whilst there were a couple of turquoise tops, there were definitely no dresses that colour. If he was honest he was bloody relieved. He didn't want to have to deal with the delusions of a would-be witness, *and he definitely didn't want to have to include it in a report to the CPS.*

On his way back downstairs, he noticed the Gale lad through the hall window trying to persuade the duty PC to let him in to the house. After the dressing down Joe Walker had got last time, this young officer was having none of it. Harry smiled…

"It's okay Thompson – let him in," he said wearily, "I'll take any rap." Andrew looked surprised with the ease in which he'd gained entry to the latest murder scene. He was even more surprised when Harry put an arm across his shoulder and walked him down the hall.

The familiar smell of chloroform filled his nostrils with every step. *Its use with Rachel, Josie and the other two women was obviously not coincidence then – it was the killer's style – behaviour pattern.*

Harry hesitated at the entrance to the living room, flashbulbs were going off, handles, switches and architraves dusted for prints and apart from Harry and a couple of uniforms, almost everyone appeared to be in white. The whole house was reminiscent of Kings Cross in a snowy rush hour.

"Do you know when it happened – when she was actually –?" Andrew broke off and turned sideways to let one of the larger SOCO team squeeze past him into the hall.

"No, we haven't got the exact time of death yet, we're still waiting for the doctor to pronounce life extinct. Not that there's much doubt of that." They exchanged a look – sombre acknowledgement of the obvious.

"The doc's late, should've been here more than ten minutes ago. It was the cleaner that found the dead girl this morning – she went ballistic, known her since she was a kid apparently." Harry paused for a moment then turned to face the younger man. He placed both hands on Andrew's shoulders and looked him straight in the eye.

"You ready for this then?" Andrew faltered for a second, but realised that DCI Longbridge was finally accepting him 'on board' as it were. He didn't know *why* he was, but he was grateful all the same. Andrew nodded, took a deep breath, and followed him into the room.

It wasn't easy to look at the body. It brought back a horrific reminder of Rachel. Andrew turned away quickly, clearly upset, but he'd still noticed she was wearing jogging bottoms and a tee-shirt – *no blue dress, turquoise or otherwise*. Harry led him to a chair at the other end of the lounge.

"Do you know *this* one, son?"

"No – no I don't, although, there *is* something vaguely familiar about her face."

"She was an actress. TV commercials and bit parts mainly, although she *had* apparently just won a role in a new saga of some sort. You've probably seen her in one of her adverts I expect."

"*Ye-a-h* – I remember now – shampoo or something? Not surprising with *that* hair. What was her name?"

"Sarrandaire, Susie Sarrandaire; real name Danielle Mogg – Sarrandaire was a stage name."

"The 'S'… in her hair…" Andrew murmured softly, eyes glazed. Harry thought about it then, he'd forgotten that part of Molly's prediction. He shuddered inwardly; he wanted to forget about it now *too*, he wasn't keen on all that 'spooky stuff'. Blood and guts and tangible crime he could cope with, weird premonitions...

"I don't suppose the dead woman... owns a long blue dress of any sort does she?" asked Andrew hesitantly.

"I suppose Miss Fields told *you* about her... *'visions'* as well did she?" asked Harry, his voice labouring on the operative word.

"She's been having them for ages to be honest;" admitted Andrew. "We... didn't think it was something you'd want to be bothered with;" he finished, uncertain of his response to their withholding information – however unusual. There was a sharp intake of breath followed by a slow release;

"We want to be *bothered* about anything and *everything* in connection with a crime, but..." he paused... "I expect the lass meant well," he conceded. "After all, she *did* have a pretty rough time of it herself. No, there's no blue evening dress lad. Look Gale – if you want to mooch around for a media report, that's fine, just don't touch anything okay?" Andrew smiled and nodded his thanks.

They both walked back down the lounge towards the door to the hall, and despite the horror of it, Andrew couldn't avoid a glance at the dead girl as he passed again. That grotesque hole in her chest, the copious amounts of blood – he was sickened by it and knew he would never forget it. *Could a woman really do that to another woman?*

They reached the door and Andrew shook the police inspector's hand.

"Thanks Harry." The DCI raised his eyebrows.

"Mr. Longbridge – *Sir*," said Andrew apologetically. To lighten the moment, Harry pointed a forefinger at him in mock disapproval as a reminder of his status, then turned back to the sombre business of Susie Sarrandaire.

Andrew took a notebook and pen from his pocket and stepped back into the hall. He looked around him and made notes on the type of house, the crime scene etcetera to ensure he captured the accuracy for a reputable piece, and finished with a carefully angled picture so as not to include the body. Since all this had started, a junior had taken over Andrew's sports column and Peter Gray had made him chief crime reporter whilst his wife Stella was still recuperating at home.

It was certainly a beautiful place, double fronted with another large room off the other side of the hallway. He nudged at a door already ajar that was next to the lounge. It was at the end of the hall opposite the front door. Most of the SOCO team that had been crawling all over the house were now congregated in the room where the body was. Still, he checked for any last stragglers on the stairs before he slipped into the kitchen, and closed the door behind him.

Andrew admired the smart designer units and top of the range electrical items. His eyes travelled along the shiny granite work tops and took in the Le Creuset storage jars and accessories. The little red heart-shaped ramekin dishes neatly stacked against the side of the fridge seemed grotesquely pertinent to the situation. Instantly *'forgetting'* Longbridge's request Andrew lifted the top one and turned it over to examine the base. *Gina would love these* he thought distractedly. Beneath it in the next dish down he saw a ticket of some sort, picked it up and turned it over. It was a dry cleaning ticket with Susie's name and phone number on. It also had *'Turquoise blue dress' written across the top.* Andrew glanced back at the door, took his chance and slipped it in his pocket. *If that was for a long turquoise evening dress, then Harry would have to take Molly's abilities seriously. It might be that one day she could help them.* Just then he heard a new voice... and she was just outside the kitchen.

Andrew opened the door and moved back into the hall to find Charlotte Peterson had finally arrived. Only a few feet in front of him she studied his face closely and seemed shocked he was there at all. Andrew held her gaze until it was obvious the woman felt very uncomfortable, mumbled something about too many chiefs and began to walk straight towards the lounge until she suddenly stopped and appeared to check something in her bag.

The looks that passed between newspaper reporter Andrew Gale and GP Dr. Charlotte Peterson, did not go unnoticed by DCI Longbridge. *What the hell was THAT all about,* he thought completely baffled. More to the point – *how did she know which room to head for…?*

Once Andrew had left, Harry showed a flushed Charlotte into the lounge where the body was. He watched her work – watched her very carefully as she went about her business. It *seemed* professional, she answered his questions and issued a death certificate in the normal way, but there was something very odd about Dr. Peterson that he couldn't quite put his finger on. It was almost as if she was partially familiar with the layout of that house – she was also extremely jumpy. For the first time in his life Harry felt unsure about another official at a crime scene, and he didn't like that feeling. He wasn't expecting it, he wasn't used to it and he wasn't sure how to handle it. One thing he *was* sure of though, he'd heard the expression **'The eyes are windows to the soul'** – *well right now Harry Longbridge wasn't entirely sure this woman even had one of those.*

THIRTY-ONE

Gina Rowlands... seethed Charlotte as she marched past two police officers on leaving the Sarrandaire house. A pair of raised eyebrows left in her wake went unnoticed, but Andrew Gale's study of her in the hall most certainly had not.

She must have contacted that reporter boyfriend of hers after I left the surgery, she deduced acidly, *well... we'll see just how smart they both are when their wings have been clipped; as for the Flood boy and that barmaid...*

Her hands gripped the steering wheel, stomach tight. Behind an increasingly mad glare a growing list of brightly coloured red names – a *Blood List.*

The Range Rover pulled away from the kerb with the eyes of Harry Longbridge bored into its rear window. Twitching the lounge curtain, he'd watched Charlotte stride down the drive in an unmistakable hurry *just like last time at the Kinkade place – only faster* he'd thought. As the vehicle's bumper rounded the corner, the name Harold Shipman came to mind. *Doctor* Harold Shipman – and he didn't want to acknowledge its presence.

There was nothing controlled about these murders, however. In the case of Shipman it was a control factor;

control over life and death; the forging of wills for financial benefit in one or two instances – *those* were the key motives. There was nothing about Kirkdale's serial killer to indicate either, the bodies of the young women found so far displayed an overly dramatic, overly staged final act. It was almost certainly the chloroform that had killed them. The gouged hole in the chest of each victim cradled a message – one that spoke volumes, echoed quite literally from the heart. That message screamed revenge – *but for what?*

Uncomfortable as it was, Harry had to consider the broadest, the most incongruous possibilities in his job – *even if casting the net that wide brought in a medical fish.*

Miles Peterson felt distinctly uneasy. He'd already cancelled the patient's first appointment for a glucose check because the man had been late, he couldn't do so again, particularly as he was waiting in the reception area.

His palms were slick with sweat, and his normally jovial chatty air had for the most part of that day completely deserted him. Whilst being entirely innocent of any wrongdoing with regard to the demise of Rachel Dern, or come to that the death of any of the women, Miles was still terrified his relationship with Rachel would be discovered. *The guy was due in five minutes.* What bothered him most were the media reports that had put Rachel's time of death at about the same time he'd left her. As the days and weeks had gone on, with no police interviews requested at the surgery owing to Rachel's practice being elsewhere, Miles had thought he wouldn't be questioned. Now by sheer bad luck, the officer in charge of the case, who *was* on their patient list, needed a genuine appointment.

He reminded himself this was a patient that needed help, not a policeman asking to speak to him in any official capacity. *Didn't mean he wouldn't make the most of it though,* he reasoned. Miles opened the door to the reception area.

"Harry Longbridge?" he called. Harry put down a two-year-old *Punch* magazine, got up and followed him towards his office. As he did so he noticed Charlotte Peterson quietly close the last half inch gap of the door to her own. Once inside, she fished the Prozac out of her trouser pocket and winced as she swallowed two down dry...

"How can I help Mr. Longbridge?" said Miles with an overly bright smile. He gestured to Harry to take a seat as his voice broke a little before he sat back down himself.

Harry noticed Miles was sweating, he seemed quite agitated, in fact he was jumpy the entire appointment. With summer behind them and the considerable drop in temperature towards the end of September, visibly sweating seemed more than a little odd. Yet it wasn't Miles he was actually interested in – *it was that wife of his that had got Harry really rattled…*

He was duly processed to the nurse's office for a blood test, and although he could cope with any amount of other people's escaping claret, was worse than useless when it came to his own. Needles and knives were both off his menu, so he wasn't in the least surprised when help was required to sit upright again after it was all over. Harry felt decidedly woozy, not helped by the thought of colleagues getting wind of his… *challenges*. Before he left he made damned sure he got an assurance from the nurse that what went on in the blood test room stayed in the blood test room. His result would be back in a few days…

Harry walked slowly out of what he'd long ago nicknamed *Dracula's Bay*, with a cotton wad on his inner left elbow and arm at a right angle. For once though his thoughts didn't linger over his long-time weakness, he knew he had to speak to Dr. Peterson *female* – but didn't want to alert her to his suspicions, which to be fair still felt fairly outlandish. He also knew he couldn't bring in a respected doctor for questioning over a collection of horrific murders when he had no concrete reason to do so. Just to run that thought around his flakey head was difficult enough, to actually follow it through with any action was another thing altogether.

At that moment Charlotte exited her office to call in her next patient, and their eyes met as Harry passed her door on his way back to reception. Just for a split second he saw a twitch of panic at the corner of one eye before her face broke into that tight controlled smile she always wore. Dr. Peterson *female,* dipped her head in acknowledgement, as Harry responded similarly then walked straight through reception and out of the building to the car park. *Double bacon and egg rolls, doughnuts and coffee time* he thought – *can't think with a light head and an empty stomach...*

Andrew waited expectantly for the dry cleaning assistant to find the item that corresponded with the ticket he'd just handed over. She disappeared amongst numerous racks of hanging dresses to look for the correct one with the right name and contact details. When a long turquoise evening number was brought out and draped across the counter, he knew for sure that Molly was a very gifted girl indeed, and whether he liked it or not – Harry would shortly have to think so too.

Back in the car he'd headed for the Carpenters Arms for lunch with the girls before he made the trip down town to Kirkdale's Police Station which was where he was now. Andrew shifted around on a hard plastic chair at the front desk area waiting for Harry to come back in, and wondered just how this sarcastic, sceptic, hard-nosed DCI who saw everything in black and white, was going to react when he handed over a long turquoise dress and dry cleaning ticket. He'd managed to persuade the cleaners to let him keep the original receipt if he signed it – *'item received'*.

Just then Harry appeared around the corner and walked briskly along the corridor towards him having satisfactorily re-fuelled en-route at Brenda's Buffet Wagon in Market Square. On reaching Andrew he gestured sharply for him to walk with him to the elevator and they rode to the 4th floor where all those wearing pips on their shoulders had their offices.

After exiting the lift they walked through a corridor and a couple of sets of double doors before Harry stopped at his own. Now inside, Andrew sat opposite him and Harry slid a white paper bag of barley sugars across the desk. Andrew took one before sliding a larger white paper bag back to the officer. He watched as Longbridge lifted the top edge with his finger. Harry's eyes widened then glanced back up at Andrew. He pulled the dress partially out of the bag until it was obvious it was going to be full length then sat back and looked at it for a few seconds. Slowly, resignedly, he leaned forward to open a top drawer and pulled out a folded piece of paper. Harry really didn't want to, but he did it anyway. The turquoise doodling from his chat with Molly three days previously was passed across the desk. After Andrew picked it up, they both sat and looked at each other with a new mutual understanding – for Harry's part it was a renewed respect of all things *'mumbo jumbo…'*

Andrew now really needed to get back to the *Courier* to write up the Sarrandaire crime report – and to check on Jenny. He figured he should also update Stella as well or she'd not be happy at all, and made a mental note to ring her later. With the discovery of the turquoise dress and the fact Harry had started to share some of his thoughts on the case, Andrew could feel the momentum… *it felt like a storm was brewing.*

***

TUESDAY SEPTEMBER 27TH

SOMEWHERE ABOVE THE HUDSON RIVER - MANHATTAN ISLAND

At 45, Ethan James had been a ferry pilot flying light aircraft to customers across the Atlantic for over 15 years. Taking the dangerous Southern route, straight across the ocean, instead of the safer Greenland, Iceland, Faroe Islands and on to the Shetlands off mainland Scotland, was just typical of his nature. That was known as the more sensible cautious *Northern route*, the one the youngsters started with, just as he'd done himself.

There had been a few seriously scary trips during the last decade, but then Ethan did tend to live on the edge. A born in the wilds Canadian, he was no stranger to the 'grizzlier' side of life, although even *he* realised he couldn't carry on with these contracts for much longer, *particularly the hazardous Southern crossing.*

This time necessitated flying his *own* Cessna 208, however, from a private airfield outside Brooklyn, and for a very different reason. As always he'd doubled checked every instrument was spot on, including the crucial GPS, and was exceedingly grateful he'd been able to get the installed ferry can re-fit done in time – to run out of fuel halfway across the pond wasn't exactly an option. Even so, a 125 litre Turtle Buddy gas pack sat behind him next to a survival kit, the vital 'bathroom bottle' on the shelf to his right – and his Provigil safely in his pocket to keep him awake. It was going to be a long flight.

Now the Hudson was five thousand feet below him, the weather predictions were fair to middling, and he felt good... well, reasonably okay anyway. As he reached forward to check a dial, thoughts turned to Emily Stone and why he was doing this crazy drop for her. He wouldn't have bothered if it was purely because she'd caught him in a clinch with his sister-in-law Jodi at that hotel. *Those McCarthy Stone book launches seemed to be bloody everywhere lately...* His wife Faithe was Emily's best friend, and Jodi her younger sister so it wasn't exactly ideal, *but no* – he was mainly doing it because she'd also discovered he'd expanded a little with a few 'extra' deliveries. This was payback time in exchange *for zipped lips.* Emily had changed though – there was definitely something

different about her, she was harder, colder, sharper...
and he suspected the content of the package on its
way to England with him was testament to that.

Well – at least it wasn't ticking...

THIRTY-TWO

Emily checked her watch. They were due to touch down at 9.55 a.m., she wound the hands forward five hours – *jet lag here I come* she thought resignedly.

As she looked out of the window a swathe of white boulder clouds gazed back, and all her reasons for coming home began to bubble like a cauldron. She'd left Gareth at the airport completely subdued, they'd not really discussed anything on Saturday evening after Jenny had interrupted what was supposed to be their crucial '*life talk*', and he'd been away at an event over the following two days. In her heart of hearts she knew if he hadn't already, he would probably be tempted to start drinking again – *and she also knew that would be entirely her fault.*

Her mother was dying, not easy news to process for any daughter, but Emily hadn't seen her for the best part of eighteen years and now deeply regretted that. However, it was other decisions she'd made back then, leading to the loss of a daughter that had increased her overwhelming feeling of guilt and emptiness. Feelings she just couldn't shake off. Three of five very important people who had massively affected her life so far – *and the other two were about to learn the meaning of the boomerang effect...*

An announcement came from the cockpit that there was ten minutes to approach, Emily folded her untouched magazine, put it into her handbag and waited for further instructions.

"Ladies and gentlemen, as we start our descent, please make sure your seat backs and tray tables are in their full upright position. Be certain your seat belt is securely fastened, and all carry-on luggage is stowed underneath the seat in front of you or in the overhead bins. Thank you."

So... soon she would see her mother, possibly for the last time, meet her adult daughter for the first time, and finally deal with the bitter and acrid memories, the ashes of her past that she'd choked on daily for all these years... Well – as Ethan would say; *"Best you suck it up Buttercup..."*

By the time she'd landed, gone through passport and customs, retrieved her bags from that God awful carousel and picked up the hire car, it was nearly lunchtime. She wasn't impressed with the deep scuff across her Louis Vuitton roller case either. Normally that would have rankled with her all the way to the hotel, but this trip there was a whole lot more than agents, authors, books, clothes and bags to worry about.

As the road stretched out in front of her with almost two hours driving still ahead, Emily seriously began to wish she'd just got a cab. She wasn't unduly tired having slept unusually well on the plane, but it would've been nice not to have had the worry, to be able to use the time to work out a few things more concisely, to be able to plan, unfettered by traffic lights, roundabouts and GPS instructions.

It was 3.00 p.m. by the time she pulled up outside the Kirkdale Grange Hotel, booked in and taken the lift to her room. Now she *was* tired. Shoes kicked off and strong coffee brewed, she lay on the bed with the realisation front and centre of what was actually about to unfold. Even Jenny didn't know – not all of it. She sat up, reached for the coffee and sipped – *good, but not as good as Elio's on the corner of 23rd*.

Emily lay back on the bed in serious thought for a moment. Had she made the right choice? She hoped she had. In all reality there hadn't been anyone else who would've understood it all, but she still prayed the somewhat flakey twentysomething would be able to handle what was to come. With her going soft on Miles again, *and she understood why – she just couldn't afford any weakness and distractions*, Emily seriously wondered if Jenny was about to become a liability.

She checked her watch for what felt like the hundredth time. 3.45p.m. Ethan would be here sometime during the evening and she didn't want those two meeting each other. That little double booking would have to be strictly organised, there couldn't be any complicated introductions and reasons given as to why he'd turned up as well. *Better text Jenny later and get her to come tomorrow instead.*

There was also the need... *want*... to go and see her mother before Ethan arrived, and that wasn't going to be an easy meet by any stretch of the imagination. Luckily the nursing home was very close by so she should be there and back in twenty minutes and still be able to spend a good two hours with her before he was due.

Emily swallowed the rest of her coffee, swung her legs off the bed and slipped her shoes back on. Reaching for her bag and car keys she took a deep breath, summoned her best power pose and walked back out of the door towards her childhood...

Old Mary knew if she returned often enough her niece would come home one day, and the girl needed to know – she needed to know everything. It was the hair that alerted her – it was completely unmistakable.

She waited in the shadow of the tall trees, watched keenly as the clearly elegant and now very rich woman exited the silver Mercedes and walked up the steps into the nursing home. It had been twenty long years since she'd last seen her and even then always from a distance, the last time there had been any physical contact was well over 30 years ago. *It was now or never.*

Rosemary Emmerson looked a good deal older than her 70 years due to her vagrant lifestyle; she was very scared and very ashamed of her appearance.

Nevertheless she walked as quickly as she could from the shadow of the tall trees, and at a safe distance, followed the redhead up the steps into the building and back into both their pasts…

Emily sat in a visitors' chair and watched her as she slept. Her mother seemed so frail, seemed so…… *old*. The nurse had said to wait for her to wake up naturally; Margaret needed to sleep as much as she wanted to. So here she was, after eighteen years, waiting the last few minutes before a historic volcano opened – *and spilled its guts all over her life.*

She got up and looked out of the window while she waited. Kirkby Pike soared majestically in the distance, dominating the landscape behind the small town that lay just outside Kirkdale. Kirkby-Over-Sands, the town where she'd grown up, where she'd been happy before it had all started, before the nightmare had begun.

She didn't even hear the door open behind her, notice quiet footsteps pad gently into the room. It wasn't until her mother stirred and she'd turned round to see if Margaret had woken, that Emily had come face-to-face with a dirty, scraggy-haired old woman with clothes that matched perfectly. Then all of a sudden she *did* notice something, the stale odour that had followed her in. Her right hand flew to cover her nose and mouth…

"What the… who the hell are you?! I'm getting security!" Old Mary looked scared then, froze where

she stood, eyes wide in horror until from the bed there came a weak voice they both knew.

"Em…no… *Em… It's Rose… it's your Auntie Rose…*"

Rose Emerson looked from her niece to her sister as tears began to well up and threaten to streak her grimy face. Margaret Rowlands lifted a tired hand and gestured for them both to come closer, she spoke very softly and breathlessly due to her weakened heart, and began to explain…

"Emily…" her breathing laboured, "it's my fault… I turned her away, all… . those years ago… and…" she was gasping now, "and I… I did it *twice.*" Emily noticed there was an oxygen mask lying on her bed, she picked it up and put it over her mother's face but Maggie Rowlands pulled it away.

"Mother *please…*" The usually hard-faced New Yorker began to feel some emotion now, the past was all becoming very real, and her mother appeared to be fading right before her eyes. Not only that, it had begun to sound like there were additional important family issues, ones she had no knowledge of. Well, why should she? She'd done a runner all those years ago…

"She… needed… my help… the second time… with the boy bairn…" All through this Rose Emmerson had sat quiet, fiddling with her hands, and even Emily had softened to her obvious distress.

Rose wiped a grimy arm across her face and pushed

a greasy tendril back behind an ear. Quietly she began to speak…

"Ain't no use in no mithering, nor runnin' tears – tis done and tis garn." Emily and her mother looked quizzically at each other over Rose's speech and dialect – it was nothing like their own.

"Rose… *why*… your *speech*?" asked her sister breathlessly; "Was that Davey? Did he… force that *too*?" She tried to sit up then, eyes wide, but Emily made her lie back down.

"It were his want, his way, an' now I can't be a changin' – even if I did want it so, even now he be larng dead an' larng garn…" She looked back at Emily again – it'd been so long since she'd swung a little girl up into her arms after she'd run up that hall to see her all those years ago…

The next hour unfolded with Emily desperately trying to compartmentalise two very different emotions. Firstly an acceptance that her mother, who she'd not seen for years, had obviously faded a lot faster than she'd imagined, and an aunt she knew nothing of who would clearly need help, and secondly… the very different and darker reason she'd flown over three thousand miles back home for – *and Emily knew she mustn't let the one weaken her resolve of the other.*

And then there was her daughter…

***

DESERTED AIRSTRIP - KENDAL, CUMBRIA
WEDNESDAY 5.00P.M.

Ethan brought the Cessna into a slow, smooth and easy descent before he skilfully landed the light aircraft on the desolate airstrip. Desolate that was apart from the pre-arranged pick-up. Once down he was more than grateful, and unusually, crossed himself as the plane slowly ground to a halt and he'd killed the engine. It hadn't been an easy flight even by his standards – it was always a challenge, but this time he'd experienced a seriously hazardous crossing. With a fast ice build up on the wings at several points it had necessitated a drop in altitude to search for some warmer air to dissolve it. Ethan had really thought that this time he was on for a fast short trip downwards.

Now though it was time to shrug all that off and just forget about it, dwelling on the negative was something he simply didn't do. There had been a couple of dodgy hours back there and now it was over, it was on to getting this job done and a damned good kip when the last lot of Provigil wore off. Well – after a large Vindaloo and a couple of beers anyway.

He zipped the package into his overnight bag, swung himself out onto the steps and jumped to the ground. The private car sat waiting. Ethan walked across, opened the door and slung his holdall onto the back seat before he slid in beside it. The deep sprung quality and soft leather felt exceptionally good – *time to relax and let someone else do the driving...*

He was asleep in minutes.

THIRTY-THREE

Jason crept stealthily through the gap in the hedge and made his way round to the back of the stables. His head was all over the place now and not with his voices. *It has to be here somewhere, it just has to be!* He repeated it over and over to himself, prayed he'd find it without too much trouble. There was only one Morgan on the drive which meant it likely Charlotte and Miles were either out together for the evening and could return at any moment, or one of them was still on the premises – time was of the essence.

He pulled back the heavy bolt as quietly as possible, opened the top, then bottom door and pulled them both open. His torch was flicked to low beam as he went inside and lit up the stable with a soft glow. It was still the same. The smells, the hay, everything was still there apart from the horses. The memory of what happened a few weeks ago suddenly hit him, what he did – *what the voices made him do.* His face flushed with shame as he stood there, head slung low, and looked up under his fringe at the empty stalls. He hadn't realised the effect his return would have on him.

Jason swung the beam slowly across the floor and

started to randomly kick at the hay. It was thick though and not a small area to sift through as it had been used as a double stable. He dropped to his knees and started to make a more detailed search through the dense covering, looking methodically now as he went across the top from left to right and worked his way down to the centre – *still nothing*.

"Is *this* what you're looking for?" He spun round with a gasp of surprise. Charlotte stood above him, back leant against the door frame, arm up as she watched the silver bracelet swing backwards and forwards from the forefinger and thumb of her left hand. Jason was too shocked to notice what she had in her right.

Overwhelming panic set in then and violent nausea threatened to deliver more than a wave. He tried to lift himself out of the hay to stand up, but his legs simply refused to support him. She advanced quickly, made use of the moment as he scrabbled like an upturned crab, his hands and feet kicked out, pushed away from her till he could go no further, until his back was quite literally up against the wall.

Then after the lunge, he felt a deep searing pain punched into his left side under his ribs, and the diamorphine began to render all the muscles in his body totally flaccid – *the roof, the walls all swirled and swam into the dark together – till they joined him on the floor...*

Charlotte thanked her lucky stars the Flood boy was a lightweight – short, slender and not too muscular at all. Even then he wasn't easy to get into the sacks she had waiting outside, or to drag round the back of the stables to the waiting car in the lane. It'd been quite a job to heave the body across uneven ground through the gap in the hedge and hoist it into the boot. *Thank God the Morgan's a low rider* she thought; *it would've been a real problem with the Range Rover. Appreciation is needed here though,* she reminded herself, *he's actually made my job a lot easier – saved me considerable time him returning to the murder scene of my darling horses. Well – now their deaths have been avenged and two jobs neatly tied up this evening. Yes, very convenient his turning up tonight – fitted in nicely with a little car mechanics that needed attention…*

Once the body and boot were secured, Charlotte slumped into the driver's seat with the exertion of it all and turned the ignition. The Roadster purred into life as she stuck a cigarette into the lighter, waited a few seconds for it to 'pop', lit up and dragged the nicotine down nice and deep. Then the Morgan pulled quietly out of the lane to take the route out towards Hill Road and St. Peter's Church.

Gina was in bits. A phone call had come from the nursing home late that afternoon to say her grandmother's heart had become a great deal weaker and could she come in that evening to see her as they didn't think it would be long. Now they were back home it was all Andrew could do to comfort his girlfriend at all. He felt helpless, she'd been so devoted to the old lady, who after all's said and done, had been a mother to her for the best part of eighteen years.

They'd arrived at Kirkby Nursing Home at about 8.00p.m. Gina had sat next to Margaret Rowland's bed with her cheek resting on the old lady's hand and an arm across her waist. Tears rolled down her cheeks whilst Andrew had sat alongside, his arm around her shoulders. She couldn't believe how quickly the end had come given the fact her grandmother had seemed quite well the last time she'd visited, although Andrew had reminded her the staff had warned on several occasions she could suddenly take a turn for the worst. Gina had to console herself with at least having been able to spend a couple of hours with the wonderful lady before she passed, a lady who as far as she was concerned had been a mother to her all her life. What was strange though, Margaret Rowlands had managed to briefly stroke her granddaughter's hair one last time, but called her Emily before her hand had fallen back onto the bed. Gina had sat up sharply then but through her tears could see it was too late for a chance to ask why…

Andrew felt it would be something his girlfriend would want to find out about in the coming days and weeks, but for now they just both lay snuggled up on the sofa with a couple of strong whisky coffees, and he held her close whilst she wept.

So many people lost in the last few weeks, he'd never known anything like it, *all* their lives had been turned upside down – *and there was still a killer out there.* Andrew reached for his drink and warmed his hands on the mug. *Something has to give* he thought as he stared across the room, *something's about to happen and it's going to be soon – I can feel it.* Gina had now fallen asleep – as he put the mug back on the table and took care not to wake her – *he felt a sudden chill cut straight across the back of his neck.*

Ethan James shut the cab door and paid the driver. He looked up at the luxury white brick hotel, shook his head slowly and smiled; *"Just like you Em – only the best!"* He took the steps two at a time and pushed at the spotless glass door, walked through to reception and booked in.

The nap on the way had paid dividends; at least he wasn't completely feeling like death warmed up. *Tomorrow though would probably be an almighty sleep fest.* Once in his room he texted Emily, threw his holdall on the bed and walked through to the bathroom. Definitely time for a shower, change and a few other necessary ablutions…

Almost immediately the reply came through:-

'8.00 p.m. is fine – don't be late'

Short and sweet he thought with an eyebrow raised. He glanced at the holdall on the bed. For some reason, although he'd wanted to, Ethan hadn't checked to see what it was she'd got him to bring over. With his concentration needed on flying it had been fairly easy to ignore on the trip, now though curiosity had got the better of him. He walked back out of the bathroom, phone in hand. As he ran the zip backwards and lifted out the package, breath held and hand poised – his phone bleeped again.

'DON'T EVEN THINK ABOUT IT…'

He released the breath and placed it back in the bag. *You always were a bit of a witch Mrs. Stone…*

Emily heard the knock at exactly 8.00p.m. and went to answer it. Ethan stood there, holdall in one hand, bottle of wine held high in the other. He gestured to the bag with the bottle;

"Just so you know I've not touched it – thought you'd like to chill out a little." Emily gave him a half-smile and stood back as he walked in. She went to get two glasses and set them on the table. Her room had more than a regular mini-bar, large lounge area and sofas – it implied she was doing very well indeed. Still, he thought, the odd undercover diamond job didn't exactly keep him penniless…

He handed over the package. Emily took it into the bathroom and locked the door. She opened the sealed box and unwrapped the 9mm Luger she'd packed in her Manhattan office the previous week, the box of cartridges sat neatly alongside. *All good*, she thought as she took a deep breath – *all good*. She packed both back up, tucked them inside the vanity unit cupboard and walked back into the bedroom.

They finished the wine and then without ceremony, Emily got up and pretty much kicked him out. From Ethan's point of view he knew he could do with hitting the sack so wasn't really bothered, from Emily's point of view, he'd paid his dues. It was time to start the next phase – *and to work out how she was going to handle Jenny.*

The following morning, although Andrew had suggested she rest at home after her loss, Gina still decided to go into work. She didn't want to sit around the flat and mope on her own, and Andrew had already said he really needed to get into the *Courier*. Jenny had got so absent-minded he was having to check half her work as well as doing his own, and he really needed to know what was going on with her. Gina told him she wanted to see Molly anyway, and would pop over to the Carpenters at lunchtime where they could all meet up as usual.

Andrew *really* hadn't wanted to leave her, but with Jenny behaving the way she was and not giving any real explanation as to why – *an affair with Miles just wasn't cutting it as far as he was concerned* – he didn't really have much choice. Gina had insisted she'd be fine and they'd arranged to meet for lunch so he wasn't unduly worried, but he would still much rather have taken her somewhere nice for the day, just the two of them.

As he drove out of the flat car park, he remembered Jenny had seemed really scared when they'd spoken about the Suzy Sarrandaire (Danielle Mogg), murder. At the time she'd managed to persuade him it was something else, but now he wondered if that was a straight-up lie.

Andrew approached the crossroads at St. Peter's Church and braked to let someone go past before he carried on down the steep, aptly named *Hill Road*. As he drove he began to break again, harder as it descended more steeply halfway, then – *nothing!* He pumped the brake pedal *again* – *nothing!* The car quickly gained speed and the tight Z-bend came up! He panicked now, graffiti was one thing – to cut his brakes quite another! Pedestrians on the nearside were open-mouthed, some jumped into property gardens to get out of the way, others flattened themselves against walls, and some dove straight over them. Andrew knew what had to be done to avoid killing someone, including himself, and yanked the steering wheel down hard right – it sent the car speeding across the grassy hill slope that ran down the driver's side of the road – *towards the lake*. He undid his seat belt in readiness, and pressed his window button so it dropped down fully open… *then eyes skyward – he let fate do the rest.*

As he hit it nose on, gallons of muddy lake water soon gushed through the opening and the car began to fill quickly, cold, dark and stinking. He just prayed it would work. Before it was above his head Andrew took a deep breath, brought his feet onto the seat, closed his eyes and pushed his way out through the open window into the lake. Arms pointed upwards like an arrow, he used his legs to kick himself up and away – his intended coffin sank quickly, deep into the murky depths. He knew he just had to keep going, just one stroke at a time and swim as effectively as he could till he reached the top, even though his clothes weighed him down, hampered every arm movement, every leg thrust.

Suddenly his upper body hit something! In the dark, cold and wet, blind to his direction, he thought at first he'd been barged by some large floating vegetation. His brain raced… *which way?! Which **way?!*** He couldn't open his eyes and it would be pointless anyway. Lungs desperate for air now, and not sure how far he had to go to the surface, Andrew lunged out as hard as he could with his arms, *thank God! Thank God it moved!*

He sensed the water pressure was a little less now and there was a muddy brightness outside his closed lids. Before he knew it, in one huge whoosh his head broke the water, his body rose up; he gave a guttural gasp for air and then splashed back down! For a few moments he just trod water and breathed slowly, evenly – in and out, to calm his mind, regain some clarity. Once he felt his head was clear, Andrew stared straight at the shore, fixed his eyes on a single point and began a steady crawl purposefully back to land.

There was quite a crowd waiting for him including an ambulance, and there had been no mistaking the clapping, whistles and shouts of; *"Hooray! Yessss!!! He's made it! He's okay!"* as one stroke at a time he swam methodically back to land. Right then he felt forever grateful his parents had made him attend weekly swimming lessons as a boy – *that was a definite.* People ran down to the water's edge to help him up now as he fell onto the shore exhausted and thankful… but he also realised that without any doubt at all – *he was a marked man.*

As he shivered in a recovery blanket, Andrew only half heard the buzz of voices around him. He stared out of the ambulance window to the lake as a mug of hot tea was pressed into his hands whilst both his blood pressure and heart were being monitored, but he barely noticed the activity.

That was no vegetation out there, it had moved far too easily. With everything that had been going on in his town lately it was likely to mean only one thing… *another body.*

THIRTY-FOUR

Harry stood on the shore with a couple of officers and watched the divers go in. When the call had come through about young Gale's accident and what he thought was out in that lake, he felt sure it wouldn't be long before the police surgeon, forensics and erection of an examination tent were in place – and unless there were *two* nutters running around this *'quiet'* Cumbrian town, felt pretty certain it wouldn't be a woman's body that was brought up. If – after his flat break-in and psychic friend's attempted murder, Andrew's suspicion of his brakes being cut was correct, then it was the same perpetrator; *but* the M.O. was completely different from the murders of all the *women*. That was of course assuming it didn't turn out to be a bundle of rags someone couldn't be arsed to run down to the recycling centre.

When a diver's hand went up to signal a find, he motioned one of the sergeants to go down to meet them. Two rubber-suited officers flanked the sides of the long tightly-bound object, swam it in to shore and hauled it onto the bank. From their exertions it was pretty obvious to Harry what they'd brought up was nothing any waste depot would accept. Their safety line was now untied, headgear pulled off, and bodysuits removed as they acknowledged the sergeant who'd arrived to take over. He'd already donned a pair of disposable gloves in readiness, and Harry walked down to see his officer cut the ropes around the large package, pull up the top bag and reveal its contents.

"We have a crime scene sir."

Jenny Flood looked jaded as she walked across the marble mosaics of the hotel reception to the lifts and pressed the call button. It had been a long time since she'd seen Emily Stone apart from the odd few minutes on 'FaceTime' and 'Skype'. Initially she'd begun to wonder how she could've even got sucked into this crazy scheme of hers – just because a man they'd both been involved with had hurt them both badly and made a choice neither of them had wanted. It had all begun three years ago when they'd met up at a publishing conference in Carlisle and discovered a common bond – Miles. It had taken the intervening time to persuade her, and now it had all begun to seem rather lame – especially as *she'd* fallen back in love with him, but now… she shuddered. Her life could never, *would* never be the same again after what she'd seen, what she couldn't wipe out of her head. What was worse, she couldn't even *tell* Miles, couldn't tell *anyone* or Jason would suffer at her hands, *Charlotte's sick, evil, blood-red murderous hands.*

And then there was the fact her brother hadn't even come home last night...

Yes, initially she'd wondered about Emily's crazy scheme, *now* though Jenny was scared and just wished someone could make Charlotte Peterson disappear – *for good.*

The lift arrived, people got out and she got in. It remained empty for the journey for which she was grateful – she didn't feel like smiling, not since that night – the nightmares just kept coming...

The bell tinged its announcement to Emily's floor and she took a deep breath and walked out into the corridor. What exactly that woman had in mind to discuss she hadn't a clue, she didn't really care anymore, all she knew was she wanted out of this crazy arrangement, whatever *'this'* was. Her sanity couldn't take much more, *and that was what she'd come to tell her.*

"Jenny! Hi!" Emily hugged her warmly; "Come in, come in I'll get you a coffee, *sit – sit."* Emily waved her hand in the vague direction of the sofas. She poured two espressos whilst her eyes darted over at the younger woman sat nervously on the sofa fiddling with the strap of her handbag. She looked like she needed a week's worth of fast food and a few large cakes – *and that was just for starters...*

"I hope you don't mind me saying Jen but... you look... really *terrible..."* Jenny stared open-mouthed in utter disbelief at the beautifully dressed, poised and confident woman who stood in front of her and held out her coffee. She had clearly forgotten that Jenny had not long witnessed the gruesome murder of an old friend, by the wife of the man they'd *both* had a relationship with, the wife that Emily had told her she'd planned for the last God knows how many years to send completely over the edge and into a long-term psychiatric unit – *at the very least*. Her brother had been threatened, she'd been blackmailed over his liberty, and her new job had suffered badly under the stress of it all – let alone her own mental and emotional health.

Jenny took the coffee, placed it on the table and fished a small hip flask out of her handbag. She unscrewed the lid and Emily watched as she poured a generous slug of brandy into her cup, stirred, and took a large gulp, shuddering slightly as it went down. *This was a new habit.*

Emily sat down slowly on the opposite sofa, placed her coffee on the table and stirred too, omitting the brandy... Well – she'd been right about one thing – Jenny Flood was going to be a complete liability. *Plan B it was then.*

Just then Jenny's mobile rang and she saw Andrew's name flash up. *Damn* that man! He was *always* on her back. She swiped right and answered the call. Crossed legged and relaxed into the sofa, Emily sipped her coffee and waited. When Jenny's face began to look even paler than when she'd walked in, she slowly replaced the espresso on the table and sat forward in readiness for what was clearly about to be bad news.

"Andrew what are you *saying!*" shrieked Jenny desperately, *"he's been pulled out of the... the **lake??!!** Where? Why? **How?!!** What do you mean? Is he **okay?!** Are **you** okay?"* This was definitely not sounding good thought Emily. Jenny pulled a notebook and pen from her bag and started to scribble.

"Yes, yes I'll come over, I'll come now, about twenty minutes I think, yes – bye – yeah got that, right, okay bye…"

She looked as sick as a dog by this point and Emily stood up in anticipation she would dive straight across the room to the en-suite then need help to hold her hair back. Instead though, she just sat in shock and stared at her phone. Emily couldn't stand it any longer…

"Well?? What the hell's going on??"

"It's… my brother… it's… it's Jason. Andrew said he's just been pulled out of… the *lake* – near St. Peter's." Hands clenched around her phone, Jenny bit her bottom lip and now stared hard at Emily. There's been an accident… with Andrew's car, I don't know the details." She snatched up her bag then and stood up abruptly.

"I have to go, right now, he wants me to drive over to his place and pick him up. He won't tell me anything on the phone." She walked to the door in a daze, then stopped and turned round.

"I don't understand why Jason would be with him though, *it doesn't make any sense.*" Emily juggled a few thoughts, *if he couldn't say what had happened to Jason that sounded bad – really bad, especially as Andrew was obviously well enough to be at home. Nobody delivers serious news over the phone.* She went up to her, gave her a long hug and a kiss on the cheek.

"Take care Jen, I hope it's not bad news but I think you should be prepared – if you need me just call." Jenny smiled weakly and nodded.

As she left she was relieved that at least one problem she felt had suffocated her for the last few weeks was now over, and without the need to actually say she wanted out. There was something about Emily that was just too full on for Jenny – she wasn't entirely sure how far she'd go, and although she wanted Charlotte dealt with – she didn't want any part of how. Now though, the only thing that was uppermost in her mind was her brother and whether he was alive or dead. The very thought it could be the latter was unbearable, but if he was… *then Charlotte would no longer have a hold over her.*

As she turned out of the hotel car park, Jenny Flood felt her entire world turn inside out all over again. How she'd coped this far was a complete mystery to her – no normal person experienced the things she'd gone through in the last few weeks. If Jason *was… beyond help…* her eyes began to fill – what had she left in her life? Her parents were dead, she had few friends, her love life was a mess and her latest job position massively beneath her journalistic capabilities. Tears streamed down her face, she felt utterly desperate as she wiped them away and drove through town past the lake and up Hill Road towards Andrew's.

Jenny turned briefly to look out over the water as she passed… in her heart of hearts she knew what news was waiting for her, she could feel the very weight of it cave in – *cave in and crush her very soul.*

Andrew opened the door as soon as Jenny rang the bell. He'd kept a lookout for her from the lounge window since they'd spoken and dreaded having to tell her what he knew he couldn't over the phone. Harry Longbridge had already rung him to confirm it was definitely a body they'd pulled out of the lake, believed to be that of Jason Flood, but would need a formal identification and had arranged to come over and take his statement. It was going to make for a difficult session all round. The minute he drew back the door and Jenny saw his face she knew she'd never see her brother's again… *Andrew caught her as she fell.*

He swung her limp body up into his arms, carried her through to the lounge, and laid her on the sofa whilst he went to make some sweet milky tea.

Missy cat seemed to sense there was something very, very wrong. Instead of doing a dance round the new visitor as usual, she sat quietly, head low on her paws, and watched through the doorway from the safety of Andrew's bed.

By the time he'd returned, Jenny had started to stir and was then suddenly awake. She sat up and remembered in a rush the assumption she'd made on her arrival and turned to look in blind hope at Andrew, but found no reassurance in his expression, no change to what she'd already guessed. Jenny began to sob uncontrollably now as he placed the mugs on the table and sat down beside her.

"I'm so sorry Jen, this whole business – it's – hell. I just don't know what to say or do to help you." He put his arms around her and gently kissed the side of her forehead, he truly didn't know how to comfort her and prayed Harry wouldn't be long with an accompanying WPC.

"How?" croaked Jenny, weak between racked sobs as her shoulders shook and head lay heavy against his chest. This was the bit Andrew had been dreading, it would be harder to explain Jason's demise to his sister than it had been swimming out of that car and back to shore… well… *almost* anyway…

"Jen –" At that moment the doorbell went for the second time. Andrew eased himself off the sofa and handed her a mug.

"Drink this – it'll do you good." He glanced out of the window and went to the door to let Harry Longbridge and Suzanne Moorcroft in as he quietly thanked the universe for their well-timed arrival. All three returned to the living room before Andrew went back out to the kitchen to make more tea. *Strange how even the hardiest of coffee drinkers turned to tea in a crisis* he thought randomly, then felt really bad for juggling mental trivia…

Harry sat himself down opposite Jenny, and with Suzanne Moorcroft now next to her on the sofa, he took in her obvious distress, and began to carefully ask her how much she knew about what had happened to her brother. She answered that Andrew hadn't actually *told* her anything yet, but had implied there'd been an accident at the lake and that he was dead. They had arrived just as he was about to explain more.

"Miss Flood…" began Harry gently, "I'm dreadfully sorry to have to tell you – but we have strong evidence to believe your brother was murdered, probably in the last twenty-four to forty-eight hours." At this revelation, Jenny would've passed out again if it hadn't been for the fact she felt like she was about to throw up – *amazingly she didn't.*

"*Charlotte!*" she said nodding her head slowly, "*Charlotte Peterson!*"

"Are you referring to *Doctor* Charlotte Peterson Miss Flood?" asked Harry. He looked over at his WPC.

"I need to make a statement – *and you better have a bloody big notebook and several pens.*" Jenny replied stonily.

THIRTY-FIVE

By the time Jenny had finished her story of how she'd witnessed Susie Sarrandaire's murder and why she hadn't reported it, *for which she was now obviously hugely remorseful, including for her own judicial situation,* several pages of rough notes and pens were indeed filled out and used. Listening to her falteringly describe the details of her old schoolfriend's murder at the hands of their GP, especially the gruesome method used, also brought back painful memories for Andrew of how he found Rachel. Jenny's account also bore out PC Joe Walker's inspirational flash at Josie Kinkade's autopsy, that maybe some kind of large ice stake had been used after the chloroform had done its job. Her testimony confirmed that this was in fact the case – *with the aid of a mallet…*

Harry made a couple of phone calls to get operational events moving and then drove them both to the hospital to identify the body whilst Suzanne took the area car back to the station. Finally he had his man, *or in this case woman,* but even with almost thirty years in the job he'd never experienced anything like it. He prayed he never would again.

Outside the morgue viewing room Jenny really did feel the nausea rise. She'd barely eaten since the previous night so was also feeling physically weak now and Andrew had to pretty much hold her up. When the morgue attendant asked if she was ready she wanted to yell; "*Noooo! Of course I'm not bloody ready – how the hell could I ever be ready? He's my* **brother***! He's only 22 for Chrissake!*" Instead Jenny just nodded quickly and dropped her gaze to the floor. The sheet was removed to the shoulders.

"Jenny?" Andrew squeezed her elbow very gently, turned round and nodded affirmatively to Harry. She took as long as she dared to look up from the floor, eyes still closed. When she finally opened them – *the room blacked out.*

Back at the station there were official statements to be taken from them both. Andrew had managed to get her to eat half a cheese sandwich and some coffee, neither terribly appetising as they were both from the station canteen and it was halfway through the afternoon, but better than nothing. Then Harry brought out a number of clear bags that contained Jason's belongings, all individually marked up as exhibits for evidence purposes – *Jenny could smell the lake even through the plastic.*

"Do you recognise these items as having belonged to your brother Miss Flood?" She just looked them over briefly at first and nodded flatly.

"Could you look a little closer, just to make sure? If you possibly can… just so you can state you don't think anything's missing from the last time you saw him, to the best of your knowledge of course." They were all set out on the table in a line – all his precious things: his black lightening shirt, his purple jeans, his silver double dragon necklaces, his gothic bracelets…

"Yes – they're all there as far as I can s… *no – wait –*" She went back along the line of bracelet bags – one was missing – the one she'd given him for his eighteenth. His JF silver fastening black Gothic bracelet that shared their initials – *it wasn't there.*

"It's missing – his special initial bracelet I gave him, he always wore it with the others, *always*, but it's not there! *What does that mean?*"

"Well, given that you feel all the rest *are* – it looks like either the culprit took it for a memento, or found or obtained it beforehand somehow, and simply forgot or had no time to put it back on his wrist before placing his… *him…* in the bags…" He tailed off. Harry really felt for this young girl, to hear these descriptions of her brother must be absolutely agonising. However, he had to continue; "Although it seems likely, at this moment in time, we still don't know for certain that Dr. Peterson is also responsible for *his* death."

"*Oh it's her alright,*" said Jenny as she looked Longbridge straight in the eye; "*I'd stake my **own** life on it.*"

Miles woke up with a jump from a rare afternoon nap on a day off. *Where on earth was all that banging coming from? And who the hell was shouting like the world had come to an end?* The front door sounded as if it was about to be caved in and with the local football supporters behind it. He jumped off the couch and started up the hall. Through the side window he could see half the town's police cars had gouged skid marks all over his spacious gravel drive.

"Okay! Hold on for God's sake!" Once unlocked, an influx of Cumbria Constabulary – *two of which now had him pinned him up against the wall* – had Miles doing a three-point head turn and air gasping like a heron stuck Carp. The rest of their colleagues poured ant-like all over the ground floor.

"Where's your wife Doctor Peterson – where is Doctor Charlotte Peterson?" demanded one officer. The stairs started to reverberate with size 12s then, as they thundered up and down and charged all around the bedrooms. He felt a twinge of guilt, but at that moment all Miles could think was *thank fuck* it wasn't him they wanted. The whole mass murder thing that had started off with Rachel had taken its toll. He'd spent the last month or so keeping a very low profile – well as low as any bloke with his particular needs *could* anyway… *What the hell did they want with Charlotte though?*

"She – she's at work why? I don't underst.." He was 'taken off the wall', marched into the lounge and 'put' firmly onto the couch.

"Stay there!" A younger officer was assigned guard duty to make sure he did, and Miles now felt distinctly uneasy. This looked serious. He didn't know what Charlotte had done, but this was more than a tad overkill for a driving offence.

"Look – all… *this*;" he gestured the craziness of what was happening in his house with open arms to the young officer as he stood up. "I *really* need to use the bathroom." Joe Walker wasn't about to get done for this one – he inclined his head sharply towards the lounge door and followed him upstairs to the toilet. He checked the window size and drop to the ground then exited and waited on the landing.

Once inside, Miles did what he had to do for noise authenticity with one hand, then fished his phone out of his back pocket and turned it to silent before texting Charlotte with the other. He just hoped she would pick it up.

I DON'T KNOW WHAT YOU'VE DONE
BUT THE POLICE ARE ON THEIR WAY
TO ARREST YOU – I SUGGEST YOU
GET OUT – NOW!

He flushed the toilet, washed his hands and came out of the bathroom.

Charlotte felt the vibration of the text through her trouser pocket. Her elderly patient couldn't understand why after she'd only just sat down her doctor had now left the room. Charlotte had mumbled something and disappeared into the kitchen behind her office through a door not visible from the main room area. She had, *understandably*, been nervy and jumpy for weeks, and checked every notification on her phone pretty smartly.

She took the mobile out of her pocket and read Miles' message. Her stomach screwed down tight. She wasn't really surprised though, her anger and emotions had lost her the only power she'd held when she sent the Flood boy to his maker. Obviously that sister of his had spilled the news of her latest 'despatch'… *and now it seemed Charlotte had to think very fast.*

She opened the surgical cabinet, took a six-inch retractable scalpel, slipped it into her trouser pocket and went back into the consulting room. She apologised to her patient, blamed a feigned stomach bug and explained quickly that another doctor would see her shortly if she waited in reception. The confused woman then got shuffled out of the door and sent back down the hall as Charlotte checked her bag for the keys she'd need later. She then phoned through to Gina to come to her office…

Everyone had been so lovely about her Gran and told Gina she should go home, even Miles had left off throwing his 'appreciative looks' in her direction that morning and kindly suggested she took some time off work. Everyone that was except for Charlotte – who'd barely spoken to her in the last week at all anyway, and Gina still couldn't figure out why. Now she'd asked her to go in to see her. To say she was worried was an understatement.

It was an anxious walk up the corridor – *why had she been summoned, and even more strangely, why had Charlotte asked that she brought her car keys? Maybe she needed an errand run*, she thought, although it had never happened before. A knock on the consulting room door brought no response and she walked in to find it empty.

"I'm in the kitchen Gina," called out Charlotte, *"come on through."* Gina walked round to the inset door into what appeared to be an empty kitchen too. Her suspicious instinct hit only a flash of a second before she felt the blade's tip in her lower back. Then Charlotte's left arm was quickly and firmly around her waist guiding her towards the exit door to the car park.

"Move – and do it naturally, *we're going for a little drive* – in *your* car." Charlotte opened the back door and moved Gina through it having first checked the rear car park was reasonably quiet. The terrified girl moved unsteadily towards her red Fiesta as the blood drained from her face, her stomach leapt into her mouth and her legs surprisingly still moved forwards despite her entire body now flooded with adrenalin.

"Wh – why are you doing this?" she stammered, shocked beyond any normal understanding of what could be happening to her, what *was* happening to her.

"Shut it and keep walking!" spat Charlotte, quickly followed by a bright smile and nod to acknowledge a patient on their way to the front entrance.

"Poorly receptionist – just taking her home, bless her," she called out as she kept moving Gina forward.

The gentleman waved and went on into the surgery. They reached Gina's car where the young girl fumbled in fear and almost dropped her keys before she managed to press the remote and unlock the door.

"Get in and stay absolutely still!" hissed Charlotte as she took the keys off her, walked round to the other side, opened the door and sat in the passenger seat. She handed the keys back to Gina.

"Now *drive* and go *exactly* where I tell you to, don't even *think* about any clever tactics that boyfriend of yours may have taught you." Somehow, she wasn't sure how, Gina managed to start the car, put it into gear, pull away from the parking space and out into the road…

Molly was in town for some retail therapy before her second shift and meeting the others in the bar. She'd ordered some gorgeous jeans online and didn't want to wait for them to be delivered so had popped down to the company's high street store to pick them up. When she saw her friend's red Fiesta being driven in completely the opposite direction to the Carpenters, away from the town altogether and on the road for the boating arena, she was really puzzled. Gina had rung that morning to say she and Andrew would be in for a late lunch – so why was she now headed out towards the arena? What *really* surprised Molly was that it looked like Charlotte Peterson was in the car too! She stood open-mouthed as she watched the tail lights of the Fiesta disappear and then immediately rung Andrew.

Her second shock of the day had her in rapid search of a bench to collapse on. Andrew hadn't been in touch with anyone apart from Jenny and the police since he'd left for work. Molly now tried to come to terms with everything he was saying, plus the fact her best friend, his partner, was in the clutches of a dangerous killer. She started to stammer... *a lot.*

"B – b – but sh – sh – she's... *got her!*" shrieked Molly hysterically, not caring who heard or saw her as she sat looking one way then the next, standing up then sitting down, then standing up again as she started to walk in the direction of the arena.

Andrew felt sick. He was still at the station and about to ring Gina himself. He knew the police were on their way and was under the impression Charlotte had no idea about that, so thought Gina was relatively safe. Somehow that crazy bitch Doctor had been tipped off and now his girlfriend was in terrible danger. He told Molly to go straight back to the pub and stay there. He'd be in touch later – and would *definitely* be bringing their girl home.

When Harry heard his operation had been completely cocked up he was absolutely livid. *If this is down to the Walker boy I'll have his balls pruned, dried and glazed for the marbles team...* it was time he got back out on the ground...

As Gina turned into the car park of the boating arena, Charlotte began to quickly scan available places nearest to the moorings. Spotting one she directed her into a space fairly close to where Miles' powerboat bobbed gently on the water. His larger and more powerful vessel, *'Babe Of The Bay'*, was anchored way outside of the harbour since he'd spent some 'R&R' time aboard the previous weekend. Charlotte loved the boat but had always hated its name and thought it a stupid risk to leave her out and unattended – *but that was men for you*. Now though she needed to get to the *'Babe'* and use it to take her to the other side of the lake.

She ordered Gina out of the car – just the threat of knowing she had a blade seemed enough to keep her compliant. The girl walked ahead of her down to the waterside where Charlotte gave instructions on how to deal with the boat's dock lines, then manoeuvred her into it. Somehow she'd have to get this kid to drive a powerboat out to the *'Babe'* without killing them both – *she needed this one to barter with*. Unbeknown to Charlotte though, Gina had actually spent quite a lot of time on the water in the past, even had a few lessons thanks to a previous boyfriend's love of all things nautical. She hadn't forgotten. Despite her obvious fear, with guidance, she managed to start the boat, get it out of its bay and headed towards the larger boat anchored in the distance, all without too much trouble. Her captor was guardedly impressed.

"Don't worry – I'm not going to hurt you," said Charlotte, as Gina brought the powerboat safely alongside *'Babe of the Bay'*. "Well – *as long as you do exactly as I say.*" She gestured with the scalpel to throw the line over the larger vessel's railings – Gina managed it on the second attempt. Once pulled in, line secured and with Gina on deck, Charlotte ordered her down to the bow and boarded herself.

"*What happens now?*" Gina shouted, as she leant on the railings not daring to move. A strong breeze had whipped up on the way out and her voice sounded a little lost on its tail.

"*Never you mind – just pray nothing goes wrong from here on in,*" Charlotte called back from the cabin. "*Now get back up here, shut up and sit down!*" Gina dutifully complied, but on the way back up the deck heard a familiar sound. She looked across the water to see harbour patrol powering across the lake but knew their rapid approach could mean this may not end well for her at all. One glance at Charlotte confirmed her thoughts as the two women stood facing each other – and she was the one without a knife…

THIRTY-SIX

Charlotte had come out of the cabin to see why Gina had stopped walking up the deck. The expression on the girl's face caused a brief glance behind her that summed up a rapid change in the situation. Harbour police were coming up fast, there was no time to faff about, she needed to act – *and act now.* She'd been having trouble starting *'The Babe'* and couldn't figure out why – the fuel gauge was correct, the keys were correct, but there was no turnover. Now the two women stood opposite each other on deck and Charlotte had only one choice.

The scalpel was in her right hand and blade slid ready. Gina swallowed hard, eyes wide in abject horror as Charlotte advanced.

"You're going over," she said flatly, "sorry – but I don't have any options here."

"But I can't swim!" screamed Gina as she backed up the deck towards the bow again, *"I'll drown!"*

"Not my problem sweety – *now jump!"* ordered Charlotte and lunged forward waving the scalpel close to her face. With her back against the railings and head turned to the water below – Gina suddenly found her strength, swung round and gave a surprised Charlotte an almighty shove before she fled to the other side of the deck. After she'd recovered from the floor, Charlotte sighed impatiently, irritated at the obvious futility of the girl's 'escape' and ran after her.

The harbour police were in plain view – there was no time to play cat and mouse – this had to happen *now*. *'The Babe'* wasn't a huge boat and Gina really had nowhere to go. With a quick reverse turn Charlotte met her portside as she ran towards her, grabbed at her flying hair and forced her back onto the railings. With a vicious swipe of the knife to her arm and immobilised by the flesh wound, Gina dropped in shock and Charlotte heaved her through the gap in the bars. She hit the lake hard and began to sink fast. Everything turned black, she'd swallowed water, she was in pain, her ears rushed and sheer blind panic grabbed her by the throat – *and held on fast.*

Charlotte knew she'd just lost her only bargaining tool but it couldn't be helped. They would have stormed the boat or taken a potshot at her if she'd held the girl hostage on deck – it would've been useless. She figured now the boys in blue would have to spend their time rescuing Gina and leave her till later. Now though she needed to get back into the working powerboat, pray there was enough fuel to reach the other side of the lake and make further plans when she got there.

She untied the docking line, threw it into the smaller vessel and jumped aboard. Once at the wheel she got the engine started and roared the smaller boat away from *'The Babe Of The Bay'* – *and as her hair fluttered wildly in the wind, realised she'd probably never see her little bit of luxury ever again.*

Finally out of nowhere self-preservation must've kicked in. Although she'd told Charlotte she couldn't swim, Gina *did* actually have a basic ability but was not a strong swimmer by any means. An image of Andrew floated across her mind together with a distant roaring sound. She began to thrash out with her legs and pull herself upwards – somehow through sheer determination, *or desperation*, she reached the surface coughing and spluttering to find several rescue divers close by to help. The relief was overwhelming, she'd never been so grateful to see anyone in her entire life as they 'swam' her to the patrol boat. But her arm was pouring heavily with blood, her vision was blurred and she felt as weak as a kitten. Now only vaguely aware of pulling, tugging and chest pressure – *she slipped quickly into unconsciousness.*

As Charlotte docked at the lone station across the other side of the lake, she actually had something to thank her philandering husband for. He must have literally re-fuelled a few days ago as she had made it with diesel to spare… *and the little cottage still sat on the shore.*

Once the boat was secure she made her way down the wooden boardwalk and up the bank to the old stone building. It still stood firm between the forest that lay behind and the water's edge in front. It had, many years ago, been a very special place to them – *and not so to others.*

As she pushed at the door of the disused building it opened easily. With a quick glance around, she slipped quietly inside and closed it behind her. Although completely deserted now, and with no lighting or heating, nothing much had changed. She could remember it… all of it… could even 'hear' the conversations as memories began to taunt her… *Suddenly her mobile sprang into life.* She swiped but didn't speak.

"Charlotte?" *She didn't recognise the voice or the number.*

"Who *is* this?"

"Don't you recognise your greatest triumph Charlotte? The girl you blackmailed into leaving her home, her family her friends? The girl *whose mother you threatened to dispose of if I didn't comply and disappear for good?*"

She ran anxiously to a dirty window lakeside, half expecting her to be lurking in the grounds somewhere. Charlotte couldn't believe it *was* her, but nobody else knew what had happened back then – *only Miles.*

"Where *are* you Emily…?"

"Well that would be telling now wouldn't it – but we *do* have to meet Charlotte. My mother is dead, you have no hold over me now and there's something you need to know."

"Just tell me what it is Emily and be done with it!" said Charlotte sharply, as she walked quickly through to each of the back rooms now and checked the windows overlooking the forest.

"No – I want to see your face when I tell you – it's *that* important. I'll drive out to you. Just give me the address."

Charlotte hesitated, but only for a minute. It was a gamble, but she needed a car – *and Emily had one.*

"Do you remember the old keeper's cottage at the base of Kirkby Pike?"

"Of *course* I do Charlie," said Emily, *unaware she'd slipped back to her teenage nickname,* "it's the last place we met… *half an hour then."* The line went dead.

Emily Stone dropped the mobile back into her jacket pocket and picked up the gun. Charlotte maybe dangerously psychotic, but Emily had become the stronger of the two. Cool-headed, confident and with a twenty year grudge… *she was about to execute her past.*

Harry Longbridge drove under the willow tree that graced the entrance of the Petersons' home and still found it easy to park, despite six patrol cars spread at all angles across the pale yellow shingle. He got out of his car and slammed the door hard, barking orders before he'd even reached the house – *this time he was mad as hell.*

"Walker!!! Are you in there??" Every time Joe heard the boss yell his name, acid literally dissolved his guts.

Surely he hadn't done anything wrong this time? He racked his brains – word had already got back Charlotte Peterson had escaped so he knew Harry would be really pissed about that, but he'd been here all afternoon and now it was early evening – he *must* be in the clear.

Harry marched down the hall, briefly checked rooms and bellowed for the whereabouts of his youngest officer.

"S – Sir? In here Sir." Joe poked his head round the lounge door – Miles was sitting back on the couch. Harry gestured to a sergeant to watch him and took Joe outside.

"Have you taken your eyes off Peterson even for a *second* without a swap out to another officer?"

"No sir – I've stayed with him from the moment we arrived, even when he went for a sla –... to the toilet, I checked the window, he could never have got out of that, I stood outside on the landing – he was a couple of minutes tops." Harry rolled his eyes and punched the wall – Joe visibly jumped.

"And where exactly is Mr. Peterson's mobile? *Do you have* it?" Joe flushed and mumbled something to the effect he thought that had been taken care of in the hall on arrival.

"Well you know what thought did, don't you?" growled his boss; "The whole operation has been scuppered and a young lady was kidnapped! *Thankfully,* despite a potentially life-threatening experience, she's recovering in hospital – *luckily for you!*" Joe couldn't

believe how stupid he'd been, but there *was* something he'd noticed only a couple of minutes before Harry had turned up, and it might well be important. *It might also just save his backside...*

"Sir there's something I think you should –"

"Frankly Walker I think *you* should take a long *holiday!*" shouted Longbridge as he started for the door.

"Sir – yes sir, but seriously though I think I've found something rather odd. It may be nothing but..." Harry stopped up short in the hall and turned round slowly as he blew another heavy and frustrated sigh. It had been a long and fruitless day...

"Okay – *okayyy...* show me – *nothing else has turned up from this damned house!*" Joe walked back into the lounge followed by Harry, and the young PC went over to the fireplace. Above it hung a large eighteen-inch Chinese dagger in its sheath. It was very unusual with its silver engraved horse head handle and walnut casing. Harry joined him to take a closer look.

"See? Along here," pointed out Joe, taking great care not to touch it. "The sheath looks like it's been repeatedly cut and glued, and there's dampness all along its length too." The boy was right, and if what he was suggesting was what Harry was thinking, together with Jenny Flood's testimonial – Joe had probably just saved his bacon and earned himself a promotion. Miles had stood up to look now, more confused than ever.

"It's just a round ended blunt knife – nobody could be hurt with it, it's just for show, the other officers have already discounted it. *Will someone tell me what the hell is going on?!!*"

"It's not the knife we're interested in Doctor Peterson – *it's the sheath.*" Harry instructed it to be bagged and for Miles to be taken down to the station for questioning. He then turned to his young P.C.,

"You never cease to amaze me Walker – *it really is all or nothing with you isn't it?!*"

It was dusk by the time Emily turned into the road that led down to Keeper's Cottage at the bottom of Kirkby Pike. She'd been wondering why Charlotte was out there at all, although an item on the news had said the police were closing in on the serial killer so it sounded like she was already on the run. Well – she wouldn't need to run anymore.

As the cottage appeared in the distance all sorts of memories came flooding back. She slowed the car down to a stop and just left the engine running for a few moments whilst she reflected on the past. It was here that she and Charlotte had fought all those years ago, in the summer of '98, the break from Uni. It was here Emily had told her she and Miles had been having an affair, that he loved *her* not Charlotte, despite Charlotte and Miles being engaged. It was here that Charlotte had threatened her family and changed her life – *and it was here that Emily had decided not to tell her about the baby...* Well now it would be here that all of that would be vindicated.

She took the gear out of neutral and continued on up the road to River Bank Lane – *and the house that had seen it all...*

THIRTY-SEVEN

Charlotte smoked and paced anxiously up and down. It had been over twenty years since they'd been in the same *country* together let alone the same house – *the same room*... she wasn't exactly relishing the idea. For one, Emily clearly had something overwhelmingly compelling to share with her that didn't sound too promising – and for two... why come all this way – *revenge?* A few more paces round the musty living room and she concluded if Maggie Rowlands had died, that must be her prime reason for returning. Em just wanted to spout off whilst she was here. Yes – that must be it. Well she could rant all she wanted... *as long as she relinquished her car.*

She couldn't help but recall their close friendship all those years ago. Emily Rowlands and Charlotte Krane had been inseparable all through school and university. As children they'd even played in the lake and woods around 'Keeper's Cottage' and were renowned for having an unbreakable bond. They had shared everything – unfortunately for Charlotte, Emily had taken the whole sharing thing too far... *It wasn't* **my** *fault* Charlotte told herself; *everything that followed* *from that day was entirely down to her.* **She** *made me the way I am!* **She** *made me ill!*

Watch checked again, Charlotte repeatedly looked for headlights and wished she'd got something a bit more effective than cigarettes to calm her nerves. Then she heard it… the clunking of tyres on the unmade part of the road that wound its way along to the lakeside cottage.

As the car bumped slowly down the lane, Emily's cool calm and collected exterior began to waver somewhat. She wondered how Charlotte would look after all this time. They'd been the fiery redhead and the mousey brown 'floppy mop' at school and university. Curiosity was getting the better of her and the closer she got to *'Keeper's'* the worse she felt. Such a mixture of emotions she hadn't expected to feel – she wanted to concentrate on just the one – the one that had brought her here.

The cottage suddenly came into view – her heart began to race. She drove up to the house, turned the car around towards the road for a quick exit, dimmed the lights and turned off the engine. The gun felt cold through her light jacket pocket – *she* felt cold. It was uncanny how it all looked exactly the same, even in the half light. Emily took a deep breath and got out of the car. She didn't bother to lock it. As she walked up the path to the house she heard the owls in the forest behind hoot loudly, it seemed they had very noisy work tonight – *she knew how they felt.*

As Charlotte watched her oldest friend walk up the path to the front door she knew it wasn't going to be easy to do what was needed in order to secure her escape. She reminded herself the woman was also her oldest adversary – even Jenny Flood didn't come close. The drumming in her ears was only outdone by the pounding of her heart – in a few seconds she would be in that house with her…

When Emily walked through the open door into the hall and stopped in the threshold, Charlotte stood silent and totally still at the other end. The atmosphere was thick with emotion, charged with… seething resentment, childhood laughter, shared teenage secrets, jealousy anger and tears – *but mostly bitterness, betrayal and recrimination…*

"Hello Emily – *welcome home.*" Charlotte waved an exaggerated arm towards what used to be the lounge but was now devoid of furniture. "I'd offer you a chair and a coffee but as you can see…" Emily's eyes swept head to toe over her former friend and rival – *she still looked good – shame.*

"I haven't come for light refreshments," said Emily crisply as she walked sharply through to a room as equally murky as the hall. The light was fading fast and she wanted to say and do what she'd come for and get out fast.

"So..." said Charlotte, standing in the doorway blocking her entrance to the hall, "what brings you to me now Emily? What is it that's *so* important you couldn't tell me on the phone?" The gun in Emily's pocket had never felt so heavy, so awkward – *so obvious.* If her coat had been transparent it wouldn't have felt any more conspicuous.

"When I – told you… twenty years ago about… about Miles and me," she began nervously as Charlotte's right eye twitched, "I didn't tell you everything when we met here that day." She took a deep breath then, stood tall and reminded herself of the misery this woman had inflicted on her.

"Go on..." said Charlotte, eyes narrowed, she didn't like where this was going and slipped her hand into her scalpel pocket…

"I was pregnant – I had a daughter, my mother brought her up. Her name… *her name is Gina* – and *Miles is her father."* If Charlotte had ever thought she'd experienced red mist before that night she was very much mistaken. This was something she'd lost sleep over, had nightmares about and tortured herself with. The possibility that Miles could have had a child elsewhere was the worst news that could come to her door – *for it to be with Emily Rowlands and that child to be in her employ was just an agony too far.*

She snatched the scalpel from her pocket flicked the blade forward and launched herself at her! Emily leapt back in total shock – with no furniture to grab she lost her footing in the worn carpet and fell as Charlotte sprang at her and grabbed her hair, her long red hair that only *now* Charlotte realised looked exactly like Gina's. She couldn't think why she'd not noticed the whole similarity before – *it was screamingly obvious!*

Charlotte plunged the blade viciously at her ribs then fell back instantly with the explosion – *she didn't know what shocked her more, the pain in her arm or the fact that Emily had a gun!* She'd managed to fire off a shot through her pocket and now took advantage of the fact Charlotte was wounded and on her back. *Emily stood over her with the gun now in plain view, the sight lined up between her old schoolfriend's eyes...*

"Before I send you to hell Charlie there's something else you should know." Emily smiled sardonically as she refined her aim even more perfectly; Charlotte in utter terror waited for yet another blow – *and death.* "Jenny and I have planned this for the last three years, *that's* why she followed you to Kirkdale *and* had Miles back in her bed – think of that as you –" *It was then that the sirens filled the air...*

Harry Longbridge had kept Miles in custody for the best part of four hours. It was now eight in the evening, and when he'd told him the direction Charlotte had taken the boat, he knew she was heading for Keeper's Cottage. What she thought she was going to do when she got there though was utterly beyond him, it had been derelict for years. Given the fact the warning text he'd sent her earlier was still on his phone, he didn't have much choice but to be helpful – *and frankly he was still reeling from the shock that his wife was suspected of being a serial killer.* He was having a harder time convincing them he knew absolutely nothing, apart from as they put it, *him trying to pervert the course of justice.*

Harry had never suspected him of being involved from the beginning but would be making the most of his twenty-four hours holding time. However, he'd ordered three cars out to the bottom of Kirkby Pike and determined to be in the lead vehicle; he wanted that psychotic bitch in a cell before ten and him home by eleven thirty. It had been an exceedingly long and tiring day, *he'd earned an early night.* This thing needed to be brought to a close as soon as possible so the real work could get started for the CPS – *at least that way he'd be going out with a bang for his retirement at Christmas.*

Emily was not a fool. She may have wanted Charlotte sent to the depths of hell but certainly had no intentions of joining her there, even metaphorically. The minute those sirens sounded she couldn't get out of that cottage fast enough, there would be very little time to get back up to the main road and take the left fork away in the opposite direction so as not to be seen driving away from the house. She made it by the skin of her teeth and saw the headlights of the police cars in her rear-view mirror as they turned off left behind her, and down River Bank Lane to Keeper's Cottage and their quarry. There was only one problem that faced her now and that was if Charlotte told them how she'd got her injury – the bullet would no doubt be lodged in the wall somewhere. *Well... she'd just have to cross that bridge when she came to it.*

Left behind and still stunned at what had just happened, Charlotte managed to hack the hem off her jacket with the scalpel to create a makeshift bandage. Her arm hurt badly, she was cold, out of pills only three cigarettes left and still had no car. However, the thought that Gina was Miles' daughter and he'd been bedding Jenny again gave her more grief than her flesh wound and the rest put together.

At the sound of the sirens they'd both momentarily frozen, but with herself injured on the floor, Emily had been the one with the advantage of reaching the car. Now Charlotte was hiking it up the through the forest in the dark, in pain and absolutely no idea of what to do next. She'd managed to climb up to the thicker region of the forest's undergrowth behind the cottage after Emily had taken off. The police had swooped down just minutes later, and from where she was hidden she could see them and the beams from their torches. This was not how she'd imagined things would pan out and Charlotte knew it wouldn't be long before they followed her up the Pike... *and they would search until they found her.*

Harry was in a foul mood. The discovery of a dark, quite literally empty house lacking any utilities, with apparently no evidence of anyone having been there apart from an open front door, and what appeared to be some bloodstains against a torchlit wall, was not how he expected the evening to wrap up. With an earlier witness statement to one of the murders and one half of the perceived murder weapon in the bag, the culprit in a possible wounded condition and almost certainly without transport, *should have* led to an easy arrest and early knock off. Now though it looked like it could be a long night ahead, necessitating a heat-imaging crew up in the air if a preliminary scout around the hillside in the pitch bloody black didn't flush her out.

Six officers started up Kirkby Pike each flashing a night searcher and all six were back within half an hour. Harry knew what he had to do next and it took less than twelve minutes to get the helicopter guys with thermal imaging launched and over the forest. He stood at the foot of the hill and scanned the slopes above him – *There's nowhere for you to hide now Doctor Peterson… it's game over.*

The beams from the torches had gone. From her 'hiding place', which was little more than a few trees closer together than some of the others, Charlotte rested a while, grateful that they seemed to have given up on her for the time being – *but her arm felt wet and heavy.* She was losing more blood than she first thought but with nothing in her bag to help there was very little she could do.

The coolness of the autumn evening had moved on to being a night with a real chill in the air, it was either that or she was not a well woman at all. Her eyelids began to slowly drop as she felt increasingly tired. Sat alone on that hillside in the dirt of the forest floor, Charlotte struggled to work out how she'd come to this. If only Miles had treated her better, if only Emily hadn't betrayed her friendship with him, if only Jenny Flood hadn't existed, *if only…* Her breathing became slower and heavier, she felt she could've slept for a month. *Maybe an hour or so would help? Even just thirty minutes might give her some strength.* She leant back against a tree, her breathing laboured, her arm pounded and her head slid sideways…

When the thrum of the helicopter blades suddenly thundered on all sides, Charlotte looked up to see exactly what she'd brought on herself. *Her heart sank.* She knew there would be heat-sensing cameras on board, she knew they'd be scouring the Pike, and she knew they would find her – *they could probably see her right now.* Well she didn't intend to give up her liberty that easily, they would have to work for their kill. With a renewed energy she slung her bag over her good shoulder and carried on slowly up the Pike. The further she went the steeper and harder it got and her heeled shoes were not exactly made for climbing. She took them off and put them in her bag but the ground was rough and stony in places, it cut into the soles of her feet and inevitably slowed her down.

All the time Charlotte climbed she could hear the helicopter's blades and engines above her. Shouts from lower down the Pike sounded very close too – for the first time in her life she understood how a fox felt when it tried to outrun the hounds.

"Doctor Peterson! We have you surrounded! Lay down flat on your stomach with your hands on your head. I repeat – we have you surrounded!"

Then Charlotte saw them. They were in all directions – *it was over.*

When she was brought down, read her rights and put in the van, Harry almost felt sorry for her – *almost.* She looked absolutely terrible. He couldn't quite put his finger on it, but given her crimes, when he looked her in the eyes he expected them to flash with anger, hatred, false pride, spite... she had none of that. As Harry Longbridge looked Charlotte Peterson in the eyes that night, there was zero emotional energy. *What he saw was a woman totally and utterly haunted.*

THIRTY-EIGHT

The day of Maggie Rowlands' funeral dawned grey and overcast, much how her granddaughter Gina was feeling as the cars arrived at Kirkby Church for the service and burial. The events of the previous few weeks had understandably left her, Andrew and Molly in a fractious and emotional state, but unbeknown to them, those feelings were about to get a whole lot more confusing…

At least with Charlotte now safely in custody awaiting trial and almost certain future incarceration at Rampton, the inhabitants of Kirkdale and its little neighbouring village of Kirkby-Over-Sands had started to settle down. Never before had its occupants suffered the terror of a serial killer, let alone one that had held a respected position in the community.

From Miles' point of view, the arrest of his wife for the horrific murders of five women, a young man, and attempted murders of their receptionist, her boyfriend and surrogate sister, was mentally just too much to cope with. He was on extended leave until further notice and under a specialist doctor at a separate private practice for his own emotional state. His decision to divorce Charlotte was pretty much immediate and he'd already instigated the initial arrangements. No amount of inheritance money could ever be high enough, *even for a man as materialistic as Miles*, to keep him in that marriage. Similarly, there would be a further shock for him that was to change his life forever…

Harry Longbridge also followed the funeral cars as they trickled up the lane to the small church. He'd become very involved with this young trio and felt quite honoured when Andrew and Gina had asked if he would attend.

Jenny had also been asked if she would come, but had declined given her grief at the loss of her brother, and the fact she'd not been allowed to arrange his funeral yet due to police procedure and Charlotte's upcoming prosecution. His special 'JF' bracelet that had been missing when he was pulled from the lake was later found in the glove compartment of Charlotte's Morgan Roadster. To make sure it wasn't left in her pocket that night she'd quickly thrown it in there, but in her haste to dispose of his body had forgotten to retrieve it to toss in the lake after him…

Under intense questioning and seriously depleted state of mind, Doctor Charlotte Peterson had finally admitted to the six murders and the attempts on Molly's, Gina's and Andrew's lives, to the relief of the whole team who had worked so hard in bringing her to justice. *Not least, Harry Longbridge and his two young officers, Joe Walker and Suzanne Moorcroft, who had been instrumental in their suggestions and observations with regard to the main murder weapon used on the five women. The chloroform, cool bag and mallet that had also been used, were later found in a cupboard under a horse rug in the stables.*

The service was quite short and the most difficult part yet to come as Margaret Rowlands had wished to be buried with her husband and parents in the family plot. It was here that only the closest of family members were in attendance, lined up either side of the open grave, now with umbrellas above them to catch the late autumn rain.

Two women, one obviously older but still very glamorous, stood opposite each other; both held yellow roses, both had flaming red hair. Molly couldn't help herself as she paid little attention to the proceedings and a very great deal on the woman facing her. It was noticeable that the owner of that other yellow rose didn't pay the attention she might have during such a solemn occasion either – instead, she stared hard at Molly's closest friend who stood right beside her – yellow rose in hand.

"Who's that woman opposite?" she whispered to Gina as discreetly as she could. "The one with the red hair… *the one who looks exactly like you!*"

Gina looked up then. She'd not really noticed anyone in particular during the church service apart from a few neighbours and friends of her grandmother's. Three or four residents from the nursing home had been able to come accompanied by staff members, and of course Molly's parents, but frankly Gina was too upset to concentrate on anyone much – she was just grateful for Molly's, the Fields' and Andrew's support.

"I – I don't know. I've never seen her before, although… there *is* something vaguely familiar… " Andrew looked up now and noticed the woman himself, glanced sideways at Gina then back across the grave. He summed up the situation immediately and raised his eyebrows questioningly at the older woman. *Emily Stone nodded pointedly back at him in acknowledgement* as Maggie Rowlands was laid to rest, and two yellow roses were thrown down…

Harry stood away from the graveside but had observed with interest from a distance. The similarity between Gina Rowlands and the redhead had not gone unnoticed by him, nor that there had been no communication between them as yet. He was aware Gina had been brought up by her grandmother in her mother's absence, now it looked like that absence might have ended.

He continued to watch as the mourners began to gradually drift away, which left the redhead and a much older shabbier lady on one side, Andrew Gale, Gina Rowlands and Molly Fields on the other. Within minutes the redhead had walked round with the elderly lady to talk with the trio, *and he would have given a great deal to know what was about to be said.*

As Emily approached them with the strange looking old lady Gina didn't know either, the young girl squeezed her boyfriend's hand tightly in anticipation of something, of what she wasn't quite sure. Somewhere at the back of her head pictures flickered in and out, pictures she had all but forgotten. He squeezed it back.

"It's Gina isn't it?" said the glamorous redhead as she held out her hand. Gina shook it automatically.

"Yes, I'm Gina but I've no idea who –" Emily took a deep breath and just came straight out with it…

"I'm your mother Gina – I'm Emily Stone, formerly Rowlands – Margaret was *my* mother." She waited for it to sink in, *Andrew and Molly waited for her to pass out.* Molly's bottom jaw dropped south at her correct suspicions and Andrew put his arms tightly around his girlfriend in case her knees buckled. Gina remained silent. The old lady next to Emily said nothing – she looked scared witless and quite out of place as her only companion. Gina's confusion was a mixture of both the ramifications of what the redhead had just come out with, and where this other woman might fit in. Andrew turned to her, concerned at how this little bombshell had just been dropped.

"Gina, are you okay sweetheart?" Gina continued to stare at her mother – she wanted to speak but nothing came out.

"Let's go and sit over there," said Andrew, his arm around Gina as he helped her over to the benches nearby where the three friends sat down gratefully. Emily and Rose remained on their feet in front of them.

"I'm afraid that's not all," continued Emily, "and this is going to come as a massive shock Gina – but now I've started I've got to tell you everything…" Gina was now seriously worried – *surely there couldn't be any more, what on earth could be more of a shock than having just met my mother at my grandmother's funeral?* Emily looked at the floor, the sky, everywhere but at her daughter. Finally she just blurted it out – *"I don't know what you've been told Gina – but your father is… Miles Peterson."* At this revelation all three of them were initially completely speechless – but Gina was having none of it!

"What? No! I don't believe you! Why should I?" she exclaimed.

"Because it's true – I'm so sorry love but it's true…" Emily knew there was another storm to come yet – this was harder than meeting Charlotte at the cottage, to see the pain on her daughter's face after not having seen her at all for the last seventeen plus years just about finished her.

"This lady is your Great Aunt Rose," continued Emily, "Margaret's estranged sister. I met her at the nursing home the day after I arrived from New York… they reconciled the afternoon before she died." Gina looked at the older woman who now gave a little half-smile, not quite sure whether she should hold out her hand, speak or just stay quiet.

"I – I don't know what to say." Gina struggled to find words for a conversation she'd longed to have for most of her life, but now it had happened the most important person to share it with wasn't there – and to learn that *Miles was her father*…

It didn't seem fair to add to their trauma further, especially on such a difficult and sad day, but she felt it couldn't be left now that she'd started. All the years had been rolled back and the last piece of the puzzle had to be put into place…

"That's not all…" Emily took another deep breath and picked up old Rosie's hand, then looked directly at Andrew before she spoke again. "I believe you're Andrew – *Andrew Gale?*" He'd been concentrating solely on Gina after the last blow, but looked up now surprised the attention had been turned to him. Molly and Gina exchanged anxious glances then waited with Andrew for… *for what? What else on earth could this woman come out with?* "Andrew I recently learnt that you were adopted as a small boy – is that correct?"

"Actually – yes, yes I was, but what's that got to do with anything?" Gina reached up to place a protective hand on his shoulder, eyes flashing through brimmed tears. Emily gently pushed Rose forward and placed *her* hands protectively on *her* shoulders.

"This is Rose Emmerson – née Rowlands… *Andrew… Rose is your birth mother.*" It was one shock too many, including it seemed for Rose who now began to weep bitterly as her shoulders shook beneath her niece's hands.

Molly took one look at her two friends, both of whom were now white and completely dumbstruck. She suggested it would be far more comfortable and practical if they all went back to the private quarters at the Carpenters where they could try and begin to come to terms with their new relationships and decide how to move forward. Gina and now Andrew remained in shock and still held on tightly to each other, but nodded quietly in agreement. Emily breathed a huge sigh of relief – *it had not been easy, but now it was done, it had hopefully been worth it and she prayed that in time everything would work itself out.*

She also hoped that Charlotte would keep her mouth shut…

And as he fished two barley sugars out of his pocket, Harry had continued to watch the group with renewed and suspicious interest –

"Now if retirement wasn't a few weeks away, I'd…"

***

398

EPILOGUE...

- TWO YEARS LATER -

RAMPTON HIGH SECURITY PSYCHIATRIC HOSPITAL - NOTTINGHAMSHIRE

Charlotte stood outside Rampton cuffed between two women prison officers as she waited to be put into a van. She'd been given leave to attend her mother's funeral and it felt good to be on the outside at last, *two years was a long time – too long.* It had been really difficult to knuckle down and accept everything at first, but she'd managed to get along with most of the other patients most of the time and had one friend in particular who would do absolutely anything for her. Eventually she would be able to show her appreciation in the best way criminals liked to receive loyalty payment – *cold hard cash.*

Her father had died the previous year due to a weak heart which had followed multiple illnesses, all as a result of shock at his only daughter's hideous crimes. Sadly she hadn't been given permission to attend *his* funeral owing to an unfortunate kitchen incident…

Her mother had been constantly unwell for the past two years, had felt eternal family shame and found the loss of her husband just too much to bear, so now Charlotte found herself in the fresh air, difficult thoughts going round and round her head as they often did.

Miles had divorced her soon after the trial which she'd found unforgiveable, *if understandable.* He'd clearly decided no amount of her parents' colossal inheritance was worth staying with her for, but as far as Charlotte was concerned it was the ultimate betrayal – after all *he* was the sole reason she was in here.

She glanced down anxiously at her cuffed hands and checked her watch – *let's hope all the arrangements are well synchronized mummy dearest,* she thought, *I've only got one shot at this.* The van came round the corner and pulled up in front of them. She looked briefly around her before getting in. *There's nothing left for me here any longer and I've always had a hankering for New York.* A twisted smile crept over her face, a previously attractive face that had considerably hardened over the past couple of years… *I wonder if those two scheming bitches are happily settled out there? To be honest, it really doesn't matter one way or the other, after all –* **Dead Girls Don't Cry…**